# FLEETING GLANCE

By Sherban Young

THE ENESCU FLEET SERIES

*Fleeting Memory*
*Fleeting Glance*
*Fleeting Note*
*Fleeting Chance*
*Fleeting Promise*

THE WARREN KINGSLEY SERIES

*Five Star Detour*
*Double Cover*

MORE BOOKS

*Opportunity Slips*
*Dead Men Do Tell Tale*s

# FLEETING GLANCE

An Enescu Fleet Mystery

Sherban Young

Columbia, MD

MysteryCaper hardcover edition first published in 2013

Cover and illustrations by Katerina Vamvasaki

Editing services by Katherine Richards from *The Reading Panda*



ISBN-10: 0-9912324-4-5
EAN-13: 978-0-9912324-4-4

MysteryCaper Press
Columbia, Maryland

www.mysterycaper.com
www.sherbanyoung.com

# Dedication

To Tom McKnight

*For your inspirational art and your warm hospitality*

# Acknowledgments

I would like to thank Yvonne at the book blog *Fiction Books* for her efforts in our "Brit-speak" experiment, as well as Lynsey Ring for her insights into the world of art. Lastly, what art-themed murder mystery would be complete without a word of appreciation to my cover artist, Katerina Vamvasaki. All your covers are masterpieces.

# 1 — Abstract Communications

I held the thing up to the light and studied it closer.

It was a postcard. 3 ½ inches high by 5 inches wide. Just a postcard. And it didn't make the slightest bit of sense to me.

The artwork on the front showed a pleasing living room scene, bright and cheery, with oodles of burgundy and gold. Left center was a Christmas tree. The artist had a nice avant-garde style with clean lines and colors. I liked it.

The back contained a short message. I give it to you exactly as written:

*John,*

*Best wishes on your impending nuptials. Things sure are liveni-ng up for you. Say hello to the old man for me.*

*Stothard Hope*

There were only a few problems with this pleasant Yuletide greeting. First of all, it was June. Second, the sender failed to break the word *livening* properly at the syllable. Not that it matters, but it should have been "liven-ing" not "liveni-ng." Lastly, I knew no one by the name Stothard Hope. I would have been pretty amazed if anyone did.

I held it up to the light one more time and shook my head. It seemed to me that spies and detectives were forever holding cryptic messages like this up to lights, but the process left me cold. Maybe I was thinking of a glass of chardonnay.

It didn't matter. I wasn't much of a detective, and I knew even less about wine. (Although, the card was a cheeky little offering, and it did amuse me.)

If it weren't for the part about the impending nuptials, I would have thought the man had gotten the wrong John Hathaway. But my nuptials were impending, impending like gangbusters. As it happened, my fiancée's parents were arriving from England today—my first time meeting the prospective in-laws—and nuptials don't get much more impending than that.

Contemplating their visit now, not one I was looking forward to with any real enthusiasm, I had barely lowered the card from my examination, resigned to put the whole Stothard Hope mystery out of my mind, when a cheerful smiling face with perfectly round specs appeared in my field of view.

We were over by the breakfast nook, me and this face, and seeing it materialize before me, all white teeth and piercing eyes, I shot back into the kitchen island, full of strange oaths.

"Hiya, Hath."

I frowned. There were many qualities about my friend Hutton I would have changed had I been consulted prior to assembly. His aristocratic demeanor. His ability to complicate the lives of everyone around him. His goatee. But his habit of popping in on a person out of nowhere would have topped the list. I figured I must have left the front door unlocked when I had gone outside to get the mail. Not that a locked door ever made much of a difference to Hutton. He enjoyed picking locks. It kept his hand in.

However he managed it this morning, I didn't give him the satisfaction of asking. I merely filled the kettle and offered him a cup of tea.

It was his turn to frown. I had never known any of my English friends to refuse a cup of real loose tea before—it's one of the few things I can do well in the kitchen—but Hutton waved it aside without hesitation. He wasn't in the market for tea.

"What were you doing?" he asked. It was the sort of pointed question you'd expect from a man who didn't believe in doorbells.

"Just trying to figure out this postcard. Do you know anyone called Stothard Hope?"

He considered the name. "Stothard Hope. Stothard Hope. Sounds like a Victorian sailing ship to me," he remarked, after a moment's reflection. *"O'erwrought in an ever-buffeting sea, thy fierce and intrepid vessel,* the Stothard Hope, *has come a cropper off the coast of Dover."*

"Is that how the Victorians described their naval mishaps?"

"Pretty much. They were an odd and fascinating people."

I looked at the card again. Aside from the details I have already mentioned, there was something else off about this message. Friends, especially male friends, tend to call me Johnny, or Hathaway, or if they're eccentric private investigators who enter people's homes without so much as a knock, just Hath. Stothard Hope had called me John. He clearly wasn't a bosom pal, and yet from his tone he acted as if we had known each other for years. Strange.

"I wonder if the 'old man' he refers to could be my Uncle George. He's old."

"And getting older all the time," agreed Hutton. He slipped the message from my grasp. "Ariadne Locke Museum," he read from the small print in the lower corner.

I had noticed that too. The card had apparently originated at the Ariadne Locke Museum, which I assumed was in Ariadne Locke State Park. I had vaguely heard of the latter. It was one of those quaint daytrip spots, the kind my fiancée, Lesley, was always chirping about visiting on weekends. You know the sort. All lighthouses and picturesque New England landscapes. If you've seen one—well, you might not have seen them all, but you've seen enough.

Hutton interrupted my thoughts. "Why were you holding this up to the lightbulb when I came in?" His visit had become a regular inquisition.

"I don't know."

"You must have had a reason."

I hesitated. I hated explaining my methods. "I thought it might reveal something."

"Revealed by way of 20 watt halogen?"

"Yes."

"Did it?"

"No."

He shook his head, as one who thought this kind of amateurish detective work unworthy of him. He gave the message another considered glance. "Hope," he mused.

"Hope, Hutton and Hath," I smiled.

"Hope," he repeated, not sharing my mirth. "I feel like I knew a Hope once."

"Bob?"

"I think it was a client. Celeste Hope, if I am not mistaken."

"Now *that* sounds like a Victorian sailing ship," I chuckled.

He continued to ignore my *bon mots*. He took an amble around the kitchen island, straightening cups of cooking utensils as he went. He had clearly gone into PI mode now. Making mysteries out of molehills was one of his occupational hazards. "It is intriguing, though. I wonder if it's a code."

I didn't know what he meant by this, and said as much.

"Perhaps this Hope was trying to deliver a message to you," he clarified.

I pointed out that he *had* delivered a message to me: a message about nuptials.

Hutton frowned. "I'm talking beyond nuptials here, Hath. Beyond the message itself. Perhaps it contains some hidden significance."

This was actually why I had held it up to the light, but declined to go into all that again. I asked him what he meant.

Hutton was growing impatient with the question. The problem was, I don't think he knew what he meant himself. He twirled a pie server between his thumb and forefinger, his eyebrow arching ever so slightly above the curved rim of his glasses. "I know, check the postage stamp. Unless I miss my guess, you'll find it's some rare and wonderful specimen, worth five hundred thousand smackers, if not more."

I checked the stamp. Stothard's choice, I showed Hutton, was a duck, worth approximately .32 smackers. "Or it was," I added, "before he gummed it on a postcard."

The great postcard debate began to wind down here. Hutton, while refusing to concede that he sought conspiracy everywhere, agreed that sometimes a postcard is just a postcard.

He glanced at his wristwatch (I don't wear one myself—never had a need). "Aren't you meeting your future in-laws for brunch in ten minutes?" he asked.

I cursed my lack of wristwatch. All this banter on cards and nuptials had made me late.

Decades of never arriving anywhere on time had left Hutton quietly unaffected. "I thought you may want a ride. The house isn't far, but it can be tricky to find for the uninitiated. GPS is hopeless."

The house he alluded to belonged to a buddy of his. It was out on the water, had ample guest quarters, and Lesley had the run of it for as long as her parents were in town. Pretty nice of this buddy, I thought. I would have had her folks here, but was put off the idea by Lesley herself. Reassuring her parents that I was a hell of a fellow would be hard enough, I was told, without asking them to interact with me on one of my groggy mornings. A ludicrous concern, really, for I rarely got up before noon.

Bruised feelings aside, I actually liked the idea of the separate house. It fit my strategy for the weekend to a T.

My plan, in a nutshell, was to smother Lesley's parents in company. I knew they would detest me, but if I could obscure myself in a swirl of humanity, ducking behind friends and neighbors and staying half out of view the entire time, I might be able to get through the visit without any bloodshed. Hutton's friend's place sounded like the perfect venue for this.

As far as the guest list was concerned, I had Hutton inked in from the start, and not simply because he was providing the house. Another Brit couldn't do any harm, even if that Brit had a wad of wavy blond hair and a tiny blond beard of the bohemian artist type.

Along with Hutton, our go-to gal was Lesley's friend, Ate Fleet (pronounced *Ah-tee*). I would have said Hutton's friend *Ah-tee,* but I had no idea where the two of them stood just then. Were they friends or something more? I had it from the female perspective—meaning Lesley, getting it from Ate—that she and Hutton had recently considered "taking their relationship to the next level." But then they had decided not to take it to the next level, then they sort of had, and then they sort of hadn't, and I pretty much tuned out there.

Hutton, meanwhile, had mentioned only last month that everything was proceeding swimmingly with Ate on the romance side, slow but steady—which, in male-speak, meant he had struck out on multiple occasions but she hadn't actually slapped a restraining order on him or shot him in the kneecap with a high-powered rifle.

Everyone has their own interpretation, I guess.

In any event, Ate was to be key for us this weekend. For one, she had offered to pick up Lesley's folks from the airport and drive them to Hutton's friend's place. This gave Lesley more time to settle in at the temporary digs and me more time not to be picking up Lesley's folks.

I know—playing chauffeur is a job a future son-in-law probably should have embraced, and I gladly would have, too. (Well, I'd have done it.) But the girls up top had benched me there as well. Ate, it turned out, did this for a living now. She had recently become some variety of hospitality specialist or something, I forget what exactly, but whatever it was, taking a load off the weary traveler was her bread and butter. I was happy to give her the work.

Running through the setup in my mind one more time, I suddenly remembered something. "Weren't you supposed to go with Ate to the airport?"

Hutton waved aside the question with a weary gesture. He was doing a lot of weary waving that morning.

"There was a little snag there," he said, selecting a plum from the bowl and giving it a meditative polish on his cashmere shirt. I could have told him it would cover it with lint.

"Snag? What kind of snag?" I didn't like snags.

"Nothing. It's fine. Ate's got us covered. She does this for a living now, you know."

I knew she did it for a living!

"But you're British, Hutton—"

He paused in his chewing long enough to tell me that he was well aware of this.

"—and I was counting on you to welcome Lesley's folks and remind them of jolly old England. What the hell happened?"

"Professional obligation. No biggie."

"I thought you said you had no cases?"

He nodded his head dolefully. The private detective business, he agreed, had slowed down considerably as of late. "Everyone is working out their own intrigues. I blame the Internet."

"Then what?"

"I thought I had a lead on something. Turns out I didn't."

"So you just abandoned her?"

"I wouldn't say that, no. In a way I was there."

I scowled at this answer. It sounded far too metaphysical for my mood.

I started to speak again, but he waved his plum at me. "Ate of all people should understand. Just look at her father."

I had no desire to look at her father, and no clue what Hutton was babbling about. It didn't matter. I had no interest in whether Ate understood or not. It was whether Lesley understood, and I already had the answer to that. She wouldn't.

"This is just spectacular," I said. "Where are my keys?"

"I thought I was the one offering you a ride?"

"Fine, I'll ride with you."

"I have the Wrangler today."

"Fine, we'll go in the Wrangler."

"Ate had me pick up a few trays of food. You don't mind balancing a few trays of food in your lap, do you, Hath?"

"I'll see you there," I said, shaking my head again. The way that woman was constantly having him jump through hoops was really pretty sad.

I grabbed an envelope of spa certificates Lesley had asked me to purchase for our guests, snagged the necktie she had told me to wear against my wishes, and located my car keys.

"I can follow," I informed him.

Between brooding on Hutton and his snags, and almost getting sideswiped by him as I backed my "Electric Blue" MINI Cooper S out from the garage, I wasn't really paying all that much attention to the rest of my surroundings. If I had been, I might have given a little more thought to the black sedan idling in a space across the street.

I had noticed it when I had gone out to get the mail, and there it was twenty minutes later, still idling. That's a long time to idle.

I hardly gave it a second look now. Hutton had the lion's share of my concentration at the moment. I could have sworn I saw him eating some kind of fancy crab doodle in his rearview mirror. He would later deny this. But that didn't change the fact that we had no fancy crab doodles at brunch.

## 2 — Portrait of a Young Couple in Love

When I arrived at Hutton's friend's house sometime later, I was surprised to find that Hutton wasn't there. He had lost me in traffic roughly thirty-six seconds into the journey, and I could only assume that he would roll in ahead of me. But not a trace. He was like a male, land-based version of Amelia Earhart. I couldn't figure it.

I didn't dwell on this mystery long. In the driveway sat Ate Fleet's champagne-colored sport utility: the one she used for shuttling clients around in her hospitality business.

The British Invasion had arrived.

I don't mind telling you, when Lesley's parents first informed us of their visit, I was annoyed. They hadn't given us any notice at all, these wandering Brits. Not very English, popping in on people like that. Besides, isn't there something in the etiquette guide about not seeing the bride's parents before the wedding? Well, if there isn't, there should be.

This wasn't simply social anxiety. I wasn't exactly pining away for the gathering, but there was more to it than that. We had plans, my fiancée and I.

I should explain that Lesley, as was her prerogative, had long ago pooh-poohed the idea of a casino-based honeymoon—which is ironic, because we had gotten engaged in one—but in a stunning show of male assertiveness I had managed to persuade her on a trip to Las

Vegas this weekend. It was to be a sort of pre-honeymoon for us, a chance to forget about the wedding for a while and spend some quality time together; by which I mean Lesley watching me play poker. That all went by the wayside the minute the folks put in their transatlantic call.

I bring this up because, at first, I found this irritation empowering. You know how it is when you're nervous. Throw a little pique into the mix and it tempers the stew. For days, whenever my thoughts would stray to what the Manchester contingent would think of me—of my erratic business endeavors, of my association with not one but two private detectives, of my jackass congressman of an uncle—I would remind myself that these were the Limeys who had cost me a seat at the World Series of Poker ($1,500 buy-in, no-limit Hold'em event), and I would come over all taut and steely eyed.

I say *at first*, because this emotional contrivance, much like the trip itself, was all off now. The letdown came as I was walking up the cobblestone drive toward the house. The crisp New England breeze played about my face. I took in the grounds and Tudor architecture. And it was then that I felt my sturdy self-righteousness draining away from me like a punctured canteen. Replacing it was a shallow feeling in the pit of my stomach and the sense that some tiny, invisible acupuncturist was sweeping over my body with tiny, invisible needles.

It's funny when you think about it. I'd been in some pretty tough scrapes in my time. There was that business at Sir Roger Banbury's estate a few summers back. And before that, the debacle with the dignitary's wife and the bowl of brandy-laced cherries. And who could forget the Wolf Valley Tribal Reservation? But, somehow, these all paled in comparison with presenting myself to Lesley's family.

I hoped she had left the door open. I possessed none of Hutton's special skills with lock picks, and the last thing I needed was to meet my future father-in-law on the threshold, like some squeaky-voiced prom date.

It was unlocked. It was the last bit of good luck I would have that weekend.

I'll pass lightly over the marble foyer and arching staircase. Take it as read that Hutton's friend, whoever he was, did pretty well for himself. I found Lesley in the kitchen, looking beautiful and annoyed.

She was glaring at a pitcher of iced tea as if it had just said something snarky about her new hairdo.

"Hi," I announced.

She transferred her glare to me. "So you're here finally."

There was no denying it. I was there. And yet, somehow, I felt like I should deny it. "Where are the folks?"

She fluttered a distracted hand toward the gigantic round window over the sink. "Ate's showing Jill and my parents the private pier out back."

"Jill?"

"My little sister Jill."

"Oh right." I'd almost forgotten about sister Jill. I hadn't seen her since she graduated. "Do we have a private pier?" I wondered.

Another distracted wave. "I don't know, how should I know?"

Well, you either had a private pier, or you didn't have a private pier. It was no good assuming you had, and then come to find that your loved ones are all bobbing around in the harbor for lack of the structure.

I changed the subject. "Where's Hutton?"

"I have no idea. Ate tells me he never showed up at the airport today."

"Yes, about that—"

"She had to handle Mum and Dad's luggage all by herself. Where was he?"

"I understand there was some sort of snag. A professional ob—"

"He's so irresponsible, Johnny. I know he's your friend, but sometimes I wonder."

"He is pretty irresponsible," I agreed.

"Of course, you should have been there to pick them up yourself," she said.

I opened my mouth to reply, but held up.

I knew what was going on here. It was the wedding plans—had to be. And this was odd, too, because when we had gotten engaged last fall she wasn't this way at all. She was carefree. Laidback. Insouciant, even. But then something changed. As the dates on the calendar turned, so too did my Lesley. She became less and less Lesley-like and more and more a caricature from a modern bridal magazine. She began fretting, brooding. Recently, she had taken to raising various points of criticism about her husband to-be which, while perfectly accurate, could only really be stated in order to wound.

"Where's everyone else?" I asked, changing the subject again.

"Not coming."

"Not coming?"

"Not coming," she said.

I didn't get this. "When you say not coming, how do you mean not coming exactly?"

"What are you, mental? I mean they're not coming. The gang from my work have that corporate retreat. None of the neighbors answered our invitation. And the party planner we hired for the wedding says she never comes to parties she hasn't planned."

I said oh. This certainly put a kink in my smother-them-in-company strategy.

"Your hair looks nice," I told her, changing the subject for a third time. Awhile back she had returned to her natural chestnut color. I've learned that it always pays to notice these things, and pass along kudos whenever possible.

She was in no mood for discussing hair (never a good sign). "Johnny, I'm worried."

I knew what I needed to do. I stepped over and reeled her in closer. "Don't fret. I just have to be extra-special charming now. I'm sure your parents will love me."

She pulled away. Evidently I didn't know what I needed to do. "It's not that! I'm sure they will detest you."

"Thanks."

"I mean, I don't care if they do. That's not what I'm worried about. It's this house!" She shivered as she said it.

I felt like I had walked onto the set of a B-horror flick. "What about the house?"

"Don't you know who it belongs to?"

"No."

"—who this 'friend' of Hutton's is?"

"No."

"I saw some bills piled up in the foyer under the mail slot." She paused significantly, and I gave her one of my impatient looks. "John Frederick Herring," she whispered.

I frowned. "The nineteenth-century English equine painter John Frederick Herring?"

"No!"

I nodded. I didn't think that was who it was either. Actually, I was pretty amazed I had known who John Frederick Herring, English equine painter, even was. I guess my time spent around my new friend Enescu Fleet, the walking book of facts, had rubbed off on me.

I considered the name again. John Frederick Herring. John Frederick Herring.

"The other nineteenth-century English equine painter John Frederick Herring?" I hazarded. There were two of them, after all.

She huffed at me. "Don't you ever read the news?"

She knew perfectly well that I didn't.

"You've never heard of Johnny 'Fishes,' the organized crime figure?"

I hadn't. Herring. Fishes. As in "swims with the…" Funny.

"The Portland kingpin?" she prompted me. "The most dangerous man in New England?"

I continued shaking my head, frankly surprised that Portland had any kingpins. ("Johnny," though. He couldn't be all bad.)

Lesley was a regular encyclopedia of crime on him: "He's most famous for an ongoing blood feud with the Vroom family of Boston?"

"Vroom?"

"Vroom."

I said ah. The Vrooms. The Vroom family of Boston. Nope, didn't ring any bells.

"That's who owns this house!" said Lesley.

I still didn't get it. What difference could it make, really?

"What if the Vrooms show up with machine guns?" she asked.

I saw no percentage in this. Why would the Vrooms bring us machine guns? "You sure you got the name right, by the way?" I wondered. Vroom? Were there people called Vroom?

Lesley seemed to think there were. "What if the Vrooms show up with machine guns and start shooting up the place looking for Fishes?" It sounded funny when she said it that way.

"Never happen," I said. "You'd have to be a real philistine to shoot up this architecture. And if anyone does show up," I proceeded, "your father can give them one of those famous lawman stares you're always telling me about, and they will shrivel up on the spot."

She reminded me that he was not a lawman. He was a barrister. And his firm back home specialized in estate law, not violent crime. "He's not used to truly hardened criminals."

"You mean other than his fellow lawyers," I said.

No one was laughing at my quips today.

I pulled her in again, softly. This time she didn't elbow me in the gut. "Look, Hutton never would have stuck us here if there was any real danger. He might be certifiably insane, but he's not an ass. I'm sure there's some reasonable explanation for it all. It's probably not even the same John 'Fishes' Herring."

"You really think so?"

"Sure, why not," I replied. (There was always a chance Hutton hadn't screwed us.)

She was beginning to soften. "I suppose I am just nervous about this weekend."

"I know you are."

She leaned her head on my chest and sighed. I was wearing the Pima cotton that morning, the good stuff. "I'm sorry you missed your Hold-it tournament," she mumbled into the fabric.

I waved aside the sacrifice with a manly nonchalance. "Hold'em," I corrected, and it didn't matter. "I'm used to it," I remarked. This was true. It seemed like lately I was constantly having poker trips turn blue on me. I guess it just wasn't in the cards for me to play cards.

She lifted her head from my chest and smiled. Her sparkling green eyes met mine, and I had the feeling that she was going to say something about my amazing, heartening nobility.

And perhaps she would have. But then the smile faded, and a pensive frown creased those soft, adorable features. "So this is what you're wearing, then?"

I stepped back. "I brought a tie," I pointed out, unfurling the item from my jacket pocket and holding it out like a gaffed salmon. "It has paisleys."

She gave the paisleys the nod of recognition they deserved. "Don't you own any trousers that aren't made of denim?"

She knew perfectly well that I didn't. "I thought the combo looked brilliant."

I had said the wrong thing. She rolled her eyes toward the heavens, or at least toward the Viking range, and brushed a strand of chestnut back from her forehead. "This is all I need!" she groaned to herself.

I gazed back at her blankly.

"Your half-ass accent," she said.

I gazed back at her again, silently wondering *What about it?*

"Your accent. They're going to think you're—I don't know what."

"Doing them?"

"Johnny, really!"

"Not 'doing them' that way, 'doing them' impersonating. Like someone 'doing' Bogart."

She shook her head, not listening. "Really, John, if you would try not to be quite so vulgar whilst my parents are in town, I would be very much obliged to you."

I felt a scowl coming on. Ever since her parents had phoned, I felt like I had become engaged to one of the haughtier British Royals.

I clarified: "You are concerned that your parents will believe I am mocking their speech?"

That was what she was concerned about, yes.

"Ah," I said.

She had a point, I suppose. I did have my accent issues. Back in my school days, and owing to the fact that my uncle/guardian (the jackass congressman) couldn't stand the sight of me as a boy, I was shipped off to England to receive my education. It was there that I met Hutton. It was also where I spent much of my adolescence, the experience leaving me with a slight, though unmistakable, British style of speaking—which most people think I cultivate, but I don't. Even now, ten years later, Americans think I'm English, the English think I'm American, and here in Portland, Maine, they just think I'm strange.

"That's all we need is for you to get off on the wrong foot because of something you say—or how you say it. My father's an orator. He won't take kindly to you—"

"Taking the Mick?"

She held up her other hand, the one not massaging her temple. "Please don't."

I said sorry.

Brit-speak or not, I thought she was going a bit overboard here. I *had* met people before, after all. I didn't like to brag, but in my time I had hobnobbed with some impressive specimens. Knights of the British Empire. Congressmen. I was once closely associated with a governor. Actually it was a governor's daughter, and she came to detest me, but it was still something.

"I'll just stick with grunts and other low guttural sounds—will that make you happy?"

"Delighted."

I said Excellent, and she said Great. I said Super, and she said Hmm. That was that.

I gave her a reassuring smile. "See, there's nothing to be on about, really."

She put her fingers to her temples again and rubbed. I think she had a headache. Just then, the patio door opened, and we could hear Ate ushering her tour inside. Lesley gasped.

"Oh God! They're back. Go. Go and meet them while I finish the drinks. Just don't sound so bloody English." She paused. "And for God's sake, don't come off as too American!"

Even though I had been denied my gambling trip, I did have one ace up my sleeve this weekend. Call it a secret talent. Some men know the right quip for any occasion, others can slip a compliment seamlessly into the conversation. With me, it's a first-class handshake.

It's the one social trait I have, in fact, cultivated. Perhaps it comes from having a relative who's a politician, I don't know. All I do know is, you're not going to find a better one. The rest of the weekend might prove an utter washout, relations might be strained and banns forbidden, but the handshaking portion would be a pure delight.

I located the family, appropriately enough, in the family room. After a quick wave to Ate, who was looking very elegant and hospitality-specialist-ish today, and a nod of welcome to Jill, looking very English-lass-y, I made my approach to Mr. and Mrs. Darlington.

Lesley's "Mum" got first dibs. This was fine by me. The quality of the handshake, I've found, doesn't matter as much to women, but I didn't let that affect my performance. A pro never does. I gave her the female version, solid but not too aggressive. For a moment I thought it might descend into a hug, but Margaret seemed to remember she was British before it was too late, and we kept it professional. This was also fine. There would be plenty of time for hugs later on. I don't know what she thought of my jeans, but I would have given her outer shell top marks. Dressed in a simple summer frock, she had kept her figure, and in many ways looked like a well-aged version of her daughters.

Next stop Lawrence Darlington. Lesley had described her father to me, but her description hardly prepared me for the man in the flesh. I'm a little over six foot myself, and he had to have at least five inches on me. If Hutton ever showed up—he's 6'4—we could have started up a pretty good pick-up basketball team. At the peak of Darlington Mountain was a mop of sandy hair, roguishly brushed and graying at the temples. He looked like a British Kennedy.

Jutting out toward me was a bear paw of a hand. I reached up and grasped it.

It was a beautiful shake. Firm but not too firm, relaxed but not overly relaxed. Personally, I don't adhere to the supporting grip on the forearm, the round-the-horn secondary grasp with the left hand. I consider it bush league. Lawrence Darlington would appear to agree. We kept it simple. Lesley came in the room toward the tail end, and what loving heart would not have been touched by the inspirational scene playing out before her: the two men in her life locked in an ancient and manly tradition.

We released hands, perfectly on cue, and stood smiling at each other. Things could not have gone better.

Well, not with the handshake anyway. As I waited there, watching the smile slowly run away from Lawrence's face, something felt amiss. I realized what this was. I had been so intent on the mechanism of the shake, so focused on making sure every little segment of it came off smoothly, that I had totally ignored the man. Throughout our shaking, Lesley's father had been speaking pretty steadily to me, and it dawned on me now that I had no clue what he had been steadily saying. Nor, for that matter, did I have any clue what Lesley's mother had said. She had chimed in about two seconds into the introductions, a few words upon this historic occasion, but for all I knew she could have been rattling off cricket scores.

I peered back and forth between the two faces, four Darlington eyes boring into me. Behind me, I could feel Lesley's Darlington eyes boring into me too. "Well, Johnny," I heard her ask. "*Do you?*"

This put a new complexion on the matter. A Yes or No question. Even odds. 50-50. Simply call all-in or fold. I could do this. "Y-yes," I replied.

Once again, I had said the wrong thing. "Oh Johnny!" she sighed, and on that note the whole gang adjourned to the enclosed terrace for brunch. I knew I should have gone with No.

I spent the next ten minutes wondering what I had said yes to, and why it had made the entire Darlington clan flounce from the room rolling their eyes. I would have to remember to ask Lesley about it later.

Eventually the tension began to ease up, if only to make room for the next argument: specifically, food and where the hell was it?

Lesley, twirling her hair nervously, said she thought Ate was attending to the eats. Ate—her round, Audrey-Hepburn-esque face flushing prettily—said she had asked Hutton to bring the trays. And Hutton, who wasn't there, said nothing.

In the midst of the mounting bicker, Mrs. Darlington turned to me and asked me how my work was proceeding. I thought it was a kindly gesture after I had failed to acknowledge her remarks earlier, showing that she had no hard feelings about the incident.

I would have answered her promptly, only I hadn't really been listening.

"Sorry?"

"Your work, John. Lesley tells us you're some kind of, what was it now—freelance courier?"

I heard Lesley's father make a low grunt of disapproval behind me.

"That's right. I mean, I am. Yes."

"It's a rather unusual occupation, isn't it? We don't hear much about couriers in this day and age, much less 'freelance' ones. How odd that you can make a living at this."

I had to agree with her there. The freelance courier game, I told her, wasn't all that it was cracked up to be in this day and age. I blamed the Internet.

"And I understand you have also been dabbling in the private investigation business?"

"A little dabbling, yes," I replied, over the sound of another Lawrence Darlington snort. "You see, I have these two friends—"

"We don't have many private investigators in the UK," continued Margaret Darlington. "Those we do have tend to get in the way of the real professionals. Or that is what Lawrence here always says they do," she chortled.

"Yes," I answered, after a short pause. "They're not so common here anymore either," I agreed, declining to dignify with a response what Lawrence there always said. "They've become rather specialized," I explained—"freelance."

"There's that word again," said Mrs. D. "Freelance. It must be nice not having to worry about the drudgery of real work," she smiled, taking up a spare celery stalk and nibbling it.

I was still trying to decide whether I had been the victim of a Darlington dig, when we were interrupted by the sound of growling. At first, I thought Lawrence had weighed in with another comment on my line(s) of work, but that wasn't it. This was a lower, fiercer growl, like a small wolverine discussing politics.

Seconds later, a tiny short-haired Maltese came scampering up the porch steps to greet us. I knew her well. It was Pixie. Pixie, the dog.

Her presence could only mean one thing. At least one guest had accepted our humble invitation:

Enescu Fleet—detective, father and the perfect man to rescue a dying party—was here.

He came around the side of the house now, his step jaunty as ever, but perhaps not quite as surefooted as I had sometimes seen it. Upon his tweedy shoulder he was supporting a tousled and limping Hutton, who looked even less surefooted, and certainly not jaunty.

# 3 — Old Man with Dog

We responded to Hutton's raggedy appearance in a variety of ways. I kicked things off with a sharp and inquisitive "Dude?" I could sound plenty American when it was called for. Ate came in a beat behind, declaring "Hut-ton!" in an astonished voice, followed by "Dad, [this directed to Fleet] what's wrong with Hutton?" I thought the blend of sympathy and concern she conveyed, especially on the second syllable of the first *Hutton*, did her credit; and if he hadn't been busy looking like something thrown out of a passing helicopter, Hutton probably would have thought so too. In fact, I'm pretty sure I spotted that winning grin of his as he shuffled past, but then he tripped on the top step, and the lovely moment they might have shared fizzled.

Lesley also said "Hutton" but in a tired and harassed tone, no doubt feeling that if anyone could show up at an already strained social gathering with his clothing torn and his person trampled, then that anyone was Hutton.

Scrolling down the list, Margaret Darlington gave a short, astounded sniff. Her husband scowled, as though to say "I don't much like the look of that trampled chap." Jill rounded out the lot by picking up the dog Pixie and showering kisses on her tiny furry face. Jill loved dogs, as any recent veterinary science graduate should. She may have also said "Oh hullo, Hutton" as he passed—I don't recall.

He gave us all a wave of hello. Very regal, very aristocratic. Always with the waving, this guy. For my part, I would have pressed down my spronging hair before worrying about any salutes, but that's just me. "Just a bit of a fender-bender as the Yanks say," he explained on the upswing. "Nothing to worry about."

Lesley wasn't buying it. "Fender-bender? What sort of fender-bender?" She didn't like fender-benders.

"Just a little smash-up," he replied.

He made his way to the door, still assisted by Enescu Fleet. Pixie brought up the rear, back on all fours and barking conversationally as they went.

"Give him a moment to freshen up, and he'll be the life and soul of the party," her owner assured the gathering.

They hobbled off into the kitchen. Ate, stiffening on the word "fender-bender," stiffened again as she remembered Hutton's role at the brunch. "The hors d'oeuvres!" she gasped, and hurried around the side of the house to assess the damage.

If I thought the concern and sympathy she had shown Hutton touching, the emotion she exhibited for our trays of food totally moved me.

I turned and followed the three-legged race inside.

I located them upstairs in the master. Fleet was sitting on the four-poster bed, rubbing Pixie's rose-colored belly. The door to the bathroom was shut, and the sound of running water could be heard: Hutton freshening up.

Fleet beamed welcomingly.

It's odd, no matter how well I get to know this man—and you can't interact with a retired private eye like Enescu Fleet, helping him solve a murder of mind-bending proportions, without getting to know him pretty well—I still can't settle on what to call him. "Fleet," by itself, is okay for our narrative, but it has never sounded right face to face. I can't quite pull off the "Enescu," and his original suggestion to call him "Ef"—pronounced like the letter *F*—has never really clicked with me. I suppose it's not important. He usually packed enough into his own salutation for the both of us: "Johnny! How are things, you ridiculous young groom-to-be!"

I hadn't seen him in almost a year. He hadn't changed. His beard was still impeccably trimmed with the perfect ratio of salt to pepper.

His eyes were as bright and twinkling as the day we met. He wore a tweed jacket and sweater vest and, all in all, appeared as fit and ruggedly well built as any man in his sixties could hope to look. In fact, he appeared fitter than most thirty-year-olds could hope to look.

He shook my hand and thumped me on the shoulder—he excelled at all forms of greeting—and asked me how the wedding plans were coming along.

I said they were coming along pretty well, as wedding plans went, and immediately switched gears to Hutton. "Is he alright in there?"

Fleet checked his own look in the mirror. "He should be fine. Splash of soap and a little peroxide, and he will be as good as new."

"Did he really have a fender-bender?"

"Not unless the other car snuck up behind him with a baseball bat."

I stared blankly, and Fleet elaborated, "I found him sitting in the driveway just now, holding a tray of finger food and looking like the dust you clean out of a coffee grinder. I don't have any details beyond that."

He stepped back from the mirror to make way for Hutton. The latter appeared nearly himself again. That peroxide was amazing stuff.

He was still hobbling. He took a seat beside Pixie and gave her exposed belly a stoic glance of acknowledgement. "Dog."

I asked him what happened.

"Miscreants, Hath, that's what happened."

"What miscreants?"

"The ones tailing us from your home, that's what. I suppose you didn't notice the car parked across the street when we left?"

Actually I had noticed it. "It was parked across the street," I said, "when we left."

"Exactly. As soon as we pulled out, it followed."

"No kidding. I remember not liking the look of it at the time."

Hutton hadn't liked its look either. "And I decided to do something about it. I led them on a merry chase. I had no sooner pulled off the most amazing Tahoma Maneuver—"

"You mean like a Toyota?"

"Not a Tacoma—a *Tahoma*. A Tahoma Maneuver."

"What's a Tahoma Maneuver?"

"The amazing maneuver I had just pulled off." He sighed. "In the private detective game, Hath, it's helpful to use shorthand expressions for these sorts of tactics. Saves a lot of time explaining, and people in the know understand exactly what you're talking about."

I looked to Fleet, who shrugged. As one in the know, he didn't seem to understand any better than I did.

Hutton proceeded, more forceful in tone: "I had no sooner pulled off the Tahoma and was in the process of concealing myself in traffic behind them—"

"Oh, you were behind them at that point?"

"Yes, Hath, I was behind. The essence of any good Tahoma is the slingshot behind."

This was news to me.

"As I was saying, I had no sooner obscured myself in traffic behind them than I saw them give up the hunt and pull down an alley. I should have known it was a trap. It had Desdemona Gambit written all over it."

I considered asking what a Desdemona Gambit was, but let it go. Hutton went on:

"I parked behind a dumpster and went the rest of the way on foot. They were just idling there, or so I thought. I crept up for a closer look, and that's when they dropped the hammer."

"A Desdemona?"

"A Tahoma, their own Tahoma. They weren't in the car at all. They were behind me. Or one of them was. He hit me with something that may or may not have been a two-by-four, and that's when I twisted my knee—pivoting to repel the assault. He started to get rough after that—that is, until I managed to get my Benchmade free and stab him in the foot. That took the stuffing out of him. From there, he went over and started poring through my Wrangler. There was a crowd forming at the other end of the alley by then, so he hobbled back to his car and screeched off, only missing my head by a whisper. I can't be certain, but he may have also eaten all the crab puffs before he went."

I massaged my temples, absorbing the finer points of Hutton's day out. I think I was getting Lesley's headache. "What were they after?" I asked. I frowned at him, letting him know in no uncertain terms not to say crab puffs.

"I don't know."

"I don't know" wasn't much better. "Could this have anything to do with your 'professional obligation' this morning?"

"I don't think so. That—that was something else," he said.

I shook my head and continued massaging. I looked over at Hutton's aged counterpart, uncharacteristically silent throughout the younger investigator's narrative. I guess, as a gifted storyteller himself, he only really interested himself in stories he was telling himself.

"Any thoughts?" I wondered.

Fleet fixed me in his friendliest steady gaze. "My only thought is we're missing an excellent party thrown for you by my daughter."

I frowned. "Are you on a case yourself?" I asked. It wouldn't have been the first time he had neglected to mention some trifling professional detail such as this.

"I'm retired, Johnny. You know that."

All I knew was few men in their prime worked as regularly and as well as he did retired. He continued open and bright toward Hutton. "You got the license plate, I assume?"

Personally I thought this was a bit much to ask of a man in his condition. Some vague recollection of his assailant, perhaps, but jot down this assailant's particulars while he was whaling on you? It hardly seemed likely. But that was why they were the professionals and I spent my time mood-lighting postcards.

Hutton replied quickly and in the affirmative. He had gotten the plates, yes.

"I have a buddy downtown who may be able to help," said Fleet. This was not news. Fleet had a buddy everywhere.

"I wouldn't bother," Hutton told him. "They're fakes. I have buddies downtown too," he added. "I called in the info before I came over. My friend promptly gave me the raspberry. The tags won't get us anywhere."

"Then it appears that we have very little to go on," Fleet concluded.

Hutton wasn't so sure about that. He did record one other item of note. "I remember noticing, just before the smackdown, that the car had one of those whatchamacallits stamped on the boot, real small. What do you call those things? Those whatchamacallits?"

Anyone else posed with this question would have said they called them *whatchamacallits* and asked you what in heaven's name you thought you were babbling about. Fleet replied coolly and without hesitation, "A dealer logo."

"Yes, that's it, a dealer logo. I detest the things normally—garish little automotive tattoos—but I thought it might help here. The dealer's a place called Wainwright Motors."

Fleet knew it well. "One of the salesmen there is a pal of mine."

Hutton didn't doubt it. "I don't know how much good it will do us, really—"

"On the contrary, it's brilliant."

"It is?" asked Hutton, frankly surprised by this.

"It is?" I echoed.

It was. "Wainwright doesn't normally sell cars," said Fleet. "They're a Land Rover dealer."

"And since this was no Rover—" began Hutton.

"It was sold there used. Correct. My friend may still know who bought it."

Hutton smiled. "Good man. See what he knows. Pry things out of him. And if he says he has to ask his sales manager first, kick him in the kneecap."

Fleet promised to keep that technique in mind. "But for now," he said, "brunch." He whistled to Pixie, and the pair headed for the doorway.

Lesley appeared in their path, a tiny barrier of indignation. "What's everybody doing up here?" She blinked at the soles of Hutton's feet, the rest of him having flopped back on the bed. "He dead?"

We confirmed the divine spark.

"Fantastic. What happened to him? Ate says his Jeep looks fine."

"I was set upon by miscreants," said Hutton, now stretching his sore knee.

"Just a little trifle," I replied, trying to ease her anxiety. (I could have hit him with a two-by-four myself.)

"One of those unfortunate byproducts of urban life," added Fleet, taking my lead.

"They were hired muscle alright," said Hutton, doing his part. "Real pros."

Lesley had withdrawn from the entranceway. She wandered into the room, twirling her hair at us. "Do you think this could have anything to do with Johnny 'Fishes'?" she asked in a low, furtive tone.

I looked at Hutton, Hutton looked at Fleet. Fleet returned my gaze.

"This is his house, isn't it? John 'Fishes' Herring, the crime figure?"

She was speaking to Hutton. And to my chagrin, he nodded. It was Johnny Herring's house. The killer Fishes, and none other. He seemed almost pleased about it. I could have hit him with another two-by-four.

It seemed that Hutton's "buddy" was Herring's real estate agent (apparently the Fish was selling the pond). In payment for some favor or other, the agent had offered Hutton the use of the place while its owner was away, and Hutton, the idiotic chump, had snapped it up.

In reply to our rising verbal abuse, he asked us how else did we think we could get such a swank residence on short notice. We had to know the Mob was involved. "And Herring's hardly a crime figure anyway," he argued. "I mean, you get involved in a few shady business deals, make a couple Vrooms disappear, and people throw out these labels. He's a pretty nice bloke actually, from what I hear. Eats lots of veggies and soy, loves dogs. He even paints in his spare time."

I sniffed. He had just described Hitler.

"And generous. Why else would his estate agent feel comfortable loaning out his house?"

My theory was a death wish, but nobody asked me my theory.

"What about these Vrooms?" demanded Lesley. I think she just liked saying Vroom.

"You mean their little blood feud?" asked Hutton. "Doesn't involve anyone here, luv. The Vrooms and Herrings have it in for each other, not us."

I didn't know what Lesley thought about this, but I wasn't all too pleased. I mean, it didn't matter to me—I've always had a kindly tolerance for the Mafia, especially the piscine Mafia—but you never knew with women.

Hutton certainly hadn't helped matters by speaking so candidly. Other than mentioning, casually, that he had stumbled upon a Vroom gunman hanging on a meathook in the wine cellar, there wasn't much else he could have done to fill her with a raging panic.

Lesley, I was astonished to observe, was taking it pretty well. "Then you don't think that's who accosted you?"

"Who, a Vroomerang? I doubt it. Like I said, the Vrooms have nothing against us. They want Herring, and for all we know they've already whacked him. I know no one's heard from the man for quite some time."

"There you are, then," I announced, and went on to argue that there was probably some perfectly reasonable explanation for the brawl in the back alley. "I mean, people try to pound Hutton into the earth every other week. He's a sort of human fencepost that way."

"It's true," assented the post, finally pulling his own weight in the ease-Lesley campaign.

"Yes, I can see that," said Lesley. "Yes."

"But if it would make you happier," I went on, "we could move everything to my place."

"No. I don't think that will be necessary," she replied. "No."

She spoke absently. I had the feeling that she would rather be gunned down in a hail of Vroom-Herring crossfire than admit to her parents that she had placed them in this situation. "The food is all laid out downstairs, and I just made tea." She wandered from the room, muttering something about gangland slayings and milk and sugar.

Fleet smiled indulgently after her. "I've always liked that young lady of yours, Johnny. She's got pluck."

I nodded. I could have used some of that pluck myself right about then.

Hutton stood up between us. "Well, that's all settled," he said, placing his arms around our shoulders in a friendly spirit of camaraderie. "Now to figure out who tailed us and who, by extension, kicked me in my tender bits."

I peered over at him. "You really think Herring's feud has nothing to do with this?"

Hutton tossed up his hands, nearly taking a header from the lack of buttressing. "That's for us to find out." He gave us a squeeze. "The team, back together again. It will be just like our casino caper last year."

I sniffed. Fleet removed Hutton's hand and shifted a few steps away. If you've ever spent any time with a pair of headstrong private investigators—one old, one young, and each with their own quirks and eccentricities—you'd know they don't always play well together. Teamwork wasn't Fleet's bag.

"Okay, perhaps not like the whole caper," said Hutton, sensing the cool reception. "Maybe just the highlights." He released the claws from my shoulder. "Guess I should go help with the foodstuffs now. It's the least I can do."

He hesitated in the doorway. "Oh, Hath, I was thinking about that old client of mine, Celeste Hope. I'm pretty sure she did have an uncle or father or something. Whether or not his name was Stothard, I cannot say, but you'll be the first to know once the recollection checks in at the reception desk."

He ankled off, under about three-quarters power, and I moved to follow.

Another hearty grip held me in place. I glanced down to see the older private eye in the room grasping my shoulder. And when he grasped, he didn't mess around.

"What's this about Stothard Hope?"

I explained about the postcard and the message from someone I had never met named Stothard Hope.

"Where is this postcard now?" he asked, loosening the clamp, but with no lessening of urgency in his voice.

"I'm not sure. Why?"

"I'm going to need to see it as soon as possible," said Enescu Fleet.

## 4 — The Bohemian Touch

Not for the first time that afternoon, I didn't follow. I couldn't fathom the request at all. What could be so important about a postcard? It was just a postcard. And not to put too fine a point on it, but it hadn't been addressed to him. What was it about private detectives that made them so unmindful of that?

"What's up?" I asked.

He took a step closer. "Let me tell you a story, Johnny—"

I checked the brass clock on the nightstand. I didn't really have time for a story.

"Do you know why I was late this afternoon?"

I didn't. Could it be that he, too, had been set upon by miscreants?

"An old police buddy gave me a call. He wanted to know if I wouldn't mind coming down to the morgue to identify a body."

I shivered. I wouldn't have liked identifying bodies myself. I can't even hack watching CSI.

"The body was a John Doe they had pulled out of the water down by Saco. Turns out I could identify him. The John Doe was a certain old associate of mine by the name of Stothard Hope."

My eyebrows jerked up here. That is, I think they jerked up. They felt like they jerked. "Were you friends?"

"More like mild acquaintances. I once shot him in Madrid."

Of course he had. "Any particular reason?"

"Just a slight misunderstanding. And I only winged him."

I tried not to judge him too harshly. As a matter of fact, I'm amazed Fleet hasn't winged more of his old acquaintances. As I came to learn on our last case, most of the people in his past could do with a good winging. It's just the way of things, I guess. When you spend your life deducing who committed which crime on whom—where and with what—that doesn't leave a lot of time for interacting with nice, regular people.

"Do they know how he died?"

"The coroner says accidental drowning. I'm not so sure about that."

I felt distinctly unsettled. It wasn't just the thought that Fleet's old associate had been found drowned—and my condolences went out to Fleet and the rest of the Hopes on that one—but the notion that I had apparently been receiving messages from the guy from beyond the grave.

"So a dead man sent me a postcard?"

"So it would seem. Although he was no doubt alive when he mailed it."

I said yes, probably so. I took a stroll up and down the lambswool area rug—I believe it was lambswool. Suddenly my own deductive juices kicked in. I let out a *Ha!* of comprehension, sending Pixie scrambling under the duvet. "You're the old man!"

"Pardon?"

"The card said something about saying hi to the old man. You must be the old man."

"I wouldn't go that far," said Enescu Fleet.

I said no, maybe not. "But why send it to me?" I asked. Of all the people Fleet knew—which was many—why pick me? What was so special about John Hathaway?

That was exactly what Fleet would like to know. "If Stothard sent it to you, he must have had a reason."

"Was he in the habit of sending mysterious messages to strangers?"

"No, but his mind worked differently than most. He was cryptic. He was cryptic the last time anyone attempted to communicate with him. Just before going off the grid, he apparently told his granddaughter he was busy 'looking for some new threads.' "

"Threads, as in clothing?"

"That was how she understood it. But Stothard Hope had never been what you would call a clothing horse. I remember, once, he wore a single pair of corduroy trousers for six months straight. I think the threads comment might have been his idea of a riddle. A code, if you like."

This was all pretty fascinating, especially the corduroy insight, but I still didn't understand why he had written to me. "I never even met the man."

"No, but he would have heard about our exploits last year: the murder, the unusual clue left behind by the victim. Your engagement. He probably figured when you got his message, you would pass it along to your pal, the world-famous detective."

It all sounded oddly reasonable, if not a bit overly complicated. Then again, most things with Fleet were. "What do you think the card meant?"

"I don't know."

There was something disconcerting about Enescu Fleet saying he didn't know. You always expected he would. (I liked how he had worked in the "world-famous" part, though.)

"Do you think Hutton was right? This card is also a code?"

Fleet inclined his head in reluctant agreement. He never enjoyed stringing along with the peers in his industry, especially if that peer was a certain young whippersnapper by the name of Hutton.

I was about to ask him more about Stothard Hope, what sort of man he had been and how often Fleet had shot him, when he cut in again, "I assume you were only joshing your elder when you said you didn't know where the card was now?"

"Huh? Oh sure. I mean yes."

A short pause. Fleet smiled. I smiled. Pixie licked her paw.

"So where is it?" he asked.

I threw my mind back.

"I know it was in the kitchen at one point, because Hutton and I talked about it."

"Then it's back at your house?"

"No. I'm pretty certain Hutton has it."

I continued throwing my mind back. If I wasn't careful, I was going to strain something. "Yes, I'm sure of it now. It's not at the house. I remember when I came back with my keys, the card—which

I had previously set on the kitchen counter—had disappeared. I didn't really think about it at the time, but it was definitely conspicuous by its absence. Hutton must have snatched it up for later study. He tends to pocket anything that's not bolted down or currently on fire."

Fleet scooped up Pixie from the covers and held her at chest height, smoothing her fur. "Then we must speak with Hutton about it without delay."

It was no skin off my nose. "I'll try to catch up with him downstairs." Anything was preferable to interacting with my prospective in-laws.

Something else occurred to me. All kinds of things were that day. "Do you think these so-called miscreants of his were after the card?"

"It's possible. Stothard had a knack for attracting the wrong sort."

I shook my head. All this over a picture postcard!

"I wonder why they tailed Hutton and not me?"

For this, Fleet did have a more definitive answer (if not a cryptic one): "They might have spotted him with it. I assume you still have those large French doors in your kitchen?"

Of course I still had the large French doors in my kitchen! Did he think I had bricked them up or something? "And how'd you know I had French doors anyway? You've never even been to my place."

"They were in the background of the Christmas card you and Lesley sent out last year."

I kept forgetting the man was a detective, a world-famous one.

"From what I could make out in the photo, a spy would have an excellent view in. I wouldn't conduct any business by those doors in the future, Johnny."

If this was what Enescu Fleet noticed in Christmas cards then no wonder he never accepted our Yuletide invitation to roast chestnuts and drink eggnog. He had all the holiday spirit of Wild Bill Hickok.

"Come," said the modern mental gunslinger, returning a squirming Pixie dog to the floor. It was like releasing a windup toy. "Before my daughter sends up a search-and-rescue team."

Connecting up with Hutton again proved a good deal harder than I would have thought. When I arrived on the veranda downstairs I saw that the party, if you could call it that, had already started. If you could call it a start.

Lesley's parents were gazing out at the bay, no doubt discussing ways of telling their daughter that marriage was a sacred affair not to be entered into lightly. Lesley was at the table behind them, silently chewing hors d'oeuvres at Jill, who was hanging around the kitchen door, probably wondering what became of Pixie. Ate was presiding at the wet bar across from them, occasionally sipping one of her own libations and basically waiting for someone to liven up the proceedings by choking on a stuffed radish.

At such an affair, you can't very well burst on the scene demanding coded communiques. Taxing Hutton about the postcard called for a certain measure of subtlety—guile. Or, if nothing else, a moment alone with the dumbass.

The real snag proved to be the dumbass himself. For reasons known only to him, he kept flitting back and forth from the porch to the house, always with his head down and never from the same door twice. He would appear on the porch from the dining room, snatch up a salmon crouton or hunk of gorgonzola in pastry, and quickly limp off again, only to pop up again from the kitchen. I couldn't get a word in with the man.

I'd had enough. I went and waited behind the pantry door for him to make his culinary journey. He swept past some seconds later, crunching a jalapeño-flavored almond.

I tackled him and pulled him off to the side.

He didn't appreciate the physicality. He'd had enough roughhousing for one day. This wasn't our old dormitory room, he said.

I had some criticisms of my own. "What's all this floating-like-a-butterfly, scarfing-like-a-bee stuff? Are you doing laps?"

"I like to keep moving at parties, Hath. You know that."

It was the second time that day someone had told me I knew something I knew, when I knew perfectly well that I didn't know it at all.

Perhaps I could rephrase that…

"Hutton, I need to talk to you."

"Talk away."

"I need that postcard."

"What, the Stothard? I don't have it. You must have left it at your house."

I was pretty sure I had done nothing of the sort and put forward my amazing powers of recollection by way of evidence.

"What amazing powers of recollection?" he asked.

"I'm a very observant person. You know that. I notice all kinds of details."

"Since when?"

"Since—never mind since when!"

"Really? Tell me, what color are Lesley's eyes?"

"Green."

"You're probably right," he said, nodding. He turned away. "Okay, what's the color of my eyes?"

"How the hell should I know?"

"An observant person would know."

"I don't spend my off-hours gazing into your eyes, Hutton!"

"No, and see that you keep it that way. But my point is, you don't observe all the details around you by a long shot. You probably don't even know how many steps there are in front of your house."

"There aren't any steps in front of my house."

"Really? I thought there were." He waved aside this petty fact. "It's not important. Look, if this is about me mocking your technique earlier with the kitchen light and the postcard, I apologize. I'm sure, with a little work, you could make a very fine detective. But the fact is, I don't have it. The card, I mean. I don't have your kitchen light either."

I began to crawl down. Hutton might have had a lot of contemptible qualities, but he was no liar. If he said he didn't have a postcard, he didn't have it.

"I guess I left it home, then. But it wasn't on the counter. That much I'm sure of."

"There you go. A compromise to satisfy all involved. The card is somewhere at your house but outside the scope of the counter. That's agreeable. So why do you want it so bad?"

I gave him the skinny on the late Stothard Hope and Fleet's trip to the morgue.

"Remarkable," Hutton concluded. He scratched his goatee. "Then Fleet thinks it's a code too?"

"Something along those lines. He's not sure. That's why he needs to see it."

Hutton said he wouldn't mind seeing it again himself, especially since it was no doubt meant for him.

"Stothard's niece or cousin or whoever she was must have put him onto my services before he died. *If you're ever in a bind, uncle/cousin, the man to call*—well, you get the idea. Everybody knows you and I are goombahs. He probably sent the card to you to give to me."

I must have appeared dubious or shuffled my feet or something, because my goombah scowled. "Why, what does Fleet think about it?"

"He thinks Stothard sent it to me, for him."

"Rubbish. Fleet's not even in the game anymore. Trust me, I'm the man the Great White Hope was calling out."

I really didn't care, as long as I wasn't the one he was calling. I did pause to wonder if referring to him as the "Great White Hope" wasn't racist in some way.

"I guess the only way to confirm it for certain is to crack the Stothard Code," said Hutton. "What are the chances of us all slipping away to confer?"

"Easier said than done," I grumbled.

Hutton scowled again; a scowl of sympathy. "Things not going so swimmingly with the Darlingtons?"

"Not by a long shot," I replied, and explained about the Lost Conversation.

He clucked sympathetically. "That's too bad. You have an excellent handshake, Hath. Seems a shame to have wasted it."

"Thanks, Hutton. It's nice to be appreciated for one's art."

We paused a moment in mutual admiration.

"Still," he remarked, "it's better than my encounter with the man."

Another of those creeping feelings began to steal over me. "What encounter?" I asked.

He smiled brightly but with a sidelong look in his eyes (which were blue, I noticed, not that it matters). I knew that smile. It was the sort of smile he always prefaced to the words, "This is going to amuse you, Hath..."

"This is going to amuse you, Hath, but I had a little run-in with Pop Darlington earlier."

"Lesley's father? When?"

"At the airport. You see, the case I thought I had a lead on was him."

For about the twentieth time that day, I asked Hutton what he meant by this.

"The fact is—" He paused to cough softly. "I thought he was this notorious con artist, a man who had been eluding the authorities for decades, and I sort of, well, accosted him about it."

I stared. There was another long pause, and Hutton carried on:

"Fortunately, he didn't get a very good look at me, and I'm trying to make sure he doesn't get a very good look at me here. Hence the flit."

I couldn't quite process this. "You thought my fiancée's father, my future father-in-law, was a notorious con artist?"

"That's right. An assumption anyone could make, really."

I stepped back, my mind still reeling. In the interim, Pixie scurried over, gnawed my shoelace and scurried off again, closely tracked by Ate Fleet.

The mistress of the hunt paused to take a breather. I was happy to see her (always am). I like to think of Ate as the sister I never had.

As I believe I've mentioned before, her late mother (Pixie's original owner) had apparently been quite the knockout—a kind of Spanish goddess from what I understand—and in looks Ate took more after the Latin mode than her father's; although I've never been clear what mode he was in exactly. (All I did know was—Enescu aside—Fleet was no Romanian.) His daughter, while not classically beautiful, had an intoxicating charm all her own. She had a long and graceful figure, and, like her dad, the mortal world was hers to command. She reminded me of some South American revolutionary, stirring up her village to throw off the yoke of tyranny.

"That dog is too much," she said. She was wearing her hair down to her shoulders now—a little longer than Lesley's and more sprightly in its presentation. Very revolutionary-y. "Why Dad has to bring her everywhere he goes, I'll never know. And what are you two doing congregating in here? It's like a morgue out on the porch. I need warm bodies."

Sort of mixing her metaphors there, I thought, but I didn't mention it.

"And what's so fascinating about the kitchen anyway?" she asked. "You expecting Guy Fieri or something? What's the big attraction?"

I fielded that one. "Hutton was explaining why he never met up with you at the airport this morning."

"Oh yeah? Why?"

"He was busy sitting on the head of Lesley's father, accusing him of being an infamous—what was it you said? Cat burglar?"

"Con artist," he replied. He glanced from my face to Ate's and then back to mine. "Perhaps I should explain," he said.

His story was a simple one. He arrived at the airport bright and early this morning. It was the crack of ten fifteen.

"I was expecting you at the crack of nine thirty," said Ate.

He waved her aside. He arrived at the airport, he said, and went to the gate to meet her. She wasn't there. Either owing to his slight tardiness, or because a certain hospitality specialist had given him the wrong gate—he wasn't pointing fingers—he continued to wait for a good ten minutes to no avail. At that point, he decided to go exploring.

"I suppose you never thought to call my cell?"

Hutton waved her aside for a second time. Mobiles were for amateurs.

Now where was he? Oh yes. He had gone exploring. And who should he spot right out of the box, but a man who was the spitting image of Gerome Lance, a notorious con artist last known to be operating out of Wales over twenty years ago.

I snorted. Gerome Lance. Stothard Hope. Where did these guys get these names?

Hutton had been shown a photo once, and due to his amazing powers of recollection—I said *harrumph*—he was sure it was he. Recently there had been word from various white-collar agencies that the man had resurfaced; and perhaps owing to getting too little sleep the night before, or possibly because he didn't have any jobs to sink his teeth into at the moment—he wasn't pointing fingers—he probably acted a bit precipitously at this point. He confronted him.

"Confronted him where?" I wondered.

"The men's room."

I nodded. Where else?

He followed him into the men's. They had words, and Hutton had determined that the man possibly wasn't Gerome, after all. "Shortly after that, we parted. I went outside, just in time to see your sports wagon zipping off. Of course, I had no idea who I had just hassled. Had I known, I would have begged off today, believe me."

I believed him. I also felt like smacking him, but that is neither here nor there.

I suppose it might have been worse. Had he taken more after the elder Fleet, he might have shot him.

Ate gave her head a shake. "You probably shouldn't hang around here," she told Hutton. "If Mr. Darlington hasn't gotten a good look at you, we might still be able to salvage things. We can say you weren't feeling well after your car accident. What really happened to you, by the way? Someone accost you in the men's room too?"

Hutton said it was a long story, and she nodded and held up her hand. She'd had enough of the Epic of Hutton for one morning. "Just slip out, and we'll explain."

It wasn't a bad idea. "I can call you later about the card," I said.

"What card?" asked Ate. I said it was another long story, and she nodded again. "Well, I guess I should be getting back." She turned to me. "Speaking of cards, you don't know any tricks or anything, do you, Hathaway? The party's dying out there."

I answered that I did know one card trick, yes, and she said it didn't matter, she didn't have a deck on her. "Well, cheers, mates, or whatever it is you people say."

I motioned her back.

"Did Lesley mention anything to you about a man called Fishes?" I was still concerned about my fiancée's mindset after our conversation in the master.

"No. Who's a man called Fishes?"

I said it wasn't important.

"Long story?"

"Long story," I agreed.

She said right and rejoined the rave on the back porch. Hutton left soon after, in the opposite direction. He refused to say cheers.

## 5 — The Master at Work

You hate to say that the departure of your best friend brings with it a warm and cozy feeling in your soul, but that was how Hutton's left mine. For once that day, I felt in control. Lesley no longer appeared to be obsessing over Fishes Herring; the mystery of Hutton's "professional obligations" had been explained and dealt with; and very shortly we'd find the Stothard Hope postcard, paving the way for a fascinating intrigue, care of Enescu Fleet. And not only would that work the stagnant brain a bit, it would provide an excellent escape from this living O'Neil play of a party.

I reentered the porch a better, happier man, and the first person I saw was Jill Darlington: another sister I never had but would shortly obtain through the magic of matrimony.

She had reconnected with her canine soulmate and was tickling her ribs, informing her that she was a "cutsie wootsie lil puppy dog."

"She's never going to learn proper English if you talk to her like that."

Jill looked up and gave me a quick Darlington smile. I had seen that smile in her mother, however sneeringly, and of course in her sister Lesley many times, though not in recent weeks. Whether Old Man Lawrence possessed it remained to be seen. "Hiya, Johnny."

I hiya-ed right back. I hadn't seen Jill since she'd come to visit Lesley on vacation from veterinary school. She had to be in her early twenties now. Despite the singular smile, she didn't look like her sister.

She had smaller facial features, rosier apple cheeks and shorter hair, curling around her face in a kind of rounded frame.

"You seem to have bonded with Pixie pretty well."

"Is that her name?" She proceeded with the tickling. "Is that your name, wittle woolly puppy wuppie?"

"That's her name," I said.

"I love dogs. Especially Maltese. They're such lambs."

I frowned. If this was what they taught her at vet school, someone might want to have a word with the dean.

"And so smart too." She pried the pup up off the floor and pointed her toward the bar. "Go. Go fetch Jill a brandy."

"I think you're thinking of a St. Bernard."

"Am I?" She glanced back at Pixie, the latter frankly nonplussed. "Go and fetch momma a vermouth, then. Go. Snag Johnny a malt while you're at it." Pixie scampered off on her errand—she probably wouldn't know my brand—leaving the humans to chew the fat.

"I read that thing of yours," she said abruptly.

"Oh yes?"

"Yes. That thing about Enescu Fleet and the Wolf Valley. He's the duffer who owns Pixie, right?"

I said he was the duffer.

"It wasn't bad. Your thing, I mean."

"Thanks."

"There was a lot about you in it, though, wasn't there."

I said I guessed there was. I hadn't really been counting.

"Not a lot about Lesley."

I said no, I guessed there wasn't. That was rather the point, I explained. Lesley had vanished, and I had no idea where she had gone.

"No, I understand that," said Jill. "Still, there was a lot about you in it," she insisted. "Kind of like that piece a few years back on Sir Roger Banbury and that artifact thingy, the Azure Star. There was a lot about you in that too, and not so much about Lesley."

I reminded her that I had no control over that piece, and she nodded and said she supposed I didn't. "Doesn't seem like you've made much of a hit with Mum and Dad." She was firing on all cylinders today, our Jill. "Why didn't you answer Dad's question better?"

I had a simple explanation for this: "I didn't know what your father's question was. I didn't hear it. What was it, by the way?"

"No idea. I didn't hear it. I thought you must have. You answered it."

I agreed I had. Boy, had I answered it.

"There you go, then," she smiled, and there I didn't go at all. "Draggy party," she sniffed. "Not that it's that girl Ate's fault. It's the atmosphere. It's almost as if there's a sense of awkwardness and hard feelings in the air."

She didn't know the half of it.

"Dogs can sense emotion, you know, and I think people can too, they just don't realize it. Of course, it would help if there were more guests here." She leaned in. "I don't wanna be a buttinsky, Johnny, but if you want some advice from your future sis, try inviting more people next time. It takes the strain off."

I said I would keep that in mind.

"I thought for a minute we had gotten a new one," she sighed, "but he didn't stay."

"Do you mean Hutton?"

"Hutton? No, not Hutton. This was some other fellow. He rang the bell while you were upstairs. I met him at the door."

"Who was he?"

"No idea. I thought he was a guest, but he didn't stay."

"So you said. Did he want anything?"

"Didn't seem like it. He just loitered about on the stoop a minute and then left."

I shivered. Not sure why, but I did. "Did he give a name?"

"I don't think so. He was an odd sort of fellow. Well spoken but hard at the same time. Square head. Anyway, if you want to know who he was, he said he'd be back around later."

And with another dreamy smile, she went to see what was keeping Pixie with the drinks.

I wasn't sure what to make of this statement of Jill's. Just because someone was hanging around John Herring's stoop with a big square head didn't automatically qualify him as a Vroom gunman. On the other hand, it didn't qualify him as not a Vroom gunman, if that makes sense. That was what got me to thinking. Typical of Jill not to have asked him his name. Sometimes I didn't know what was becoming of the younger generation.

In a sort of fog, I wandered out into the throng of brunchers, if you'd call it a throng, and pondered these new developments. As I drifted, a strange sound floated past my ears. So alien was it to my senses that it took me a minute to place it.

Laughter. It sounded like laughter. I looked up and confirmed it. It was laughter. Small laughs, big laughs, laughs of every shape and size. Perhaps Ate had tracked down that deck of cards, after all.

It wasn't a card trick. It was Enescu Fleet, the hospitality specialist's best friend. He was standing left stage center on the porch, regaling the party about the time he had met the queen or saved the Duchess of Digby's life or something of that variety. I didn't catch all of it.

The gang was eating it up. Ma and Pa Darlington, Lesley, Jill: all of them standing by, soaking in his remarks. Evidently what Margaret Darlington had said about the British view of private detectives did not apply to debonair retirees with salt-and-pepper beards and twinkles in their eyes. Even Ate, who'd probably heard the one about the queen fifty-eight times before, was gazing up with sincere appreciation at her father, the man of the hour.

I had half a mind to edge away and let them have their fun, but before I could, the great raconteur observed my arrival and without missing a beat segued to the tale of the murderer he had nabbed last year: a devious killer he could never have brought in without Lesley's and my assistance in the matter.

The audience turned in my direction. Rather than boring into my very soul, as certain parties had done earlier, all eyes rested on me warmly. Some were moist with tears of laughter, others dancing to the beat of the man's lively narrative, but they were all good-natured and welcoming in their intent.

The Hathaway stock was on the rise.

As I drew ever closer to the herd, I learned that Lesley and Ate's fathers had met before. Fleet really did know everyone. Apparently, he had assisted on several fraud investigations for Lawrence's firm. Not only that, but the only case of murder that had ever crossed their desks had been cleared up quickly and efficiently by Ef without any duress to the earl involved. (Not that there was an earl involved!) If you had asked Lawrence D, it was a near thing that the city hadn't commissioned a statue in the PI's honor. Or words to that effect.

Unfortunately, not every private investigator was made of this kind of quality material. And here Larry glared down at the ceramic tile, and I could tell he was thinking long, dark thoughts.

"Tell them about the young scalawag," prompted his wife.

Her husband thought he would. This young scalawag, it seemed, had been the impetus behind the negative feelings the Darlingtons had toward all other private investigators. The man had come into the firm a few years back—he couldn't have been much older than thirty—and using the name Enescu Fleet of all things as his referral, proceeded to make a hash of one of their more delicate insurance cases. Lawrence had not interacted with him directly, but the man's technique, as related by the rest of the staff of the firm, had become the stuff of legend.

The man ended up solving the case well enough, Lawrence supposed, but not before ruffling every single person on the premises. This included their best client, none other than Sir Elton John, there to discuss a matter concerning one of his charitable foundations. It appeared that the scalawag had mistaken him for a comic juggler—who, oddly enough, they also had at the firm that day giving a deposition. It was a scandal, how the PI had spoken to one of Great Britain's most valued entertainers—Sir Elton, not the comic juggler—and this young man, this so-called investigator, evidently always conducted his business this way. He was a scalawag.

I couldn't tell you why, but the depiction of this scalawag sent a shiver up my spine. And Lawrence Darlington's next words suggested the reason. We'd hardly credit it, he continued, but the man had actually looked an awful lot like a deranged individual Lawrence had encountered earlier today. We'd hardly credit this as well, he went on, but this man, this deranged individual, had accosted him in a washroom of all places. And not only that—

I don't know what suggested that Hutton was standing behind me. Maybe it was the eyes of the crowd, back in boring mode and focused on something over my shoulder. Perhaps it was my basic sixth sense and detective-ness bobbing to the surface again. Whichever it was, I turned, I looked, and there he was. Hutton, a.k.a. the scalawag PI.

He was leaning over the buffet table, hastily assembling a bag of veggies and nuts inside a napkin.

"Just a little nosh for the drive," he whispered to me, scooping in his grab-bag of goodies.

And then he went. The Hathaway stock, I observed, was on the decline.

The remainder of brunch, to use Hutton's own term, did not go all that swimmingly. Not even Fleet's good-natured presence could salvage the party now. He recounted several more anecdotes over dessert, carting out some real gems I thought, but the response to these was tepid at best. The audience was not in the mood.

I tried to explain about Hutton. I really did. But I had the distinct feeling, surveying the crowd, that my explanation wasn't going over. It was like trying to explain Mr. Hyde. By the time I had finished, all I seemed to have communicated was that Hutton and I were great friends, that he was a private detective—odd, even a little freakish in his methods—and that Elton John had some very nifty songs. Not exactly the way to win back friends and influence people.

And I hardly helped my cause a couple minutes later. The folks had finally shifted gears and moved on to a new topic. They were telling Lesley about the latest exploits of her brother Theodore, the apple of the Darlingtons' eye, and I had to go and butt in and say that we hadn't heard about Teddy since his actions nearly got Lesley and me killed at Sir Roger Banbury's estate a few years back.

My comments were not well received. I should have kept out of it. I was merely attempting to infuse a sort of cheerful camaraderie at the table—one large happy family, laughing about the time that one of the tribe almost got two of his fellow members murdered. The result came out more along the lines of an outspoken court jester making wisecracks at the expense of the crown's favorite prince. The Darlingtons did not abide any criticism of their Teddy. Teddy—that's Theodore to you, Hathaway—could do no wrong. And as my friend Hutton and I had already demonstrated that we could do plenty, I would have done well to have kept my mouth shut.

This I did now. I didn't pipe up again for twenty minutes, at which time I was asked, peevishly, if I was listening or wasn't I?

I peered up, a dollop of some custard-like substance quivering on the end of my fork.

"Pardon?"

Lesley had the mic. "Mum asked you a question, Johnny," she said from the far end of the table. "So, *did* you?"

It was a close thing whether I would burst into tears or laugh hysterically.

I did neither. I wasn't about to be scuppered on this again. I had it all taped out this time. I would simply reply, urbanely, that I was sorry, but I did not hear that last question, as I was otherwise engaged wondering if we had any arsenic on hand that I could slip into my custard.

I was all set to give this urbane reply, when young Jill galloped up to my rescue. Returning to her seat, she answered promptly (and, in the event, officiously), "Oh no, Johnny never would have done that. Absolutely not."

A layer of ice settled over the table. Various Darlingtons grumbled under their breath.

I was 0-for-2 on the $64,000 question, even if it was a proxy reply this time. I asked Jill later what this question had been, and she told me she wasn't sure, she hadn't heard it herself. She just figured she'd take a shot and lend a hand. It was a 50-50 chance.

Some ten minutes later, I found myself in the foyer in another one of my fogs. I wasn't completely clear how I arrived, or what had facilitated my escape, but it felt good to be free.

Fleet stepped up and gripped my shoulder.

"There you are," he said. "That wasn't all that pleasant. Any chance of you marrying someone other than a Darlington daughter?"

I said alas, Lesley was the only woman for me, which was weird because I never say alas, and he nodded and said it was just as well. He had always liked her. She had pluck.

"And I wouldn't concern myself about what her parents think. All prospective grooms go through a rough patch with the in-laws."

"Did the parents of your wife like you?"

"Adored me, but you can't go by that."

I said no, of course not, and fell into another reverie. Fleet interrupted it.

"Did you retrieve the card?"

Card? Card? Was I retrieving cards? "Oh, the postcard. No. Hutton didn't have it."

"Then it's at your home. Shall we slip away?"

I glanced down the hall. "Yes."

"Do you want to explain to the party that you're stepping out?"

I glanced down the hall again. "No."

We took my MINI. As I drove, Fleet asked if it was hard having such an eccentric friend, meaning Hutton, and I gave the speaker and his little dog a glance and said you got used to it. I then asked if he, Fleet, was finally embracing retirement, and he answered that a man is only as retired as he feels. Whatever that means.

I spent the rest of the drive brooding on Lesley. I knew if we could just get through this rough patch—the stress of the wedding, and meeting her people, and proving to everyone that I wasn't a waste—everything would be jake. There was no point in fretting about it. That's the secret of happiness, I've always found. Sit back and wait. Things have to get better at some point.

We pulled into my garage. Fleet de-lapped Pixie and followed me inside. The pup had enjoyed a ripe old time on the drive over, barking at passing motorists who had incurred her displeasure, and almost causing me to swerve off into a ditch no less than four times.

It was a hoot.

"She isn't going to piddle now, is she?" I asked, watching her run in circles at our feet. That would not have been a hoot.

Fleet replied that she had been very aloof in her piddling gesture lately.

We headed upstairs, whereupon Fleet passed along his compliments on my little home, and Pixie launched herself into an involved sniff of my hallway.

"Did you hear something?" I asked. Fleet, too busy extracting the pup from my umbrella stand, said he hadn't, no.

I went down the hall to the kitchen and peered around. Nothing.

I reported back to my guest, now busy disentangling Pixie from my ficus.

"Card?" he asked.

"No card," I said. At least not on the counter. "It's got to be somewhere," I added.

Fleet agreed that, for most things, this was invariably true. "While you're looking, I'll go check outside. See if you dropped it in the street or something."

I told him to knock himself out, or have a lovely time with it, or something like that, and he went. It was just me, alone with my thoughts now.

I could have sworn I could hear that noise again, a sort of creepy ruffling sound, and it wasn't simply the visiting wombat devouring the ficus. This was something else.

I poked my head out the window and saw Fleet had vanished. I didn't know where he thought I might have let slip the postcard, but apparently it wasn't anywhere nearby.

Standing there soaking up the creepy silence (even more creepy than the ruffling sound), I was once again placed in mind of some old horror film. You know the kind. One member of the camping party goes out in the woods for some idiotic reason, and of course never returns, and then one by one the rest of the hapless chumps follow—only to vanish themselves. (I guess it never occurs to them to go in a mob.) I was the next hapless chump.

I returned to the kitchen. Pixie jogged up and tugged on my pant leg. I knelt down and gave her head a pat.

"What's this?" I asked, discovering something under her collar.

It was a tiny vermouth bottle, such as a certain traveling Brit might have picked up in a hotel minibar. It came loose under my examination and rolled over toward the sliding door.

"Jill," I snorted, and would have gone on to soliloquize pretty freely about that scamp of a sister-in-law, had the bottle not fetched up beside the linen curtains—or, more specifically, beside the large-toed boot parked beneath those curtains.

Fleet was right. Those doors were dangerous.

# 6 — Surrealist Movement

I was in a quandary on how to deal with this boot, or—more specifically—the rest of the body attached to the boot. It was no good waiting till I could hail Fleet and canvass his thoughts. Who knew when this boot-man might decide to spring out from his hiding place and *phut* would go my strategic advantage then. I had to act.

Meanwhile, I couldn't understand why Pixie hadn't gone bananas over this. I mean, how often does your average Maltese come across such an unexpected treat? An alien boot, no doubt fragrant, sticking out from a wad of curtains? It should have had her barking her head off.

I was beginning to think that Hutton had been correct. He had stated once that there was something wrong with the girl's sniffer, and watching her tool around the kitchen, snuffling at the pantry and generally missing the point of the man behind the curtain, I felt there might be something to this assessment.

Strong-and-silent Maltese aside, I found it harder and harder to snap into action here. The problem was, how to snap? There were plenty of knives lying about, I supposed. I might not cook, but that didn't keep me from buying every knife I saw, provided it looked cool and was endorsed by the right Food Network celeb. But could I run this man through in cold blood? There was something altogether too Shakespearean about heedlessly jabbing daggers at figures through draping linen. I would have liked to have employed something a little less Elizabethan. Whacking him in the head with a frying pan had attractive possibilities, but where was the head?

There was nothing else for it. Selecting my pan, I hauled off and let him have it.

Except I didn't. The pan hit something loud and clunky and ricocheted back, clipping me on the tip of the nose. Cursing freely, I whipped aside the drapes and saw that not only had I missed the man's head, but the rest of my would-be assailant as well.

Nobody was there. Literally. No head, no arms or legs, not even a decent shoe tree. Just a pair of boots staring up at me and the giant shimmering windowpane. I was lucky I hadn't smashed the glass.

I hated to admit it, but I owed Pixie an apology. No wonder she had kept her cool. What could be more mundane than a couple of disembodied boots? She may have thought it odd, spotting them under the curtains, but Maltese don't concern themselves with these details long.

They concerned me. I was still contemplating what to do about them—wondering who had left them there and why—when a giant weight landed on my back. And unlike the giant weights I had been shouldering all morning, this one was not figurative.

I saw the windowpane rushing toward me. I bounced off this with surprising buoyancy—man, it was durable—and then I was on the floor. The next thing I knew, my assailant was looming over me, his fist cocked back from my face.

"Hath?"

"Hutton?"

We had it worked out. I was Hath. He was Hutton. (Evidently, he was taking the concept of popping in on me to a whole new level.)

He helped me up, asking me what the hell I was trying to do; and I got up, asking him what the hell he was trying to do. He ignored my question. "Do you routinely try to bash figures in the head before you can identify them?" He spoke haughtily, pushing his glasses back in place.

I returned his hauteur with some of my own. "As strange as it may sound, Hutton, it's not my routine to find phantom footwear lurking under my drapery."

"Well, if I had been there, you would have cracked my skull."

As opposed to my nose, I retorted.

I stepped over and opened one of the French doors. Things were getting heated in the kitchen, and I could use some fresh air.

I supposed I had acted a little hastily with the pan. I apologized for going all Hamlet on him—or trying to go all Hamlet—pointing out that it could have easily been a sword in the arras instead of a pan in the noggin, and he agreed that that was something.

I still didn't understand what the boots were doing there. "Whose are they?"

"Yours."

I gazed down at them. He was right. They were mine. "But how'd my boots get behind the curtain?"

"I stuck them there. It was a ploy, Hath. I placed the boots there as a distraction and then hid in the pantry behind you. Modified Desdemona."

I would really have to learn what a standard Desdemona was sometime. Whatever it was, it apparently outdid a Hamlet. "But why?" I asked. "Why a Desdemona?"

"I was setting a trap. There's someone in the house."

I think I must have goggled at him again, because he told me to knock off the startled codfish routine. People were going to start calling me Johnny Codfishes if I wasn't careful.

"There's somebody in my house?" I replied.

Sensing excitement, Pixie jerked in place, but before she could shoot off, Hutton snatched her up and muzzled her impending yaps. "They were here when I arrived," he said, wincing as her fangs met flesh. "Didn't you notice your alarm was off?"

I hadn't at the time, being more concerned with Pixie's piddling traits than dead keypads. "Who are they?"

"That's what we need to find out," he whispered. Handing me Pixie, he made a move toward the hall, but I arrested him with a grab to the back of the sweater. He wasn't the only one who knew that maneuver.

"We should call the police."

He shook his head. "Mobile phones are out. They must have a jammer. They definitely cut the landlines. Kiboshes the alarm system," he explained, in reply to my goggle.

And so saying, he hoicked Pixie from my grasp, paused to straighten his sweater at me, and then went over and stuck her in the half bath in the hall.

"She'll bark," I whispered.

"She'll nap," he whispered back, and continued to creep along. He was right. The pup kept quiet.

"I have a Glock," I said.

"Where?"

"In my nightstand." I actually kept it in a special hollow thesaurus Fleet had given me for Christmas. It fit the gun perfectly. (As Fleet had written on the tag inside the gift—*When you can't think of the mot juste, a Glock does nearly as well.*)

"So it's all the way on the other side of the house?" Hutton asked.

"Pretty much, yes."

He scowled and muttered something under his breath. I didn't catch these remarks in their entirety, but the gist was, this was why, at his place, he had a gun hidden in every room. Sometimes two.

We decided to split up and divide our efforts. I'd fetch the cannon, while he'd keep an eye on the living room and den, kicking in the tender bits any hoods who came his way.

It was a plan. Parting in the living room, I crept upstairs, crept into my bedroom, and crept to the nightstand and slid open the drawer. I said a bad word.

The drawer was empty. My Glock Model 26 was gone. So was my thesaurus. (So much for the mot juste.) I said another bad word.

"Looking for something," said a man behind me.

I stood frozen on the spot, as silent as a Maltese in a half bathroom.

Once again I had to act. Setting my feet under me, I whirled around with a mighty fist. The mighty fist whizzed past a debonair face, and I whizzed along with it. Failing to compensate for the shift in weight, I stumbled off balance and careened across the carpet. Had a major league umpire been present, he would have called me out on both the swing and the slide.

I gazed up at the debonair face peering down into mine.

"Do you always take swinging potshots at your guests?" asked Enescu Fleet.

I declined to explain myself. If I felt like taking swinging potshots at my guests or, alternately, hitting them in the head with pans, that was my business, and I didn't want to talk about it.

"There's people in the house," I told him, as he helped me up.

"You might need this, then," he replied, displaying my Glock Model 26. He twirled it around to hand it to me, barrel pointed down. He really was a modern gunslinger. He also handed me the trick thesaurus, adding that he was touched that I had been using his gift.

"Hutton's waiting for us downstairs," I remarked.

Except he wasn't. The living room and the hallway adjacent to it were vacant. Hutton had left his post.

This bugged me. Not only had the man let the side down, but now it looked like I was going to have to spend the afternoon poking inside drapes and on top of wardrobes and things. Anywhere his fertile mind might consider a strategic position.

"If there is someone in the house," said Fleet, "there is one way to know for certain." He stepped to the half bath and opened the door.

Out came Pixie. Scrambled might be a better word. She came bounding into the room, bouncing along the hardwood like a furry grenade, barking and snarling, snarling and barking. She darted to me, from me to Fleet, Fleet to me, and then back to Fleet. She finished by coughing up a hairball, sniffing my coffee table and roaring off into the den.

She began barking uncontrollably.

"Easy does it, girl," Fleet declared, asking me for the gun. He headed for the fray. Before he could lend a hand, a crash drifted out from the den. Following this crash was a smash, then a thump, a few clangs and a thud. Finally a man emerged: sadder, wiser and sporting several pretty contusions.

This pretty contused man was Hutton. Pixie was scampering about in his wake, describing in yips and yaps how she had worked the body, worked the body, then jab, jab, jab, and then back to the body again. It was an impressive account, but I was inclined to believe that Hutton, in his panic, had fought much of her fight for her.

"Oh, there you two are," he said, booting Pixie away from his ankles. "Den's all clear. I was about to check the basement. I think they might be down there. I heard a noise earlier."

Fleet explained that that was him.

"Ah. Well, there was some commotion somewhere a minute ago—"

"Also me. And Johnny."

"Right. Then that just leaves the kitchen—"

"That was you."

Hutton nodded. I think he was out of ideas. "Nice Glock," he said, eyeing the piece.

Five minutes later, we could state unequivocally that the house was clear. (Whether it was still clear of dog pee was a topic for another time.)

"I guess they're gone." I couldn't speak for the Ef-man, but I was beginning to wonder if there ever was anyone in the house.

Hutton took it philosophically. "Go figure," he said, and disappeared into the hall bathroom to freshen up from his tangle with Pixie.

"Woof," added the pup, advising him to watch out for the knob. It was a real bitch to get open, that one.

While Hutton freshened, Fleet and I repaired to the den. Fleet sat in the overstuffed club chair in the corner, the one I spent most mornings/afternoons eating breakfast in, while I took a seat on the edge of my desk. "What were you saying about having eccentric friends?" I asked. Hutton might be no liar, but I was starting to think that maybe he couldn't help himself. Maybe the strain of having his client list go *kaput* on him had compelled him to create these elaborate fantasies for us. Maybe he was just mental.

Fleet made no comment. He had folded his hands on top of his chest and closed his eyes. Pixie took this as her cue to jump on his stomach and nod off in his arms.

"Do you think the man in the alleyway was real?" I asked.

"I think he was real to Hutton," Fleet answered, without opening his eyes.

I snorted. "That's more than we can say for his so-called prowlers."

Fleet wasn't so quick to mock. "Things are not always as they appear, Johnny."

I snorted again. When it came to Hutton's whimsy, nothing was.

"Why are you here?" I asked the whimsical one, once he had returned.

The question took him aback. "You knew I was leaving the brunch, Hath."

"But not to come to my house. Don't you have a home of your own?"

He replied that he did have a home, yes, but he figured he'd stop here on the way. "And it's a good thing I did. Otherwise, I might never have stumbled on those miscreants."

I snorted for a third time. Him and his miscreants! "Where's your Jeep?" I asked. Or had desperadoes made off with that too?

"It's right out front. Didn't you see it?"

I hadn't. I guess my powers of observation weren't all that dazzling, after all.

"The funny thing is," he tacked on, "the car that tailed us this morning wasn't. But the occupants of the car were. The miscreants, I mean."

"Stop saying miscreants!"

"Well, that's what they were. Or that's what they sounded like, anyway, charging about the house. You do believe there were miscreants here, don't you, Hath? Intruders?"

"You want an honest answer?" I asked.

Hutton said he would. He'd love it.

"I don't believe there ever were any intruders or miscreants."

Hutton stepped back. I had wounded him.

"Fine. No intruders. No miscreants. That's brilliant. I made them up. I fabricate miscreants, that's what I do. But if I am so far gone, so utterly loopy that I see faux hoodlums all over the place, answer me this. Where's the card?"

"Huh?"

"The postcard, Hath. Where is it?"

I had to hand it to Hutton, he had succeeded in getting Fleet's attention. For the first time in five minutes, the man's eyes opened. He peered intelligently in the speaker's direction. Even his pup rolled over on her back and smacked her lips in canine awe of his reasoning.

"He has a point, Johnny. It wasn't anywhere I found. You didn't notice it in the kitchen?"

I hadn't. Of course, between dogs running amuck on one side, and loons flipping me ass-over-tea-kettle on the other, I didn't have a whole lot of chance to concentrate on cards.

"You definitely don't have it?" I asked Hutton.

"Didn't I say that I didn't?"

"Does seem odd," said Fleet, setting Pixie down. "Perhaps someone was in the house. There was definitely someone spying on you two this morning."

"What?"

"I confirmed my theories while I was outside. As I suspected, there's an excellent sniper's perch across the street, a hill with trees for cover. It has a perfect view of the French doors in your kitchen."

I hadn't forgotten about the French doors. "But how can you be so sure there was anyone out there?" (I was doubting everybody that afternoon.)

Fleet didn't mind explaining. He could never pass up a good exposition.

Upon examining the hill, he said, he had noticed that the lawn cover—a particular variety of New England bluegrass—was pressed down in such a way to suggest that a man of medium build had knelt on it for a period of ten, maybe fifteen minutes. The reeds growing on the ridge were divided, as they might have been drawn aside by a pair of muscular hands, possibly manicured. And several pinecones were snapped, consistent with a size-nine shoe or thereabouts landing on them with moderate weight.

"Also, I bumped into one of your neighbors, and she thought she saw a man crouching there this morning."

I gave a derisive sniff. Very scientific, very detective-y. "And you could see into my house from there?"

"Up to a point. I saw you open the door, and that gave me a view inside. Anything to the right, where the glass was, I couldn't make out. Everything was reflected. Were the doors open or closed this morning?"

"One was open, the other closed."

"Just like now. Then your snoop would have had the same problem. After watching you two discuss the postcard, he no doubt assumed Hutton had it and followed him."

I understood. Another 50-50 gone awry. Of course, considering that neither of us had it, it was actually not 50-50. 0-0? I'm no good at statistics.

Fleet took a position between us. He rested a hand on both of our backs, just as Hutton had done this morning in John Herring's bedroom. (That sounds weird.)

"I need to know what was written on that card," he smiled.

I had that one covered. I went to the desk, took out a pen and paper, and wrote.

"There," I replied, handing him the scrap.

John,

Best wishes on your pending nuptials.
Things sure are livening up for you.
Say hello to the old man.

Stothard Hope

Hutton viewed it over Fleet's shoulder. "It was 'impending' not 'pending.' Also not 'hi' but 'hello.' And wasn't one of the words hyphenated?"

I took his criticism on board. He was right, one of the words was hyphenated.

"Actually, it was kind of funny," I said.

I took out another paper and rewrote with the necessary corrections:

John,

Best wishes on your impending nuptials. Things sure are liveni-ng up for you. Say hello to the old man.

Stothard Hope

"He broke up the word 'livening' weird. Just remembered that."

Fleet's eyes had lit up. "Not weird, Johnny, not weird at all." He stood fanning his beard with the paper scrap, gazing toward my book-case. "You have an encyclopedia?" he asked. (Fleet had always been an aficionado of encyclopedias, having once read a complete set of them while marooned on a desert island—long story.) "I don't see any on your shelf."

That was because I didn't have any. I did have one on my iPhone, however, which he found acceptable. "Cool beans. Look up the word 'Liveni' would you."

I looked up the word Liveni. *Liveni. Village in Botoşani, Romania. Best known—*

I gaped and read on:

*Best known as the birth place of George ENESCU. Renamed GEORGE ENESCU in 1955 after the composer's death.*

"Enescu!" I whirled around. "Then he hyphenated the word that way on purpose. It *was* a code!"

The composer's modern namesake nodded. "Now do you believe that the card was meant for Stothard Hope's old associate, Enescu Fleet?"

I was about to reply "You betcha," or even the Enescu Fleet special—"Cool beans"—when we were interrupted by the clearing of a throat.

"Excuse me," said Hutton, "but are we forgetting something here?"

Both Fleet and I turned.

Hutton rolled his eyes. He took off his specs, polished these slowly and significantly, and returned them to his nose. "My name is also Enescu Fleet."

I gasped. Can't say why—strikes me as kind of girly now—but that's what I did.

Hutton was correct: he was Enescu Fleet. Enescu Fleet: Part Two. I had just learned about this awhile back, the dick-weed having kept it a secret for the better part of two decades.

If I have my facts straight, it went something like this. Thirty years ago, an English cousin of Old Fleet's—I think it was a cousin—adopted a son, and figuring that one name was as good as another, called him Enescu, in honor of his famous cousin. If it was a cousin. Young Enescu subsequently went to school, as many children do (even those called Enescu), and not appreciating the treasure trove he had in his name, insisted friends and associates call him by his initials, E. F. Not to be outdone, we began referring to him as "Hutton," after the E. F. Hutton brokerage firm, whose commercials were very popular at the time. And so the Hutton nickname had been born.

Mark the sequel, however. Upon graduating and starting to make his way in the world, Hutton had taken up the mantle of private eye, just as his adopted cousin thrice removed (or whatever it would be) had done before him. Quickly discovering that the name Enescu Fleet carried a certain weight in that quarter, he got over his youthful aversion and started letting the label slip wherever it would do the most good. And if people thought he was THAT Enescu Fleet PI, amazingly well preserved for his age—well, that was all for the better.

Hutton was looking pretty pleased with himself. "You know perfectly well that, since your retirement, I've helped make that name famous again."

"Infamous, you mean," said Fleet: Part One. He had never been a fan of this namesake business, and if he'd had his druthers his cousin would have dubbed his adopted child *Wolfgang*. "And I fail to understand what this has to do with Stothard's card."

"Don't you?" asked Hutton. "Or rather, do you?"

Fleet did. Or maybe that should be *didn't*. "You didn't even know the man."

"But I knew his niece or daughter or whoever. Or is the wench not called Celeste?"

Fleet remarked coolly that Stothard had a grown granddaughter named Celeste. Hutton said precisely. That was exactly what he meant. "We never actually met, but she phoned me a few months back, and thinking I was you, engaged me on a certain matter which I don't, at the moment, recall. However, I did a bang-up job, whatever it was, and I remember her leaving me a message saying that the old man—you—could hardly have done better himself."

"I highly doubt that."

"Well, she paid my fee, which is more than I can say for most of my clientele. If that's not a ringing endorsement, I don't know what is."

Fleet had the look of someone who did know. "The card said 'old man.' You said it yourself, I'm the old man."

This wasn't consistent with what he had told me back at the Herring estate, but I didn't correct him.

Hutton sprang on this bit of reasoning: "There you have it, then. The postcard said 'Say hi to the old man.' An afterthought—a P. S., in other words. *Once you have finished solving my challenge, Young Fleet, say hi to the old man for me*. That proves it."

"It proves nothing!"

I stepped in before there could be any Enescu-on-Enescu violence. "I think we can all agree that Stothard Hope meant the card for one of the world's great Enescu Fleets. Let's just leave it at that for now."

"Fine," said Enescu One.

"Okay by me," said Enescu Two.

"Spectacular," said I.

Something still bothered me. I turned to Fleet (original recipe). "If Stothard Hope had a grown granddaughter, he couldn't have been younger than you?"

"He wasn't."

"Then how could you be the 'old man'?"

"That was his little joke. He always thought it was funny that I had retired, while he, twenty years my senior, had carried on in his business."

I said oh. "Funny." Back to our business: "So we have this card mock-up, but what about it? What's the rest of the code?"

I had them there. We took turns gazing at the scrap and looking baffled by it. I was pleased to observe that, at one point, Hutton held it up to the light.

"What was on the other side?" Fleet asked.

A good theory. The artwork.

I described what I could remember. I mentioned the clean lines, the reds and golds, and the avant-garde style. Also the Christmas tree. Couldn't forget the tree.

"Anything else you can recall?"

I gave the brain cells another churn. "There was a fireplace, a mirror, a bookshelf reflected in the mirror, houseplants, vases, flowers in the vases and a fancy throw rug. Oh, there was also a logo stamped on the bottom of the card. It said 'The Ariadne Locke Museum.' "

"Ariadne," repeated Fleet. It seemed to resonate with him. "Was the painting signed?"

I figured he was going to ask that. I didn't remember seeing a signature, but I did recognize the artist. "Pretty sure it was a McAlester. No, not a McAlester. McCoy? No, not a McCoy. McGuffin?"

"The gentleman's name is McKnight," said Hutton. "Thomas McKnight."

Of course! McKnight. Forget my own name next.

I actually had one of his prints lying around the house somewhere. "I believe it's in the exercise room upstairs," I told them, which explained why I hadn't looked at it in a while.

"McKnight," commented Fleet. "That's very interesting, very interesting indeed."

I was glad. I didn't know why it was interesting, but I was glad anyway.

"From your description, it sounds like it was one of three McKnights commissioned by the Clintons in the nineties for the presidential Christmas cards." He paused, taking a twirl around my den.

"So, do you know what the card means, then?" I asked him.

"No idea. But I have a notion I know something else." He pivoted my way. "Do you recall, Johnny, what Stothard said to his granddaughter before he disappeared?"

I didn't. People had said so many things already…

"He said he was 'looking for some new threads.' "

I did remember that—and didn't get it.

The word 'threads' was the significant part," Fleet remarked.

"Ariadne," whispered Hutton.

"Precisely. In Greek myth, Ariadne helped Theseus escape the Minotaur's labyrinth by providing him a ball of thread to lead him out. The word 'clue,' in fact, comes from 'clew,' literally meaning a ball or mass of thread."

My head felt like a ball or mass of thread. "Then there's something significant at the Ariadne Locke Museum?"

"Significant and possibly dangerous."

"Oh good."

"It deserves a glance."

"Cool beans," I said.

Hutton was already halfway out the door, with Fleet close behind.

I followed well enough. I still didn't get everything. I mean, had there been any miscreants in my house or not?

And what did Minotaurs have to do with Stothard Hope's new clothes?

## 7 — Exhibition at a Museum

It was going on five when Hutton pulled his Jeep up at Ariadne State Park, home to the Ariadne Locke Museum. With the detectives Fleet in the driver and passenger seats, and myself crammed in the back with a highly strung Maltese, it wasn't the most pleasant forty-minute ride I had ever spent. The MINI would have been just as cramped, I suppose, but at least there I would have had the helm, and Pixie's tiny claws would have been digging into somebody else's thigh.

Once the Wrangler had scuttled across the bar of sand connecting Ariadne with the inlet, we found the park pretty much as advertised, very quaint and day-trippy. It was surrounded by water on three sides, had many pine and birch trees, ample craggy hills and the mandatory lighthouse. Next to the lighthouse was the museum, although this was really more of a rugged old mansion of uncertain architecture (not Tudor).

We got out, stretched and, in my case, shivered. "Should we just go in?"

Other than a half-faded sign bearing the locale's banner, there was nothing to suggest that the museum was actually open to the public. (Or could support human life.) It was a large, chunky structure, with huge stone bricks the size of compact cars and very few windows. It looked vaguely tomb-like.

"You two go," suggested Fleet. "Pixie and I will be exploring the grounds."

I figured he would take that route. After all, getting torn to shreds by ancient apparitions thirsting for human blood was young man's work.

The museum's interior proved just as old and dilapidated as its exterior. The foyer was jam-packed with paintings, sculptures, heirlooms and trinkets of a long-forgotten and dusty past. The whole place smelled of paint, clay, tobacco and, oddly enough, orange marmalade. There was an elaborate set of stairs on our right, curved and in need of a good carpenter. Straight ahead, stretching off into the murky distance, I could discern a series of rooms and corridors, containing, one could only hope, exhibits *not* worth dying for.

A knocked-about old sideboard with cracked marble inlay and a wonky leg, propped up on a stack of brochures, greeted us as we drifted inside. More brochures were stacked up on top, beside a sign that read "Welcome." I enjoyed the irony.

Hutton snatched one of the leaflets—hopefully not one of the supporting ones—and read aloud as we strolled: " 'Built in 1931 by Daniel Rose Locke'—now there's a manly label for you—'the Locke Mansion was…' Filler, filler, filler… 'Endowed by Ms. Ariadne Rufus Locke in 1998, the property would later become…' More filler… Now this is interesting: 'In recent years the museum has served as—' "

I waved him off. This was partly due to the fact that I detest people reading at me, but mostly because we had unearthed a fellow traveler: a woman of fair-to-middling countenance, hair blondish, dress golden and presentation harried.

"Oh hi," I said. It felt like an *Oh-hi* moment.

I wasn't certain she agreed. She gave us an alarmed look, shook her head, first at Hutton then at me, and hurried off. I tried to follow, but as I came around the corner she vanished. It seemed we had met our first apparition at the Ariadne Locke Museum.

"What were you doing bothering my wife!"

As long as I was cataloguing alarmed looks, I might as well include Hutton's and mine at this point—though mine was probably more startled than alarmed, and Hutton's more perturbed with a trace of whacked-knuckle-on-sideboard.

The speaker was a lot older than his wife. She couldn't have been much more than forty, whereas he was a sour old man in his early thousands. He had a drooping countenance, a butternut-squash-shaped head and large, circular glasses (about five sizes larger than Hutton's). These surrounded large, goggling eyes. Take Munch's "The Scream," add a few layers of wrinkles, and picture him not so much screaming as expressing his dissatisfaction with his electric bill, and you'd have placed him perfectly. He had on a baggy cardigan sweater, baggy pants and what looked to be a professional-grade camera dangling from his baggy hip—though not any model manufactured this century (both the camera and the hip).

I felt a pang for his vanishing spouse. If this peevish picture-taker was all she had to gaze at day in and day out, no wonder she went about the place starting at sudden noises.

"Oh hi," I said.

The butternut didn't care for the greeting any more than the missus had. "I asked you why you were bothering my wife," he grunted, adjusting his camera lens like an assassin screwing on his silencer.

All I could formulate to say was, "Who, us?"

I deferred to Hutton, who spoke for the landing party. "We weren't so much bothering," he said, "as hoping to cadge a tour."

"She doesn't work here."

"No. No, of course not. Perhaps you yourself—"

"I don't work here."

"No, and why should you? As it happens, I don't work here myself. Nor does Johnny—this is Johnny. Four wandering souls and not a single one of us works here. Seems to unite us somehow, does it not?"

I believe the old man's vote would have been *Not*. He never got a chance to cast it.

"Now, now, Chris," said yet another new addition, "is this any way to speak to guests?"

The newcomer was no young buck himself, but unlike the heebie-jeebie-inducing *Chris*, he wore his years well. His head was completely bald and shaved, his jaw firm, his eyes soft. He smoked a pipe, an affectation he only barely succeeded in pulling off.

"Niles Brisbane," he said, placing the pipe between his teeth in order to shake hands. "This is Christopher Cotton," he added, speaking through the bit. "Tell me, what brings you young fellas here?"

"Nothing special," answered Hutton. "We'd heard tell of your wondrous museum and had to see the place for ourselves."

Christopher Cotton snorted. It was a very sour snort. "Nobody comes here for the museum," he harrumphed, "and anyhow, we're closed up. Nothing to see here," he concluded. And on this note of unfettered congeniality, he wagged his head at the pair of us, first at me then at Hutton, snapped our portraits, and left.

"Don't mind Christopher," said Niles. "He's not a bad guy once you get to know him."

I didn't intend to try. "Do you work here?" I asked. I figured somebody had to—a place like this didn't stay stale and moldy all by itself.

"No. Just visiting. We're here as—"

Whether the next words out of his mouth were "honored guests" or "reluctant pagan sacrifices," we shall never know.

He fell silent, his pipe-less lips drooping ever so slightly at the sight of something in the near distance.

I had seen that look in Pixie's eyes when she would spot a squirrel, or in the faces of visitors to the Louvre the summer I popped over to Paris from school. It was the look of one gazing on some spectacular something, some special treat they had seen many times before and were gladly seeing again. (If that's not a buildup, I don't know what is.)

Hutton and I turned and were immediately glad that we did. A young woman had joined our gathering. She was standing in an arched doorway behind us, beyond which there was an artist's studio of some sort. Not that I was paying that much attention to what was beyond her. She had long brown hair, matching her long and curvy frame. Her skin was a lovely olive tone, her stomach muscles taut, her features sculpted and proud.

She was also nude. I remember that part distinctly.

# 8 — Nude Not Doing Anything with Staircase

What was I saying? Oh right. The naked chick. She moved away from the doorway and said things to us. Words, if I recall them correctly.

"Are any of you listening to me?" she asked at one point.

She had an exotic flair to her speech. Italian perhaps or Eastern European. Maybe Wisconsin. I liked it. She repeated her question. Amazingly, I was able to page back through her comments, a skill I could have used with the family of my fiancée this morning.

(Lesley. Yes, that's it. My fiancée Lesley.)

Piecing together her remarks, I could recall our nude newcomer saying, "What's all this talking?", followed by, "We cannot work with all this talking," and finally, "Of course. We are always at work"—this in reply to Niles Brisbane asking her something, possibly whether she had been at work or not.

"This is Jelena," he stated, chomping on his pipe bit again.

It was Hutton's time to shine. Show me a beautiful naked woman—seriously, any beautiful naked woman—and it would be Hutton I would want at my side to keep the conversation flowing. He had always had a way with the women we met. It just came naturally. This Jelena, though nakeder than most, was no exception.

He stepped into the batter's box, dispelling the momentary impression that his bones had turned to jam, and said, "Good afternoon. Jelena, is it?"

Jelena nodded, declining to comment on the goodness of the afternoon one way or another. "Just Jelena?" he inquired.

"Just Jelena," agreed Just Jelena.

Hutton said splendid. "Enescu Fleet here. Friends call me Hutton. Just Hutton. This is just Johnny," he remarked, indicating yours truly with a nod of the head. [Just Johnny just waved.] "You can call him Johnny H," he said.

Jelena turned and gazed at me. "Johnny H? This is Johnny Herring?"

I said no, not that Johnny H. "Wait, you know Herring?" Surely she hadn't mistaken me for the nineteenth-century painter.

Jelena shook her head. "I know no Herring," she responded curtly. That cleared that up. Back to Hutton: "Enescu Fleet. I know this name Enescu Fleet."

"As well you should," he replied.

"He is a detective."

"He is—am. I am."

"But he is the much older man?"

"Common misconception."

"And you are not Romanian. I was certain Enescu Fleet was the Romanian."

"A man is only as Romanian as he feels," explained Hutton, pausing. "So," he remarked, after another stretch of silence, "walking around in the buff, are we, Just Jelena?"

"It is naked, this buff?"

"It certainly is."

Jelena accepted the colloquialism. "It is necessary that I work this way."

"I understand completely," said Hutton. Whatever this naked work was, he was on board with her doing it. He looked to me, and I nodded. She had my support.

"But not everyone does understand," she said. "They carry on. Men in this country, they are such children about the breasts."

Hutton could well appreciate her struggle. It had to be very difficult for her. "Did I mention I'm British?" he asked.

Niles Brisbane excused himself here, gnawing his pipe some more and whispering something to Jelena about putting some clothes on. I found myself no longer liking Niles very much.

He had no sooner gone than the void was filled by a long-haired young man, fairly good looking—okay, exceedingly good looking—with a goatee to rival Hutton's, and dark Mediterranean features.

"I'm getting impatient, Jelena," he told her, barely acknowledging the rest of the room. "I cannot continue our work alone." He stepped up behind her and slipped a long velvet cloak around her shoulders. I found myself not liking this handsome young man very much either.

"You're an artist?" Hutton asked him.

The young man glanced back. He had to blink once or twice, as if reassuring himself that we were three dimensional—not some ill-conceived wall mural.

"Malcolm Rosso," he replied. He spoke in a sort of half-whisper. "I am he," he added, somewhat unnecessarily.

Hutton said this made sense. After all, who else would he be but the he that he was? "So you're one of the artists here?"

"I am."

Hutton let me in on a secret: "That's what I was starting to tell you before, Hath. The Ariadne has become a sort of freewheeling artists' colony in recent years."

"Artists' retreat," corrected Malcolm.

"Whatever. According to the leaflet, it's still open to the public but only by appointment. I suppose we're gate-crashing."

I had a feeling that old man Cotton, had he been present, would have agreed with this assessment wholeheartedly.

"If you're an artist," continued Hutton, "then you must be his model?" he asked Jelena.

"Of course." She spoke as if the fact had no need of confirmation. "You are the artists as well?" she wondered, and I realized she was speaking to me.

"Who, us? No, not the artists," I said, though I might have mentioned that my handshake was very well thought of in certain quarters. "I'm an occasional courier. Freelance. Own my own business and all that."

"Never mind, then," said Jelena. She had no interest in couriers, freelance or not so free. "What are you doing here?" she sighed. She was speaking to Hutton again. He played it coy.

"At the moment we're trying to track down a friend of ours. Perhaps you know him. Stothard Hope? I think he paid this place a visit awhile back."

"I do not know this Stothard," said Jelena. I couldn't tell if she was acting coy herself. On the whole, I thought she was acting coy.

Malcolm also seemed coy. (Maybe everybody just seemed coy, I don't know.) "No, you remember him, don't you, Jelena? He stayed in the guest quarters. Oh, that's right, he left before you arrived. We occasionally take in guests," he explained for our benefit. "Helps pay the bills. He didn't stay long—which was too bad because he had expressed an interest in buying one of my smaller sculptures. But you know how it is?" he said.

All I knew was Malcolm had said more in the last ten seconds than he had during our entire discussion, and all at the mention of the name Stothard Hope. Psychologists have a term for that kind of sudden outpouring of unsolicited information. I don't happen to know what this term is, but they gotta have one. Those guys got a term for everything.

I honestly couldn't tell if he knew that Stothard Hope was dead or not. I couldn't tell if he knew that we knew that Hope was dead. I couldn't tell anything.

Jelena was looking pouty. I sensed she was growing bored with our discussion.

"I grow bored," she said. "I am going back to the studio now."

She let the cloak slip from her supple shoulders and strolled slowly away. Perhaps "swayed" might be a better word. Not exactly sashayed, but—

"Hath."

Silence.

"Hath, old man."

More silence.

"HATH!"

I swung around and blinked at Hutton. We were alone in the foyer now. Malcolm had evidently tailed Jelena back into the studio—lucky bastard—and was even now, depending on his medium of choice, resuming to paint, sculpt or construct a Tinkertoy model of breathtaking depth and symmetry.

I could hear the subtle *ting, ting, ting* of a sculptor's hammer. Sculpture it was, then.

"I think we should be going," said Hutton.

This was fine by me. Frankly, I didn't know what the holdup was.

The gravel crunching beneath my feet outside worked to revive me somewhat. I found myself thinking less of Jelena and more of Lesley Darlington, soon to become Lesley Hathaway. I reminded myself that she was an amazing woman—Lesley—and while she might not become spontaneously nude as much as one might like, she made up for this by possessing many other fine qualities.

I mentioned some of these to Hutton as we walked, and he replied, "Yes, Hath," and, "You bet, Hath," and at one point, pausing to take some gravel out of his shoe, "Put a sock in it, Hath." This was probably just the gravel abrasion talking, however.

We wound our way down from the museum and past the lighthouse. I could see Christopher Cotton's dour face peering out at us from one of the small lower windows.

According to Hutton's intuition when it came to his namesake, Fleet had probably made a loop around the perimeter. He would, therefore, be returning to our location from that direction there. He pointed to a hill (craggy).

"Come," he said, and I grumbled something and went.

We had hardly reached the crags when our path was impeded by the yellow and flowered form of Mrs. Christopher Cotton.

It occurred to me that she wasn't half bad looking. She just needed to cool her heels a little and knock off the crazy eyes. Even if she had kept her heels hot and goggled at us into the wee hours, she was still far better looking than her husband deserved.

"You shouldn't have come," she blurted out.

"Say again?"

"You shouldn't have come." (I walked right into that one.)

I won't say that it was my time to shine, for who wants to shine when it comes to dealing with the neurotic wives of ancient relics, but I handled the situation well enough.

"Actually, we're just leaving."

"You seek a man," she said.

"Stothard Hope? Yes, we heard he, uh, left."

"He's gone," replied Mrs. Cotton, "but he never left." There she lost me.

"When you say gone—"

"Gone," she insisted. "Gone with one rapid slash of the brush." Now she was just speaking in riddles for the sake of it. "It is simple fate. If only that could be blotted away so easily." She really dug the artist imagery, this lady.

"Are you well?" Hutton asked her.

"Gone, gone, gone," said Mrs. Cotton, which didn't answer the question at all. "Gone, and now it's time for supper."

I didn't get it. Supper, as in—

"It's dinnertime." She spoke quite frankly now. "Time to eat." She began to wander off, one presumes to have her dinner. She paused at the top of the path, the receding sun at her back. "The tide is coming," she announced, returning to the riddle-speaking portion of our program.

Or so I thought.

Hutton tapped me on the shoulder. He jerked a thumb over the ridge where Enescu Fleet was glaring up at us. He was standing in an inch of water, in a spot where previously there had been nothing but sand and seaweed.

Pixie was lingering a little to his left, growling at a hermit crab.

Apparently—and this would have been a good thing for somebody to have mentioned earlier—the innocent-looking bar we had driven across on our way in had a habit of becoming covered in about three feet of ocean, twice daily. This, evidently, was one of those times.

We hurried back to the Wrangler and rolled down the hill to grab man and dog, leaving the hermit crab in status quo. We probably kicked up more gravel than was absolutely necessary, not to mention trampled on a few too many beds of New England bluegrass. But you know how it is.

Anything to avoid spending another moment alone with these artistically minded lunatics.

# 9 — Dabbling in Intrigue

If nothing else, I got to ride shotgun on the trip back, which cheered me up some. Fleet didn't seem much in the mood for sharing his findings, though—what, if anything, he had learned on his walk—and that depressed me.

It wasn't for lack of effort on our part. We told him all about our experiences inside. About Jelena and her contributions to art (Hutton rubbing this part in quite a lot). About Malcolm Rosso and his peculiar manner when Stothard Hope was brought up. And Mrs. Cotton's bizarro comments on the path outside the museum.

Fleet took it all in as he always does, occasionally nodding his head and smoothing his beard in thought. When we mentioned Jelena he did perk up momentarily, like a retired sommelier recalling some wonderfully rare vintage. But the Cotton female seemed to plunge him back in his depths, the way that same sommelier would feel gulping down a shot of rice wine vinegar.

He asked to be dropped off shortly after that, not at home, but in town—this town consisting of a service station, a boat rental shop and a man in overalls called "Rudy," evidently the proud proprietor of both establishments. I couldn't figure whether this sudden desire to get out and stretch his legs again had anything to do with what he had seen back on the island, or he simply had a hunch. Maybe he just liked Rudy's face.

We left him at the station, and he tooled off without saying another word. (That is, other than asking if we would mind watching Pixie for him for the evening. I knew then that something was up. He also mentioned that he was pretty certain that she had piddled on Hutton's seat, leading me to believe that maybe things were not as up as I had thought them. There was a certain normalcy to Pixie's piddling.)

Hutton personally saw nothing unusual in the man's behavior. "You can't assess an Enescu Fleet by other men's standards," he explained, as we drove off. "If he wants us to watch the Pixie dog, then he's up to something. If he's up to something, it means he has a plan. And if he has a plan, I for one am glad somebody does."

"I suppose. But how's he going to get home?"

"I wouldn't worry about that. He'll figure it out. Ate tells me he once chased the Palm Beach Poisoner two hours in a convertible jammed with beach bunnies, the latter of whom happened to be passing by on their way home from spring break."

"Is that how she described them?" I asked. "Beach bunnies?"

"Probably not. She probably said young ladies on their way home from the seashore. It doesn't matter, it was the style of the thing that I was pointing out. Fleet has style. If you're gonna go somewhere, you might as well do it right."

I didn't doubt it. Of course, if you're an Enescu Fleet I guess no one ever bothers to ask *What if there aren't any cars full of beach bunnies waiting to chauffeur you around?* I gather that question never comes up—when you're Enescu Fleet.

All this talk about hot babes reminded me that I had one such in my life, no doubt growing hotter and more curious about my absence with each passing hour. I gave her a call, and sure enough her first question was where the hell had I gone? I explained that I had been working—she said Who, *you?*—and I told her Yes, *I*—a job had come up. She said no, seriously, what had I really been doing? I persisted in my explanation, trying mightily to conceal the recent nudity in my voice, and she eventually accepted my story, which also happened to be the truth. She wrapped it up by calling me a slew of British slangs, several of which I had not heard before, and we rang off with mutual esteem and respect.

From there, Hutton and I got a bite to eat at Charlie's Bistro, a charming little boîte with small portions and hefty prices. I wasn't very hungry and it was Hutton's turn to pick up the check, so it was all good. (Also, the maître d' was an old buddy of Fleet's and offered to have one of the busboys watch Pixie out back while we supped; even going so far as to provide her with the liver snap *du jour*.)

It was still light out when we left Charlie's. We had spent most of the meal discussing the inmates of Ariadne Island, with special emphasis placed on Malcolm Rosso and the Cotton wife. They, more than any of the other denizens, I theorized, seemed to have something to hide. The batty Mrs. Cotton, in fact, appeared to have definite knowledge of Stothard Hope. Maybe even his demise.

Hutton refused to speculate one way or another. According to him, we couldn't go by anything the Cotton woman had to say. She probably didn't even know what a Stothard was.

One thing we could agree on, something was afoot on that island. We had begun sketching out a plan for learning what form this size nine took, but then the check had come and Hutton insisted he had paid last time—burgers with the girls two Sundays before last—and we spent a good ten minutes working that out.

It seemed to me, as we rode home, that Enescu Fleet wasn't the only Romanian-themed detective keeping his thoughts to himself. Even though Hutton had participated well enough in our discussion over dinner—at one point waving his hands with such gusto that he sent a sliver of thyme-encrusted ahi flying—he had become less outspoken as the meal drew on. By the time we were back in his Jeep tooling along Cumberland Avenue, he had gone positively pensive.

At first, I attributed this lack of dialogue to professional musings. Wrapped in thought and not especially talkative, he was clearly rolling things around his mind: pondering Mrs. Cotton's odd comments, pondering Stothard Hope's odd clue, pondering how Charlie can get off charging fifteen bucks for Melon in Season. Something. The case had plenty of ponder points, and I didn't feel it was my place to interrupt. If he wanted to spend the entire drive in a pensive silence, shifting his Jeep from third gear to fourth, fourth gear to third, third to second, and once, if I observed it correctly, second to third to fifth—then all this pensive shifting was okay by me. I made no mention of it.

Patience has always been the Hathaway motto.

It wasn't until we had traveled approximately six-point-four miles up Cumberland, a long six-point-four miles by my calculations, that I thought the hell with patience and asked him what he was being so damn quiet about.

He answered calmly and with only the slightest hint of a smile, this mostly directed at the rearview mirror, "We picked up an entourage a ways back."

"Entourage?"

"A tail."

Pixie and I turned in our seat. We hadn't spotted any tail. Nor entourage. This was the first we had heard of any entourage or tail. "Where?"

"Give me a minute and I'll show you," said Hutton, suddenly turning off Cumberland Ave onto a side street. "Now for the fun part," he remarked, and in a flurry of wheel-twirling and shifting, not pensive at all, he spun the Jeep up on the curb, up onto somebody's front lawn and down a bumpy hill.

We roared across a short valley next—it could have been a drainage ditch for all I knew—up another hill, over somebody else's lawn, down their curb and onto the street again. "There!" he announced.

I hitched myself up in my seat. For a second, I interpreted this "There!" as an expression of triumph, what a lesser man would have worded "Tada!", and I found this comment grating and difficult to take. Once I had a little better look around, however, I saw that he was only indicating our tail (also known by some as an entourage).

About a hundred yards behind us, right about where we had made our first curb-jump, I could just make out a black sedan. Unless I missed my guess, it was the very sedan I had seen idling outside my house this morning.

The driver's head was protruding from the window. He glared across the valley at us, then down the hill and then back at us again. He looked put out.

"How'd you spot him?" I asked.

Hutton didn't reply. We tore off again, Pixie and I goggling all the way down the street. "Now that's a perfect Desdemona," he said, and there was no mistaking the trill in his voice this time.

Funny, I could have sworn it was a Tahoma.

## 10 — An Artist and His Tools

We returned to my house after that. It seemed like the last place we should go, but Hutton's house was halfway across town and Fleet wasn't answering his phone. We had to go somewhere.

Once inside, I made a point of steering clear of the French windows in the kitchen. I didn't know whether the hill across the way was a valid sniper's perch or not, but I wasn't taking any chances.

Hutton appeared as calm and collected as ever.

"It was the parking space," he said at last, and I stood blinking at him. "You asked me how I knew the man was tailing us. The sedan dude."

I said right. "What about the sedan dude?" I asked, prodding shut the drapes with an outstretched baguette.

"When we pulled up at Charlie's tonight, there were two prime parking spaces in front of the restaurant."

I said I remembered them. I didn't, but I said I did.

"We took one, but the car behind us—a black sedan—did not. It drove in only thirty seconds after we did, but went out of its way to take a space on the other side of the lot. That's when I knew something was up. Anyone who would give up a primo parking space like that would have to have something to hide."

I just nodded. In a more fanciful mood I might have heckled Hutton about this stream of thought, for on the surface it sounded like complete hogwash to me. There had to be a thousand reasons why someone might pass up a good space. They might—well, there were a thousand reasons why.

What had really happened, of course, was he had simply recognized the sedan from this morning, and was only handing me all this psychological snoopery to make a good story of it.

"What should we do now?" I asked.

"No idea."

"Any idea who these guys are?"

"No."

"Want a piece of baguette?"

Hutton shook his head, and I tore off a hunk of bread and offered it to Pixie. "We shouldn't stay here. They know where I live."

Hutton didn't follow. "I don't follow," he said, pouring us out a couple shots of my scotch.

"The sedan. It followed you from here this morning. It must know how to get back."

Now Hutton was the one goggling. "Are you talking about the vehicle from the alley, the one containing a miscreant and/or miscreants, one of whom jumped me and bruised my gonads?"

"Yes?"

"That was no sedan, Hath. It was a little white sports whosit."

"A little white sports whosit?"

"A little white sports whosit," said Hutton. "Two door convertible. That's the car from Wainwright Motors." His eyes suddenly widened. He grasped my shoulders and shook, causing the baguette to sail off into the offing. "You mean to say there was another tail?"

"I don't know. Maybe?" I was shaken up. Literally and figuratively. "I mean, it was idling in a space across the street. Black sedan, darkened windows."

Hutton was pacing. "I knew there was something else this morning! There *was* a strange sedan idling across the street. It's actually what got my mind working on a tail. I checked to see if it would follow when we left, and it did. But then I noticed this little white sports thing, and I forgot all about the sedan. The sports must have been for me and the sedan you. It makes perfect sense."

"Then you mean—?"

"The sedan must have followed you to the Herring house!"

I grabbed Hutton and rattled his shoulders. Without the flying bread, it was nowhere near as satisfying.

"Do you really think someone would try something there?"

"Why not?"

He was right. Why not!

I gurgled "Lesley!", Hutton gurgled "Ate!" and Pixie yipped "Jill!" (or so I assumed).

Hutton and I both scrambled for our phones. No signal.

"Nothing," I said.

"Nada," agreed Hutton.

I was down the stairs and into the garage in a matter of seconds. Hutton was a step behind, holding Pixie under his arm like a furry football. After the garage door had opened—damn thing was so slow—he sprang to the shrubs beside the driveway and yanked something out from the power plug.

"Mobile jammer!" he said, showing me the unit. "They must have forgotten it this morning."

I took it and smashed it on the cement. "Come on!"

Hutton didn't budge. "Let me drive. You know I'm better."

It was no time for male ego. I handed him the keys, he handed me Pixie, and an instant later we were roaring off in the MINI. I just hoped we weren't too late.

We took Cumberland Avenue at a clip and arrived on State Street in a matter of moments. We were only on State for about a minute. At that point, Hutton jerked the wheel to the left and the next thing Pixie and I knew we were whizzing down a side street, an Electric Blue blur.

"You'd better hold onto something," said Hutton.

The dog and I were still scraping ourselves off the passenger window, when Hutton threw it around another curve, this time to the right. Slaloming a little through the bends and swerves, we eventually arrived upon a short incline, where he really dug the spurs into the supercharger.

"Why didn't you stay on State?" I quavered.

"Roadwork," he said, and I nodded—not that you could tell with all the jiggling in the vehicle. "Hold on," he said again, and we held on.

He took us up Pleasant, down Maple, across a small handful of thoroughfares and then back to Maple again. If you asked me, Maple hadn't seen this much excitement for centuries. We finally took another quick left, nearly clipping a mailbox, and with a skip and a bounce were back on State Street. The MINI's movements had become a work of art, and Hutton was the gifted craftsman spraying motor oil all over the canvas.

"I'm going to try calling Lesley," I said over the sound of all the artistry.

I took out my phone and slid to unlock.

"Hello? Jill? Why are you picking up Lesley's phone, Jill? You were just passing by, and it rang? Oh. Well, I need to speak to Lesley. What? No, I'm not in the house. What's that? No, I can't explain now. No, I can't. Say again? Because I can't. Yes, Pixie's with me. Yes, she's a cutsie wootsie little doggie. No, I will not give her an itty-bitty kiss for you. Has anyone been in the house today, Jill? No, I don't mean you. No, not Mum or Dad either. What? No, you're breaking up. I can't hear you. I need to know if you've seen anyone lurking. What? Yes, like the square-headed chap. No, I can't explain why I'm asking. I can't. Because I can't. I'm not fooling about. I'm not. What? Because I'm not! What was that noise? Why are you looking inside closets, Jill? I tell you I'm not in the house. Jill? Jill? I need—Jill?"

I lost the connection.

"Was that Jill?" wondered Hutton. I said it was Jill, yes, and Hutton said he had deduced as much. He made a skidding ninety-degree turn next, and Pixie and I slammed against the passenger window again.

We were in the home stretch. We had just come up over a hill, which I knew from experience led to the J. Herring mini-mansion, when Hutton suddenly pulled the J. Hathaway MINI-car to a screeching halt.

Up ahead, someone was trying to back a truck full of gravel into a driveway, and they were not doing a very good job at it. Our path was completely cut off.

"Hold on, Hath."

I had grown so accustomed to these words from Hutton that I didn't give them a thought; not until I felt the *kathump* in the bucket seat and looked around to see that we had jumped the curb and were careening down another hill into the grassy meadow below.

Everything went swimmingly for a while—if you'd call it swimmingly clumping over boulders and branches and basically churning up the suspension like a paint shaker. Then we hit bottom. Both literally and figuratively.

Without consulting an expert first, I couldn't say whether we snapped an axle, or tore off some precious gizzard from the undercarriage, or just plain got stuck. But the fact remained that there we remained, and there wasn't much Hutton, the MINI or Pixie could do about it, no matter how much the trio of them squirmed and growled. We weren't going anywhere.

Steadying Pixie in my lap, I looked over at Hutton. Hutton looked over at me.

"Bit my tongue," he said.

More silence. Hutton looked at me, I at Hutton.

"We're not in my Jeep, are we?" he asked.

I shook my head. We were not in his Jeep.

He nodded. He peered out his window, then mine. "That would do it," he agreed.

I handed him Pixie. I unbuckled my seatbelt, opened the door and climbed out.

"Where you going?"

"We're only about a mile away from the house. I'll take it on foot."

I had assumed with his bruised ankle/gonads he wouldn't be joining me, and I was correct. As I vanished into the distance I could hear him shouting Godspeed after me, adding that he would catch up as soon as he was able.

As soon as he was *able*. Now, see, I would have called him Cain.

It's a funny thing, covering distances on foot. When you're buzzing along in your MINI, you would never think that a length of terrain like a mile would stretch on and on. But it does. After what felt like an hour, I came huffing and puffing over the ridge. I could see the Herring mansion about a hundred yards ahead.

Even then, it took forever. There were no jump cuts to me bursting through the door, shouting Lesley's name. Only me stumbling onward, pausing every couple feet to catch my breath or twist my ankle on some slab of turf.

Eventually I arrived. The sun had just begun to set as I staggered into the marble foyer like a truckload of gravel inexpertly delivered. I tried to call out Lesley's name.

"Le—"

No good.

"Lesley!" I rasped.

Jill appeared with a couple martinis in her hands, Boston Bullets from the looks of them. I took this as a good sign. If her entire family had been knocked off by miscreants, she might well have poured herself a drink, but she hardly would have bothered with the almond-stuffed olives. That would have been too much.

"Oh hullo, Johnny. I knew you were here all along. Have you finished messing about?"

I hadn't finished, not by a long shot. "Where's Lesley?"

"Upstairs I think, why? Where's Pixie?"

I didn't answer. I blundered over and accepted the cocktail in Jill's right hand, drinking it in one gulp.

"That wasn't for you."

"Not safe," I huffed.

"Swiping my cocktails? You're probably right."

I rattled out another no on the old kettledrum. "The house. It's not safe in the house."

"What are you on about, Hathaway? Not safe in the house how? You mean it's got dry rot or something? Speak sense."

"It's dangerous."

"How do you mean dangerous? What could possibly be dangerous—"

The word hung out over the empty martini. A high-pitched scream had split the air. I knew the timbre. It belonged to Lesley.

Bounding over the remains of the cocktail glass, which I had let slip from my grasp immediately following the screech, I shoved past Jill and was up the stairs before the shards could settle. Down the hall and around a corner and I burst into the room at the far end. I wasn't huffing or puffing now, just scanning and searching. Searching and scanning.

Lesley was standing by the window.

"Oh, Johnny!" she exclaimed, rushing into my arms.

"What is it?"

She kept her face pressed against my shirt. Her hand went out, pointing at something on the floor. I detached her from the Pima and knelt down. There was a small pool of red gunk on the hardwood. It was almost dry.

"It's blood," Lesley gasped.

As a principle, I've always questioned the sanity of characters in cop shows and the like who, scooching down, dab, sniff and taste the substances they find on the ground. This goes on all the time, and I'm constantly amazed that their last words aren't "Yup, poison," as they keel over in agonies.

In this instance, however, I strung along with their technique. I didn't taste the stuff, but I had no problem dabbing and sniffing it. I was pretty sure it wasn't what Lesley thought it was. Chalk it up to a life spent around the wrong sort of people, but I knew blood dried a dark brown. This was far too bright and candy-apple colored. Cherry syrup perhaps, blood no.

"It's paint," I said.

"Paint?"

"Red paint," I remarked, and stood up. Now I needed something to wipe off my hands.

"What the bloody hell is bloody paint doing on the bloody floor?"

That I couldn't tell her. I almost wished it had been blood. It would have made my story about roving miscreants a lot easier to explain. "Where is everyone?"

"Down at the private pier watching the sunset."

I should have known. I would really have to find out what made this pier so riveting. Apparently it was a sight to behold.

"Listen, I have to tell you something."

"Tell me what?"

"This house," I said.

"What about the house?"

"I don't think it's safe. I think we should move everything to your place or Ate's place or somewhere like that."

She frowned. "How can we move everything to my place, Johnny? The thing's the size of a shrunken postage stamp. And Ate's place isn't much larger. If we were going to move, it would be to your place, and I'm not saying we'd even want to do that."

I agreed with her there.

Lesley frowned again. "What's going on?"

Once more, I didn't have a chance to answer.

Jill stood in the entranceway. Evidently the sound of her sister screaming her head off had not affected her in the slightest. Perhaps this was a sibling thing. Never having had any of my own, I wouldn't understand.

"That guy's back," she said, sipping her drink. I noticed she had refilled the cocktail in her other hand. "You know, the square-headed bloke. He's asking for you, Hathaway."

Lesley looked at me. "Do we know a square-headed bloke?" she wondered.

"You do now," said Jill. "I stuck him in the library. Oh, and I got a name this time. Vroom. Can you beat that? Cornelis Vroom."

## 11 — Wrong Medium

Lesley looked at me, I looked at Lesley. Becoming a regular routine, that.

"Vroom?" I said. "As in the locked-in-a-deadly-blood-feud-with-John-Herring Vroom? You're certain you got the name right," I asked Jill—"he wasn't describing his engine sound or something?"

She said no, he wasn't describing his engine sound or anything. She drank from her cocktail again, frowning over the rim at us. "What's gotten into you two?"

I looked at Lesley, Lesley at me. "I knew we never should have come here," she said. "It's a death trap, that's what it is."

I resisted the urge to reply, "Yes, honey." There would be plenty of time for that once we were married. "I guess I'd better go down."

Lesley quivered. "What if he's armed?"

I appreciated the sentiment. It was nice to know that my fiancée was thinking along the right lines.

"What if he guns you down when you can't deliver Herring?"

"There's always the chance," I agreed, realizing again how funny it sounded when she said things like that.

I stepped over and drank Jill's other cocktail. I wiped my mouth and went.

I was remarkably calm on my way downstairs to meet this so-called Vroom. Maybe it was the alcohol, or the thought of what the mechanic's bill would be for my MINI (which, at the moment, did not go vroom), but I didn't care anymore. I was sanguine. What could he do? There were witnesses in the house. True, most of them were outside occupied with the ever delightful dock, but someone would have to hear the shots. (Or at the very least a splashing sound as my corpse is dragged out and dumped in the harbor.)

I arrived back in the marble foyer, and after several wrong turns, I homed in on the library door, which was large and ornate and appeared to have been fashioned out of heavy oak. It was strange, but I hadn't noticed all the aquatic motifs before then. As I made my way down the corridor, I spotted fish, fish and more fish. There were fish paintings lining the right wall, fish tanks on the left, and when I entered the library the first thing I saw staring back at me was a bookshelf full of our liquid-loving friends done up in porcelain.

The crowning achievement in subject matter, however, began and ended with the oil painting hanging on the back wall. It depicted a gorgeous mermaid (topless), her proud face half shaded by her tail, her body curled seductively around a wood post poking out of the water. Now this was a fish I could get on board with.

I had to respect the dedication to theme. Evidently the notorious gangster "Fishes" Herring had a nice sense of humor about his name. It remained to be seen whether Cornelis Vroom would.

He watched me enter. He was standing over by a red velvet settee. He was probably only thirty odd years old, but he carried himself with the confidence of a much older man. You'd expect a guy in his line would. He had the squarest head I'd ever seen. Jill had not gone astray in her description there. His hair was closely cropped in a crew cut, adding to the illusion, and the lines of his jaw were perfectly perpendicular to his shoulders. These were fairly boxy as well, as was the rest of his body. He could have been fashioned out of heavy oak himself. The human cube I might have called him. I didn't, but I might have done. He was dressed in a suit, charcoal gray, and a red tie.

"Johnny?" he began, speaking with a slight European accent.

"Yes?"

"You've not been an easy man to locate, Johnny. I should have known you would be here all along. I thought as much on my visit this morning."

I nodded uncertainly. It was always the first place you looked, I guessed.

"I expect you know why I'm here?"

I really didn't. I was also struck by his familiarity. I suppose you've already spotted the snag, the laughable misunderstanding we were both participating in. I'm sorry to say I hadn't stumbled on this myself. Attribute it to the rides with Hutton, or Lesley's nerves, or all the almond-stuffed olives I'd been eating, but I didn't get it. According to Jill, this man had specifically asked for me and now here he was calling me Johnny. What other explanation could there be?

I muttered a polite response to his question. I think it was "uh." I started to speak again—well, speak might be going too far. I made a sort of gulping noise, like one of Herring's pets perplexed by a tapping on the tank, when the door opened, and Ate came in.

She handed our guest a sherry. "As I was saying, Mr. Vroom, I don't think—" She paused. She looked at me, I at her. Yup, definitely becoming my regular routine. "What are you doing in here, Hathaway?"

I might have asked her that myself.

Vroom looked confused. "Hathaway? Who is this Hathaway?"

"John Hathaway," sighed Ate. It was as though she had been all keyed up to introduce The Beatles, but got stuck with doing the honors for Kiki, the Dancing Cocker Spaniel instead.

Vroom let out a guffaw. It sounded a little like an engine roar. "Then this isn't Johnny Herring I have been speaking with! Ha! But of course. I asked for a Johnny when I arrived, and it is the wrong Johnny I get, ha-ha!" He went on laughing.

Ate gave a faint titter. I did my best to join in but fizzled on the backend.

"Cornelis Vroom," said Cornelis Vroom, as we shook hands. "A strange name, I know, but helpful in my line of work."

This surprised me. His line of work? I would have thought the other mobsters would have teased him something fierce about it.

"My family has not always been Vroom, you see. My father called himself this when we relocated to the Netherlands many decades ago. He named himself after the painters Vroom, who lived and worked there in the 16th and 17th centuries. But you are no doubt familiar with them?"

I raised my head vaguely. I wasn't all that familiar, no.

(I have since looked them up, and he was right, there really were Vrooms of old. Who'd have thunk it? People called Vroom.)

"Cornelis Hendrik Vroom the Younger, and his father, Hendrik Cornelis Vroom the Older," said Cornelis Vroom the Modern. "Those were our namesakes."

I nodded a second time. Good thing those ancients had switched up their Hendriks and Cornelises. Otherwise it would have just seemed weird.

"It is a very proud name Vroom," concluded our guest. "It means 'pious,' you know."

Now I really was confused. Were there pious gangsters?

Ate took over from here. "Mr. Vroom owns the Vroom Gallery. He runs it for his father. I believe you two are also artists in your own right?"

"A very minor one myself," simpered this baffling brick-body.

"Artists?" I asked. I rubbed my head. "Then you're not a gangster?"

Both he and Ate gawped at me, though I think Ate's gawp edged out his by a nose. I was beginning to think that Cornelis Vroom was not a gangster.

Ate's gape was still going strong. "Hathaway!" She looked to Vroom and apologized. She glared back at me. "What gave you such a ridiculous idea, Hathaway?"

There were so many reasons. I went with the easy explanation: "My fiancée just figured you were," I told Vroom, trying to convey in my tone that fiancées are forever thinking that their houseguests are prominent underworld figures.

Cornelis seemed hip to it. "I comprehend. It was a misunderstanding."

"Just a laughable misunderstanding," I agreed, and the three of us enjoyed another quick chuckle. Vroom's ended first.

I decided to share the whole picture with them. Or most of it. "Sorry for the mix-up, but a friend of a friend of ours wound up dead recently, and it's made everyone a little on edge around here."

"I'm not on edge," said Ate, continuing to show oodles of that helpful spirit. "What friend of a friend?"

"Stothard Hope," I replied, though I didn't see how this was any of Cornelis Vroom's business.

"Stothard Hope?" she asked. She sounded surprised.

I drew her aside, dropping my voice to a whisper. "You know him?"

"Vaguely. But I thought he died a long time ago. Didn't Dad shoot him in Monaco?"

"Madrid—and apparently he only winged him. He's dead now, though."

"Ah," she concluded, and there the matter rested. Not exactly Tennyson's *In Memoriam*, but it got the point across. Ate and I were up to speed.

It was more than I could say for Cornelis Vroom. When we returned to our guest, he had the look of a man who had selected the wrong language on his Blu-ray subtitles. I couldn't blame him. I was having trouble keeping track of everything myself.

"I think I should be going," he said.

Ate led him to the door. "If Johnny turns up we'll be sure to let you know." She turned back to me. "The Johnny Mr. Vroom is looking for is called Herring. This is his house."

I knew all this already. "The gangster," I replied simply.

As with my pronouncement about Mr. Vroom, this didn't go over very well. Ate stared, no doubt feeling that not even Kiki the Dancing Cocker Spaniel would have gibbered quite so much.

Vroom pieced together another smile. "It is strange how you persist in believing everyone is a gangster, Mr. Hathaway. Why do you think this is?"

I had no answer to that. "Then he isn't one either?" I asked. I felt like somebody should be.

"Not exactly. He is a painter."

That actually made sense. "Just like the John Frederick Herring of old."

Vroom brightened. "Aha. You *are* a student of the arts, then?"

I didn't know about that. One likes to stay abreast.

"And it is clear that you have heard all about the Vrooms and the Herrings?"

I said "Well" and invited him to continue. He would probably tell it better than I would.

He came back into the room. He heaved a sigh. "It is not so ridiculous what you have said here," he admitted.

"It isn't?" I asked.

"It wasn't?" asked Ate. I don't know who was more astonished.

Vroom waggled his large head. "No. Many decades ago, our fathers, Johnny's and mine, were what you might call 'gangsters.' Not anything major, you understand. But they did not always stay within the law. They were working together in Europe at the time, but they both wanted something more. They wanted to start anew. My father, as I say, relocated to the Netherlands and began calling himself Vroom. Johnny's father immigrated to England. He also decided to honor a past master by christening himself (and later his son) John Frederick Herring, another father and son team who had excelled in their field."

"That's a beautiful story," Ate whispered.

"Neat," I agreed.

"For a while, our fathers remained friends," continued Vroom. "When they later met up again in this country, they became rivals. First as artists, then as gallery owners. As artists, they constantly tried to outshine each other. As patrons, they would never miss a chance to poach artists from one another. You might even say they were involved in a figurative blood feud."

I laughed despite myself. A *figurative* blood feud. Why didn't somebody say that before? I knew all about the figurative versus the literal. This explained what Lesley had heard: she had mixed up the fathers' past with the sons' present. It also explained why Hutton had thought the Vrooms were taking out Herrings, and Herrings Vrooms. There were no contract killings, only better artist contracts.

"Recently," said Vroom, "I've been trying to put our families' pasts behind us. My first step was to offer Johnny work. The Herring Gallery closed a long time ago, after Herring Sr.'s death, and I thought we could all benefit from young Johnny's contributions. He is quite gifted. Unfortunately, there was also an obstacle to this. Johnny is an eccentric."

"Must be something in that name," said Ate.

"He is a recluse. So much of one that he and I have never met in person. Nevertheless, he agreed to help out on a certain matter at the gallery, but before he had fulfilled even a fraction of his obligation, he vanished. This was over two weeks ago, and no one has seen him since."

Seemed to be the pattern, that. "Bummer," I said.

I probably should have been more sympathetic, but I couldn't help feeling relieved that Vroom hadn't whacked the master of the house, nor would he apparently be whacking any of us in Herring's stead.

I broke off from my meditations to see that I was alone in the library. Evidently the Vroom had vroomed. I did recall hearing words of departure now that I thought about it.

Our resident hospitality specialist had also vacated. I discovered her out in the corridor.

"If you want to accuse Jill of being a gangster," she said, "she's in the kitchen."

I didn't want to speak to Jill, I wanted to speak to Lesley. But as Lesley was in the kitchen with Jill, I had to go that way anyway.

"Well, that's all settled," I remarked, and would have gone on to explain matters pretty concisely (leaving out the choicer bits of my idiocy), when Lesley interrupted to say that she had heard all about it. Ate had explained.

"It makes perfect sense. I can't believe you ever thought there was anything to worry about with John Herring."

I stared. "You're the one—" I let it alone. "Right. Well, touching on our stay—"

"Jill told us about that too," said Lesley, and the other witness for the prosecution slipped out the back: perhaps to avoid my beaning her with a porcelain fish. "She says you want us out of the house. Why do you want us out of the house, Johnny?"

This was complicated. "There was a little unpleasantness earlier. I'm concerned the person or persons responsible might know we're here."

Lesley was looking squiggly eyed at me. "This wouldn't have anything to do with your parcel-posting business, would it?"

She was referring to my freelance courier enterprise—the same one her mother had sneered about earlier today. "What do you mean by that exactly?"

"I don't mean anything by it. Only that you know how it's wont to get you into trouble."

I was well aware of this. I was also well aware, as she was herself, that it had once, thanks to a little jeweled dagger called the Azure Star, supplemented our income very nicely.

"You know my parents think you're a drug mule," she said.

"Oh yes?" I retorted. "Well, I'm not."

"I know you're not, Johnny. That's just one of the things they say."

"One" of the things!

"And you know that it does tend to bring you into contact with an undesirable element."

If she meant Congressman George Hathaway, my uncle, I agreed with her. I laid my cards on the table. "Honestly I don't know what's going on here, Lesley. I rarely do. All I do know is I might be in danger, and I may have passed some of that danger onto you. It's probably Hutton's fault," I said, lashing out at my poor absent friend.

Lesley rolled her eyes. "Well, you know what my parents say about *him*—"

I had some idea, yes. "Then again, it could indirectly be Fleet's doing, and your parents *love* him."

"I guess they do."

"There's no guessing about it. He's their dream man. You mix their hatred of Hutton in with their love of Enescu Fleet and you come out with a nice even British insouciance."

"How do you mean it could be Fleet's doing?" she asked, listening selectively again.

"It all depends for whom Stothard Hope meant the postcard. Him or Hutton."

"Who's Stothard Hope?"

"The guy who either meant Hutton or Fleet to get the card."

"What card?"

"The card that's the clue."

"What clue?"

"The clue in Stothard Hope's postcard," I replied.

Lesley rubbed her forehead. "So you're delivering postcards for people now?"

I rebutted this easily. I explained that I didn't deliver the postcard, no. Stothard Hope had mailed it. So there. I was pleased to see that Lesley had no reply to this.

"What is it that you *are* doing?" she wondered.

This was also complicated, and there we were, back at the beginning. "Look, maybe the smartest thing would be for me to leave."

Lesley, to my surprise, thought this a splendid idea.

"You want me to leave?"

"Well, not exactly *want*, Johnny, no. I don't mean it like that. It's just that—well, it might be easier. Dad's still pretty heated up about things."

"Why? Because of that Hutton thing? He thought your father was a notorious con man. Assumption anyone could make."

"Oh no, Dad's forgotten all about that. Well, he says he doesn't want to talk about it anymore, which is nearly as good. It's just—well, he was hearing about our adventures at Sir Roger Banbury's estate earlier—you know, where you and I first met—and he realized that you were the one who had spirited me away for weeks and weeks all those years ago. You remember how annoyed my family was about that at the time."

I did remember. I knew Lesley's disappearance had caused quite the scandal in the Darlington household. It was why she had always maintained, up until now, that she had gone off on her own in order to clear her head. That somehow sounded better than her shacking up with a degenerate nephew of a congressman who, when he wasn't dealing in stolen goods, was apparently muling drugs for the underworld.

"How'd he hear I was the spiriter?"

"Jill told him. She didn't mean anything by it. She just thought it would help."

I knew all about Jill's help. "Then I should go?"

"I think it might be best. You can always stop in in a couple of days and say goodbye. They have to get used to you eventually—they're going to see you again at the wedding."

One could always hope.

"And if some miscreant whacks me in my sleep before I can stop in?"

"Oh Johnny, don't be so dramatic. You'll be fine, you always are. And don't forget you have Hutton and Enescu Fleet to keep you out of harm's way."

Hutton and Enescu Fleet. One to get me killed, the other to save my life. You mix them together and get what exactly?

I didn't like to think about it.

## 12 — The Clue Seekers

I did think about it, though. I thought about it a lot as I walked along the darkened streets outside. There was no sign of Hutton, and with nothing better to do but head off to where I had left the MINI, I headed off to where I had left the MINI.

I don't know what irked more as I strolled along, that Lesley had essentially booted me out—a fine preview to our married life that was—or that there was still the chance that someone had followed me to the Herring mansion this morning.

I think it was more the booting thing.

I was still brooding on this more than the other when, oddly enough, I realized someone was following me now. I peered back and saw a car on the horizon.

It looked like a station wagon or possibly an SUV. Call it an SUV-wagon. I didn't like it. In my current state of mind, nothing short of a couple wise guys hanging off the running boards, sporting tommy guns, could have affected my nerves more profoundly.

I increased my pace to speed-walking proportions. I came up over the hill like a barrel of Prohibition whisky cut loose from the delivery truck, tripped over my own giant clomping feet and took a spill into somebody's marigold garden. The SUV-wagon screeched to a halt, the right passenger door flew open, and a figure sprang out. Rather than a wise guy sporting a machine gun, however, I perceived Hutton sporting a Maltese.

"Don't look now, Hath," he said, "but you're covered in posies."

"They're marigolds."

"I bow to your expertise."

Pixie also bowed. And bow-wowed. She must not have liked marigolds.

Hutton indicated a pair of blondes in the car window. "Meet Tiffany and Jenny. They happened by after you headed for the Herring house. And if you think that's easy to say with a bitten tongue, it's not. They very kindly offered us a ride."

I had to say, I was impressed. It wasn't a carload of spring-breaking beach bunnies, but not bad for 8:36 p.m. in Portland. He had learned well.

He helped me up from the shrubbery, apologizing for not signaling to me earlier. "I meant to holler hello when you came out of the house, but I was distracted. Pixie had just licked Tiffany's neck, and I had to intercede on the pup's behalf."

I was sure he did. As long as it was Pixie who had done the licking. I climbed in the backseat, said hello to Tiffany, hi to Jenny, and immediately pooh-poohed a suggestion from Hutton that we all go grab some margaritas. I was tired, he was supposedly dating Fleet's daughter, and I was engaged to be married. Supposedly.

It was almost midnight when I got off the phone with the tow people. By the time I had explained where they could find the MINI, explained how the MINI had wound up where they could find it, and explained what I wanted them to do with the MINI once they found where it had wound up, I was exhausted, thirsty and my right earlobe was all sweaty from holding my phone up to it all evening. I needed a good stiff drink (and possibly a washcloth).

Hutton provided the drinks—whisky. We were at his house now, Tiffany and Jenny having graciously dropped us off. "Johnnie Walker Black?" he offered.

I shook my head. I couldn't deal with another Johnny at the moment. Not tonight.

"Even though it has an 'ie' in it?"

"Especially because it has an 'ie' in it," I said. The "ie" was only mocking me. We settled on Famous Grouse. I drank it down and asked him where I could sleep. I was exhausted.

He kindly offered me the master bedroom for the night. He said it was the least he could do, and I agreed with him, but that was before I had seen the room.

Hutton always had been a bit light on furnishings. He liked to take his time choosing his pieces, weighing the merits of this one over the other, the result being that you could tally up his appointments on one hand.

The entire master suite consisted of—let me see if I can remember—a nightstand, a chair and a mattress. The rest was all cherrywood floors, beige walls, white crown molding and air.

It didn't matter. I was tired enough to sleep anywhere. I flopped down on the mattress and almost immediately zonked out. I remember thinking, just before slumber overtook me, that I wondered where he was going to sleep. I also remember not caring.

Shows that it never does to go to bed angry, though. I woke up an hour later, my mind racing and my T-shirt all in a bunch. I kept dreaming that black sedans and white sports cars were hunting me down on the beach during spring break. Pretty blondes were sitting in SUVs keeping score, and Pixie was the lineswoman. When I awoke there had just been a penalty called for excessive use of coral.

I sat up and looked out the window, rubbing my face. It was hard to make out, but there appeared to be a Mercedes or BMW parked across the street. A black sedan. Still half asleep and determined not to fret about every random vehicle I saw—there were a lot of black sedans in the world—I flopped back on the mattress, my leg immediately striking some strange solid object on the edge. I looked up and observed a shadowy figure looming over the "bed."

At first I took this to be Hutton, come to ask if he thought the blonde Jenny fancied him. But no. It was not my host disturbing my rest. The interloper was a hard young man dressed in fuchsia running togs. They had actually looked more eggplant in the moonlight, but then he switched on the overhead lamp and they shone more vividly.

I felt like I had seen his face somewhere recently. He had a small round head, too small for his body, a small furrowed brow and a few days of stubble on his face. He looked like an angry coconut. "Johnny?" he said.

"Yes?" I said.

"Good," he said.

## 13 — Artistic License

The moment I said it I realized the more sensible reply would have been No. There are a lot of Johnnies in the world, after all.

The intruder didn't give me a chance to qualify mine. He half-grinned, took a seat in the chair and remarked, "Expect you know why I'm here."

I don't know why people are always asking me this. I never know why anyone is anywhere. "Who the hell are you?"

"Name's Basil." He spoke with a cockney accent. (Just what this case needed, I thought, more Brits.) "And I wouldn't worry about how I nipped in here. That's my specialty, idn't it." He paused to take a gander around, rubbing his hands together. "Wasabi and rose petals," he said, exhibiting what was evidently some boutique variety of hand cream. "Fancy a dollop?"

I said no thanks, and he nodded placidly—to each his own. He took out a toothpick and chewed this thoughtfully. "Nice place you got here. Kinda spartan, though, the decor. Don't you find it kinda spartan, chum?" He was evidently under the impression that this spartan space was mine. In no agreeable mood, I replied that I didn't find it all that spartan, no.

Basil frowned. He couldn't let this one pass. "I mean, as a new guest I gotta ask myself, what is the vision behind this space. I don't know, do I?"

"This is where I keep the chair," I said, and Basil smiled broadly and without charm.

"And a nice chair it is, too. An Eames, yeah?"

I replied that I wouldn't be surprised, and Basil said yeah, it was an Eames. "You really don't know what this is all about, do you?"

I told him I did not.

"Then I'd expect you'd like to know why we're paying you a visit?"

I did confess to a momentary spasm of curiosity.

"It's a simple enough reason, mate."

I said good. Simple reasons were my specialty.

"Where is he?"

I assumed he meant Hutton, and a line about my best friend's keeper sprang to mind. Instead I just laughed bravely. I didn't feel brave, but that's how I laughed.

"Somefing funny, friend?"

I said more like whimsical. I climbed to my feet, stretched, and tried to guess where Hutton may have hidden all those secret guns of his. Basil glared up at me from the Eames—let's assume it was an Eames. He wasn't tall, especially seated, but his glare added about six inches to his height. "I don't 'fink you're taking this very seriously, chum."

"Oh yeah? Well, you know what I *'fink* about that?" I said.

Basil didn't give me a chance to say what I *'fought* about it. In a blur of brutish little knuckles he gave me a solid jab in the stomach, propelling me backwards and onto my ass. Luckily somebody had placed a mattress there.

Basil stood. He stared down at me, massaging more cream into his hardened fist. (Great, now my stomach was going to smell like rose petals.)

"Seems to me," he drawled, "I asked you a very simple and polite question, and you're going to look slippy about the answer."

He was quite wrong. I was not going to look slippy about the answer. I was going to sit back against the pillows, massaging my tummy with a baffled and pained look on my face.

"What do you want him for?"

"That's our business, idn't it."

"*Idn't it* what?"

"Idn't it our business, chum." He sighed, rather a pitying sigh.

I moved to stand again. "Look—"

He laid another serving of wasabi into my breadbox. He had a nice easy release point, I noticed, but tended to favor the body a little too much.

"Knock that off," I coughed, not favoring any of it.

He proceeded dryly, "We can make this simple, yeah. You tell me where he is, and live."

That did seem fair. There was an even simpler solution, however. Basil's last punch had sent me into the nightstand, and if I was any judge of Hutton and his obsessions, that stand would contain some form of firearm. It could be a Glock, a SIG—I wasn't picky. Thanks to Basil's roughhousing, all I had to do was lean back, pivot and I would be in the drawer with my hand wrapped around its soothing polymer grip in a matter of seconds.

I leaned back. I pivoted. And in a matter of seconds I had my hand wrapped around an Itty Bitty Book Light, Volume One of the *Complete Works of William Shakespeare* (which I had loaned to Hutton over eighteen years ago), and a *Book of Suggestive Limericks* (which I hadn't).

There was no gun. Not in the Shakespeare, not in the *Limericks*. Fleet's thesaurus, they were not. I had a passing thought that the book light might, in fact, be an Itty Bitty Bazooka, but it wasn't. I shined it on Basil, who appeared unamused.

"Read much Shakespeare?" he asked, gazing down at the tome through lazy eyelids.

"Not as much as I should," I confessed, "I'm more of a thesaurus man myself."

"There's a good line in Shakespeare," said Basil.

"I've heard that."

"In Macbeth. This hired assassin in there says the blows and buffets of life have so incensed him that he's reckless to what he does. That line really speaks to me, mate. Because that's me. I don't care what I do or how I do it, but you can take it as given that I won't abide any more fancy moves like that. My employer asked me to get some answers from you, he never said in what condition to leave you, now did he?"

I couldn't say, I hadn't been present at the time.

"Get up," Basil grunted. I got up. "We'll see what he has to say about this."

"Aren't you going to call me 'chum'?" I asked.

"I ain't your chum," said Basil, shoving me out into the hall.

I paused at the top of the steps. I couldn't believe all this bustling hadn't woken Hutton. Where the hell was he sleeping? Saturn? And what of the ferocious guard puppy Pixie? Where was she—the moon Dione? (I was feeling rather astronomical at the time.)

"I should probably freshen up first," I said, making one last effort for a gun, any gun.

I had been eyeing the linen closet. I seemed to recall almost blowing my index finger off one afternoon when Hutton had run out of hand towels. "Shan't be a minute," I remarked.

Once again, Basil's hands were quicker than the eye, and even quicker than they had been in the bedroom. They snagged his chum, or not his chum at last count, and sent him toppling down the stairs, through the railing, and onto a decorative glass shelf which had, up until that point, held knickknacks. I landed in a burst of crystal shards and fancy bric-a-brac. (The only piece of furniture in forty square feet, and I had nailed it.)

"Now, now," advised Basil, following me down the stairs, though without all the thumps and whaps. "Don't break anyfing serious. I could get in trouble for that." He lit a cigarette. Holding this up to the skylight, he mused, "What is it with this country and the cigs, chum? Can't smoke these anywhere anymore."

I rolled over and stared at him. It would be a great relief to Basil that I hadn't broken anyfing serious. "I thought I wasn't your chum?" I asked.

"I'm warming to you," he said.

He puffed a few smoke rings, then flicked out the cig on the rug: an obvious fire hazard, but trying telling Basil that. He took out one of his toothpicks next and gnawed on it in a philosophical vein. He seemed to have a lot of nervous energy.

"I like your bravado, mate. It shows bollocks, it does, but you know what Shakespeare says about bollocks—"

What The Immortal Bard may or may not have said about bollocks would remain in the exclusive domain of literary scholars for now. A familiar voice cut in on our discussion.

"That will be enough, Basil," said this familiar voice. The light was still out so I had a hard time making out a face. But the voice was definitely familiar. "Let's see if we can locate our host." He made a signal to Basil, who herded me down the hall and into the kitchen.

We discovered Hutton at the center island, rinsing out our whisky goblets in the sink. He betrayed no surprise at our arrival. In fact, he greeted us warmly. "Howdy, Hath. Howdy, fuchsia man prodding Hath. Hello to you, large square-headed dude."

I couldn't help twirling around on this cue. Sure enough, standing beside the free-punching jogger was Cornelis Vroom.

He gestured me over to the sink. Hutton shut off the tap. I appreciated his cleanliness, but I could have done with his presence out in the hall. Assuming we got out of this alive, I'd be picking knickknack slivers out of my backside for days.

I also couldn't help noticing, as I took my position at the counter, that the door to the guest room was ajar. There was a finely appointed sleigh bed there, turned down for the evening. It looked mighty comfortable, that bed. Following my stare, Hutton leaned in and whispered, "You didn't want that one, did you, Hath?"

Basil told us to hush up. He wasn't armed, but the tone of his voice compelled us to jerk our hands up. We stood there a moment behind the counter, hands raised like a couple of line cooks in a stickup, before Basil told us there wasn't any need for that. "Just shut up," he said.

Hutton was never one to take orders. Leaning in again, he whispered "Glock," like a line cook looking to return fire.

I hated to disappoint him, but it had to be done. I had no weapon. I didn't even have the book light. I whispered back "No Glock" and Hutton said "No. *Glock.*" I didn't get it.

"Shut it," insisted Basil. "We got some questions for you."

This was convenient, because we had some questions for them too. As hosts, it was only polite to let them go first. "I expect you know why we're here," Vroom began. (I sighed.)

Hutton, not standing on ceremony, replied, "You're the blokes from the black sedan, aren't you?"

The Living Cube confirmed this with a bow of his car battery of a head. They were the blokes. He turned my way. "Aren't you going to ask if we're gangsters?" he inquired.

I hesitated. "Are you gangsters?"

"We are indeed," laughed Cornelis Vroom, and Basil frowned at him. He seemed annoyed, as if he and the boss hadn't agreed they were telling people. "Although I tend to prefer the term crime lord for myself. Gangster is such an outmoded word. It puts one in mind of trilby hats and pinstriped suits." He paused to straighten his pinstriped suit. "But call us what you like. Your fiancée, she referred to us as gangsters, did she not, so we'll be gangsters for her sake. You should really learn to listen to her, Johnny. She knew all along what we were."

I nodded. She was a pippin alright, my Lesley. (Even if she did abandon her theories the minute they appeared to be going south on her.)

I paused. If Cornelis Vroom really was a gangster/crime lord, not an artist/gallery owner, or maybe a gangster/crime lord first and an artist/owner in his off-hours, then that could only mean one thing. It was the old mistaken identity trick.

"Listen, I'm not the guy you're looking for. I really am John Hathaway. I know it's very inartistic having the same first name as this Herring fellow, and the same last initial for that matter, but it's the truth. I left my wallet at home—I'm always doing that—but if I had it, you would see that I'm not him. I'm just staying at his house."

"I know all this already, Mr. Hathaway. I might have been deceived momentarily at our initial visit, but I quickly realized you could never be John Herring's son. The boy is a genius. From what I've heard, he exudes brilliance with every word he speaks."

"Right," I said. That would do it. "Then it's not a laughable misunderstanding?"

"Not so much, no."

"Oh," I replied. That was too bad. I liked the old mistaken identity trick.

Vroom perched himself on Hutton's one-and-only barstool. "It is well that you brought up the subject of Johnny Herring. Johnny, you see, is key for us."

I tried, once again, to explain that we had no idea where the man was, eliciting Hutton's assistance on this. Hutton said nothing.

Vroom smiled. "I was inclined to believe you. At the house I was certain you knew nothing about Johnny Herring's whereabouts."

I had another *Then why—?* all poised for the ready, when Vroom continued: "But then you mentioned Stothard Hope, Mr. Hathaway. *Stothard Hope.*"

"And this is a problem?"

"Not in the slightest. Stothard Hope is key."

I was getting a little annoyed with this Cornelis Vroom waffling. "I thought you said Herring was key?"

"They are both key. They fit the same lock, let us say."

We could say it, but it still meant nothing to me.

"We'd like to know what became of him."

"Hope or Herring?"

"Both."

I nodded. "Hope is dead."

"So I understood you to say earlier. What of Herring, then?"

I un-nodded. "We told you everything we know."

Vroom glanced at his tiny thug, who wrinkled his pug nose. "We think you know much more than you're saying."

This was a bloody lie! I never knew anything more than what I said.

I looked to Hutton, who picked up a salad fork from the sink and polished it. "What is it you want from us exactly?" About time he spoke up.

There was a pregnant pause, during which Basil twirled his toothpick back and forth in his mouth. "Enescu Fleet," said his employer.

Hutton looked as baffled as I was.

"There is no one more uniquely positioned to help us," Vroom explained. He unperched himself from the barstool and straightened his tie. "Do we have an understanding?"

If he wanted us to understand this understanding, we didn't. Before I could reply in that vein, Hutton answered for the both of us. "You're set on securing Enescu Fleet's services?"

"We are."

"Then you need look no further." There was another pregnant pause, this one of his own fathering. "I'm Enescu Fleet," he remarked.

Even with the knowledge that he was Enescu Fleet, of a sort, I was astonished. I couldn't figure what he was playing at.

Neither could Vroom. "Really, Mr. Hutton, if you expect us to believe—"

"It's the truth. Take a look." He handed over his wallet and ID, not to mention his EGO. "Hutton's just the name I use around the place."

Vroom refused to accept what he had been shown. "My father used to speak of the great detective Enescu Fleet when I was a boy."

Hutton was ready with an explanation. Not the actual explanation, but an explanation.

"Enescu Fleet was my grandfather. You probably heard they used to call him the old man. Well, he was certainly that."

"He is alive?"

"Not especially. He was sadly eaten by sharks trying to swim to Barbados. This was decades ago. You knew he was shipwrecked on a desert island?"

"I heard he escaped."

"Escaped? No, no escape. Does anyone ever really escape from a desert island?"

"But I have seen his picture in papers as recently as last year."

"Him? The dapper man you see schmoozing at cocktail parties and shaking the DA's hand is an actor I hired to play the part. I use him to give myself some rest and relaxation. No sense getting mobbed by hordes of adoring well-wishers everywhere I go."

"But why? Who are you?"

"Just the greatest private detective who ever lived," said Hutton. "I took over the family business when grandpappy went full fathom five."

Vroom tried to speak, but Hutton steamrollered over him. "My father was a circus strongman, my mother a Romanian ballerina. Once, when I was six—"

Vroom wasn't too pleased—no mistaking him for an adoring well-wisher. "And his daughter? The woman I spoke with at the Herring household?"

"You mean Gigi Rodriquez, the Mexican stage actress? She's good, isn't she?"

"Then she is not your—his daughter?"

"Well, she's somebody's, I'm sure. But Fleet's? Don't be ridiculous. I ask you, would anyone name their child Ate?"

Vroom grumbled an obscenity under his breath. I was surprised he wasn't taking this better. I'd have thought men like him would have been more accustomed to disappointments. Getting outbid on a new casino by a competitor. Having your accountant dispute "gats" as a business expense. Things of that sort. I guess there are moments when even your most hardened don wonders if it is all worth it.

"Let us say, for the moment, that you are who you say you are."

Hutton bowed. Very regal, that bow, very Romanian.

"Then you've had no interaction with The Artists' Colony, a group functioning in Madrid twenty years ago?"

"Twenty years ago," said Hutton, "I was in school in England, in a tree, trying to get a peek at the headmaster's wife undressing in her bedroom."

I could support this. I was out on the limb alongside him.

Vroom voiced another expletive.

"So," asked Hutton, pushing his bluff, "shall we get started on your little assignment, or would you rather just give it a miss?"

Vroom peered up; to Hutton's amazement and mine, he replied, "Yes."

Hutton blinked at him. I had a feeling this was not part of his plan. "Did you say yes?"

"Yes."

"Yes, you said *yes*, or *yes*, we should get started on your little assignment?"

"I shall expect Herring found before the 6th," said Vroom. "That gives you two days." And just like that he and Basil collected themselves. Vroom paused in the doorway. "And lest you two get any clever ideas, remember we know where you live. All of you." He nodded back at Basil, who grinned all over his disgusting toothpick.

"We won't get any ideas," Hutton muttered.

"We aren't clever," I agreed.

I waited until the door slammed shut before speaking again. "That went well."

"A very apt observation," said Enescu Fleet—the real Enescu Fleet—speaking from about five inches behind my head.

# 14 — Student Becomes the Master

I probably should have been used to people breathing down the back of my neck by now. I wasn't. I sprang back, scattering Hutton's one pot and pan.

Fleet smiled. "You're very jumpy tonight, Johnny."

I riposted that he would be jumpy too if he had spent the evening getting flung about and talked cockney at. "Were you here the whole time?"

"More or less. I missed the opening remarks."

"Where? I didn't see you. Wait, you weren't behind the drapes, were you?" I didn't feel I could take another modified Polonius or whatever you call it.

Fleet replied that he had not been behind the drapes, no. "Don't be ridiculous. I was crouched down behind the piano in the dining room." He turned to Hutton. "You don't have much by way of furniture, do you?" he scowled, and Hutton replied that he preferred to hold off on buying items until he had settled on the "perfect piece" to complete the space. This did leave things pretty sparse for visitors, he acknowledged, and Fleet said sparse was right. It probably made sweeping up after parties pretty easy, though, and Hutton agreed that there was always that.

I gazed back and forth between these two peerless PIs, trying to focus in on their highly technical shoptalk. I was going to need another drink.

Hutton fetched me a small batch bourbon in an attractive Waterford glass. He might not have much by way of furniture, but he always did have the right alcohol for any occasion.

"Start with the piano," I told the old man. "Or right before the piano, maybe."

Fleet said he would be only too glad:

"After my errands, I returned to the Herring house to look for you. You weren't there. My daughter said you'd lost your mind, and Jill said you'd gone on a bender and were in a dangerous mood. Having learned from Lesley that you were out gallivanting with Hutton—"

Gallivanting! I liked that.

"—I tried your place first, then came straight here. I had hardly let myself in, when I stumbled on your conversation. I would have made my presence known then, for it sounded like this Vroom was all keyed up to confer with me, but then Hutton went off on his flight of fancy, and I thought it best to wait and see where it took us."

"And?"

"It proved very interesting, if not a little peculiar. Sharks off the coast of Barbados?" he asked Hutton.

"Yes?"

"Romanian ballerina?"

"No good?"

Fleet suggested that these details would not have been his first choice, especially the grandfather part. Hutton conceded that he might have gotten a bit swept up in the role.

"Still, you understood the motivation for the lie?"

Fleet said he had gotten the gist of it, and I waggled my goblet at them, calling the meeting back to order. Also calling for another bourbon.

I didn't have the gist at all. Not a speck of it.

Hutton elucidated for me. The ploy, he explained, was the perfect way to delve into the Stothard Hope case. By agreeing to assist Vroom, we would be privy to everything he knew. With Fleet absent, or so Hutton thought, this meant posing as the man in order to win Vroom's trust. He hated to do it—*ha!*—but it seemed like the only path to take.

I wasn't so sure about this. I also wasn't certain that we had learned anything.

Hutton continued to point out the nuances of his plan, not to mention the nuisances.

"I agree, it would have been nice for them to have begged off. That was my initial plan. But we can still salvage something. Thanks to my maneuvering, Fleet is now free to investigate without interference. It's like one of those whatsit passes in rugby."

"What whatsit passes?"

"How should I know? That pass where the whosit goes up the middle and there's some other whatchamacallit sneaking down the sidelines."

I shook my head. "Never mind whatsit passes. All you've done is thrown us in the thick of it with Vroom. How's that for interference?"

Hutton said he could deal with that kind of interference, as long as we had Fleet going down the sidelines unobserved.

The aging fullback supported this. "He's right, Johnny. It was a good play."

I snorted and shook my head again. I didn't get Fleet-reasoning.

"And you are not in the least bit concerned," I asked, "that these men are cold-blooded killers?"

Hutton said you would think he would be, but no. "They have every reason to keep us alive now."

Very gratifying! "And unless we find Herring, how long will that last? And what about Lesley and Ate?"

"What about them?"

"They're at Herring's house for God's sake!"

"Exactly. The safest place in town."

"But Herring's a gangster! And a painter. A gangster-painter."

Hutton asked what if he was. "His house is in an upscale neighborhood, there are barristers on the premises. Besides, he's already determined Herring's not there. That's why he hired us."

I supposed his argument had merit, as bizarre arguments went. "Speaking of safe houses," I frowned, "what the hell happened with you tonight?"

"Say again?"

"Why weren't you armed? What happened to having a gun concealed in every room?"

"Oh that. I do have a gun concealed in every room. Sometimes two."

"Not in the master you didn't."

"Did you check under the Eames?"

"No."

"How about in the nightstand drawer, behind the trick back?"

There was a trick back? Didn't matter. "What about you?"

Hutton asked what about him? He couldn't very well shoot them in cold blood, now could he? It's not like they had gotten violent.

"Basil threw me down the stairs!"

"Well, there's that."

"And what about letting them leave? You could have held them up. Called the cops."

Hutton asked to what end? "We wanted them to leave, remember? They go, and then Fleet here checks them out unobserved. Sees what clues they might be hiding of their own."

"Was that the plan?"

"Of course."

I said oh. That was a pretty good one, actually. "Tahoma?" I asked.

"Perfect Tahoma," replied Hutton, and I nodded. I was glad to be on the right page for once.

"I still think you should have been armed," I said.

"Who says I wasn't?" answered Hutton, and so saying reached back into the sink.

There was a splooking sound, and a second later he came to the surface with a Glock Model 26. It looked vaguely like…

"Is that mine?" I gurgled.

As a matter of fact, it was. Hutton had taken the liberty of securing it from my place earlier today. Whatever wasn't bolted down or currently on fire…

"I have always dreamt of concealing a Glock in a sink," he said wistfully.

"You have?"

"Absolutely. Consider it. Menaces are surrounding the kitchen. I make like I'm reaching for a scrubby tool, and *blam!* I blow them away through the stainless."

"You've always dreamt of this?" I asked, also wondering, if he had always dreamt of it, why he didn't fulfill this dream with his own damned pistol.

"Well, maybe not *always*," he admitted. "Since this afternoon perhaps." He glanced over at Fleet, inviting him into the conversation. "They shoot underwater, you know—Glocks."

Fleet said yes. Yes, indeed. "The amphibious Model 17 does anyway," he commented. "Shoot this one in your sink and you might have blown your fingers off, not to mention cracked your finest whisky goblet."

He took the soggy 26 off Hutton's hands and placed it on the dish strainer to dry. He asked for the dishrag next, dried his own powerful hands, and then flung the rag on the hook behind Hutton's head.

"Now then," he said, and I could infer from his tone that serious matters were about to be discussed. "Where, pray tell, is Pixie?"

I had wondered this myself. I knew she wasn't much of a guard dog, but there are limits. I hesitated to ask whether Hutton had always dreamt of concealing a tiny Maltese in a breadbox, a clever ploy to unleash on assailants who simply wanted a nice bite of rye.

He put our qualms to rest. "I gave her to some neighbor kids to play with while Hath was on the phone with the auto shop. I figured we'd pick her up from them in the morning."

Fleet gazed back at his junior—the man entrusted with the care of the royal pooch.

"Or we could go get her right now," said Hutton. "I'm sure the little tykes are still up. It's only two a.m."

# 15 — Local Color

I was up bright and early the next morning, if the 9:55 on my phone could be believed. I was still a bit hazy as to our plan of action. I suppose that was my fault. I never should have had any more drinks on the heels of all those whiskies and martinis. You gotta have something to help you get back to sleep, though, and a couple more small batch bourbons seemed like a good idea at the time.

On the plus side, Fleet did not insist on waking the neighbor children in the wee hours. In fact, he waited until lunch before retrieving Pixie. I figured he was enjoying the peace and quiet himself. With Vroom and Herring and Hope all floating about in a colorful investigative swirl, the detectives and I still had matters to discuss. The chowder house down the street seemed indicated. It would have to have more expansive seating than Hutton's place.

There was a momentary clash with management as Fleet strolled in with the pup, but a few well-chosen words and the anti-Maltese sentiment went by the wayside. We took a table in the back with a view of the ballgame on TV. Pixie stayed on her best behavior throughout; except once when the right fielder failed to hit the cutoff man on a play at the plate.

Between the 4th inning and Hutton's second basket of clams, Fleet showed me some McKnight paintings on Hutton's iPad. He was hoping I could identify the picture from the postcard. We began with "The Red Room," went from that to "The Blue Room" and closed with "The Green Room," all from the artist's Clinton Christmas series, '94, '95 and '96.

I enjoyed them all, and would have gladly toured the entire McKnight collection; but, as Fleet pointed out, it wasn't for my edification that we were doing this. He never got frustrated, however, not even when, in a moment of punchiness, I indicated Socks the cat in one of the pics, urging Pixie to catch the "li'l kitty." Once the canine had disengaged her fangs from the screen, I knuckled down as best I could.

The Blue Room I could dismiss immediately. Too blue. The Green Room also wasn't it. The tone was—wait for it—too green. It had to be the Red Room. It had the right color, the right Christmas tree, the fireplace, the flair. It had it all. Even still, there was something not quite right about the picture. Something missing. Or perhaps something there that hadn't been there before. I couldn't figure it. Then again, what did I know about art?

A few more looks at the piece and our art discussion came to a close. I have a vague recollection of Pixie running up and down the bar counter after that, chasing a peanut Hutton had thrown for her amusement. Sometime later, I slipped away from the herd and attempted to sleep off my hangover on the pool table in the back room. Just myself, not Pixie. The dog would have just been ridiculous.

About half an hour later, Fleet woke me from my felt nap. He wanted to tell me that he had gotten in touch with his buddy at the car dealership. I asked Car Dealership Who?, and he replied Wainwright Motors. I asked Wainwright Motors Heh?, and he poked me with a pool cue. He was in no mood for my cross-talk impersonations. He had gotten the scoop on the white sports car and the man who had out-Desdemona-ed Hutton in the alley.

"He used a false name and paid cash, but my friend did remember him. Based on his description I'd say the buyer was none other than Tony Rudd."

And this was supposed to mean something to me?

"Tony Rudd is a dangerous criminal for hire, ex-mercenary and assassin."

I said gotcha and lay back on the slab. The palette was certainly thickening here. "Sort of a non-cockney Basil, this Rudd?"

"More of a Basil plus. Basil threw you down the stairs. Tony Rudd would have been more inclined to use a wood chipper. It's no wonder he was driving around with fake plates. Men like Tony Rudd are always up to some nefarious criminal act. Hutton's lucky he didn't kill him in that back alley."

Hutton was often fortunate in that respect. I stretched out and yawned. "I was thinking, maybe we can find this granddaughter of Stothard Hope's. She might know something."

Fleet puffed at his beard. "I expect she might, although I gather Stothard and she were never very close."

"Have you talked to her?"

"No. Oddly enough, no one can find her now. She has also gone off the grid."

That made three and counting. "What do you think is going on?"

"There's some kind of job in the works—has to be." He paused. "I wonder if the stories about the—" He shook his head. "No, I'm getting ahead of myself."

I didn't pry. If Fleet was getting ahead of himself, then there was no point in asking either one of them for any insight.

I lay back down. It seemed to me, as I curled up against the eight ball, that there was still something he wasn't sharing with me. "What's The Artists' Colony?" I asked. "Vroom mentioned it last night. Something about Madrid, twenty years ago?"

Fleet took a deep breath. He assumed a near recumbent position in his chair and put his feet up on the pool table. "The Colony was a criminal syndicate. One of the most notorious bands of art thieves no one has ever heard of."

"You investigated them?"

"Our paths crossed." He leaned farther back. "Some bright-eyed lieutenant came up with the name. He dubbed them that after we realized everyone in the gang had chosen an alias in reference to some past artist. Cornelis Vroom Sr. and John Herring Sr. were the leaders. Stothard Hope was their utility infielder."

I jerked up, my leg sending the nine ball into the six, sinking both. It was actually a pretty good shot. "Hope was an art thief?"

"More of a consulting thief. At his height, some of the biggest names in organized crime hired him for his expertise."

I could dig it. A fellow freelancer. The only way to go.

"He was more or less the brains behind the Art Colony operation. Some say he was the greatest con artist who ever lived."

I frowned. Seemed to me we had discussed some other great con artist recently—someone who was a con artist, or someone we thought was a con artist and wasn't a con artist. In my enfeebled condition I couldn't place it. Probably wasn't important. What did I know about con artistry?

"Stothard, of course, chose the structure of his alias for my benefit, a gibe at my expense."

I said right, a gibe. I didn't get it.

"He was always goading me, that man: the alias, the little taunts he used to leave behind after heists. He was always trying to lure me out of retirement. Interestingly enough, it was something in one of his messages to me in Madrid that led me to foil a much more significant heist later on. I always wondered if he had sabotaged their efforts on purpose."

"Why would he?"

"Who knows? Stothard always had an odd view of justice. It's possible he no longer approved of the syndicate's actions. I don't know. Not long after Madrid, the Colony disbanded. Herring and Vroom became artists, and later gallery owners, and later-later enemies. Theirs had not been an amicable breakup. Stothard Hope retired. After mocking me for years about my retirement, he had finally done the same himself."

"And then you shot him."

"Not precisely at that moment," said Fleet. "But yes. I had to show him I still cared."

I could see that. "So, fast-forward twenty years, and Vroom and Herring's sons have gotten the gang back together again?"

"Perhaps." Coming from Fleet that was unbridled enthusiasm. I could live with *perhaps*. "Which means Stothard was probably up to his neck in it," he added.

"I thought you said he had retired?"

"He had. But men in his line of work often have a hard time hanging up their tools."

I knew the type. "So let me see if I got this straight. A few days ago Stothard Hope, with his unusual views on justice, got in the gang's way, and they killed them. But not before he got off one last taunt, this in the form of a modified SOS, to his old nemesis Enescu Fleet?"

His old nemesis said perhaps (again).

"And then Vroom Jr. got greedy and killed Johnny Herring—no wait, he wants Herring found. Unless that's a bluff. Anyway, Herring is missing, and Stothard Hope's granddaughter is missing, and—hey, do you think the house was a setup? Herring's place?"

Fleet remarked that a coincidence of that caliber would hardly seem likely.

I jerked up again. "Then the girls *are* in danger!"

Fleet shook his head. "I don't think they are. I don't think young Herring was behind Stothard's death. Nor do I really suspect the Vrooms. I think something has gone awry with their plans, but I don't think they have killed anyone. There is definitely a party yet to be heard from here."

Well, I wished they would hurry up and get on with it.

"Any idea what kind of job they're planning, if there is a job?"

"No. Although I have a pretty good idea *where* they're planning it. A picturesque spot."

I squinted at him. "You don't mean—"

"The Ariadne."

"Ha!"

"It *is* an artists' colony, Johnny."

Actually it was a retreat—according to Malcolm Rosso it was, anyway. Even still, it was a little on the nose, wasn't it?

Fleet didn't think it was. "You yourself said Stothard stayed in a guest room at the museum."

"Sure, but lots of people visit museums, lots of people stay at weird-ass B-and-B's. That doesn't mean they're looking to loot the place."

"Most people are not Stothard Hope," said Enescu Fleet. "While I was in town, I learned quite a lot about the residents of the Ariadne. They're a strange group. They've been there months. They never go out, they never interact with the townsfolk. They just stay holed up in their colony and receive food deliveries two times a week. They might be protecting something of value, something Stothard and his gang were looking to heist."

I sighed. I stretched my leg again, but to no good advantage on the felt. "We're talking about stealing *art* here, right?"

Fleet nodded.

"Then the Ariadne has to be out. I've seen the place inside and out, and the only thing of any value in that museum wouldn't fit in a frame. Not without a fight anyway. Not without receiving a supple European knee in the cojones."

Fleet didn't seem to be listening to me anymore. Whatever flight of fancy he was on, my observations were just a pleasant background flitter, best ignored.

Our conversation more or less dwindled down from there. Fleet wanted to look into the postcard a little further, determine any symbols or whatnot the painting might have contained. Apparently he knew a McKnight expert in Connecticut. We left it that I would sleep it off, Fleet would check out his art history, and I would sleep it off some more.

We would watch Pixie for him of course? Cool beans. He departed, adding that we should do nothing until he returned.

No problem there.

I can only guess that Hutton felt guilty finding me sprawled out among the chalk dust. Shortly after Fleet left, he collected me off the table, offering me the bed in his guest room. The real bed. I woke up a few hours later, feeling refreshed and well rested; though with the strange sensation that someone had tried to rack me during my nap.

I discovered my benefactor on the kitchen stool eating a bowl of afternoon cereal. He acknowledged me with a nod and a rattle of the box of oats.

"Yummy O's?"

"What time is it?"

"Four thirty."

I asked him to make mine a double.

"It's a good thing you're up, Hath. There's been a development."

"What development?"

"You got a text."

"What text?"

"Text on your mobile, twit."

"Oh yeah? Where is it?"

"Not sure, but the text was from a blocked number."

"You read my text?"

"Of course."

"Don't read my texts," I said, wishing I had somewhere to sit and eat my Yummy O's. I took a bowl from the dish strainer. It looked like my Glock was almost dry.

Hutton remained firm. "I have to read your texts if I'm going to know who texted you. And you'll be glad I did. The message was from a potential client in your courier business, someone looking to hire you."

"Give them a miss," I said, sitting on the counter.

"I wouldn't. The text was signed Stothard Hope."

It just goes to show the persuasive power my friend has over me that half an hour later—and against my better judgement—I found myself outside a seedy little shop down by the wharf. The address given in the text.

I used the drive over to point out a flaw. "It's unlikely, nay impossible, that the message came from a dead man." Postcards, maybe, but not a cellphone text.

"All the more reason to find out who did send it," said Hutton.

"But Fleet told us not to do anything until he returned," I reminded him, not liking the look of the neighborhood—nor the reddish-brown stain on the sidewalk outside the shop.

"Oh yes?"

"Yes. And Vroom told us not to try anything clever."

Hutton scowled. "And the bartender told us not to let Pixie lick all the pimentos out of the olives in the condiment tray. If I listened to everything everyone told me never to do, I'd never do anything. Come on."

The place didn't look any better from the inside. I'd have called it a cross between an old-fashioned dime store and a pawn broker for your more fanciful assassin. There was merchandise scattered hither and thither, all of a rugged and violent nature—knives, battle swords, things of that sort. Also sleeping bags and other camping goods, no doubt featured in some of the state's lesser known ax murders. And then, as you reached the end of the shop, an old and weary-looking gentleman leaning against the counter, reading a local newspaper.

"Yes?" he asked. His lips may have said yes, but his leathery brow said no.

From what I had heard about Fleet's old nemesis, a less Stothard-looking man I could hardly envisage (even if he was dead). Right-looking or not, Hutton spoke the name to him: whispering it like an undercover agent meeting up with his liaison in a 1950s potboiler.

The man shook his head. He wasn't Stothard Hope (that much we knew).

He told us to wait there, and disappeared into the back. A few minutes later, two men stepped out and stood glaring at us.

I rescind my previous statement. The least Stothard-looking men ever were them, either one of them. They appeared to be in their early thirties, wore various shades of plaid and denim, and looked like enforcers for the local Elks Club. The one on the right was about 6'9, with limbs and chest to match; his buddy maybe 6'8, and every bit as robust.

"You take the little one," Hutton whispered.

"Understand you're looking for information on Stothard Hope," said the man on the left. He had a hefty Maine accent, and pronounced Stothard *Stahdud*.

Hutton and I looked at each other. "Maybe we are," he replied.

"You Hathaway?" the man asked.

"Maybe I am," said Hutton. Anyone but himself, that was his motto.

"We're supposed to give you this," said the man on the right.

He handed Hutton a parcel wrapped in paper, about the size of three quality paperbacks.

Hutton turned it over and gazed at it. I gazed at it with him. If this was all that was left of Stothard Hope then Fleet might not have been too far off with that Tony Rudd wood chipper comment.

"What are we supposed to do with this?" Hutton wondered.

"Look at the stickah," said the man on the left.

We looked. The sticker was addressed to "AR" from Stothard Hope. Evidently John Hathaway—I—was supposed to deliver this package to an AR, whoever and wherever he was.

"Then you don't know anything else about him?" Hutton asked.

"About who?"

"Stothard."

"Stahdud Hope?"

"Yes, *Stahdud Hope*, the man on the *stickah*. Is Herring behind this?"

"Herring?" They knew no Herrings.

"Yes, Herring!" said Hutton. "And I don't mean the fish *chowdah*."

The man on the right glanced at his associate. "He doing us?" he asked, and the man on the left said he was wondering that himself. I assured them that Hutton wasn't doing anyone.

"He's got this speech impediment, you see."

"What kind of speech impediment?"

"England."

Back inside the Jeep, Hutton immediately began tearing open the parcel. Pixie helped.

"What are you doing?" I asked, aghast.

He asked me what I thought he was doing.

"But you can't open that!"

"Why?"

"Haven't you heard of the Freelance Courier's Code?"

Hutton hadn't. "Is it a long code?"

"No, quite short. It says a courier shall never open a parcel he is delivering."

"I thought you always opened your parcels. What about that one your uncle gave you several years back?"

"That was before I realized I had a code," I explained.

Hutton waved aside the Courier's Code. "I'm sure Stothard Hope would have wanted you to open it. How else are we supposed to know what's inside it?" His argument had a specious allure.

"Okay, open it, but just to see if there are any instructions."

He opened it. It contained a fancy inlaid lockbox. "I'm going to need better light," he said.

"What for?"

"Picking the lock."

Half an hour later, I was happy to say the Courier's Code was still safe. "Won't open," he grumbled, tossing down his tools on the kitchen counter. "I guess we go with Plan B now."

"What is Plan B?"

"Deliver the parcel."

He handed me the delivery instructions he had neglected to show me in the Jeep.

According to the sheet, John Hathaway—still I—was to leave this package for AR at the Ariadne Locke Museum.

We were heading back to the Minotaur's lair.

## 16 — Rough Landscape

By 6:00 p.m., Hutton and I were standing beside his Jeep at the familiar Ariadne inlet. It felt raw out. The sun was keeping its distance, the air had a languid brine to it, and there was a breeze coming up off the current that made my tender bits curl up and hibernate for the evening.

I had exchanged the blazer for my leather jacket ("borrowed" by Hutton the week before). Hutton had swapped out the cashmere for his Scottish Highland pullover, and we both had on woolen stocking caps, which, speaking for myself, made me feel like a longshoreman who had taken to smash-and-grab raids.

"The path is already beginning to disappear," he said. "Once we get across, we'll only have an hour or so before we're trapped on the other side."

I could see what he meant. Little sections of sand and turf were already starting to dip down below the sea.

"We could just wait until tomorrow," I suggested.

Hutton didn't want to wait until tomorrow. "There are too many imponderables in this investigation already. We owe it to Fleet to learn what's going on."

I knew as well as anything that this had nothing to do with Fleet. Not *old* Fleet anyway. This was all about young Fleet proving he could hack it as a private detective in a down market. I could already answer that question. He couldn't. No more than I could hack it as a freelance courier, or Pixie could hack it as a woolly little lambkin, or whatever it was Lesley's sister Jill kept calling her.

Personally I could live with the mystery here. This was especially true if uncovering it meant traversing the Ariadne State Parkway again, with nothing but a few helpings of Yummy O's to fortify me.

Nevertheless, we pressed on through. The crossing went pretty well. We crawled and sputtered a few places, but we got across without mishap, climbed back out and looked around. There was a handful of craggy rocks nearby, with an offbeat path snaking up the side. Once we had scaled to the top—Hutton and I each tripping over our own personal crag in turn—we surveyed the landscape.

I took my turn with the binoculars. The museum and lighthouse were pretty much where we had left them yesterday.

"There's nobody about," I told him, realizing after I had removed the lenses that he was one of those who was not. I followed him back down the craggy path, stumbling only once.

"I really don't see what this is going to prove," I said. "We should wait until Fleet gets back from talking with his McKnight expert. He's bound to have some insight."

Hutton shook his head. We had to explore this angle, tomorrow could be too late. And with these words of wisdom, he opened the passenger door and unleashed the dogs of war. Or the Maltese of war, anyway.

Hutton's plan was a simple one. I would drive the Wrangler up to the museum, ostensibly to deliver Stothard Hope's package. We didn't know who "AR" was and Hutton didn't care. His idea was for me to claim the parcel was for one of the residents—any of the residents. I would choose whoever was the least accessible when I arrived and explain that I had been told to hand them the package personally. That should buy me some time to explore.

Hutton, meanwhile, would employ Pixie as his cover. (What could be more natural than a man taking his dog for a stroll around the park?) While I went down the middle, he would go around the outside. It was just like that rugby play—he didn't know which one.

And so, after wasting several minutes chasing Pixie around the Jeep, we set out separately. I took the high road and Hutton the low. (It remained to be seen who would be in Scotland before ye.)

The lobby of the Ariadne was as deserted as ever. Somewhere in the near distance the *ting, ting, tinging* of the sculptor's hammer drifted out into the foyer: Malcolm Rosso hard at work.

I stepped deeper inside, and on cue Christopher Cotton came popping out.

"You again?" he asked.

Well, it was. No sense denying it. "I have a package to deliver."

"Oh yeah. Who's it for?"

Hutton had stressed that I should *not* choose Jelena as my patsy, no matter how tempted I was to do so. We knew from our previous visit that the artist's studio was only a stone's throw away from the foyer. Picking her or Malcolm Rosso wouldn't grant me any sort of maneuverability. I should choose Christopher Cotton—or, if he was the one who greeted me at the door—I was to go with Niles Brisbane or Mrs. Cotton. It was all very simple.

"It's for Jelena," I replied simply. (So I liked seeing Jelena. Was that so wrong?)

The geezer photographer sighed. He seemed more impatient with visitors than usual. "Trying to get a shot of that sky," he grumbled. "Girl you want is in there." He pointed and left. Apparently capturing the stunning grandeur of a New England evening was more important than ogling a naked model for a fleeting moment or two. I guess I just don't understand the older generation.

*"Did you say Jelena?"* spoke a voice in my head. It was not my conscience. Hutton and I had an open link on our phones.

"Maybe."

*"Stick to the plan, Hath, stick to the plan."*

"You stick to the plan," I snarled into the tiny headset in my ear. Not exactly a snappy comeback, but I wasn't at my best at the moment.

*"What are you doing now?"* he asked.

"Heading down the hall."

*"So you can ogle Jelena,"* he stated. *"We're not here so you can ogle Jelena, Hath."*

"I know we're not here so I can ogle Jelena," I replied. "Who said anything about ogling Jelena?"

"Who is it that is ogling Jelena?" asked Jelena.

I hadn't gone to the artist's studio. I honestly hadn't. It had meant exercising all my iron self-control, but I had headed off in the opposite direction to explore. Just as I had agreed to do. But there she was.

She was fully clothed—or as fully clothed as she ever was. Satin kimono (red); fuzzy slippers (green); small birthmark on her upper right thigh (silky).

"*Parcel*," I blurted out.

She nodded. "You are the courier."

"You remember me?"

She did not. "The courier delivers the parcels. It is his job, is it not?"

I said no. I meant yes. I delivered the parcels, yes. I was the courier.

"And this parcel, it is for whom?" she asked, letting her kimono dip dangerously open at the sash.

I forgot what we were talking about. "The parcel? Oh. It's for Mrs. Cotton." The Cotton wench seemed the logical choice.

She pointed me down the hall. That was where Mrs. Cotton resided. I said cool.

"I enjoy your hat," Jelena commented.

I peered up. The stocking cap. I pulled it off and ruffled through my hair. "Forgot I had it on."

"I enjoy it," said Jelena again. "You look well in hats."

I thanked her. We had broken the ice.

"That man," she asked, becoming conversational, "the one you arrived with earlier. He was truly Enescu Fleet?"

I said no. And yes. "It's a long story," I explained. "You do remember us, then?"

"I have always admired Enescu Fleet," she replied. "He is a great Romanian. But that man, I do not believe it was he."

She removed her kimono and hung it on a brass hook behind her. "I have to return to work now."

I half-turned. (Okay, I didn't turn at all.) "Work?" For some reason, I had trouble speaking the word. My uncle frequently said that I did.

"You might need to hurry yourself." She indicated the sun out the window: a lovely nude spokesmodel of nature. "The tide. Unless you wish to stay?"

I said yes. Or rather no. I snapped out of it.

"Take care of yourself, Johnny H, courier man," she declared, her taut flesh disappearing behind the studio door. *Johnny H.* She did remember!

Hutton tactfully maintained radio silence for a good five minutes after Jelena had left me. I checked to see if we had lost our signal.

*"Still here,"* he said. *"Just jotting down a few notes for* The Hathaway Guide to Birds. *I'm working on a chapter now called* How to Flirt with Naked Chicks.*"*

"I wasn't flirting," I insisted. "And she wasn't naked. Not at first anyway," I added.

*"That woman has you under her spell, Hath. I don't blame you, she mesmerized me too, but you need to keep your focus here. You're losing your edge."*

"I never had any edge."

*"Perhaps not,"* he conceded. *"Find anything interesting?"*

Actually I had. In five minutes of exploring I had discovered the kitchen, two linen closets, a small public restroom, a dead grasshopper and yards and yards of folksy local art. There was also a large locked door, arched and heavily carved, but judging from my explorations so far, it probably just contained more dead grasshoppers.

I circled around the hall and frowned. If there was anything of value hidden among all this folksiness I couldn't see it (not unless Stothard Hope knew a fence yearning to purchase large, chunky sea captains, carved out of driftwood).

Across from one such cap'n was a room that smelled of raw earth and looked like it had been excavated from the side of a mountain. In the back corner, hard at work on a bust (not the good kind of bust), was Mrs. Christopher Cotton.

I slowly backed away. I was pretty sure she hadn't spotted me.

"You again?" she asked, following me out into the hallway.

I turned and said yes, it was me. "I'm looking for Niles Brisbane," I explained, working my way down the list. "Got a parcel for him."

Mrs. Cotton looked intrigued. "What kind of parcel?"

I made a weary gesture. Perhaps she was familiar with a little something called the Freelance Courier's Code?

"Who sent it?" she asked. All I could do was shake my head.

She took a step closer. I thought for a second she was going to try and mold me. "Malcolm showed me some bust techniques," she remarked abruptly, crazy eyes dancing all over my face. "Have you seen it?"

I replied that I had. It it was right there. George Washington, wasn't it, or possibly Gertrude Stein.

"Not the bust. I don't mean the bust. Have you seen *IT*?"

"I, uh—"

"Come," she said, pushing me down the hallway.

She twirled me around and shoved me through a door of hanging beads. Who knew that frail neurotics had such upper-body strength? As I stumbled to my appointed mark in the room, I discovered a single oil canvas under spotlights. The pic showed a bull-like creature, done up in yellow: half man, half monster, all hideous. I was standing face-to-face with an amber Minotaur.

"You like it?" she asked breathlessly.

I said sure, why not? It was as if she had captured the soul of the golden calf after the government had conducted secret genetic experiments on it. What wasn't to like?

"Neat," I said.

Mrs. Cotton seemed pleased with my assessment. She reached out to touch the canvas then quickly drew her hand back.

"You'll never find your way out now," she said. "It will crush you, just like it crushed everyone else here."

I nodded and took several steps away. I backed out through the hanging beads and continued out into the hall. Once there, I maneuvered around the dead grasshopper and kept up the fancy footwork until I had discovered an exit behind me. "All part of the life of a courier," I called back through the beads, and shot out into the open spaces.

I was happy to be outside again. It was considerably cooler now and had started to rain. I didn't know what this was going to do to Christopher Cotton's sky, but I welcomed the cold.

"That woman freaks me out," I whispered, pulling my hat back in place over the headset.

*"Cruf…snurk…crumbly…"* replied Hutton. *"Damn reception…snurk…can't ever get a decent…cruf…nails whiz-bang…"*

I waited patiently while he made several other interesting noises and then went silent. "You find anything out here?" I asked.

*"Curble."*

"Me neither. We should probably meet back at the Jeep now. Oh hey, there's Brisbane."

That distinctively shaved head shone like a newly laid egg over by the rocks. He was sitting with his back turned to me, watching the horizon. The rain was softly pelting his noggin.

"I'll see what he has to say for himself and then let's get the hell out of here."

*"Flipflop,"* Hutton agreed.

I made my approach to Niles. I had the eerie feeling, as I got closer, that he wasn't moving. Not even a little. I crept slowly around to face him and saw his eyes closed, his mouth half open and a little wisp of tobacco smoke drifting up from his favorite affectation, cradled in his hands. The rain continued to fall.

Corpses were nothing new to me. I wouldn't say they were old hat or anything, but I had seen a dead body before (sometimes the same dead body multiple times).

I moved in for a closer look.

Novices, at this point, might have chalked up his demise to natural causes, for I was having a little trouble detecting any signs of a struggle. But I wasn't fooled. I examined him for a pinprick—such as might have been left behind by the poisoned dart of an Incan blowgun (another area these novices never bother to check). There were no Incan-blowgun pricks.

I gazed up at his big shaved head.

"I found this here, you know," said the head, and I bounded back, nearly taking a pitch over the side of the cliff. "I found it here," he went on, opening his eyes.

He lifted the pipe to show me. "It was in one of the dresser drawers in my bedroom, and I took a shine to it. Hadn't smoked in forty years before I came here."

First things first. I was happy he wasn't a corpse. Well done, Niles. Point, Brisbane. But sucking on some old pipe you found in your room? Yucky.

"I suppose you think that strange?" he asked, still speaking in an odd, empty tone.

"Oh no," I lied. Not at all. What could be strange about that?

It occurred to me, as I shuddered over the man's hygiene, that if anyone wished Niles Brisbane out of the way, all they would have to do is leave a poisoned cigar lying on the floor, and that would be that. Game, set, match.

"I find things, you know," said the odd one. "I find things and make them art, but now I'm the one—" He paused, blinking at me. "You're back?" he asked. It was better than "You again?", I suppose, but not much better.

"Got a parcel to deliver," I said. I was getting tired of saying that.

"Parcel?"

I waggled the package at him. He understood. I had a parcel. "Is it for me?"

I was half tempted to say sure, here you go. But I didn't. Whatever was in that lockbox might still prove useful to us.

"Sorry, it's for—" I scrolled down the list. Who hadn't I picked yet? "Malcolm Rosso," I concluded.

"What's for Malcolm Rosso?" asked Malcolm Rosso. The egotist had arrived.

I noticed he was a little gamy-smelling from all his hammer and chiseling. I guess these brilliant sculptors just can't make time for a bath.

"When I say Malcolm Rosso," I said, "I of course mean Mrs. Cotton."

"You said it was not for Mrs. Cotton," said the Cotton female, sweeping in from the other side of the lawn and closing in on me. It was like *Night of the Bohemian Zombies*.

I turned and gawped at her. I may have said crap, can't recall.

"You seem muddled," observed Niles Brisbane.

I took another step back. It seemed like all I was doing lately was taking steps back.

"You know, let me check my invoice." I pulled out my receipt from Charlie's Bistro. "Oh right, here it is. The parcel's for AR."

The crowd stared blankly. Niles repeated the initials in a deadpan voice: "AR?"

"That's right—AR." Let him put that in his pipe and smoke it.

Now Mrs. Cotton got in on the fun. "AR," she stated.

Malcolm also said "AR." He spoke it with a certain flair.

AR, whoever it was, really seemed to spook them.

"AR," I confirmed. "Or *Arrr*, if you feel a sea chanty coming on. Well, take it easy, all," I remarked, and beat a hasty departure over the ridge.

*"That went well,"* said Hutton, wasting no time in advancing his opinion.

"Nice to hear the reception has cleared up."

*"Yup, clean as a whistle now. I could hear every word of your brilliant maneuvering."*

"Thanks. So where are you?"

*"Around the side of the lighthouse. Pixie is sniffing up a storm on some gull poop."*

It was good to know that our time here hadn't been wasted. "You know, something just occurred to me."

*"That it's raining?"*

"Not just that. I bet I know who this 'AR' is." I waited a moment in order to generate the appropriate dramatic tension for my thesis. "Ariadne Rufus," I said.

Hutton considered my theory. *"Ariadne Rufus? As in Ariadne Rufus Locke, founder of the Ariadne Locke Museum?"*

"The very Ariadne Rufus. How creepy would that be?"

Hutton agreed that it would be pretty creepy. *"Considering that she died in the 1990s."*

"I know. But you heard how spooked everyone got when I said AR, and those *are* her initials."

*"They aren't her initials, Hath; a person's initials are their first and last name. AR would be her first and middle name."*

"Initials can be first and middle. Look at all the authors that go by their first initials. Athletes. The original E. F. Hutton for goodness sakes."

*"Okay, okay."*

"And maybe it isn't initials at all. Maybe it's not A. R. Maybe it's 'Ar,' short for Ariadne."

*"Or the start of a sea chanty,"* replied Hutton tartly. *"Of course, in New England,"* he said, *" 'Ar' would be pronounced 'Ah.' We should really be looking for someone with the initials A. H."*

"Do you think so?"

*"No!"*

He had come back so emphatically, so brusquely, that I declined to share any more of my theories with him. Not that I had any more theories to share.

*"I'd say I'm about done with this island for the evening,"* he said. I heard him chiding Pixie about gull poop. *"It might mean fighting off the wraith of Ariadne Locke, but I'm heading back to the—guk!"*

"You're heading back to the *Guk?*" I asked.

Silence. Guess he was heading back to the Guk. "Hutton? You there? Hello?"

More silence.

"Hutton, if this is your idea of a—"

I held up. If Hutton wanted to spend his time playing childish pranks, pretending to have his throat torn out by deceased female dilettantes returned from the grave, let him. I had more important matters to investigate. I had just come up over the ridge leading back to the museum. As I crested the hill, a white sports car, just like the one he had described tailing us yesterday, hurtled past.

I didn't like the looks of it. I know what you're thinking—there are lots of white sports cars in the world—but I wasn't concerned with other white sports cars at the moment. I was concerned with this white sports car. It disappeared around the corner, and I picked up my feet and jogged behind.

Arriving at a clumping of trees, I peeked out and spotted the vehicle down the hill.

The car was stopped, its trunk open. I couldn't make out the license plate. The tire jack was out, lying on the ground next to the rear tire. I'm no expert, but it looked like it was having a tire problem (which you will if you insist on going a hundred on these country roads). I moved in for a closer look.

Aside from the tire, it also appeared to be having a people problem. There were none around. I pulled the trunk door down, and spoke slowly and clearly into the headset: "Hutton, if you would knock off your foolishness for a minute, I need your help. What was the license on that sports *cah*—"

I froze. Next to the license on the trunk—also called a "boot"—was one of those whatchamacallits, stamped real small. This particular whatchamacallit said Wainwright Motors.

I staggered back. I continued staggering backwards until I rammed into a tall man with an elongated jaw. He had on a dark gray suit vest, white shirt tails and a tie (also dark gray).

"I believe you have a parcel for me," said this tall dark stranger.

"Who, me?" I turned and backed away, banging my elbow on the open boot. "Ouch."

"I am AR," said the man.

I frowned. He didn't look like an Ariadne Rufus.

"My name is Anthony Rudd."

Rudd. Rudd. Where had I heard of a Rudd recently?

"Tony Rudd," said Tony Rudd.

Oh, *that* Rudd. Tony Rudd, ex-assassin. The one Fleet had told me about, the one who owned the white sports car and liked wood chippers. Cool beans.

"And you are Johnny H."

"No!"

"I think that you are," said Tony Rudd, limping toward me.

He laid a giant hand on my shoulder. Before I could fight back, I found myself twisted and turned and shoved inside the car trunk—or boot. These ex-assassins know how to move. I was lying on top of the spare now. As I said earlier, I'm no expert. But I was beginning to think there was nothing wrong with that rear tire.

## 17 — Silencing the Critics

A couple of thoughts on spending the evening inside a car trunk or "boot." First of all, it's dark. Second it's hot. Mostly it's dark.

I would have used my phone to light things up, but about a minute after I had landed in these economy digs the trunk opened and Tony Rudd took this off me. Roughly thirty seconds after that, the trunk opened again and he tossed the jack in. I guess he'd forgotten to do this earlier, because he seemed annoyed about it. Then we were on our way. The courier had become the package.

If you're wondering if I could find a decent jimmy or bludgeon during this time, I couldn't. The jack was a nonstarter on both counts, and the only other items I could lay my hands on during the journey were small and squishy, not unlike old figs or possibly globs of grease. Old figs are not exactly effective levers. Nor, for that matter, are globs of grease.

I would have loved a tire iron or two, but the trunk seemed unequipped with any of these. I was completely iron-less. I tried to lie back and think but found this difficult within the confines. I was basically tangled up in a ball. My back was crunched, and my ankle itched. I wasn't having a good time.

Finally the car stopped. The engine shut off, and I heard a key slide into the back lock. We had arrived. I think I had some vague notion of springing out and attempting to overpower my captor through the use of some well-honed martial art, but this never came off. Between the stiffening of the joints and the jack impeding my movements, it was all I could do to topple out onto the ground. (Besides, I didn't really know any well-honed martial arts.)

The first thing I saw as I hit the turf was Rudd's shoe: a reddish-brown stained loafer. Now *that* was blood, I could have told Lesley.

I was lifted off the ground and pushed through a doorway into a dimly lit room. Even though I had been locked up in a trunk, I figured I could guess my approximate location. From the bumps and shimmies I had experienced in the back, to the slight shifting of weight as we made right turns and left (six right and four left), to the displacement of the gull calls, I was pretty certain we had traveled due north for some considerable duration. We were no doubt deep inside Cumberland County now, possibly as far afield as Oxford.

The lights came on around me. I was in the kitchen of the Ariadne Locke Museum and Artists' Retreat. (I may have been a little off in my calculations.)

I was shoved into a chair by Rudd. "Talk!" he said.

I hadn't noticed it before, but he had an accent. I couldn't quite place it but it was an accent I felt I knew. What I didn't know was what he wanted me to say in mine.

I thought for a second or two, and then happened upon an item that he and I should really clear up before we went much further. "Look, there has been a lot of talk about Johnnies lately," I said, "and I just want it understood that I'm Johnny *Hathaway*, not any other Johnny you might be looking for."

"I know this."

"You do?"

"Of course." He limped over to the table. He picked up my parcel and tore it open, tossing the paper on the butcher block behind him. I stifled a slight shiver. Anything with the word *butcher* in it, in conjunction with the man Rudd, gave me the willies.

"What is the meaning of this?" he demanded, showing me the lockbox underneath. He stared up from it with cold dead eyes.

I said I wish I knew.

"How do I open this?"

There he had me. "Don't you have the key?"

"Of course I do not have the key!"

I said no. Why should he? "I guess we're in the same boat here," I remarked lightly.

Rudd was busy strangling the life out of the lockbox. It seemed to be his preferred method of obtaining information. "You came by boat?" he asked.

"No, no boat. It's just—skip it," I said.

Rudd went back to his interrogation of the lockbox, and I looked out the window. Evening had come to the Ariadne, and with it went my chance for an easy escape. The tide would have seen to that.

"What is the meaning of this?" he insisted. "Where did you get this?" He seemed all atwitter over the box.

I straightened myself up in the chair. The Freelance Courier's Code could take a holiday. "This is going to amuse you," I began. "The thing of the thing is—"

I paused. There was some kind of racket going on outside. Raised voices. Clanging of fence gates. Then the grinding of gravel as footsteps approached the door.

"Up," said Tony Rudd. He pulled me out of the chair and swung me around to the basement door. "Down," he instructed. (I wished he would make up his mind.)

I stumbled down, and heard the door shut and bolt behind me. I crept further down the stairs, found a dangling light cord and pulled it. Rudd's technique might not have been very genteel, but it was more genteel than Basil's (for now). Looking around the basement, I was happy to see there were no wood chippers present.

The raised voices had found their way into the kitchen. I could hear them through the exposed ceiling, although not what they were saying. Eventually they died down, and there was just the sound of creaking as someone stood on an especially squawky floorboard. There was some kind of scratching noise next, which put me in mind of rats, then the voices filtered through the beams again. They sounded different. Party A was the same, but Party B had stuck on an understudy: a deeper, more resonant understudy.

The voices suddenly became heated. There was a THUD!, then a WHAP!, and then SILENCE.

I didn't like the look of things. I had no idea who these heated parties were, but they didn't sound good. My only solace was that Hutton (assuming he hadn't gotten ensnared in Ariadne Locke ectoplasm) would have realized that I had been captured, gotten away before the bar flooded, and would even now, I hoped, be getting help.

I was still consoling myself with this when someone undid the bolt, the door opened and Hutton came stumbling down the steps. The door shut behind him. I heard it lock.

"Hiya, Hath."

He looked damp and tousled but otherwise none the worse for wear. If he had been set upon by the ghost of Ariadne Locke, he didn't look at all bad for it. "What happened?"

"It's a long story," he said.

For once I didn't mind. He and I weren't going anywhere.

"It all starts with Pixie," he began, waving me off when I asked where the dog was. He was getting to that. "Do you recall me remarking 'Guk' while we were on the phone earlier?"

I did remember something about a Guk, yes.

"Well, while we were speaking, someone snuck up from behind me and grabbed me. That's what made me say Guk."

"A Tahoma?" I asked, and Hutton said not now; he wasn't in the mood.

It wasn't so much the grabbing from behind, he explained, as the method the person employed. "He grabbed my ear."

I chuckled. Just like our old headmaster when he discovered us spying on his wife's bedroom. "Who was it?"

"Who do you think it was? Christopher Damn Cotton. He grabbed me and dragged me over under the eaves. It was raining harder by then. I asked him what he was on about, and he said the dog, that was what he was on about. 'No dogs,' he said, and I said 'No dogs?' and he said, 'No dogs on park property.' Apparently it was a regular obsession with him—dogs. At this juncture, no doubt sensing that she wasn't wanted, Pixie slipped her collar and went charging off. The geezer told me I'd have to go too. I retorted that I wasn't going anywhere without the pup. He said the pup was gone, and I said whose fault was that? He had no answer. I think he was beginning to warm to me. A few minutes later, we convened in the kitchen, where he grumbled something about getting me a torch and some rain gear, and left me drip-drying by the sink. I had no sooner squeegeed the water from my glasses than a lean, mean son-of-a-gun stormed in."

"Tony Rudd," I said. "Or Anthony Rudd as he prefers it, a.k.a. 'AR.' The parcel was for him."

"Oh, you figured that out, did you?"

"He explained."

"He didn't explain anything to me. He asked me what the meaning of this was."

"He likes to ask that."

"I mentioned the dog, he said no dogs allowed, and I said yes, we'd gone over all that. That's when he recognized me from the alley. There was a scuffle. I acquitted myself pretty well, especially when I remembered his wonky foot. Eventually he tied me into a modified Windsor knot, despite the foot, and gave me a shove down here—and that brings us up to the present moment. So what happened to you?"

I brought him up to speed on the white sports car, the fake car trouble and Tony Rudd's antisocial behavior. Hutton nodded knowingly.

"They call that one a Lucida. Lures the subject in. If you take the wheel full off the axle, it's a Lucida Grande."

"Fascinating," I said. "What do we do now?"

"We escape," replied Hutton. He always did have a nice simple answer for things. He crept up the stairs and examined the sliver under the door. "I don't think there's anyone in the kitchen now."

"Can you pick the lock?"

"There's nothing to pick. It's bolted from the other side. Even I have my limitations."

I had a sudden inspiration. "The Glock!"

Hutton grumbled that there was no lock. "What did I just say?"

"Not lock—*Glock*. You have my Glock on you?"

He asked me why he should. It was my gun. "I figured you'd bring it if you wanted it."

He came back down the steps and peered around the room. I could have told him there was no wood chipper, if that was what he was looking for.

"Do you still have your phone?" I asked.

He didn't. He had lost it outside when Christopher Cotton had jumped him. I replied that Rudd had taken mine off me, and Hutton asked why I let him do that?

He looked around the walls, at the piles of old wooden crates, at the staircase again and at a washer and dryer on the back wall. He looked up. The open ceiling seemed to fascinate him. "Give me a boost," he said.

"You're doing great."

He frowned. He climbed on top of one of the crates and made a standing spring in the air. A couple of bounds and he had managed to snag an exposed pipe above us. He swung his feet up and began working his way across.

He reached the opposite end and paused. Hanging by one hand, he reached in his pocket and took out his handy Benchmade, flicking it open with one thumb. He placed the blade between his teeth, took it out again and spat, and continued on to the space between the top of the drywall and the bottom of the first floor.

He squeezed through and disappeared onto the other side.

There was some creaking here, a bit of clumping and banging, and finally a curious grinding sound. Something cracked, and I heard a loud thump, perhaps indicating that a tall, gangly body had fallen down behind the frame. I grimaced. Sucks when you've got a dead Hutton rotting behind your wall. Takes forever to get rid of the smell.

I didn't hear any more of his racket for the next couple minutes, save one muffled popping noise, which could have been his bones snapping. I tried whispering "Hutton" into the drywall, but no answer came. Funny, when I wanted my space free of Hutton all I got was Hutton and nothing but the Hutton, but now that I could have done with his company—nada. It was annoying.

I could hear that *scratch, scratch scratching* again. The rats must have gotten to him.

Someone tapped me on the shoulder, and I jumped.

"Fleet was right," said Hutton. "You're very jumpy."

I blinked at him. I turned and blinked at the open basement door at the top of the stairs and then back at him. "Did you cut your way out?"

"Nope. Couldn't get through the floor. They made their floors tough in 1931."

"Then how?"

"It occurred to me that the door might not actually be locked. We were only going on the assumption that it was. I tried it, and it opened right up. Lock-picking 101—always try the handle first."

Now I really was confused. The door had definitely been locked. I had heard Rudd bolt it behind him. "Maybe someone heard you wriggling around and let us out."

"Maybe," he remarked. "Either way, we're free. Come on."

I held him back. "Do you have any clue what is going on here?"

"Not a one," he replied, and I said good. Up we went.

The kitchen was deserted. I noticed a few rainwater footprints on the checkered tile, but no Tony Rudd.

"The tide's got us trapped," said Hutton, looking out the window, "but we can still call in the cavalry."

"Don't you mean the Fleet?" I asked.

Hutton nodded, adding that he still wasn't in the mood. "Tony has your phone, so we'll have to find mine. I'll look for it outside, while you check for yours in here just to be certain."

He went, and I checked for mine. My phone wasn't in the kitchen, not that I noticed anyway, but I did find something nearly as good: an old-fashioned landline. I had just picked this up, listening for that quaint old sound—a dial tone—when I heard something a little more chilling. *Scratch, scratch, scratch.* That eerie noise again. It was coming from the back door. Figuring it would have taken a very domesticated rat to have asked for admittance, I stepped over and turned the handle. Pixie came darting in, shaking off moisture from her body.

She stared up at me with mild disapproval, and I said "What?" I wasn't the one who had left her out in the rain. She rubbed up against my jeans to finish drying and then turned and charged off down the hall. I sighed and staggered after her. She was always doing this.

She led me on a merry chase. I eventually caught up with her in a mini-lobby of sorts. It was small but well lit and had a closed door on the left and an open corridor on the right. Pixie was in the middle, panting up at me, obviously enjoying every minute of the hunt. I lunged. She scooted, and off she zoomed down the corridor again.

There was only one room at the end of the hall. I stepped inside, turned on the row of lights and was almost immediately blown away.

For the first time in two visits, I was favorably impressed with the Ariadne Locke Museum and Artists' Retreat. The room Pixie had led me inside was truly exceptional. Clean cement floors, bright white walls, plants, flowers and other vegetation, and tons of shapely windows curving up along an inner dome.

But that wasn't all. There were paintings, lots and lots of paintings, mostly the work of a single artist. And I recognized these too. Not McGraws, not McGuffins. McKnights. There were tons of Thomas McKnights on the sparkling walls. After all the shabby folk art, and Mrs. Cotton's yellow monster, it was as though I had fought my way through some musty jungle and landed in a bright and soothing oasis. Finally something of value in this dive.

I had seen plenty of McKnights in my time, but only prints. These were originals.

There's nothing like real paintings: the warmth of the texture, the gleam of the brushstrokes, the shades of color you only seem to find on a canvas. I liked them.

The McKnights weren't the only treat in here. Over on a maple table in the middle of the room sat the infamous lockbox from my parcel. The lid was open, revealing a lush red lining—very chic. There was also an odd, L-shaped indentation in the velvety folds—very strange. The box was empty. Very curious.

A Maltese cheer brought me out of my trance. Pixie had discovered something in the back of the room, down behind an array of orchids.

I stepped over to investigate. And there we had it. The real showpiece of the evening.

At my feet lay our captor, that cold dead look in his eyes—colder and deader than ever. He was in a sort of L-shape himself. His legs were prone in front of him, his back propped up against the paneling. He was slumped beside an open cabinet door. It looked like he had been reaching inside it when he expired. And expired he had.

Tony Rudd was dead.

# 18 — Framed

There could be no question of the body's deadness this time. There was a red splotch soaking through the white shirt just above the vest and a tiny trickle in the corner of the mouth. Add to that the bloody loafer and Tony Rudd had not had a good week. Oddly enough, it was only now that I realized he had a mustache. I suppose this was the first time I had relaxed enough in his presence to notice such things. Or maybe it was the lighting. Nevertheless, there it was. Sort of a Fu Manchu. Looked good on him.

I stood up and dusted off my jeans at the knees. (Might seem a cold reaction upon discovering a dead body, but my dusty knees weren't going to help Tony Rudd now.)

"Do you have something you wish to tell me, Hath?"

It was only Hutton. I turned and gave him the once-over.

"Might ask you the same thing."

"What do you mean?"

"Well, you're the one who brawled with him."

"We didn't brawl that much."

"And you're also the one with the knife. How am I to know you didn't run Tony through with your Benchmade dagger?"

"First of all, it's not a dagger; a dagger blade is sharpened on both sides. Second, he wasn't stabbed, he was shot."

"How do you know?"

"You can see the powder burns from here. In fact—" He stepped past me and knelt at the body, examining the wound. Pixie helped. "Whoever shot him pressed the barrel to his chest before pulling the trigger. Muffled the sound." His eyes shone insightfully as he said this. "Aha! Then *that* was the pop."

"Pop?"

"Whilst I was climbing, I heard a popping noise."

I, too, had heard a popping noise whilst he was climbing. "Thought it was your spine."

"Well, it wasn't. That means Tony must have been shot moments before I freed us."

"And you're certain you didn't have my Glock with you?" I asked. He gave me a look, and I figured he'd had enough of my sardonic wit for now. "Who do you think shot him?"

Whoever it was, it was Hutton's theory that the killer hadn't used a Glock. Or any modern handgun. "From the wound, I'd say it was something pretty rustic. Maybe an antique."

I fancy my eyes also shone insightfully here. "Antique?" I turned and pointed to the lockbox, drawing his attention to the L-shaped indentation.

"Could be," he agreed. "Pretty revolver-like, that shape. Wait, are you telling me we brought the murder weapon with us?" Sounded bad when he put it like that. "See if it's still here," he groaned.

Locating a theoretical revolver in an open sunroom isn't as easy as it sounds. There are junk drawers, dingy old cupboards and nothing is where you would expect a rational person would store it. I mean, Fig Newtons in with the turpentine. Brilliant!

Nevertheless, I was the one to snag it in the end, and Pixie didn't help. She and Hutton were on the full other side of the room when something seemed to beckon to me from inside one of the other cabinets. I opened the door and sure enough, there it was: nineteen cans of tuna, six spare paintbrushes, orchid food and—perhaps most importantly—one gun.

There was a pair of gardening gloves lying on a nearby table. I slid these on, to prevent fingerprints, and lifted the exhibit out.

I had seen this kind of piece before. Our old school friend Walter "Ditters" Dittersdorf, a well-known collector of ancient crap and antiquities, had an old six-shooter like this once. His had a longer barrel and was in better condition, but otherwise they could have been cousins. If Ditters' tastes were any indication, we were dealing with a real lunatic here.

I held the gun up to show Hutton. He didn't seem all that pleased. "Hath, where did you get those?"

"The gloves? They were on the table—why?"

"And you just slid them on?"

"Of course. No fingerprints." John Hathaway was no idiot.

Hutton wasn't certain of that. "Sniff them."

"Huh?"

"Smell the gloves, Hath."

I smelt them. "Smoky."

"You're wearing the killer's gloves."

Sounded bad when he said it like that.

"Take off the gloves, Hath."

I took off the gloves.

That is, I eventually took off the gloves. First, I stood there like a lummox, giving ample time for Christopher Cotton to bound in from an outer door. He was wearing a nylon poncho and rain hat. After Cotton came Mrs. C., goggling; then Jelena, un-nude; Niles Brisbane, sans pipe; and finally Malcolm Rosso, mallet in hand.

Then and only then did I snap out of it and take off the gloves.

I set the gun down on the table first—couldn't forget the gun—pulled off the gloves and set them beside it. I looked down at the dead body. I stepped away from the dead body.

The gathering was growing restless. I expected some kind of outburst: Christopher Cotton shouting *By cracky I knew he was a bad 'un*; Mrs. Cotton having hysterics; Niles shaking his head and saying he was *Sorely disappointed in this behavior, young man*; Jelena shedding her clothes—don't know why—and Malcolm—well, not sure what I expected of Malcolm. Malcolm looking pungent and handsome, I suppose.

But I got no outburst. What I got was both Cottons grumbling; Niles shaking his head; Malcolm fixing his hair; and Jelena frowning down at the dead man.

"I know what you're all thinking," I announced to the room, "but I didn't do it." I looked over at Hutton, holding Pixie. "I'm pretty sure Hutton probably didn't do it either."

"Thanks, Hath."

The gang remained silent.

"We already know you're innocent," said Niles. He made a gesture of reaching for his pipe, seemed to realize it wasn't there, sighed and continued, "It was the same for us."

"What do you mean?"

No one answered.

"Would someone please tell me what the hell is going on here!" I shouted. Guess we were to have our outburst, after all.

Malcolm slammed a grungy palm down on the maple table. "Don't you get it, my fine little fool? He's got you right where he wants you. You've been framed!"

"F—" I stumbled over the word. It was too ridiculous.

"Somebody get him a drink," said Chris Cotton. I never would have pegged him for the hospitable sort.

"A drink," spoke Mrs. Cotton with a harried nod.

Mr. Cotton answered her nod with a nod of his own, not very harried, paving the way for Niles to jump in with his own nod, not harried at all.

"Yes, get him a drink. Both of them."

Jelena left the room, returning a minute later with the beverages. Looked like sherry. I took a quick sip and then downed half the glass. I don't really like sherry, but Cotton was right, I needed that.

Hutton appeared uncharacteristically aloof from the partaking. He sniffed the snifter and made a face, and then looked at me. He must not have liked sherry either.

"What's all this about framing people?" I asked.

"Everything will become clear soon enough," said Niles with a smile.

I doubted that. "Okay, let's try this. Who are we talking about? Framed by whom?"

Again nobody answered. I noticed Jelena was gazing at the body again. Suddenly she pointed at the dead man's hand. It was loosely curled around something, this mystery item glistening in the overhead lights. "Something is there."

I hastened to her side.

"There is something in his hand," she whispered. I looked. She was right, there was something in his hand.

"He must have grabbed it out of the cabinet after he was shot," I theorized.

"Give us a look," said Hutton, crowding in.

"Shouldn't we wait for the cops or something?" Seemed to me there was something about not touching a crime scene in the detective's manual.

"Might be a clue to get us out of this," said Hutton.

I didn't need any more encouragement than that. I jerked forward, experiencing a slight head rush as I moved. "We should really—" I stumbled. Fortunately Jelena's breasts were there for support. "We should—" I looked over at Hutton. He was frowning again. I turned and looked up at Jelena. "You—drugged—"

I was fading fast but I could have sworn she replied, "Of course."

"It's for your own good," said Niles Brisbane, coming up from behind. For some reason he was speaking in a spooky echo. "You will understand why later—"

*Later*

*Later*

I slumped over the maple table.

This might have been for my own good, but I highly doubted I would understand it.

# 19 — A Certain Flair

I awoke sometime later, blinking up at a pale yellow ceiling with finely carved beams, also yellow. Sunshine was creeping in through the window on my right. It had to be about five or six in the morning. There was a throbbing in my skull, and my face was sore from where I had landed on it in the conservatory. I felt like hell.

Rolling over on my other side, I spotted a baby grand in the corner; a light blue side chair with two throw pillows (one purple, the other yellow); several houseplants scattered about on various tables; and then the floor rushing toward me at I toppled off the four-poster bed with a splat.

There was a rustic area rug here. Very Aztec. Not all that soft.

I continued to peer around. The piano was just like the one Hutton owned, a violin and some sheet music perched carelessly on the bench underneath it (just as Hutton would have done had he ever taken up either instrument). Baby grand or not, I knew I couldn't be at Hutton's place.

Too much furniture.

There was a quartet of windows in the corner behind the piano, two on each side: French. A few feet from them sat the blue chair, large and puffy, with arms that came to a swirling cinnamon-roll design at the ends. Beside the chair was a round table covered in peach cloth with another houseplant on top. There was also a plate of fruit—plastic, as I would come to find out. Beyond the table was some kind of indoor tree, maybe a ficus. It also had fruit, probably also plastic.

Wrapping things up, there was a mauve-colored sofa; a painting of a young couple fooling about in a swan-shaped gondola; a curved sideboard with inlaid doors; and a basic sense of peace and harmony throughout.

I recognized where I was now. I had somehow landed inside a Thomas McKnight painting.

I was still trying to place the name of the piece when I was interrupted by a voice. "They stuck me in *Antibes*," said Hutton, also up to speed on the motif. "A sprightly work from the early 1980s. Lots of oranges. Quite nice."

He was standing in the entranceway, twirling the doorknob he had just picked. As he would go on to explain, we were still in the museum, or to be precise, inside Ariadne Locke's homage to her favorite artistic visionary.

"We're in the museum?" I repeated, speaking with difficulty. My mouth was dry.

"We never left. We're in the bed-and-breakfast portion now. Well, at least the bed. There's been nary a suggest of breakfast as of yet."

"What the hell is going on?"

"Unknown."

"Did somebody drug my drink?"

"Yep."

"How did I get here?"

Hutton muttered something to himself. I think he took issue with my method of inquiry. I definitely caught the phrase "like a kangaroo on speed" as he stepped past. Arriving at the armchair, he gave a plastic kiwi a sniff and replaced it on the platter. "Malcolm and I lugged your sorry arse halfway across the museum last night. Niles, the Cottons and Pixie brought up the rear. It was quite the little parade."

"Did they drug you?"

"They tried," Hutton replied, and so ended Part One of our question-and-answer session.

I moved on to Part Two. "I remember a body," I said, rubbing my temples in a swirling fashion, not unlike the sewn pattern in the arms of the chair. "Other than my body I mean. Wasn't there a body?"

He nodded. "Six bodies to be precise, one of them less alive than the other five."

It was all coming back to me. Somebody had killed Tony Rudd in the McKnight gallery last night. Somebody had said we had killed Tony Rudd in the McKnight gallery. "We—"

"—wuz framed," Hutton agreed, concluding the thought for me.

I was up to speed now—whether I was a kangaroo on it was a point open to debate. "Who—how—why—?"

Hutton waved me off. He had no idea.

"I'm afraid no one knows exactly what is going on," answered another voice, speaking from offstage. It was one of those busy weekends for offstage voices.

Niles Brisbane entered the room, followed by Jelena and Malcolm. She was in her satin kimono; his oily hair was tied back in a ponytail. "We have no idea who is calling the shots here," said Niles (his head was still bald).

I didn't understand. Calling the shots how? What shots? Who said anything about shots?

He took a seat in the blue armchair. He took out his pipe, which he had apparently dug up somewhere, and smiled. "We have never met our host. All we know is he is a criminal genius. You almost have to admire what he has managed here. I despise him—but I also admire him."

"Admire him for what? What has he managed?"

"He has assembled the ultimate team of criminals: people who are not actually criminals. Ordinary men and women, all chosen for some unique ingredient they bring to the equation."

"What equation?" Math had never been my strong point.

"That is the question we keep asking ourselves," answered Malcolm, taking the floor. "All we know is we are going to participate in it."

"Participate in what?" I demanded. Why wasn't anyone explaining anything! "And what if we refuse to participate in whatever it is we're supposed to be participating in?"

"Then the evidence that you two killed Tony Rudd finds its way to the police," said Niles.

"But we didn't kill Tony Rudd!"

"Well then, that should be a very interesting conversation," he concluded, puffing away at his pipe.

"I mean, why should we kill Tony Rudd?" I persisted.

"Motives are never hard to find once the authorities have set their minds on a suspect. An argument you three had and couldn't resolve. An altercation about money. A—" He hesitated. "A disagreement over a woman."

He glanced at Jelena when he said this, and suddenly something occurred to me. Tony Rudd's accent, the one I fancied I had heard before. It was the same as Jelena's accent. Pretty good detective work on my part, I thought, considering she had yet to utter a word since coming in the room.

"You and Tony—"

"Knew each other," she replied.

"You were—"

"Not lovers." She looked at Malcolm "Tony told me he loved me, always he loves me, but of course it was only adoration on his part, which is not at all the same thing."

"No," I agreed. Not at all. Who would want to be adored? "So you knew each other?"

"We were from the same village."

I nodded. Small world. "Do you know who killed him?"

"That would be our host," interrupted Malcolm. "Tony was our host's mole here. He claimed to be a simple guest, but it later turned out that was just a bluff."

"But if he worked for 'our host' why did 'our host' kill him?"

"Apparently they had a tiff," said Malcolm.

Apparently so. "And what about this host? Is he here too? At the Ariadne?"

"Oh, he's here alright. He is always here," he sneered, echoing Mrs. Cotton's words from the end of our first visit.

"But not literally," tacked on Niles. I was beginning to feel like a ball in a three-way game of Ping-Pong. "Call him a sort of absentee owner of our poor hides. He occasionally sends word to us, gives some cryptic order—like drugging you—but he never makes himself seen. That was what he had Tony for. Clearly his henchman proved more valuable to him in death."

"As a snare for me and Hutton?"

"Precisely. Everyone you see here at the museum has been 'snared' in some way."

Malcolm looked to Jelena, Jelena to Malcolm. They both looked to Niles.

The older man laughed. "Some of us are more sensitive about our predicament than others. I will gladly tell you the hold our host has over me." He took a breath. "I was framed for embezzling from my previous employer. The evidence, it seems, is quite compelling."

"But you didn't do it?"

"No. If I had, it wouldn't be framing."

"So our host did the actual embezzling?"

"Did it, or knew enough about the crime that he could arrange for me to take the rap. If need be. That is the significant part. I'm safe as long as I play ball."

As we all were, apparently. "So what does this criminal genius want with me and Hutton?"

Niles and Malcolm couldn't say. Nor could Jelena. Either that, or they didn't care.

"You should hear from him soon enough," Niles replied. He stood up and knocked out his pipe in the potted plant. Probably wouldn't do the plastic any good.

As the gang went to leave, Hutton asked abruptly, "Who moved the body?"

The welcome party turned and stared at him. "It was the first thing I checked when I got up this morning. The corpse is gone."

Niles was the most impressed. "We were instructed to shut you in your room for the night. The door was locked."

"But not bolted," said my friend.

Niles smiled—a weary, amused smile. He punctuated it with a little shrug and headed through the doorway. He never answered Hutton's question. Jelena followed, but not before giving my fellow framee's face a sympathetic tap as she passed. Lucky bastard. She also whispered something in his ear.

"Well, that was fun," I said.

Hutton wasn't listening. He was holding his cheek between the goatee and sideburn. The spot the goddess had touched. "Sorry, what were you saying?"

"Would you like that cheek bronzed?"

"No, bronzing will not be necessary. And don't be jealous. The tap had a most practical application. She was relaying information."

"What sort of information?"

"Apparently, while we were dragging your poor hide around last night, Jelena stayed behind for another look at the body."

I shook my head. "Crazy kid. She really did love him."

"Not so much. She wanted to see the object in his hand. Remember the dying clue?"

I had almost forgotten it. The clue. Or *clew* if you like it old school. "And?"

"It was gone. Someone must have snatched it up while the rest of us were deciding which end of yours went up."

The significance was not lost on me.

"Then somebody in that room wanted to be sure we didn't see what Tony was holding?"

Hutton, still holding his cheek, nodded.

The rest of the day was something of a blur. I guess anytime you arise five hours early, smack dab in the middle of a living landscape as painted by one of our leading artistic visionaries, you're wont to feel a shade on the wonky side. I know I did.

The blackmail wasn't helping. According to the other residents, we could leave whenever we wanted, tide permitting; but if we did leave, our host would take a very grim view of our departure. He would be especially put out, it seemed, if we were to go before he had a chance to give us the details of *his plan*—whatever that might be. Not to mention our roles in that plan—whatever these were. So we stayed. You hate to slight your host. Even an invisible host.

As to the murder of Tony Rudd, it was discussed, analyzed and discussed some more, and the upshot was our blackmailer had me and Hutton by the short hairs. That was the consensus view of Jelena and Malcolm during breakfast; Niles and Mrs. Cotton over lunch; and briefly Christopher Cotton as he lay on his back in the main foyer, trying to get a close-up photo of a spider dangling from the bannister. This was around two thirty.

As Chris put it then, it looked every bit like we had tracked down Tony Rudd, used the parcel as our ticket inside the museum, and then in payback for some disagreement, gunned him down in cold blood with the contents of this parcel.

As Hutton would put it in reply, "And that would be wrong, yes?"

Judging from the evidence, we had motive and opportunity. And if the former was a bit thin, Chris agreed with Niles Brisbane: the authorities could always stitch together something at a later date. We certainly had enough thread on hand for them to hang us with.

One of the pieces of evidence against us, the gloves used in the shooting, we had already identified. It was Mrs. Cotton who recognized them. It was a pair the residents regularly shared, worn by any and all of the household at some time or another. It was all common property here at the Ariadne Artists' Commune and Murderers' Den. DNA evidence wasn't going to help us any with the gloves; although it did help tighten the noose around my neck, considering I had been the one to wear them most recently. I liked it better when all you had to worry about were fingerprints.

So that was how I spent my day: fretting about the murder, the frame-up and what the villain, our host, had on the rest of the gang to keep them all here. Hutton spent his time brooding over the Disappearing Clue.

Around three, we headed back to the McKnight gallery for another look at the scene of the crime. Pixie came along for the ride, having made the Cottons' room her base of operations. (Evidently Chris Cotton liked to keep his friends close, and his enemies closer.)

Hutton was right about the corpse. It was nowhere to be seen. The gun and lockbox were also gone. It was almost as if none of it had ever existed—a pretense I was more than happy to string along with.

"Do you think there's a chance Tony Rudd was faking?"

Hutton lifted Pixie off the stone floor and set her out of his field of investigation. No, he said, he did not think Tony Rudd had been faking.

"Still, you never know," I argued. "Sometimes bodies aren't as dead as they seem." I related my experience with Niles Brisbane the previous afternoon.

Hutton wasn't satisfied. "Niles has that dreamy look. Couple of times I thought he might have popped off myself."

"Then Tony Rudd really was dead?"

"Tony Rudd was really dead. You can't fake a hole in the chest."

Well, you could. But who would want to try?

He had moved on to rifling the cabinets. Pixie was napping in the sunshine. It was a lovely scene.

Left to my own devices, I continued to acquaint myself with the surrounding artwork (I could do with a diversion right about then). I concentrated my attention on the output of Thomas McKnight most of all. There were other artists represented—Maine-born painters like Earl Cunningham and Eastman Johnson—but the McKnights were the star attraction, no question. It didn't take an expert to see that TM had been Ariadne Locke's favorite. For starters, there was the sheer volume of canvases. Also our rooms, remade in these paintings' images. And then there was the fact that the residents had told me he was.

From what I gathered, the Lockes had always moved in arty circles. Ariadne's grandfather had been quite the social butterfly in his time, hobnobbing with all sorts of Salon types in the mid to late 1800s. Her father, not to be outdone, had chummed around with the likes of Renoir, Cézanne and Picasso. Then came Ariadne's turn. She had known of McKnight's work since the early 1980s, but it wasn't until she received one of the Clinton Christmas cards that her devotion truly blossomed. From that point on, she snapped up all the McK's she could get her hands on.

And if you asked me, she could have done no better thing. If you're going to be held against your will in a decrepit old mansion, threatened with taking the rap for a murder you didn't commit, it helps to have some nice paintings to look at while you're waiting.

I awoke from my reverie to check in with Hutton again. He was stooping at the cabinet where the body had been found. He shook his head in disgust, more at the lack of organization on the shelves than at anything else. I half-expected him to spout *I cannot work this way!* as he squatted.

"Problem?"

He sniffed. "Lord knows what Rudd might have grabbed in his death throes. Or whether he grabbed anything at all. Cabinet's so stuffed to the brim, junk might have simply tumbled down on him as he fell."

He wasn't kidding. As I had observed the previous night, the Ariadne crew didn't have much of a flair for tidiness. The cabinet was most certainly chockfull of crap. There were cans of pudding, cans of sardines, a few energy bars and what looked like some kind of dried fruit (let's hope it was dried fruit). As you moved along the shelf, there were cleaning supplies, plastic forks and knives, brushes, a porcelain porcupine I think you were supposed to stick loose pens and pencils inside, a few loose pens and pencils, and more pudding. It was quite the stash.

Kneeling there, poring over the horde, I wasn't sure why anyone bothered to shoot their enemies in this joint. All you would have to do is offer your victim a snack, and chances were he would end up accidentally washing it down with a swig of turpentine.

"Maybe it was just a lark," I agreed. "Maybe Tony's hand simply landed on something as he crumpled to the floor."

"Maybe," said Hutton—and then showing that he could never completely concur with anyone, not even himself, "but then why would someone go to the trouble of retrieving it?"

There was that, of course. If you're going to be technical about it.

"Speaking of the residents," I said, "I've been thinking. What do you think our host has on everyone here? We can infer from what Niles told us that they've all been framed for something, but other than his embezzlement, we don't know for what."

Hutton said he had been musing on that inference himself. It was a poser. "There are plenty of things one can be framed for. Murder, theft, fraud—"

"Assaulting a man's future father-in-law in a public restroom?"

He perked up at the mention. Framed. He had never thought of claiming he was framed. "Of course, there is one foolproof way we can learn everyone's situation here."

"And what is that?"

"Ask."

I didn't care for the suggestion myself. This was merely an academic exercise on my part; there was no sense prying. Besides, it didn't matter what they'd been framed for; it was what Hutton and I had been framed for that worried me.

I'd been thinking about that too, and the more I thought about it, the less I liked it. Even if we could prove we had nothing to do with the murder, how was this all going to look to the very refined Mr. and Mrs. Darlington? And to Lesley? Jill would probably have no problem with it, assuming no animals had been harmed in the commission of the crime, but Lesley would definitely look askance. Just the merest suggestion of an infatuation with the sexpot Jelena, whether I had killed Tony Rudd over her or not, would be enough to sink my marriage before it had even begun. Just Jelena, plain and simple, would have been enough.

No, I couldn't care less what the Ariadne gang had gotten themselves ensnared in here. We had our own problems.

"They're not our enemy, Hutton. Our host is."

"Is he?" he asked.

"Is he what?"

"Is he our enemy?"

"Isn't he?" I wondered.

"I don't know. Maybe he isn't. Not our only *only* enemy, I mean."

I frowned. My head was throbbing again. "What are we talking about?"

"We're talking about our host. He might be our opponent, but he may not be as secret as he appears. Think about it. Someone grabbed Tony's clue right from under our noses, in a room full of people. That can only point to one thing."

"Our host has another spy at the Ariadne," I said.

"Precisely."

"And it's one of the residents," I tossed out. Actually that was two things.

"Exactly. One mole killing another. And you know moles. They eat everything, and their bites are venomous."

"I think you're thinking of shrews."

"Moles, shrews, they're all a bunch of weasels."

I wasn't sure that they were. I would have to ask Jill.

Nevertheless, as usual, I found his theories drawing me in (just like the Minotaur's maze). Also as usual, I had no idea how these theories were going to help us. But I figured there was no harm in musing. As long as we didn't do anything to make matters worse. Fortunately, for once, I couldn't envision any way that we could do that.

"Come," said Hutton, envisioning a way that we could. "There's nothing for us here. Let's go ransack everybody's rooms while they're downstairs finishing lunch."

A few minutes later saw us back on the bedroom level again. There were eight rooms here, spanning up and down the corridor and around the corner. These Hutton and I would divide up and search. (I didn't even bother to argue.) "So what are we looking for?"

Hutton sighed. "A clue, Hath. We're looking for a clue."

"*The* clue?"

"Any clue. *The* clue, a clue to our host's plans, anything that might give us an upper hand, point out who his spy may or may not be, and/or lead us out of this rattrap."

Or weasel trap, I quipped, bringing it all together. "So we're searching for Ariadne's thread, then?" I asked, putting it rather neatly.

"If that helps you, then yes."

I was musing again. Had to be the locale. "You know, what I'd really like to find is one of our phones."

"Good luck with that. Mine was lost in the storm, and yours is probably at the bottom of the ocean by now, in Tony Rudd's pocket."

These logistics meant nothing to me. "I need to call Lesley. The last she and I spoke, you and I were 'gallivanting' about town. What's she going to think when I don't call? I saw an old landline in the kitchen last night, but I don't think there was a dial tone."

"I haven't had a phone with a dial tone since 2006," said Hutton, this admission not really helping me.

Pixie was at our feet, taking a great fascination in this discussion of the telecommunications industry.

"Who gets the pup?" I asked.

Just as he had in the conservatory, Hutton lifted the canine off the floor and set her several yards away from him, at my feet.

"You do, Hath. Look at her. She adores you."

If this was adoration, I could see why Jelena objected to it.

Pixie was sitting back, staring up at me with that unblinking expression of hers. She seemed to be thinking that I had a very unusually shaped head for a Maltese.

A moment later she trotted over to where Hutton stood. She always did like men named Fleet. "Come on, then," growled the Fleet of the hour, and man and dog ankled down the hallway to begin their search.

For roughly half an hour, I wandered from Manhattan to Greece, from Greece to France, and onto New England: the world of McKnight. Each room was a faithful recreation of a painting, masterful in every detail, but none of them had any details I was looking for. I wasn't even clear whose room was whose, though I was pretty sure I scoped out the Cotton abode in Manhattan—from all the tripods and Maltese hair and whatnot—as well as Jelena's in Greece, from the lack of clothing. But as far as smoking pistols, mysterious tidbits recently gripped in the hands of expiring assassins, and furtive notes back and forth to a mystery man—nothing.

I had arrived at one room, and was just thinking that the soothing yellow walls and gleaming black piano could tell me a lot about the guest, when I realized it was my room.

I paused. Something had changed here. It wasn't the fruit. The fruit hadn't moved. The ficus also remained in status quo, if it was a ficus.

It was the sideboard. There was a sheet of paper on the sideboard which had not been there before. As I stepped closer, I could see it was a heavy card stock, quite expensive looking, with typewritten text.

I picked it up and perused its contents.

"What is it?" said Hutton, back from the hunt. Pixie was up on the armchair, showing us her belly.

I handed Hutton the paper. "Now we know why our blackmailer wanted me here."

Hutton gave the page a look-see. "Well, ain't this a hoot," he said. When called for, he could sound vaguely American himself.

# 20 — A Certain Flare

Dear Johnny, [it read]

By now you're probably wondering why you're here. A very good question. It seems I have a favor to ask of you. I would be very much in your debt if you would arrange for the arrival of your charming father-in-law to-be, at this address, on the evening of the 6th. Formal attire will be worn. Please understand that if you fail, your charming wife not-to-be will be looking for a more suitable mate than a charming accused murderer. Awaiting your reply in the conservatory.

Charmingly Yours,
Your Host

"I liked Stothard Hope's communiqué better," said Hutton.

"You betcha."

"Not as pithy, this one."

I agreed with him there. Very short on pith.

"And all the *charmings* and whatnot. Pompous."

I nodded. Very high on pomp. "Why does he want Lesley's father here?"

"I don't know."

"And in formal attire! The evening of the 6th? That's tomorrow. Why does he want him here in formal attire tomorrow?"

Hutton had no inkling. "Perhaps he has a history with Larry Darlington's firm and is looking to leverage it somehow. Perhaps he needs a barrister to bless his plans—how should I know? There's no explanation for it. Unless—" He shook his head. "No, it would be too ridiculous," he muttered, and said no more. I really hated it when the Fleets did that.

"Now what?" I asked him.

"I guess, now, we see what awaits us in the conservatory."

We arrived at the arched doorway of the McKnight gallery (as I would always know it), but I delayed our reentrance. "Do you really think our host is in there?"

"Only one way to find out," said Hutton, and went in.

There was no one there. In the last twenty minutes, something had changed, however. On the maple table in the middle of the room lay a single iPhone.

"Is it mine or yours?" asked Hutton, examining it.

I reached out and tentatively poked the home button. Ate's face shone up at us.

Hutton squinted at it. He turned this squint on me. He had obviously forgotten that he had changed his wallpaper two nights ago, over his fourth whisky. He was wondering what I was doing with Ate Fleet's picture on my phone.

"It's yours," I growled.

He nodded again, sufficiently soothed, and went on examining the unit. Confident that it contained no booby traps, he reached out to pick it up. It wouldn't move. "It seems to be glued down."

"Seriously?" I made a grab for it myself, but it wouldn't budge.

Hutton was enraged. He called out over his shoulder, to anyone who might be listening: "It's one thing to mistreat us, but our phones were innocent! What sort of heartless bastard tortures phones!"

He continued peering around angrily, but received no balm for the injustice done here. I nudged him. There on the table, next to the immobile mobile, was an invitation to an art gala. It was printed on the same heavy card stock as our note and announced the hootenanny here at the Ariadne on the 6th. The pieces were all coming together—all the jagged little pieces.

Also on the invite, written in a carefully printed hand, was the phrase: "No funny business."

There was nothing else for it. For reasons I didn't know, and under pressure from something I didn't do, I would have to find a way to invite a man I didn't like to an art gala I didn't understand.

I dialed Lesley's number. Hutton put it on speaker. Clever of him. Much easier than bending my head down to the table.

*"Hullo."*

It was good to hear her voice. "Honeybun—"

*"Hutton?!"*

"No." I turned and squinted at my friend.

*"Oh, it's you, John. I saw Hutton's picture come up on my screen and couldn't figure out why he was calling me honeybun. Why are you ringing on Hutton's phone?"*

"Mine got lost. Can't explain now. I'm glad you're the one who answered—"

*"Why wouldn't I be the one to answer? It's my phone."*

"I know. It's just, the last time I called, your sister answered. It's not important—"

*"Jill answered my phone?"*

"Yes. It's not important—"

*"When did Jill answer my phone?"*

"Yesterday, the day before. I can't remember. It's not important—"

*"But what was Jill doing answering my phone? I've told her not to answer my phone—"*

"I don't know. It's not important—"

*"She knows I hate it when she answers my phone."*

"Look, it's not important—"

*"She has a perfectly good phone. I gave it to her last Christmas. It's the same model, in fact. Wait, is that why she answered my phone? Did she think it was her phone?"*

"It's NOT important!"

A short pause. Lesley continued, slightly put out, *"There's no reason to shout."*

"Sorry."

*"I have enough to put up with here without your shouting."*

"I understand."

Another pause.

*"So why did you say you were using Hutton's phone?"*

I looked at Hutton, and he smiled back at me. I wondered if all this would come under the heading of funny business.

With a tap on the shoulder, he left me to it. From the furtive expression on his face, I gathered he was going to have a look around. See if there really was anybody else there.

Lesley was still at it: *"Where have you been all this time? I texted you about fifty times. Are you at home?"*

I didn't have time to explain about this either, and somehow I felt she should know that. "There's this gala," I said. In retrospect, I could have prefaced that somewhat.

*"A gala? What kind of gala?"*

"Just a gala. I was calling to invite—"

*"You want to invite us to a gala? What gala? Why a gala?"*

Somehow I hadn't considered this. Pretty stupid, I know, but it had never occurred to me. Of course I couldn't invite Lesley's father to an art gala alone, without inviting everyone else. He and I didn't have that kind of relationship. (I'm not sure any son-in-law would.) Now I would have to bring Lesley into this too? I didn't like it. Not one bit of it.

"It's an art gala," I said, trying to stall while I thought. "At this museum place upstate. You've mentioned it before, in fact. The Ariadne Museum and Something. It's upstate. There's a gala here. At the museum."

*"So I gather. But why do you want us to go?"*

"Oh well, you know."

*"I do?"*

"I thought it would be, you know—"

Hutton made a passing sweep, whispering a suggestion. I reluctantly took it.

"I thought it would be a hoot."

Lesley sounded impressed. *"You thought it would be a hoot?"*

"Yes, you know, a hoot. Something for the whole family."

*"A hoot for the whole family?"*

"Something like that. Your father is still there, right?"

*"Of course he's still here. Where else would he be?"*

I tried to infuse a merry tone into my voice: "Bring him along!"

Of course she would bring him along! What else would she do with him? Him and Mum and Jill, she supposed, although she was getting pretty fed up with Jill. She'd been acting very peculiar on this trip. *"You honestly want us to go to this gala?"*

"You know it," I sighed.

Something sprang to mind here. Not a solution. Just a tiny high note I could pluck out from the chaos.

"I've been hard at work arranging this. That's what I've been doing these last few days."

*"Is it? Well, I'm glad you're doing something to help me. After I never got those spa certificates from you—"*

"Yes, never mind about the spa certificates."

*"I mean, it wasn't that difficult. All I asked—"*

"Forget about the spa already! This will be way better than any ratty spa."

*"If you say so. Text the address."*

I went to key it in, only the pop-up keyboard had been disabled. The text app already had the information. (Our host had thought of everything!)

I hit *Send.*

I was running out of time here. I had to think of something. Anything! Dragging Mr. Darlington into God-knows-what was bad enough, but he was a lawyer and therefore expendable. Lesley, though—that simply wasn't on. Even if she was in no real danger, I couldn't risk it. As Hutton had spoken so eloquently a moment before, our host could do what he liked to me, but Lesley was innocent. She didn't need to be involved. Not to mention I loved her (just as Hutton, I could only assume, had loved his poor brave iPhone).

I needed a plan. I needed Enescu Fleet.

Suddenly I had a thought. An inspiration, really. It shot across the landscape of my mind in a splendor of old-fashioned ingenuity. All around me there were paintings, paintings and more paintings. There were also plants, lots and lots of plants—and flowers, and a good deal of sunshine despite the overcast skies—but mostly there were paintings. I stared at them.

Paintings. Postcards. Coded messages on postcards. That was it!

I would send a coded message!

The trick was sending something innocuous enough that our host wouldn't pick up on it, but with enough clarity that Lesley would recognize it and tell Fleet.

But what code, you ask? How could I possibly think up an innocuous code, on the spur, with our host (and/or his secret minion) listening in the offing? It can't be done, you say? No one could manage such a feat?

It can be done, I say, and here's how. I already had my code.

Earlier, while others mucked about looking for clues, I had been busily studying the artwork in this gallery. One of the paintings I had seen here was a pretty little Earl Cunningham called *Blue Sail Fleet Returns*. The title had stuck in my mind at the time—Fleet, Fleet returning, oh, that he would, I had sighed to myself then—but now I could use this *Blue Sail* whatsit to my advantage.

Consider it. I needed Fleet to return, and now I had a method for expressing this desire. All I had to do was communicate this painting to Lesley without clueing in our host, and Bob would be your uncle.

There was the rub, of course. Some of my enthusiasm trickled away. Okay, most of it trickled. How do you communicate the title of a painting over a phone without actually saying the title? It can't be done. No one could manage such a feat. It was hopeless.

Luckily Lesley, who had been talking all this time, showed me the way.

*"... anyway, I spoke to the wedding planner again, and—"*

That was it! Wedding planners, wedding photographers, Chris Cotton taking photos...

Photos. The theme of my new inspiration was photos. I would take a photo of the painting and send it to Lesley. The keyboard had been disabled but the photo button was still there. I grasped for the phone. It didn't move! The glue! I'd forgotten about the damn glue!

*"She hasn't returned my calls, and I really do wonder—"*

I continued clawing away to no avail. It was Hutton who came to my rescue this time. He had just stepped out from some rushes with Pixie, and immediately homed in on my distress. The man was intuitive, you had to hand him that. One look at the open camera app on the phone, and another at the row of paintings on the opposite wall, and he had it. Without pausing, he stepped past me and flipped the maple table on its end.

THUD!

Turning the flank toward the artwork, he hung over the side, aimed and fired.

CLICK!

*"What in blazes was that noise?"* asked Lesley from the other side of the heap.

Hutton dangled over the edge. "Did you get the text?"

*"Of course I got it. Is that you, Hutton? It looks like you also sent a picture. I—"*

The line went dead.

I helped him replace the table on its legs. No reason to be untidy.

"At least, if she does figure it out," I said, "she'll be sure to relay the message to Fleet."

"We can only hope."

"But how could she fail? It's right there in the title."

"What's right there in the title?"

"Fleet!"

"Is it?" he asked.

"Isn't it?" I wondered.

"I don't know," he repeated, "is it?"

"Let's not start that again." I drew his attention to the Cunningham hanging on the wall. "Am I wrong, or is the title here not *Blue Sail Fleet Returns*?"

Hutton said I was not wrong.

"So there you have it. Granted, Lesley won't be able to make out the plaque underneath, but with a little luck she'll ask Fleet, and the human trivia bank can identify it."

Hutton wasn't disputing any of that. It was beautifully argued. "There's only one glitch."

"And what's that?"

"That's not the picture I sent."

I turned and stared at it. "Wasn't it?" I asked.

Hutton escorted me down the row to another painting on the wall, darker and more brooding in its appearance: like a latter-day Rembrandt. This one showed a young person in pioneer garb, kneeling at the foot of a tree, fooling about with a box of some sort.

"Eastman Johnson," he announced.

I gave it a careful look, nodding intelligently at the brushwork and the use of ambient light.

"I made a mental note of it earlier," said Hutton. "You see the title."

I saw the title. "*Setting the Trap.*" I nodded thoughtfully. That was good too.

I spent the next twenty minutes in deep thought. Like Lesley, I had a lot on my mind. Eventually Hutton roused me from my meditations. We were sitting in the kitchen. I was poking idly at a tuna-fish sandwich; he was scrutinizing a sardine (apparently one of the museum's awesome food deliveries had arrived this morning). He banished the critter to his plate, and broke the silence with a question. "Are you still worried about Lesley?"

I answered that I was somewhat worried, yes.

"Are you concerned that she won't have a clue what we were driving at with the photo?"

"Somewhat concerned, yeah."

"Are you thinking that Eastman Johnson was a melancholy old duffer—what? What's really on your mind?"

I rotated around to face him. "I was thinking about our host."

"God bless him. The founder of our feast."

"Yes, but is he?"

"Well, I can't say for sure that he picked out each sardine personally, but he is certainly the reason we're here."

I leaned in closer. "I'm not so sure there is a host."

His brow crinkled. He took off his glasses. "A bold statement. Explain."

I kept my voice low. "I realize everything points to some mystery man. That's what everybody keeps telling us. But maybe too much points to him, if you know what I mean."

"I don't."

"It's like someone is forcing the host card on us. If there really is a host, then why haven't we seen him? What's he afraid of?"

Hutton opened his mouth to reply. I could tell he was thinking that there were a thousand reasons why a host might choose to remain unseen. He might—well, there were a thousand reasons why.

"And what happened to Stothard Hope?" I asked. "No one has even mentioned him since we arrived."

"In a book, it would turn out that Hope is still alive and has secretly been pulling the strings here while we search vainly for other suspects."

"Fleet saw his body."

Hutton agreed that that did make it less likely.

I continued to concentrate. "If only we knew what Rudd was trying to tell us. Unfortunately that clue is lost forever. Unless—" I bounded from the table.

Hutton grumbled that he hated when I did that. "Unless what?"

I didn't reply. I sprang into the pantry, nearly steamrollering over Jelena as she came in from the back porch. Hutton followed at a gentler pace, the slinky model close behind.

"What's all this, Hath?" he asked, closing the door behind us.

I was busy rifling the items on the shelf. I turned and hastily explained.

"We know that whatever Tony Rudd grabbed, it likely came from the cabinet, correct?"

Hutton and Jelena said correct.

"We know that this one object had been removed, but what if other examples of it had been removed as well, just to throw us off the trail. That would be a logical precaution, and it would explain why we found nothing significant in our search, right?" They said right. "Let us further suppose, then, that these duplicate items had not actually been thrown out, but merely moved. They were probably food stuffs, judging from the rest of the contents of the cabinet, which means—ha, found it!"

I had snagged my quarry. Stepping away, I settled the object in my grasp behind my back and then brought it around for them to see.

Hutton nodded appreciatively. So did Jelena. "Could be, Hath, could be. I'd say the edges look pretty much like the mystery item. What is it?"

I opened my palm.

Jelena stared. So did Hutton. "Kippers?" he asked.

I nodded. Kippers. My pantry pals were frankly stunned.

Hutton shook his head. "Trained assassin Tony Rudd's last act on earth was to reach out and grab a can of kippers?"

I nodded again. I was certain of it. "The sardines are what gave me the idea. I figured if the residents liked tuna, and they liked sardines, then they might, just might, like kippers too."

"We do enjoy the fishes in the can," agreed Jelena, who also remembered seeing kippers in the conservatory on more than one occasion. "You would think with the ocean so near we would catch the fishes, but no."

Hutton's face lit up. Finally he had it. "Kippered herring?" he said, slapping his thigh.

"Kippered *herring*," I repeated, almost slapping Jelena's—"Johnny Herring killed Tony Rudd!"

## 21 — Lovely Artifice

The rest of our deductions would have to wait. No sooner had Hutton spouted, "The weasel Herring, we meet again," than a tentative knock came on the pantry door. Mrs. Cotton asked in a bleating voice what we were doing in there. She seemed concerned that it was nothing lewd.

We took our leave shortly thereafter: a tiny parade of two male guests and one scantily attired artist's model. For Jelena, it was just as well. She had to get back to Malcolm and their work in the studio. She was very curious to learn what other items of fish we might discover, and asked us to keep her apprised of our progress. A second later, she was skimming down the hall in her fluffy green slippers. I had never seen a goddess scurry before.

Hutton and I continued our conversation in a more secluded corner, away from the kitchen and the prying Mrs. C.

I got the ball rolling: "I guess I was wrong, we do have a secret host."

Hutton peered around suspiciously. "Maybe we do, maybe we don't."

"What do you mean?"

He peered around again. The carved wood pelican on the back wall was definitely giving him the creeps. "I think one of us is not who we say we are."

"You mean—"

"Herring is among us."

I sniffed. "So you agree: one of the residents here is actually a killer and blackmailer?"

Hutton nodded. "What better way to keep tabs on your victims than to blend in among them. It's the oldest trick in the secret blackmailer's book. And who better than John Frederick Herring to blend in? He's a recluse. No one knows what he looks like."

It sounded far-fetched, but on this case what wasn't?

The answer was easy, then. "It's gotta be Malcolm. He's young enough and remember Vroom mentioned that the real Johnny Herring paints. Malcolm's gotta be our man."

My fellow deducer wasn't so certain. Apparently the answer wasn't easy. "Herring's a painter, Hath, not a sculptor."

"Well, maybe Malcolm paints on the side." It had to be him. "No one else is the right age."

"Unless we're thinking of the wrong Johnny," said Hutton. "Remember, there are two John Frederick Herrings."

Actually there were four, counting the Herrings of old. But I took his point. "Are you talking about the father?"

"The original Don Herring, yes."

"He's dead."

"Only according to Vroom Jr., and we've already seen how good his word is. If alive, he could be either of our duffers here. In fact, I'm not sure he'd have to be completely alive to be Chris Cotton."

This was getting convoluted. "Well, at least we know it can't be the ladies."

Hutton wasn't so sure. "What's to say that Johnny Herring is a man? No one has ever seen him. And Johnny can always be a girl's name."

"I've never known it to be a girl's name," I frowned.

"Well, it can. Look at the song *Frankie and Johnny*."

"Johnny was the dude."

"Oh really? I suppose you're telling me, then, that Frankie was the girl? Ridiculous. No, Johnny can definitely be a bird. See it all over the place."

I grumbled something under my breath. There truly was nothing about that name that wasn't annoying me on this trip. Perhaps it was time to start going by my middle name.

"I agree it's a long shot," he continued, "but we have to consider everyone. Anyone here could be Johnny Herring. Anyone here could be a killer. Even the ladies."

"Mrs. Cotton, maybe, but not Jelena. I refuse to suspect Jelena."

"That's only because you're a horn dog."

"On the contrary." If anyone was a horn dog, then that horn dog was he. As far as Jelena went, my argument was pure logic. If you can't trust a naked lady, then who can you? "My money's still on Malcolm," I said. He smelled like old herring; it fit perfectly.

"I would be more inclined to go with Brisbane," retorted Hutton.

"That kindly old geezer? Nonsense."

It was his kindliness that made Hutton suspect him the most. "It's always the kindly ones you've got to look out for."

"You're nuts. If Niles Brisbane is the—"

"If Niles Brisbane is the what, Mr. Hathaway?" wondered Niles Brisbane. The residents never tired of that shtick.

He was standing in the archway behind us, glaring in. It occurred to me that he didn't look very kindly, after all. Even his pipe appeared sinister. "Is the *what*?" he asked again.

"—is the man to ask about this lock," said Hutton. He stepped away to reveal a door, the one I had spotted in my travels the previous day. He rattled the handle emphatically. "What's in here?"

The duffer glanced between the door and us and back to the door. "That's not for you," he stated. "Not for any of us here."

"*Ours is not to reason why, ours is* something something *do or die*," quoted Hutton (almost). Niles Brisbane didn't sing along. "Then you don't know what's in there?"

"No," said Niles, and left us.

I may not be the best detective who ever lived. I might miss clues and jump to false conclusions, but I knew one thing for sure. Niles Brisbane knew exactly what was on the other side of that door, and he wasn't happy about us snooping around it. Maybe Hutton was right. He could be our killer.

Once he had trudged out of view, I turned to Hutton and commended him on his fast wit. I wouldn't claim that Niles had bought our explanation completely, but he had purchased enough of it to save us from explaining.

"Good one."

Hutton wasn't receiving compliments at the moment. He was busy picking the lock. "You knew about this?" he asked.

"Yesterday—why?"

"I've never seen anything like it. Look at the design."

He moved aside so I could look. It was a little on the peculiar side, perhaps, sturdy and mysterious, but nothing to write home about. "What of it?"

"It's unpickable—practically a mini-vault. And I thought the lock-box we delivered was tough." He straightened up and glared down at it. "I need—" He paused and glared even further down. "Where's Pixie?"

I wouldn't have thought a tiny Maltese all that helpful at picking locks, but he knew best. "She was with us in the conservatory."

"She's probably still there. Come on, with any luck we'll discover her with her teeth clamped on the trouser seat of the real Johnny Herring."

She wasn't in the conservatory. The trouser seat of Johnny Herring, whatever size, sex and age that might be, also wasn't present.

Hutton didn't pause for a roll call. He went straight to the back, slowing only when he had reached a pair of giant outer doors. They were open. "Just as I figured," he said, and charged on through and across the expansive lawn. I jogged to keep up.

He eventually dropped anchor at the edge of the meadow, behind a birch. "There," he announced.

I hated to be contrary, but this wasn't a Maltese. It wasn't any kind of dog. It was a tree. There's a difference.

"Not the birch, Hath, look at the gravel."

I was getting a little tired of him telling me to look at things, especially low things. When I assisted Enescu Fleet in his investigations last fall, he didn't make me look at low things.

"What?" I snapped.

He pointed. "This is where Herring stood and spied on us during our call to Lesley."

"How do you know?"

"The gravel is disrupted."

I snorted. Disrupted gravel. What a load of—

"Also, this tree gives a perfect view of the conservatory."

I snorted again. "So where's the dog?"

"She's out here somewhere. She must have run through the open doors while we were on the phone—the doors I knew would be open."

"And how'd you know they would be open?"

"Because Herring had to leave them open in order to see inside—in order to see us. It's just like Fleet said a couple days ago. During the day it's hard to see in through a window because an interior tends to be less bright than outside. The conservatory has a lot of natural light, but not enough to make a difference."

I half-snorted. "Anything else?"

"Just that Herring no doubt availed himself of a parabolic mic to listen in on our conversation. We should keep that in mind. The Fish is always listening. He or she also had some kind of mobile phone jammer—something more sophisticated than the one we found at your house—which is how she or he ended our call. It's obviously good for the whole park."

Obviously. "So why didn't he just bug the gallery?" I asked. I was sticking with a *he* for now. I refused to play pronoun footsie.

"Hard to do without being observed. Remember, if our theory is right about Herring, he—or she—is trying to keep his or her identity a secret. Also, there would always be the chance that we would spot the bug and dispose of it before making the call."

"Bug the phone, then."

"Even harder. The parabolic mic makes the most sense."

I didn't know what a parabolic mic was—other than it was a mic and it was parabolic—and I didn't intend to find out. "We should look for Pixie," I said. "Better we find her before Chris Cotton does."

"Before Chris Cotton does what?" asked Chris Cotton.

He was holding the dog up against his cardigan. The Maltese was out of the bag.

"I've talked to you about keeping an eye on this animal," he said, patting her head softly. For an enemy of canines everywhere, he was giving the beast some pretty gentle treatment.

"Sorry," I replied, taking hold of the furry package.

I didn't have her long. I had hardly grasped her around the gut when she elbowed me in the solar plexus and sprang off onto the lawn.

She charged the birch next, barking suspiciously at it, as if unpersuaded of its bonafides.

Cotton continued, "I've been trying to get a photo of this magnificent tree, but every time I get my shot in line you all gum it up."

I apologized again. I could see why he wanted to immortalize the birch. It was a lovely tree: tall, full of birchen goodness. And other than the commemorative "1834" someone had carved in the bark, it was unmarred by human hands.

"Wait," said Hutton. "You say *we* gummed up your shot earlier today?"

"One of you did. Didn't notice it till later on, after I had the photo and was back at my studio. Gummed it up proper. Damned nuisance."

Hutton stepped closer. He rested his hand on the photographer's bony shoulder. "When was this?"

"How should I know? Around three thirty maybe."

Hutton gave his new friend an amiable squeeze. "Who was in the photograph, Chris?"

"I assumed it was one of you rapscallions."

"Of course. You did say that. When pics are gummed, one always blames the rapscallions. You've developed this photo?"

"No need to develop it. Was using the digital this afternoon."

Hutton bowed his head in honor of the grouchy-faced modern man. "Can I see it?"

The grouchy-faced modern man said nope. "As soon as I saw the figure, I deleted the picture lickety-split." And with this endorsement of modern technology, he ankled off.

"Of course, I could be wrong," said Hutton, roughly fifteen minutes later. We were at the land's edge, right about where the tide would soon cover the path leading off this berg. He was atop one of the crags. I was glaring up at him, wondering when he might topple off this crag. Pixie was lagging back, spying gulls.

Hutton had apparently forgotten all about our talk with Christopher Cotton. Forgotten about the geezer's itchy trigger finger on the delete. Forgotten about the one piece of photographic evidence we might have had. Forgotten it all.

He was onto new horizons, cheerfully taking the rough currents with the smooth.

I had moved on myself, pondering that empty feeling you get when life kicks you in the seat of the pants and then goes off and laughs about it to its friends. We were officially trapped here for another evening (as opposed to the unofficial trap we had been in ever since the assassin Tony Rudd had gasped his last). We were no closer to a solution than the day before, or the day before that. We were no closer to extricating ourselves from this frame or fashioning our escape. We were stuck. And soon Lesley and her family would be here, and they would be stuck too. I looked out at the closing tide and sighed. I knew what Ariadne Island reminded me of now. Alcatraz.

"I could be wrong," Hutton was saying. "Such things have happened. But even if I am wrong about a few details, I am certain of one thing: someone here is on the wrong side. Someone here is working against the whole. We need to find out who."

And so it was decided that we would divide up the residents between us. Apply a little psychological technique.

Anything was better than standing around and waiting.

Hutton would take the Cottons, Mr. and Mrs. I got Niles and Jelena (I won the toss). Malcolm Rosso we would tackle together later on. Pixie—well, Pixie had her gulls.

Our priorities: learn everyone's background, learn what crime we could possibly be assembled here to commit, learn what they knew of Johnny Herring—and by extension if they happened to be Johnny Herring—and lastly, learn what was behind that locked door.

If you asked me, the locked door was of the essence. Now that we had seen most of the museum, inside and out, The Door, and what was beyond it, had become irresistible. Before, it had merely been intriguing, a curiosity. Now it was downright baffling. What could be in there? Herring's secret lair? A congregation area for Locke family ghosts? An additional supply of kippers? What? It could be anything. And I couldn't abide any more teasing. We'd already seen halfway up the museum's skirt, we might as well see the Full Ariadne.

"It is true, I have often pondered this door," Jelena said to me as we walked. It seemed strange, taking an evening stroll along the shore with a beautiful, kimono-clad girl who was not my fiancée, but I tried to make the best of it. "It is a mighty door, that. An impenetrable door."

I pondered it myself. *The Mighty Door of the Ariadne.* All very mysterious and parabolic-sounding. (Maybe that was what a parabolic mic was.) "What's on the other side?" I asked.

Her answer came quickly and without any doubt in her voice: "Ariadne's secrets are buried there." She spoke with a far-off gaze, the sun accentuating the highlights in her hair.

I said cool beans.

"So there are secrets buried there?" I asked Niles Brisbane half an hour later. He had mellowed considerably since we last spoke. He puffed at his pipe as we stood on the same stretch of land Jelena and I had covered earlier.

"Secrets?" he remarked, kicking off his shoes in the sand and blinking at me.

"Behind the locked door."

"Oh, that." He nodded thoughtfully and puffed. "No one knows what's behind that," he answered, the waning sun bouncing off his giant bald noggin. "It was locked when we got here, and no one's been able to budge it."

A short pause. Overhead, a gull swooped down and made me yip like a little girl.

"So you're an artist too?" I wondered, shooing it away.

"Oh yes. Yes, yes, yes."

"Paint?"

"Sculpture. Oh, nothing like Mr. Rosso, you understand. Malcolm works with stone, old-school sculpture. I don't have the upper-body strength for that kind of work. My focus is on 'found art.' "

"Found art?"

"The assembly of everyday items into wondrous living collages!"

I said ah.

"The splendor of the mundane," he tacked on.

I said you betcha. "Sounds fascinating."

"Oh, it is. Yes." He bent over to roll up his pant legs. "Yes, yes, yes." While he was down there, he noticed something in the sand. He dusted it off and showed me. Looked like a window crank from a 1972 Buick Skylark. "I can use this," he announced, twirling it happily.

As he toddled away, crank in hand, I reflected back on the parallel conversation I had had with Jelena earlier.

"I am the art," she had said, in reply to my question about her work. I had asked her if she had ever dabbled on the other side of the canvas or slab, and that had been her answer. "I am the art, John. You ask me do I do the art. I answer, I am the art."

You had to admire her opinion of herself.

"Work with Malcolm a lot?"

She shook her raven strands. "Malcolm is a, what do you call it, an off-one."

"One-off?"

"Yes, he is the one-off."

I was happy to hear it. "Where did you work before, if you don't mind my asking?"

"I was the studio model for the Vroom Gallery," she answered matter-of-factly, hurrying down to the edge of the turf and dipping her painted toes in the water.

I came out of my reflections. Niles was dipping his toes in the water now too.

The Vroom Gallery, I thought to myself. I had almost forgotten about the gangster Vroom. Jelena's knowing him couldn't be a coincidence.

"What do you know about Cornelis Vroom?" I asked Niles.

The duffer looked up from his wiggling tootsies. "We've met."

That was a lot of help. "Met where?"

"At his gallery. I contributed to an exhibition he held once."

"I see. How about Johnny Herring? Was he there?"

Niles looked uncomfortable. He walked along the shore. He wanted no part of these questions.

My mind went back to Jelena. She had not been as unyielding:

"You refer to the gangster's son, Johnny Herring, do you not?"

I did. "You know him?"

"No. But I have heard of him. I have heard Mr. Vroom, the gallery owner, speak of him. He paints."

He did a hell of a lot more than paint, if you asked me. "Everywhere we turn," I said, "we come up against this man Herring. You remember what we found in the pantry?"

"We found the fishes."

"The *herring* fishes," I corrected. "Rudd's dying clue. Could John Herring have killed Tony Rudd? Could he have assembled the residents here?"

"These questions I do not know."

"Why do you think we're here, then?"

"I do not know, John. I hear things, whispered theories, but that is all."

If you asked me, she did a hell of a lot more than hear. The moment had come for straight-talking. No more deception.

"What hold does the Ariadne have over you, Jelena? You can tell me that, can't you?"

She turned and placed a hand on my face. Hutton was right. It was neat. "It is better that you do not know, John."

Usually this wasn't hard for me, not knowing. Today it wasn't so easy. "But we might still be able to help you. We might be able to help everyone here."

She responded with a lovely little wiggle of her lips. "You and your lanky friend cannot even help yourselves! Do you really believe you can help anyone else?"

Maybe not, but I wanted to know. I had to know.

"I will tell you, then," she declared. "I know I can trust you. I have been framed for stealing state secrets from my home country."

I was relieved. I thought it might be something serious. "But you're here now. If the secrets are any good, I bet our government would embrace you with open arms." In fact, if she let loose that satin kimono, they might let the embrace go on a little longer than was appropriate.

"It does not work that way. I would be deported, deported to face the justice of my own motherland. And my motherland's justice is not something I wish to face."

Before I could respond—not that I had any sparkling reply—she lit up at the sight of a school of tuna in the near distance. With a resounding Oooh!, she let loose her robe and dashed down to the water to swim with the fishes. Au naturel.

That was pretty neat too.

I was still thinking about it an hour later. Not just her modified, nude biathlon—I would be thinking about that for a long time to come—but what she had said. Perhaps she was right. Perhaps Hutton and I were kidding ourselves. How were we going to solve anything here? We couldn't even open a locked door.

I snapped out of my trance to see Niles in one of his own. His pipe was in his shirt pocket, and he was staring out at the ocean. I decided to level with him, man to man.

"Look, we're all trapped here," I said. "It would help to know what you know. What everyone knows. Put our heads together and figure a way out of this. Take this embezzlement against you—"

He turned to me and smiled. He put his hand on my head. "You're a nice fella, Johnny. But it's too late for us. All that matters now is art."

And on that sentiment, he spotted the perfect piece of driftwood floating a hundred or so feet out. Explaining that it would make an admirable addition to a piece he was working on, he stripped down to his boxer shorts and ankle garters, declared Tally-ho! and waded out to retrieve his rustic treasure.

Watching this was not as neat.

## 22 — Behind the Frame

I went inside after that. The first thing I saw as I entered the musty hall off the kitchen pantry was a trio of painted naval statues: sea captains in various poses. (Some salesperson of nautical camp must have made a real killing here at one point.)

One of the figures, the farthest from the door, appeared a bit more stiff and wooden than the other two. "Hutton?"

"Hath?"

"What are you doing?"

"Ducking Mrs. Cotton. I thought she was on my tail. You haven't seen her?"

"Sorry, no. I was too busy watching Jelena frolic naked in the sand."

"Lucky stiff."

"And then Niles Brisbane frolic."

"Ah. That's not as lucky."

I agreed that it was not. Not as lucky at all. "Why are you ducking Mrs. Cotton?"

He stepped out from his stolid cohorts, ushering me back outside and into the evening air.

"I tried, Hath, I really did."

"Tried what?"

"Tried to question her. Tried not to lose my marbles in the process."

"Not on?"

"Not in the slightest. Nobody could converse with that woman. She's a loon."

I was somewhat peeved. If I could watch Niles in his skivvies, the least he could do was endure a few minutes alone with the Cotton clan. "Did you learn anything at all?"

"Very little. I spent most of the interview with the old guy. He used to be a professor. He was at the same university as Brisbane, in fact."

"Niles Brisbane was a professor?"

"Of course. You didn't know that?"

"No."

"What did you two talk about?"

This was hard to say. Litter, mostly.

Hutton continued, "Anyway—yes. Chris Cotton and Niles Brisbane taught together at some university, the very university Malcolm Rosso also worked at, though I'm not certain he was a professor. More like guest lecturer slash wandering mad genius."

"Malcolm worked at the university?"

"Pretty sure. I think that's where he met Jelena."

I declined to contribute to our cross-talk act by asking, "Jelena was at the university too?" But I thought it. I thought the bejeebers out of it. She had "never" worked with Malcolm before—that was what she had said. He was the one-off, she had told me. She lied.

Hutton was still talking: "Cotton and Brisbane worked in the art history department. The future Mrs. C was their assistant. Chris swept her off her feet, they married and, sometime later, he took up photography. This was after he retired. Retired was the word he gave anyway. Personally I think the university forced him out: boinking *inappropriatus*."

I shook my head in confusion. Latin terms always left me fogged. "Why shouldn't he boink his assistant?" I asked—although it was hard to think of Mrs. Cotton (or Mr. Cotton) and boinking in one breath.

"No reason, except she was the university president's daughter. Didn't I mention that? Oh—well, she was. His daughter. Old guy pegged out a few years back and that helped set up the dilettantes in their current life of leisure. Cotton has had a few of his photos exhibited, though mostly he just diddles. Mrs. Cotton, meanwhile, in the mode of a true dabbler, tries her hand at a little of everything. She keeps butterflies, she paints, she communes with whales—that is, if the poor beasts don't see her coming first. She and her hubby also run some charity: The Cotton Thread Foundation. Apparently the fund has grown quite hefty as of late. I can see why. Who'd take money from them?"

I considered the label. Cotton's *Thread*.

He read my mind. "As in Ariadne's thread. That did occur to me. Curious choice."

I agreed that it was. Very curious.

"Anyway, that's all I learned," concluded Hutton. "Oh, except for the Cottons' frame job."

That was pretty significant. "So what were they framed for?"

"Just Mrs. C. Chris is only here because the Cotton men always stand by their birds. The latter, apparently, has been framed for tax fraud. From what I learned, she used to do all the filings for her family—her father didn't trust accountants. At some point, somebody got whimsical with the figures. If it comes out, all fingers would point to her."

I didn't see what the big deal was. She would just goggle at them.

"That concluded our interview," said Hutton. "I slipped out a short time after that, whilst the missus' back was turned. She had the look of a woman about to try her hand at some sort of interpretive dance. She was holding silks."

It seemed to me he had done the right thing. It also seemed like he had learned a lot more than I had. I barely knew anything about Niles. As for Jelena, I had picked up that Vroom detail (assuming that wasn't a lie too) and that was pretty much it—other than she enjoyed the fresh air on her skin and was a good sprinter on the turf. I didn't even know her last name.

We had put some distance between us and the house now. Hutton spoke calmer: "You can say this about the detainees here, they like to keep busy."

I had noticed that as well. They made the best of their confinement at the Ariadne Museum and Artists' Retreat. Mrs. C with her oil painting. Mr. C with his photos. Jelena and Malcolm and their sculpture. Niles and his chunks of driftwood. It was like the latter said, standing there in his pinstriped boxers, pasty flesh shimmering in the breeze: it was all about embracing the true beauty in the world.

We had reached the lighthouse. Hutton jerked open the weather-worn door, stooped and went in. I followed, not stooping, pausing to clip my forehead on the doorframe.

It was the first time I had been inside the landmark, having previously only enjoyed its hoary charm from afar. Apparently it was a gift shop. Also Christopher Cotton's studio. The curved walls—parabolic?—were covered in framed shots, some black and whites, but mostly color, mainly landscapes. His stuff wasn't bad, brighter and more vibrant than I would have expected from the geezer. The shutterbug was standing in the aisle examining negatives, looking like a close-up of sourness personified.

"Shh!" he instructed, pointing to Pixie, sound asleep atop a makeshift bed of pillows. I couldn't be sure, but they looked a lot like my pillows. "If you're here to ask me any more of your damn questions—" he began.

We assured him that we were fresh out of damn questions for the moment. He let us pass with a nod, and we climbed the spiral stairs to the level above.

Here the gift shop really spread its wings, offering T-shirts, sweatshirts and taffy. Hutton held up one of the tees, but it wasn't his size.

He took a few trips around the room, coming to rest by a table of calendars from the early nineties. He began flipping through one. On the next shelf there were travel guides and a row of bookends in the shape of—three guesses—chunky sea captains.

Poring through the pages of decades-past seemed to jumpstart his mind. "Tomorrow's the sixth, Hath, the night of the so-called gala."

"I know."

"Who would want to *gala* here?"

I couldn't tell him.

"What was Stothard Hope trying to tell us?" he asked.

The last question appeared to send a charge through his wiry frame.

He tossed 1996 aside and rushed to a rack of memorabilia at the top of the stairs. We had walked right by it on our way in.

I was only a step behind him. "Postcards! Do you think this is where—?"

"—Stothard selected his clue? I do. And with any luck—" He trailed off over the sound of the revolving stand creaking on its axis. "Ha!" He flicked one from the slot. "The Christmas section is almost depleted, but there's one card here that might interest us."

He handed over a McKnight: the Red Room from the Clinton Christmas collection.

"Stothard Hope's clue, without the message on the back, of course."

I nodded. The tree, the windows, the fireplace—they were all there, right where the artist had left them.

"Come," he said, hurdling a table of ceramic mugs and scattering taffy to the four winds. "I have a plan."

A couple hours later found us scrunched up behind the blue chair in my bedroom, slightly under the piano. Hutton was on my left, Pixie on my right. The lights were dim, and the trap was set. His plan was on the books.

We had spent the evening putting it into place. I hated to admit it, but it had potential. Over dinner Hutton had casually mentioned the original Hope postcard to the rest of the residents. He had casually mentioned that it was in my bedroom now, casually implying that it had never left our side these past two days. He concluded by mentioning, casually, that immediately following the meal he and I were going outside to look for Pixie—falsely stating that she had made a dash for it again. She was quite the scamp, he had added, tossing out one last mention (casual) that we would likely be out there for quite a while.

It wasn't a bad little plan. Whoever the real villain was, he or she would know—or would think they knew—that the card had been retrieved from my house days ago. They would want to discover how we still had the thing in our possession.

Interestingly enough, the gang all seemed to remember the original postcard. Outgoing mail, we learned, was left out in the open at the Ariadne, where any of the residents could see it. The brightly accoutered McKnight had not gone unnoticed. The Cottons had appreciated the high-quality stock, curious if they could use that weight for Chris's smaller photos. Niles had thought it odd that one of the residents should be corresponding with anyone on the outside, whereas Jelena had wondered when they had changed the month that we celebrated Christmas in this country. Malcolm, barely aware of any artist other than himself, had found the painting on the card quite stirring in its way, but lacking in the weighty anguish of a Rosso.

No one would admit to turning the card over and looking at its contents, which I could hardly credit. It was a postcard—everybody turns over postcards.

They also wouldn't speak about Stothard Hope. They were still maintaining that he had been a guest and nothing more.

We knew at least one person at the table was lying.

I came out of my thoughts to attend to an itch on my right ankle. I was beginning to feel silly camped out under the piano. There was no denying that we were out of place in this McKnight homage. There were definitely no PIs or Maltese in the original work. Although, who's to say what the artist had left out due to time restraints?

From my angle, just below one of the full-length windows, I could see straight out at the moonlit ocean. We were completely surrounded by water now.

I shared my Alcatraz analogy with Hutton. He said he could see why I would say that, but if you asked him, the place was more like that Scorsese film, *Shutter Island*—the one where Matt Damon digs around at the 1920s mental institution.

I agreed that the Ariadne was certainly somewhat mental-institution-ish, in its way, but took issue on one point: "Matt Damon wasn't in *Shutter Island*, dude. That was that other guy. The guy from the *Italian Job*."

"Michael Caine?"

"Not that *Italian Job*, the new *Italian Job.*"

"DiCaprio?"

"No, no, DiCaprio was the one in *The Adjustment Bureau*."

"I thought that was Mark Wahlberg?"

"The *Antiques Roadshow* host?"

"Not Mark L. Walberg, the other Mark Wahlberg. The action Wahlberg."

"Oh," I said. "Well, I don't think either one of them was in *Shutter Island.* I think you're thinking of the guy who was in *The Basketball Diaries.*"

"Maybe that was Matt Damon."

Perhaps. I was very confused now.

So was Hutton. "Which one was in the *The Departed*?" he asked.

We shelved the Damon-DiCaprio-Wahlberg enigma until we could consult IMDB.

I peered up over the chair to make certain the decoy postcard was still on the side table.

The card was still there.

"By the way," I asked, slipping back into position, "I saw you scribbling on the back of the dummy postcard earlier. What did you write?"

"Not write, *drew*."

"What did you *draw*, then?"

"A sketch of a hedgehog mooning the viewer. I felt the artistic instinct. I would have drawn something else, but I only know how to draw hedgehogs."

I nodded. Didn't quite have the flair of Stothard Hope's original message, but the sentiment was good. For a dummy card.

I leaned back, checking the position of the moon in the sky. I couldn't determine the time from this, but I could tell it was late. We had been at this for hours.

"Has it occurred to you," I said, "that we might be too clever for our own good?"

"Frequently. Why do you ask?"

"Just this. Whoever we're after was fooled by Stothard Hope's postcard once. They didn't realize it was a coded message, correct?"

"Correct."

"Well, what's to say that, after retrieving it from my house, this person—"

"Call him Johnny Herring."

"What's to say that this person, this so-called Johnny, would even care. In other words, he gets the card back from my place a couple days ago, can't make heads or tails of it, and therefore pays no attention to your mention of a dummy card now. He can't be too concerned about something he doesn't understand."

Hutton refuted this argument, as vigorously as he had refuted my assertion that Matt Damon had started his career as a rapper.

"He would never have gone to the trouble of retrieving the card the first time, Hath, if he wasn't concerned about it. He (or she) would be irresistibly drawn to our claim of another card. Human psychology."

"As opposed to canine psychology?" I asked. Pixie growled.

"As opposed to no psychology," said Hutton. "We will get a visitor tonight, Hath. You can bank on that." He tapped his head knowingly. "Psychology. Human."

I peered over at the door. We had no visitors. Human or otherwise. "So what do you think the card meant? What was Stothard Hope trying to tell us?"

Like all art, Hutton felt the card's message was open to individual interpretation.

"In other words, you still don't know?"

"No."

I had a few ideas myself. "Maybe we're looking at it the wrong way. We've been focused on the text. Maybe the message is in the picture. Like the message we sent Lesley."

Hutton agreed that that would certainly make things more baffling.

"If it is the picture," I continued, "then what could it mean?"

Hutton had no idea. Pixie sniffed to indicate that she was also out of theories. She licked her paw thoughtfully.

I mused: "The painting is very colorful. Very red. It depicts the White House. The White House Red Room. White. Red." I slapped my forehead.

Pixie jerked up from her paw-licking and stared reproachfully. More roughhousing like that and she was going to ruin her manicure.

"It's so obvious. Red room—*red*. Malcolm *Rosso*. Rosso means red in Italian."

Hutton wasn't as astounded by my reasoning as I was. "You've always been down on poor Malcolm. What did he ever do to you?"

"Nothing. But you can hardly deny that his name means red."

"Sort of. So, for that matter, does Rudd."

"As in the assassin Rudd?"

"Do you know another Rudd in this adventure?"

"No, but how could Tony Rudd be the man we're after?" How could I put this?—"He's dead!"

"So?"

"So! He couldn't be the killer. He's the *killed*."

"You never said we were talking about the killer, Hath—only people whose name means red. Besides, if Stothard wanted to demonstrate red, there were plenty of other cards that would do that. Why pick a Christmas one? It's confusing."

"Okay, maybe it had nothing to do with red," I conceded. I went back to musing. Hutton shut his eyes. Pixie licked. "Wait a minute," I said. "Christmas! Maybe that was the message."

Hutton opened his eyes. "It *was* an unusual time to send a Yuletide greeting. So where does that get us?"

I would have thought it obvious. "*Christopher* Cotton of course!"

Hutton blinked. "Because Christopher means Christmas?"

"Of course it does."

"Does it?"

"Sort of."

He gave a careful nod. "You're very hip to words that *sort of* mean things, aren't you?"

I supposed I was. "You have to admit, though, it's a thought."

"Is it?"

"Sort of."

Hutton *sort of* had to admit that it was. "But why couldn't Stothard have been indicating Mrs. Cotton just as easily?"

"Why, what's her name?"

"Christine."

This dampened my theories somewhat. Christopher and Christine Cotton. How quaint.

What was this investigation's problem? Two Red names. Two Chris names. Two past masters' names (twice). Two Johnnies. Two Mark Wahlbergs (sort of). All we needed was another Pixie, a second Lesley and a backup Jill, and we would be all set.

"Fine, what's your idea?" I asked.

Hutton didn't have one. He reminded me that he didn't like blurting out his working theories until he was certain they had a chance of—how could he put this?—*working*. It was a trait he shared with the older Enescu Fleet.

I continued to ponder. Pixie closed her eyes. Hutton chewed on a hangnail. The night wore on.

I was still weighing the plausibility of Chris and Christine Cotton as a latter-day Bonnie and Clyde when a creaking floorboard sent a jolt through my body. Hutton knocked off his gnawing, and Pixie shot from the spot in an explosion of barks and yaps.

Our trap had worked!

I don't know who was more startled, the three of us behind the chair, or Christine Cotton, seeing us pop out at her from the furniture.

She staggered back, panting freakishly. "Who—? What—? When—?"

We were the ones asking the questions around here! "Where—?"

Hutton cut in ahead of me, "How did you get in here, Christine?"

She continued to stumble backwards, eventually landing on a creaky daybed in the corner of the room (another detail thankfully left out of the 2D McKnight).

Pixie bounded into her lap and started licking her forearm. You're not going to find many guard dogs this ferocious.

"You scared me half to death!"

"And you didn't answer our question," said Hutton.

"I thought it was the beast Cerberus!" she gasped.

"Well, it wasn't," he remarked. "So how about it?"

The panting had slowed to an even keel. She was able to speak semi-coherently now. "I was out exploring and must have come into the wrong room."

"Likely story," I said.

"It's true. You don't know how easy it is to get turned around in there."

"In where?" asked Hutton.

She flailed a distracted hand in the direction of the far wall. There was a slight opening in the wainscoting, a narrow crevice leading into the inner recesses of the museum. A secret passage. (I would have expect nothing less.)

Hutton stepped to the opening and together with Pixie peered inside.

"Um, Hut," I said.

They continued their examination. Hutton stared, Pixie sniffed.

"Hutton," I repeated.

Still no reply. Hutton snuffled, Pixie blinked.

"Young Enescu Fleet!" I shouted.

He turned my way. "Yes, Hath, what is it?"

I pointed at the side table. The dummy card had vanished.

Who was the dummy now?

## 23 — Under Wraps

We looked to Christine. Once we explained what had disappeared—as if she didn't know—she jumped to her feet, quivering from head to toe. "You don't think I have it?"

Hutton answered by submitting her to a careful search. More respectful of married women, I pointed out ripples and bulges in her dress for him to pat down.

There was nothing there.

"I said I didn't have it," she huffed at us. "Did it ever occur to either of you that someone might have slipped in here while you two were nestled behind that chair?"

"Nope," said Hutton, who didn't care for the word *nestled*. Nor did I. "Our faithful guardian would have sensed it." He pointed to the pup, currently rolling about on the floor like a furry wiggle-worm. "Or not," he sighed. He peered back at the secret passage. I knew what he was thinking. "Whoever they were, they couldn't have gotten far. Come on." He led us in.

Christine galloped ahead with a tiny pen-sized flashlight. It really was the Minotaur's labyrinth, this joint. The passage was long and murky and looked like something out of a home contractor's mock-up for a haunted house. Dim and cobwebby with framing material for walls.

About fifty yards in, we heard a noise. Sort of a tender rustling sound. Pixie heard it first. Always happy to do her bit, she lurched forward and chomped me on the ankle. Not exactly Cerberus, but it still smarted. Stupid dog.

Kicking off my Maltese ankle bracelet, I barreled down the musty passageway. Christine and Hutton followed, with Pixie barking at our heels. The next thing we knew we had met up in a collage of arms and legs. I was aware of the smell of orange blossoms, the sensation of Mrs. Cotton elbowing me in my back, the sound of Pixie squeaking underfoot and the sight of a silhouette taking a tumble right in my path. Shortly after that, we all toppled through a trapdoor in the wall and out into another room. We were in a heavily windowed hallway on the second floor of the museum.

Jerking myself free from the pile of humanity, I took a poll. Hutton. *Check.* Pixie, gnawing on Hutton. *Check, check.* Christine Cotton, crazy eyes a-goggle, incoherent gasps. *Check.* Jelena, robe strewn open. Lovely supple skin glistening in the moonlight. *Ch*—wait.

"Jelena?"

The model joined me among the perpendicular. "John."

This was no time for *Johns*. "What were you doing? You weren't spying?"

"I was not spying, John, no. I was exploring."

I nodded. Exploring. Made sense to me.

Mrs. Cotton was not so easily persuaded. "I guess you're not going to bother searching *her*?"

Jelena peered across at her accuser in pouty inquiry. She transferred this inquiry to us.

"What is this searching?" she wondered.

"We're missing a little something from our rooms," Hutton explained. "You remember the Stothard Hope postcard we mentioned at dinner?"

"It has disappeared?"

"Like a disreputable second cousin with the family silver."

"What is this?" asked Jelena uncomprehendingly.

"It has disappeared," he said.

Jelena could see where this was going. Without a word, she undid her sash, lifted her silken robe off her shoulders and let it slip to the floor.

"The clue you seek, it is not here," she informed us. We could see it was not.

"She's good," said Hutton.

I nodded. "Yup, good," I confirmed, my mouth suddenly dry. It felt warm in there. Did anyone else feel warm?

This little trick of hers, shedding her clothing and looking all slinky and naked and all that, it was getting old. I mean, I was an affianced man. How many times did she believe she could bewilder us with that maneuver? Seriously, how many? Five, six more times? Ten?

An instant later, after I had cleared the sweat from my eyes and Hutton had picked up the robe and checked the pockets, we were able to focus on what we were doing.

"If Christine doesn't have the card, and Jelena doesn't have the card, and Pixie—" He hesitated. "No, not even a real wombat could consume 300-gram card stock that fast. If we don't have it," he went on, "then the person who has is still inside. Right. Back into the breach."

We filed back in. Hutton led the way again, and I brought up the rear. "If you didn't come for the card," I whispered to Jelena, "then what were you doing in here?"

It was a plan, she replied. After we mentioned the postcard, it occurred to her that one of the residents might know more about it than they had let on. They might try to retrieve it. She was lying in wait for this person.

Very cunning, I thought. The old lying-in-wait trick. Good one.

The light got better in the next section. It looked like we were inside the belly of a great wooden frigate. Not that I had seen many frigate bellies, mind you. We met up together in a dank corner, jam-packed with copper piping.

I took Jelena aside. "If you were in the passageway, then you must have seen who took the card?"

She shook her head. "I am sorry to say that I saw no one. When I heard Christine approach, I made myself what do you call it—scarce. I skedaddled."

Up ahead, Hutton cleared his throat. We had a decision to make here. We had arrived at a fork in the frigate. One path led up a set of rickety stairs, the other down a set of rickety stairs. It was decided that the girls would take the high rickety stairs, the boys the low.

"What did you learn from Jelena?" he asked as the two of us headed onwards and downwards.

I frowned, choking on a cobweb. Learned? Was I supposed to have learned something?

"Personally I learned why Christine has been exploring these passages," he said. "I got her to open up while I was helping her step around that dead rat."

"There was a dead rat?"

"You've gotten most of it off you by now," he remarked. "Anyway, that small act of chivalry helped defrost Mrs. Cotton's reserve. She told me what she has been seeking."

"And what is that?"

"Treasure. With a capital T. Seems her husband and she have heard that there is gold in these thar museum walls. I guess our blackmailees aren't having such a bad time here, after all."

I guess they weren't.

I smacked at an invisible spider on my neck. "Have they found any?"

"No. She was making another pass at it tonight, but then she saw Jelena and hightailed it out of there. That's how she wound up in your room."

I told him that was funny, because Jelena had said the same thing about Christine. Except she had featured a skedaddle instead of a hightail.

Hutton found this interesting, very interesting indeed. He would have thought Christine more the skedaddling type. "Now what's this?" he asked, focusing the lamp.

He was using Christine's penlight. And oh what a mighty beacon it was too.

In the middle of the wall there was a knob. A small decorated knob, gleaming in the light.

"Should we turn it?" I asked.

"Only one way to find out," he said, reaching out and twisting. Actually there were other ways. Plenty of others.

Nothing happened. Then there was a creak, then a clunk and then the wall gave out behind me. I fell.

"Where are we?" Hutton whispered, climbing over me with the support of my spleen.

We had never been in this room before, but I knew it immediately. Large rugged space, cloths strewn here and there, all around the mild smell of rock quarry and contemporary artist. We had arrived in Malcolm Rosso's studio. Had to be.

It was quiet, chillingly quiet. I had gotten so used to the *tap, tap, tapping* of the man's hammer and chisel day and night, that now that we were inside, the complete silence was oddly unsettling.

"What have we here?" asked Hutton. He had worked his way around the room, pausing at a six-foot-high mound of lily-white drop cloths. "I believe we have stumbled upon the infamous marble Jelena. Shall we have a peek?" He bent down and lifted up the corner of the cloth.

"Hands off!"

And just like that the artist was among us. He had sprung out from a sort of improvised pup tent in the back of the studio. A couple drop cloths and an old standing lamp and there you had it: a pile of crap fit for a king.

"Just what do you think you're doing?" he yelled.

Hutton released the cloth and faced him. Evidently the genius slept in his studio—all the better to be near his baby. He was dressed in a sleeveless white T-shirt, striped pajama bottoms and a hairnet. Yes, a hairnet. The man seldom showered, never changed his clothes, and only shaved every other Wednesday, but preserving his coif during slumber—that was essential.

"How did you get in here?" he demanded.

That was a very good question. An excellent question. I turned to Hutton and put this excellent question to him. It was a long story, my friend indicated with a gesture.

"Just what do you think you were doing with my statue?" As he asked this, he removed the hairnet and ruffled his hands through his greasy locks.

Hutton took up the query. "We meant nothing prurient, I assure you. Just wanted to see how it was coming, pass along any constructive criticism that might occur to us. I'm no artist, but I should think that the *gluteus maximus* in particular—"

"Get out!"

He took each of our shirt backs in hand and ushered us toward the door. I seemed to get there faster than Hutton. The sculptor's left was definitely stronger than his right.

"No one sees the piece until it is finished!" he bellowed, flinging us out into the hall.

The door slammed shut. We were alone.

But not for long. The sound of a particularly grumpy throat being cleared brought us around with a start. Christopher Cotton was standing in the main entranceway, peering in at us from beneath the brim of his floppy rain hat.

"What was that all about?" he grunted, pushing his glasses back on his crooked nose.

Hutton ignored the question and asked one of his own. "Little late for a stroll, isn't it?"

"I was out searching for that blasted dog of yours."

"Were you really? Why would you do that?"

"You said she'd run off, hadn't you?"

Hutton's face cleared. "I do recall saying that, yes. And you went after her? Good man."

Cotton clearly resented the term. (Still, better than his wife and her *nestling* comment. Stupid woman.) "Can't have her freezing her tail off out there," said the geezer.

"No, we cannot," agreed Hutton. "You're a kind man, Chris Cotton. So, did you find her?" he asked—a rather facetious question, I thought.

Cotton shook his head.

"Ah well, suspect she will turn up eventually," Hutton declared, and in what I have always considered especially good timing, at that moment she did. A whooshing sound between our ankles and the mutt had appeared. Christine and Jelena followed.

There was an unusual air about them. More unusual than usual. Christine greeted her husband with a distant nod. When he asked her where she found the dog she said *she'd love a cocoa, thank you*. When he said she looked a mess she replied *marshmallows would be lovely.*

Jelena, on the other hand, while not quite as super-goofy as Mrs. Cotton, was hardly the free-spirited proud beauty we had come to know and love. Her robe was tied tight, her *gluteus maximus* locked away from the world. She seemed distracted. If I didn't know better, I'd almost say she and Christine had just seen a ghost.

Cotton took off his hat and hung it on the hook. "Shall we go up?" he asked.

"Third cupboard from the right," answered his wife absently.

Absorbing this bit of dialogue, Hutton turned to Jelena. "Any luck in your explorations?"

She raised and lowered her shoulders. "I would not say we had luck, no. We arrived at the dead end."

"Did you?'

"Yes. Very much the dead end. Yourself?"

Hutton said, "Dead end, yup."

We were all on the same page, then. About what, I couldn't tell you.

"Well, I'm going to bed," said Cotton with determination. "See you upstairs, dear."

"I guess I should be leaving as well," said Jelena. Christine followed, babbling something about marshmallows and shortbread.

"That was weird," I commented.

For once Hutton and I were in complete agreement. It *was* weird. Completely weird. He picked up Pixie and brushed back the fur from her eyes. He peered in at her with a penetrating gleam behind the specs.

Another minute and he'd be inquiring where she was on the evening of the 5th and whether there was anything she wished to tell us.

She yawned. She only wished to tell us that she was tired.

I was feeling pretty unrested myself. Hutton, however, required no sleep.

He had a hunch.

"If it involves playing good cop bad cop with the dog," I said, "you can count me out."

It didn't involve good cop bad cop, but Pixie did have her role. With the mutt still in hand, he reached in his back pocket and removed Malcolm's hairnet. He must have swiped it while the artist was giving us the bums' rush. "Hold this for a second, would you?"

"You hold it," I recoiled. I had already stepped in dead rat that night. I had to draw the line somewhere.

Hutton frowned at my lack of cooperation. With a dignified snort, he took the squirming animal to the studio door, opened it, stuck the net in her mouth and booted her softly inside. One Maltese cocktail, shaken not stirred. (My bet was it would be pretty stirred as well.)

"Wait for it," he instructed, retreating to a sensible distance. I followed.

We waited for it. A moment passed and Pixie came darting out of the studio, with Malcolm a couple steps behind. It was hard to tell with her mouth full, but she seemed to be saying, "Come and get it, stinky." They disappeared down the hall, one after the other.

"Let's go," said Hutton. "We don't have much time."

As soon as we were inside the studio again, he went straight for the statue: examining an ankle under the sheet with long, sensual caresses. Seemed pretty prurient to me. He let the veil drape back in place and went over to Malcolm's tools. He selected a mallet. He stared at this, turned, looked at the covered statue a moment, and then unceremoniously smashed the man's sleeping accommodations into rags. And he said I was the one who had it in for the guy.

"That was mean."

He assured me that this was not wanton destruction on his part. He crept up to the wall, running his hand along the seams of the grout in the exposed brick. "Get me the chisel."

This I could handle. Hairnets no, chisels sure. I passed him the tool, and he made a few quick calculations. He placed the chisel in place, wound back on the mallet and let it fly.

One shot Hutton, that's what they call him. As soon as he hit, a section of wall came loose and landed in a thump on his right. Once the dust had cleared I saw he had revealed another passage: only more rustic. Actually, it was more of a tunnel.

"I wonder how long the tapping we've been hearing was this," he said.

I didn't get it.

"The ankle was smooth and polished," he explained.

And the crow flies at midnight. His point?

"The detailing on the statue is complete, Hath. Malcolm wasn't trying to keep us from seeing an unfinished product. He was trying to keep us from seeing that it *was* finished."

I got it. "Then the statue was his cover?"

"For the last few days I would guess, yes. He didn't want anyone to know about this little side project of his."

I nodded. Just as I had thunk—Alcatraz, right down to the escape plan. "He was tunneling out!"

"Not tunneling out. Tunneling *in*."

I was back to not getting it. He gestured me to follow. He would explain it to me on the other side.

I've been in some pretty tight spots before, but none quite as tight as this. I missed those luxurious corridors we had explored with Jelena and Christine. We inched along—dust, grime and who-knows-what other wall innards grinding up against us. We eventually came to another dead end. Hutton shined the penlight.

"Go on, then."

"Go on then, where?" I snapped. He reached out and tilted my head at a crevice. It was about ten inches wide, five feet high, ragged and torn, like a crack in a boulder. "You're joking!"

He never joked about crevices. "Slide through. It's not as bad as it looks."

It was. Every bit as bad.

I made it through somehow and staggered out from behind a wall tapestry—a wall tapestry, I might add, in need of a good beating out.

I was still spitting out bits of lint and finding dust bunnies in my hair (nowhere near as fun as beach bunnies), when I felt a hand on my shoulder. It was Hutton. I wished he would quit touching me.

He clicked on the lights and turned me around, and I was suddenly face-to-face with the most outrageous display of fine art I had ever seen in my life.

## 24 — Hidden Meaning

I needed a moment to soak it all in. Other than the paintings crammed across the midsection of the wall, the place didn't look like much of a gallery. It was more of a parlor, with fifty-foot ceilings, dry and neglected sticks of furniture all around, faded settees, murky lounges and lots and lots of garish wallpaper. Not that you could see much of the paper for all the frames. There were also no windows. I'd known casinos with more access to the outside world.

It was one crazy room-o-art, that was for certain.

"There's more back here," said Hutton, poking his head around the corner. I gave him a quick nod of acknowledgement, but didn't join him. I was good where I was.

Even I could tell we were in the presence of masterpieces (over three hundred of them, spread out over five rooms, I would later learn). I strolled down the line, taking in landscapes of pastel grandeur; still lifes that had more animation than many of the people I knew; portraiture of men playing cards, portraiture of women in white stockings and very little else; men in funny hats; women in funny hats; men and women in no hats at all; and tons of abstracts that looked like nothing from this world.

One of the headshots resembled a realist approach to Christine Cotton.

This was because it was Christine Cotton. She was standing at the tunnel entrance, gazing in at us from behind the edge of the woolen tapestry. She squeezed forward into the room, causing me to jump a foot.

Behind her was Jelena, wearing a T-shirt and khakis.

Jelena looked at Christine, Christine at Jelena. The latter spoke for them both. "So you've found it too," she said.

"What is this place?" I asked them.

I would say roughly a minute had elapsed between Jelena's last statement and mine. Nobody had felt like ruining the moment.

"You are in the main collection room of the Locke Foundation," Jelena replied.

"*The treasure*," added Christine Cotton, drawing the word out.

Jelena rolled her eyes and continued, "It spreads out over five rooms. These are the rooms we could not get inside. Behind the *door*."

I checked behind me and sure enough there it was. The door.

I was annoyed. "How long did you plan on keeping this a secret?"

Christine shook her head vigorously. "We found it tonight, we swear. We knew about it, of course. But it wasn't until tonight that we finally got around the locked door."

"And what was so special about tonight?"

"It was something he said," she chirped, pointing at Hutton. Hutton peered behind him.

"And what was that?"

"He said something about taking the high road while we took the low road."

I frowned. Actually it was the high staircase, but who was counting. "So what?"

"It's from that old song, the song about Scotland."

"And old Celtic folk songs always make you remember hidden art treasures?"

"No. But Scotland always makes me think of Ireland. And Ireland makes me think of green, and green of greenhouses, and greenhouses of arboretums. And of course arboretums are like conservatories, and from there my mind went to the conservatory in this house. So, you see, his remark told me everything I needed to know."

It wasn't all I needed. "That explains why you went to the McKnight gallery—sort of. How did you wind up in this room?"

"Oh." She laughed. "I realized the conservatory was the one room I had never looked for a secret passageway in. I had accounted for every other inch of the museum, but I never tried in there. Most of it doesn't share any walls with the house. Also, I didn't want to disturb all the wonderful paintings. But there is one inner wall, just as you come in, and Jelena and I gave it a try and wouldn't you know it, we found a new passageway. It led straight here."

Wouldn't we know it.

"Well, maybe not *straight* here," she qualified. "It got pretty narrow in there, but still wide enough to move. I think they left the space between the walls extra wide in order to allow for all the passageways. They say Mr. Locke had these passageways built so guests could tour the house without disrupting the layout of the rooms. You could see inside the rooms without actually going inside."

I nodded. Nothing disrupts a house like a bunch of people in it.

"I don't think he liked his fellow man very much," continued the prattling Christine. "He was very particular about guests, people asking to come here. They say he used to pee on letters from those he didn't like and mail them back, COD. One of these, I understand, was from the head of the Architectural Society, arguing that the hollow walls were compromising the integrity of the house's design."

Hutton cut in to say he had observed this himself: not Locke peeing on anything, but the hollow walls. It was this extra hollowness that paved the way for our death-defying escape from the basement the other day. (He forgot the part about someone opening the door for us.)

"Of course, the puppy helped," said Christine, uninterested in our death-defying escape. "Once we got inside the passage, she sniffed out a path to this opening. And here we are."

I knew the Maltese breed had to be good for something. "And where is *here* again?"

"The Locke Collection."

"And what is that?"

Christine stared blankly at me. In the microsecond between the words "Locke Collection" and my question she had become completely absorbed in a Renoir. "Huh?"

Jelena took up the slack. "The Locke Collection is the second-largest private collection of modern art in the history of the world," she answered blandly.

"Second largest?"

"It is said that there was a larger one in Philadelphia a while back, but ours is nicer."

It did seem pretty nice. "What's it doing locked up in here?"

"That wasn't our doing," said Christine. She was goggling at a Cézanne now. "Vroom installed the lock."

"And did the Lockes install the *vroom*?" I quipped. Nobody got it. "Wait a second! *Vroom?* As in Cornelis Vroom?"

The very Vroom, agreed the ladies.

"The Vroom Gallery is trying to absorb the Locke Collection," Jelena tossed out.

"Absorb it? How the hell—"

"It's really very simple," said Christine. "For three quarters of a century the Locke family had amassed this amazing collection of art."

"Yes?"

"The Vroom Gallery wants it."

"Sure. Who wouldn't?"

"Well, that's all there is to it," she said.

The rest of the explanation—or any explanation—would have to wait.

There was a tapping at the arched door behind us.

Everybody froze. When you're holed up in a gigantic makeshift gallery at one a.m., surrounded by yards of secret priceless art, you're not exactly yearning for visitors.

"Nobody say anything!" exclaimed Christine Cotton. I could see she was new at this.

"*Hey,*" came the voice of Niles Brisbane through the door, *"is there someone in there?"*

"Don't answer!" exploded Christine.

Jelena went to the door. She spoke distinctly: "We are in here, Niles. We cannot open the door. You will have to come in through the conservatory."

Here Hutton interrupted again to say the studio route would be faster. She motioned him over to give instructions. I'd known him to give the same detailed directions to lost motorists, men and women who were never seen or heard from again.

After a couple false starts, a few muffled oaths and several pulls from Christine Cotton, Niles Brisbane popped out to greet us. It was like extracting a giant bald bottle plug. Stumbling out into the center of the room in his PJs, he stood staring up at the surroundings, agog. If he had thought ahead to bring his pipe, it would have toppled out of his open mouth.

"You didn't have any trouble with Malcolm, did you?" Hutton asked him.

Niles turned and blinked. "What?" he whispered. "No. He wasn't there. Is this—?"

"It's the room," gushed Christine, returning to his side and dusting him off. "We finally got inside!"

He stared at her. He had no words.

Hutton frowned. "Was there something else you needed, Niles?" He didn't like to be rude, but we had matters to discuss and the man's continued goldfish impersonation wasn't getting us anywhere.

Niles closed his mouth. "We have a guest," he replied.

"At this hour? Who?"

"Says his name is Gerome Lance."

This struck a chord with me. Gerome Lance. Gerome Lance. I had heard the name Gerome Lance before.

Hutton nudged me. He took me aside at the tapestry. "Gerome Lance! Remember Gerome Lance, Hath?"

"Sort of…"

"The con artist who has been eluding the authorities in Europe for decades!"

Oh, *that* Gerome Lance. It was all coming back to me. "The dude you thought you were accosting in the men's room the other day?"

"The very dude. He must have gotten word of all this."

"How?"

"Lesley probably told him."

I raised an eyebrow. "Why would *Lesley* tell him anything?"

"He is her papa, isn't he?"

It was my turn to stare. My pal had finally lost what little mind he had come here with. "But Gerome Lance *isn't* Lesley's papa, remember? Remember, you went to great pains to prove that?"

"But maybe he is," said Hutton. "Maybe I was wrong, which is to say right. Maybe that's why our host requested him. Maybe Lawrence Darlington was Lance all along."

"He wasn't," replied a new party from behind the tapestry.

We whirled around. In stepped Enescu Fleet.

## 25 — Fleeting G. Lance

I noticed he wasn't covered in any bits of fluff. His tweed was pristine.

Fluffy or not, he was a welcome sight. I only had one question. "Gerome Lance?"

He didn't miss a beat. "In the flesh." He shook my hand. "You must be Johnny."

I rattled with the shake. I supposed I must be.

He gave Hutton a glance. "Enescu."

Hutton said, "Hi." For all his pretensions as the new and improved Fleet, he appeared unusually nonplussed at accepting the role.

"And whom have we here?" wondered our visitor, turning to the rest of the room.

Hutton played a cautious emcee: "This is Niles and Jelena. Christine Cotton on drums."

"Charmed," said Fleet. "And who is this little rascal?" he asked, peering down at Pixie. Evidently she had followed him in from the studio passageway. She bounced about, pawing his trousers. Then she piddled. That seemed to cover the introductions for now.

"I'm not interrupting anything, am I?"

No one had an answer. Maybe he was interrupting, maybe he wasn't.

He looked around the room. "I see you have unwrapped your gift a day early."

No one confirmed this. Maybe we had unwrapped, maybe we hadn't.

"And now you are no doubt wondering how I come into the picture?"

"As a matter of fact…" spoke up Niles Brisbane. There was no *maybe* about it.

Enescu Fleet pursed his lips. Or Gerome Lance pursed, or whoever the hell he was did the pursing. I was totally confused. "As you know, my name is Gerome Lance." [See what I mean, totally confusing.] "What you may not know is, I'm your host here."

Everyone stared. Christine, Jelena, Niles—people in the paintings. Everyone.

"So it is your thumb we are under?" asked Jelena.

"It is," said Fleet—let's call him Fleet.

"And it is the Locke Collection you are here to heist?"

"Again, it is. But you're frowning. Don't tell me you're going to shed any tears for these long-dead Lockes?"

She didn't appear to be shedding any; one of the few things she hadn't shed this weekend. "And we are going to help you with this heisting?"

"You are indeed. But not just me." I felt a hand on my shoulder. Fleet's right. His left went to Hutton. He brought us together.

Jelena was shocked. Shocked and appalled. (She wasn't the only one.) "*Them?*"

"Of course. Who better to assist in this magnificent heist than Enescu Fleet, master PI?"

"And *him*?" Her eyes had gone all flinty, focused in my direction. There was such a wealth of heat and disappointment in them that it reminded me of my loving fiancée. (I missed her.) "He is part of this too?"

"A huge part. You know who he is, don't you?"

Jelena wiggled her lips to suggest that she only thought she did.

"Who is he?" wondered Niles Brisbane. Christine seconded the question with a nod. I was rather curious myself.

"You've heard of the Herring crime family?"

They had.

"I give you the son, the infamous Johnny Fishes."

And he punctuated this reveal with another friendly shoulder grasp.

Like that helped.

The three of us were alone in the room-o-art now. Just Gerome and the boys. Everyone else had been sent to bed without their cocoa.

"That should settle their hash for the moment," said my cheerful christener. He picked up Pixie (the only creature in the room he hadn't actually named) and gave her head a pat.

I couldn't speak for my fellow residents, but my hash was still plenty unsettled. "Johnny Herring?" I asked. "Seriously?" He had done this to me before. He seemed to take a perverse pleasure in assuming names on my behalf.

"It had to be done," said Fleet, still patting Pixie's head. He'd probably get to mine next.

"It may interest you to know," I clued him in, "that I've already been told by one person this weekend that no one would buy me as Johnny Herring."

"The eccentric recluse with possible homicidal tendencies? Don't sell yourself short."

"Thanks." I paused. "Are you actually Gerome Lance?"

"No."

That was something. Not a lot, but something.

He set Pixie on a marble podium at his elbow—*Maltese Overlooks Her Subjects.* "We don't have much time. We all have questions. Let us speak them quickly and in low voices." Why he was sounding like a Shakespearean conspirator all of a sudden, I couldn't say.

"How'd you get here?" I wondered. "The tide's still in. Or is that out? Doesn't matter. How'd you get here?" I wondered.

"It would be a pretty poor Fleet who couldn't reach a simple island, Johnny."

Of course. He had a boat. Probably stowed somewhere, ready for a rapid getaway. Good. Next question: "Did you get our message?"

"I did, and I must say I was astounded by your ingenuity. I take it the call was bugged?"

"Something like that."

"It would be. But you out-thunk the bugger. The photo you sent was sheer genius."

Hutton stuck his oar in here. He could never leave a thing alone: "I had a hand in that, you know."

Fleet commended him. Nicely done times two, he remarked.

"Hath and I had a bit of a disagreement on which painting we should send."

"Did you? Well, I'm glad you compromised and sent both."

Hutton and I shared a look. "Compromised?" I asked. "Both?" he said.

Fleet nodded. "*Blue Sail Fleet Returns* together with *Setting the Trap*. It was brilliant."

We supposed it must have been.

"I mean, either by itself and I might not have understood. But side by side? Masterful. How did you manage to frame the shot of those two paintings so perfectly?"

I made a gesture, indicating that it was just a knack. Hutton replied that it took some heavy jockeying. You don't just stumble on a brilliant code like that by accident.

With that settled, I asked Fleet where he had been all this time.

The question seemed to startle him. "For some of it, I was consulting with my McKnight expert in Connecticut."

I nodded. He was still on that, then. Even still, he might have wrapped it up a little quicker. "The last time I checked, Connecticut and Maine were basically in the same area."

"It depends what part of Maine and what part of Connecticut. For me, the drive took just over four hours each way. But it was worth it. You'll be pleased to know that it was a fruitful visit."

"You learned something?"

"Not yet. But I expect we shall. I've planted a few ideas. We just have to wait and let them flourish."

Didn't sound all that fruitful to me. Sort of seed-related, but not fruitful. "Did you just get back?"

"Somewhat recently, yes."

"Then how in God's name do you know so much?"

"About our situation? Speculation tempered with common sense. I've not been idle this weekend. Even while driving I've been stitching everything together in my mind."

That was super. "Care to take us through it?" I inquired.

He said he'd be only too happy. "You and Hutton arrived here two days ago. You were lured in by a text message from Stothard Hope—or that was how it was meant to appear. Since arriving, you have been set upon by Tony Rudd, discovered his corpse and have been framed for his murder by the very person my recent arrival was meant to disrupt."

I stood blinking at him. "How could you possibly know all that?"

"Simple PI work. I retraced your steps to Ye Olde Weapon Shoppe. I've reconstructed your movements here at the museum." He paused. "Also, Cornelis Vroom told me."

Hutton and I both blinked. "You've talked to Vroom?" we asked.

"Not exactly talked, no. Thanks to Hutton's claim that he was me I've been able to move pretty freely in this investigation. Some of Vroom's men followed me initially, but once I had convinced them that I was nothing more than an actor playing a part, they pretty much left me alone. I've had carte blanche."

"How'd you convince them you were an actor?"

"Oh, you know. A few trips to a local theater where a friend allowed me to run through some lines from *Our Town*; several visits to the neighborhood spa. You know how it is."

Actually I didn't. But I got the gist. (I was glad someone was getting use out of the spa.) "And because of this, Vroom took you into his confidence?"

"Oh no. He would never do that. He just wasn't as wary as he might have been. I was able to make my investigations of him unobserved. He knows quite a lot, our Vroom. But I have been dominating the conversation. If you have been here two days, you have no doubt learned something as well?"

Actually we had. "Would you like to hear what we found?" Hutton asked him.

Fleet said he would be delighted. He leaned back and listened as Hutton shared our experiences. I was pleased to see he gave me credit on the can of kippers.

"So, if Tony Rudd's dying message is worth the tin it was written on," he concluded, "it looks like John Herring is our main suspect here."

Fleet offered no complaint with our interpretation.

It was nice not having him shoot down our theories for once. I don't know how Hutton felt about it, but the old guy sometimes made me feel like we were the Hardy Boys' slow-witted cousins, just marking time until Papa Fleet could arrive and set everything right. It was refreshing to be seen *and* heard.

I did have one question, though. Now what was it? Oh yes—

"What the hell is going on here?"

Fleet was waiting for someone to ask him that. After a glance at the door, and then the tapestry, he went over to an ancient gramophone in the corner. Selecting a record that had not quite turned to dust (and I thought CDs were old-fashioned) he cranked up some Haydn. I wouldn't have been surprised to learn that the LP had been recorded by Franz Joseph personally.

With the crackling music on to mask his speech, he took a seat on a sagging settee. Pixie bounded from the podium into his lap, and he began his tale.

## 26 — Signature Move

"Interestingly enough," said Fleet, "this story of murder, bribery and blackmail does not begin with Cornelis Vroom or John Herring or even master art thief Stothard Hope. It begins with the most savvy kingpin of them all."

"And who is that?" asked Hutton.

"Daniel Locke."

I didn't get it. "Ariadne Locke's father? He was no gangster."

"Perhaps not. But how much do you know about his collection?"

Hutton and I glanced between ourselves. "It's pretty," I offered.

Fleet agreed it was. Very pretty. And peerless. "The Lockes had always been good at spotting talent, especially talent others had yet to discover. Consider any legendary artist from the last hundred years or so, and some Locke somewhere knew them before they were anybody. And not just knew them; they bought up their work before they were anybody. Hoarded might be a better word. It was this hoard that drew Cornelis Vroom onto the scene."

"We're talking Junior here?" I clarified.

"We're talking Junior. The truth is, the elder Vroom is not much of a force anymore. After the Artist Colony disbanded, he more or less went straight. He's largely retired now. And unlike certain parties, he stays retired. He's into Greek pottery, restoration and collection. If you asked him, he probably would have preferred his son followed in those footsteps. As a boy, young Cornelis had quite a knack for painting. But it was not to be. The man you've met is every bit as devious as his father was in his youth, although not quite as given to violence as his pop once was. Discovering the Locke Collection was young Vroom's criminal masterpiece."

"So he's looking to swipe it?"

"Not exactly. A smash-and-grab would have been too bourgeois for him. This isn't his father's heist. He's *absorbing* it."

I didn't quite get this absorbing business. Jelena had used the term as well, and I couldn't help wondering how you absorbed art. Sounded vaguely fresco.

"After Daniel Locke's death," explained Fleet, "the entire collection went into trust. By rights it should have gone to his daughter Ariadne, but Locke didn't feel she could handle the responsibility."

"But it's the Ariadne Locke Museum and Whatsit?" I pointed out.

"True, but the collection is separate from all that. It's one of the many baffling things about the Locke family legacy. The house and the retreat belonged to her, as did all the art she would accumulate after her father's death. The collection is the collection."

"And it was this collection the old goat didn't feel the girlie could shoulder?" asked Hutton, champion of sexual equality.

"Correct. For that, he preferred a dispassionate third party, a board of right-minded men and women selected by his alma mater. This would turn out to be an ironic choice, because it was this very board that young Vroom would use to force his way in. By manipulating the trustees, he would end up getting his mitts on one of the most extensive collections of modern art the world has ever known."

I held up a finger. I hated to interrupt, but I didn't understand something. "If this collection is so damned famous and extensive, why haven't I ever heard of it?" I mean, I wasn't a complete cretin.

"Few people truly know of the collection. Locke made sure of that. Even before his death, it had always been one of Maine's best kept secrets. He used to invite special guests here, but they were never allowed to speak of what they saw. And few ever did. I'm sure most were afraid of him. He had that kind of personality. Rumors of its existence did get out, however, and when Locke died, some people wondered if the stories they had heard were true. Unfortunately, very few have been given an opportunity to investigate. That was his true legacy. Even the current trustees haven't had a proper tour. Of course, that wasn't Locke's fault. That was Vroom."

He stood up to attend to a skipping piano trio.

Poking the needle into place, he proceeded, "Ever since Daniel Locke started collecting, there have been rivals who wish to plunder his treasure trove. After Ariadne Locke died, and details of her father's collection became more widely known, museums began lining up as well. The Vroom Gallery was one of these museums."

"With Cornelis the Younger spearheading the operation?"

"None other. He brought just the right combination of traits to bear. He is obsessed with art and thanks to his own family's legacy, he knows how to steal it. As I've said, he didn't go about this the traditional way. He chose a semi-legal method. He went after the board."

"More blackmail?"

"More like good old-fashioned bribery. Knowing that Locke's alma mater controlled the board, and the board controlled the collection, Vroom made the former an offer they couldn't refuse. I'm not certain of the exact dollar amount he donated, but it was sufficient to establish the 'Cornelis Vroom' wing in the Fine Arts Department—named for his father, of course. It got young Vroom in the door. From there, he was able to ingratiate himself with the powers that be, eventually convincing them to allow him to add his own trustees to the board. Art department business became Cornelis Vroom business. Over the years, through coercion and reward, sometimes both, he managed to populate the entire board with people he could control."

"This board sounds like a real lot of weak reeds to me," said Hutton.

"You can decide that for yourself," Fleet offered. "You've met most of them."

"You mean—?"

"The current residents of The Ariadne Locke Museum. Christopher and Christine Cotton, Malcolm Rosso and Niles Brisbane. Those are four right there. Vroom employed varied techniques to get at them. Malcolm got shows to exhibit his own art, a campaign of underworld support that would have made Frank Sinatra blush. Niles was promoted to department head at the university. The Cottons got their charity—a real charity. They already had their foundation, but with Vroom's connections they could go mainstream, become preeminent givers."

Hutton whistled. "I had no idea charities and trusts were such a dog-eat-dog business."

Pixie perked up. She looked like she could go for a dog snack right about now—something small. A Chihuahua perhaps.

"So now," said Hutton, still pondering the finer points of the Art of the Vroom, "our square-headed friend can do what he likes with the Locke Collection?"

"As long as he remains inside the frame of the law, yes. And he chooses to have the entire collection moved."

"Into his living room?"

"Not exactly. He is not actually taking ownership of the art. He couldn't. He is simply moving the collection to a new facility associated with his gallery. Call it a permanent loan. There are parties fighting the move, claiming it violates the terms of Locke's will, but they don't have the wind at their backs. The government supports the relocation. And why wouldn't they? It's good for tourism."

Hutton said amazing.

I concurred. Made repelling down the side of a building and futzing about crawling under laser beams seem ridiculously old school.

"Once the board had approved his wishes," said Fleet, "Vroom no longer had any use for them. He had the rooms here locked up pending the relocation. And as you have just observed, not even the trustees have access."

"How come there's no security system?" I asked.

"Too much red tape. Changes to the house are not Vroom's to dictate. The collection rooms are under board control; the house and all the rest still belong to a separate trust established at Ariadne Locke's death."

I sighed on Vroom's behalf. Life as a white-collar gangster wasn't easy. "When is he moving everything?"

"Tomorrow evening."

This time I whistled. "The gala."

"The gala indeed. Vroom wants all of society's elite to witness his triumphant acquisition."

I smiled. The world's first public art heist.

"Meanwhile," inserted Hutton, "he has no clue that his board of stooges has been turned against him. It's funny in a way. Cornelis Vroom bribed the trustees, and Johnny Fishes is blackmailing them."

"Or someone is," agreed Fleet. He didn't like to commit to any working theory.

I had a question (just the one). "How did Stothard Hope enter into things?"

"Stothard was part of Vroom's scheme. They knew each other through Vroom's father. He helped manipulate the board. His natural charm would have come in handy. Young Herring also helped—although, from what I can tell, without so much charm. He played his role somewhat reluctantly. Originally he was the only one with a legitimate seat on the board. It was through him that Vroom first got the idea for his 'legal' heist. When Johnny and Stothard both vanished, Vroom got nervous that something was up."

I couldn't blame him. When your cohorts start disappearing, it would make any thug nervous. I had another question (just the two). "Why did our host request Lesley's dad? He asked for him specifically."

"Not specifically as it would turn out. The blackmailer asked for him because he believes he is Gerome Lance." He gave Hutton a look. "And apparently he is not the only one."

Hutton half-smiled. "You heard about that, did you?"

"Yes," said Fleet. "Ate told me about your little restroom adventure. That would have been helpful information to have a couple days ago."

Hutton said sorry. "He really does look like him, incidentally. From the photos I saw."

Fleet didn't argue. He had never met Lance in person, but he too had seen pictures. Evidently the man did bear a remarkable resemblance to my future pop-in-law.

"But what's his role here?" I wanted to know. "Who the hell is Gerome Lance—really?"

"Lance was another member of the Artist Colony syndicate," said Fleet.

Another one. Was anyone *not* a member? "Where is he now?"

"I've been wondering that myself. I'm sure Vroom offered to bring him in when he began assembling the old gang. It's a poser."

I sniffed. Apparently not enough of a poser to prevent him from impersonating the man. "You've explained why the blackmailer wanted Lesley's dad here. He thinks he's Lance. Fine. But why did he want Lance in the first place? Where does Gerome Lance come into this?"

Fleet nodded toward the door. "This is no time for levity," I replied.

"Not levity, Johnny. The lock."

"Ariadne or Daniel?"

"Neither. The lock-lock. Our host believes Gerome Lance has the key to the lock."

I frowned. What was so great about unlocking the door? "Why not just carry the art out through the secret passage?" Assuming the masterpieces didn't mind a bit of fluff.

"I'm sure that was the blackmailer's idea behind getting Malcolm to tunnel. That was his contingency plan. But the crevice, as it stands, is too thin. We could barely fit through ourselves, let alone carry out armloads of priceless art. As you can see, there are no windows, and there isn't enough time to make the passageway wider. That's two feet of stone each way. The only way the art is leaving this room is through that door."

"Jimmy the lock, then?"

"Not so easy. The lock uses a combination Abloy and Chubb. It's impossible to pick, or virtually impossible. There are probably only a handful of experts in the world who could handle it. Ironically, Stothard Hope was one of them. Equally ironic, he was also the man who had the key."

"He stole it from Gerome Lance?"

"No."

Of course. No one was really stealing anything here. Everything was perfectly legal.

Fleet continued, "Wherever Gerome Lance is, he never actually had the key; that's only what the blackmailer was led to believe."

"Then Stothard had it the whole time?" Hutton wondered.

"He did. Vroom trusted him more than anyone on his payroll. And this trust was nearly repaid in kind. Stothard is the one who figured out the conspiracy, the heist within the heist. That's when the blackmailer turned his guns on Stothard himself. We all have our soft spots. For Stothard this was his granddaughter Celeste. The only family he had. It's hard to say what scheme the blackmailer would have hatched against her, but with her welfare in play, Stothard's hands were tied."

I knew how he felt.

"Stothard warned Celeste, but he could not get word to Vroom so easily. He tried the next best thing. He sent out a coded postcard to the one man likely to decipher it. Then he hid the key, telling the blackmailer that he had given it to Gerome Lance."

I frowned. And now the key was lost, Hope was dead and the one man likely to decipher the postcard hadn't deciphered a damn thing as far as I could tell.

"Vroom only had the one key?"

"He only had one because there is only one. He didn't install the lock; he simply availed himself of it. Ariadne was the original installer. She had it put in in the mid-nineties. She also had a small lockbox designed. I believe you have seen this box?"

I had seen it.

"Daniel Locke himself never had any use for locks—his formidable demeanor was the only security he ever needed—but Ariadne Locke liked locks."

I let this sink in for a moment. Sometimes I felt the names in this investigation were just trying to be funny on purpose. "And no one thought to make a copy?"

"The key is an exceedingly complex design, difficult to duplicate. Ariadne probably thought it was more secure that way."

She was always thinking, that Ariadne. "Can't Vroom simply knock the door down?"

"He can, and he will. But that disrupts his plans for the gala. Should he fail to recover the key in time, he will have the door forced open. In which event he will cancel the gala and have the art moved without the fanfare. Admitting the key had been compromised would be a public embarrassment for him. As would blowing open the door."

I could see why. Dynamite does tend to cast a pall over a cocktail party. "And that would be so bad, canceling the gala?"

"For the blackmailer's scheme, it would be fatal. Our host doesn't have the resources for strong-arm tactics. In order for the heist to work, the door must be opened, the art must be moved. The blackmailer is depending on it. So are we. If Vroom cancels, who knows if we'll get another chance to nab the killer."

I did want the bastard nabbed, it was true. But how? That key could be anywhere now.

The Haydn piano trio had come to a close in the background. So had our trio.

"So we're stuck?" I said.

"Perhaps," answered Fleet. "Or perhaps not," he added, reaching in his trouser pocket. "You see, I have had the key for some time."

## 27 — Master of the House

It was a very toothy specimen, with a long, jagged blade and a triangular bow. A lovely key.

I took the initiative: "Where the f—?"

"Stothard Hope left it for me."

I felt slighted. All he had left me was a stinking postcard. "Left it for you where?"

"Here," he replied simply. I gave him a hard look, shared by Hutton. It was a look that said he would have to do better than that. Fleet gave in. "Do you remember noticing a certain tree on the property, Johnny—?"

I said I had noticed trees.

"—with the year 1834 carved into it? I saw it on my walk on our first visit. It was in the vicinity of this tree that I found the key."

I actually remembered the tree he spoke of. The birch. That tree had keys?

"It had been marked," said Fleet. "Obviously the date had not been carved in 1834, or anything like 1834."

"Obviously," I remarked. I paused. "Why?" I asked.

"As I'm sure you are aware, birch trees rarely live longer than 50 years. The carving had been made much more recently, and from the look of it, very recent indeed. Seeing it, I knew it had to be a signal from Hope. 1834 was the year the artist Thomas Stothard died."

So that was where he got the name Stothard. It was all coming together.

I tallied things up in my head. We didn't have much—no postcard, no murder weapons, no Herring. But we had a key, and that would at least open a few doors, so to speak. The show could go on.

"It all comes down to the gala?"

"It all comes down to the gala," agreed Fleet. He re-pocketed his keepsake. It was time for bed.

We opted to leave the hard way. According to the man who would be Lance, it would be better if the residents weren't aware we had the key. You never knew who might be watching.

Just before climbing back through the tapestry, he paused. He pulled out the key again and handed it to Hutton. "This needs to be returned to Vroom. It would be better coming from Enescu Fleet. The Fleet he hired. I'll get word to him on your behalf to expect the key tomorrow before the party. I'll explain that Herring and Hope have been hauled in for questions for some unrelated crime—it shouldn't be hard getting a phony police report. That should leave things open for Vroom to have his gala without concern for the Locke Collection's well-being."

Hutton accepted his sacred obligation. "Should I say a few words on the occasion, or—"

"Just give him the key," said Fleet.

We climbed on through, arriving on the other side relatively dust and fluff free. I was getting used to that passage.

There was still no sign of Malcolm in the studio. The man took the loss of his hairnet pretty hard.

"I don't know what bedroom you should take," I said, as we came out into the foyer. Hutton had already wandered upstairs with a vague wave of good night.

Fleet answered with a wave of his own, brushing aside my concern. "Don't worry, Johnny, I'll find something to my liking."

I had no doubt.

I paused on the steps. There was one thing I had forgotten to ask him in the collection room. Just a small question (number forty-six):

"How much is this art worth anyway? It's got to be in the hundreds of millions."

Fleet shook his head. "Oh no. Nothing like that."

"No?"

"No." He picked up Pixie and tickled her tummy. "From what I gather, something like five billion. Night, Johnny."

I don't know how well the man and his dog fared among the vacant rooms, but I slept fitfully in mine. Five billion. That's what he had said. Billion. He had definitely said *buh*. It was because of that *buh* that I tossed and turned the rest of the night.

The next morning Fleet had run out for some last-minute errands. He didn't say what. You couldn't expect a five-billion-dollar heist to keep him idle.

I spotted Hutton out on the property when I came down to lunch: looking for more trees with clues carved in them, no doubt. The rest of the residents were getting ready for the gala. According to a message left pinned to my pillow by Fleet, Vroom had agreed to a "request" from the board, allowing them to exhibit their own art during the party. It was good PR, the big man felt. Showed the board was on board. (All part of the blackmailer's scheme, or just more torture for the non-artistic residents? You decide.)

Malcolm was still not among the assembly. Several caterers and other party officials had arrived. Christine was busily forcing a recipe for tofu hors d'oeuvres on the chef. Jelena was ignoring advances from the male wait staff (and a few of the female). Niles was overseeing the arrangement of the resident exhibits in Malcolm's studio. And Chris Cotton was sulking because nobody had woken him last night to show him the amazing room of art. I was staying out of everyone's way, trying mightily to avoid sampling any tofu hors d'oeuvres.

Lunch came and went, and still no Malcolm. The man really had vanished. That meant one of two things to my mind. The blackmailer had done away with him or—as I had suspected from the beginning—Malcolm Rosso was the blackmailer himself. Or both. Well, maybe not both.

I returned to my room.

I had become pretty good at detecting things out of place in my quarters by now: cryptic messages from blackmailers, missing postcards, Maltese. This afternoon was no different. There was a tuxedo laid out on my pillow.

I picked it up, and a voice spoke behind me. I didn't even flinch. "Lesley helped with the measurements," explained Enescu Fleet. The man had returned (again).

"She gave you my size?"

"Yesterday. Meanwhile, my daughter supplied Hutton's measurements, a fact I would prefer not to dwell on."

I tried on the jacket. It was a pretty good fit.

"I'm sure the blackmailer would have provided you something to wear, but I couldn't chance it having a bad cut. I had my tailor work overtime to get this today."

I wasn't interested in haberdashery. "She's not coming, is she?"

"Lesley? No. I arranged a clambake for her family instead."

That was good. "Did she wonder where I was?"

"She did seem a little perturbed about that; but then her mother made a comment about how she and her father simply want what's best for their daughters, and the subject turned."

That was fine. A little off-putting, but fine. "Did Hutton give the key to Vroom yet?"

"Not yet. The man of the hour is due here in twenty minutes."

I continued getting ready. "Where have you been all day? Not arranging clambakes?"

"Not entirely. I had a few last-minute matters to contend with."

"Well, it's annoying not knowing what's going on. And it's not like I can call you." I hated not having my phone. I felt half-naked without it.

I looked in the mirror. I *was* half-naked.

Fleet handed me my trousers. "The blackmailer is no doubt hanging onto your phone, most likely to put with Tony Rudd's body. It will help incriminate you in his murder."

As long as it helped. "So where were you?"

"You keep asking that." He examined himself in the mirror. I wondered if he was planning on slipping on a tux himself, or would he be rolling out the dress tweeds this evening. "I've been looking into our fellow blackmailees, building on what you and Hutton learned."

"And?"

"For one, Christopher Cotton isn't here simply to support his wife. I'm not certain she knows this herself, but the blackmailer has evidence framing him for his father-in-law's murder."

The murder of his father-in-law. "And that would be wrong," I agreed, pausing. "Was her father murdered?"

"Not likely; but our blackmailer's evidence has certainly made it look possible. He is quite the artist. Cotton, you see, was guilty of one crime against his father-in-law: embezzling from the university."

Embezzling from the university? But that was Niles Brisbane's crime. Or his supposed crime anyway. So Cotton was the real embezzler. "How do you know all this?" It was becoming the question of the hour.

"I had a very interesting phone conversation this morning," answered Fleet, tearing himself away from his reflection. "It came in from your number, as a matter of fact. The blackmailer was using it. He told me to tread very carefully here. He then outlined a few of his frame jobs, such as the one surrounding Cotton."

"Whose voice was it?"

"Difficult to tell. He was disguising it."

"But it was a man?"

"Difficult to tell."

I sneered. "What did you say?"

"I set his mind at ease that Vroom would have the collection rooms open at six. He thanked me and hung up."

At least the villain was polite. "Is that all you learned?" He didn't even need to go out for that. I slid on my shoes and tied them. Pixie helped. "You still have that boat, right?" When the tide came in, or out, or whatever it was it did, I wanted to be certain we could still make our getaway.

"Actually, I've had to ditch the boat," said Fleet. "That was another of the blackmailer's provisions."

"And you complied?"

"Why not? He was so polite about it."

I shooed Pixie away. She wasn't getting the bows on the laces right at all. "He doesn't have something on you, does he?"

Fleet laughed—a rich, melodious laugh. "Really, Johnny? What could he have?"

"You have family."

"I do, but they're not here. And thanks to Hutton's convolutions, the blackmailer doesn't know who I am. He might suspect that I'm not Gerome Lance, but that's it."

I strode up and down the area rug. It was all well and good for him to be sanguine about it, but I wasn't settled. "We need a plan here. At least a plan to make a plan."

Fleet treated me to a melancholy smile. "You really don't know how to live in the moment, do you, Johnny?"

"Huh?"

"You're always looking to the future, when everything will magically improve and all your problems will be solved. They never are. You need to live in the present. Look at art. It freezes a moment in time. When are you going to start enjoying a moment that way?"

I replied, rather tartly, that I supposed I would starting enjoying the moment when the moment was worth enjoying.

"But isn't it worth enjoying now? You're in a nice old house. There's billions of dollars of art afoot, society's elite, the occasional naked woman. What more do you want?"

I did enjoy several of those things, he was right—

But no. I couldn't think about that now. Too much on my mind.

"Is it really worth $5,000,000,000?" I asked. I don't know why, but the whole idea of all those commas under my feet was making my pores sweat. Or maybe that was just the tux.

Fleet reflected. "Perhaps not five billion, no. People do tend to inflate their figures when dealing with art. It's probably only four. Three or four billion."

I said was that all?

It's hard to pick out any one thing at the gala and describe it. There was a lot going on. Most of New England's wealthy had arrived. As I came down the arched staircase an hour later, I was immediately thrown into a sea of Armani and whatever the equivalent evening wear would be for women. There were several local celebrities I vaguely recognized in the crowd; lots of politicians I wouldn't know from Adam but they looked like politicians; several pretty young ladies with dissipated old men; several pretty young men with dissipated old women; and Christopher Cotton.

He was standing over by the wonky sideboard in the foyer eating tofu. (And his wife wasn't even there. Now that was love.) I elbowed my way through society's elite and took refuge beside him.

He sniffed at me. "So it's Johnny Herring now, is it?"

I said sure, why not?

"Our reclusive board member finally reveals himself. Guess you had us all fooled."

I guess I had. More so than he would ever know.

"You're not what I would have expected from a crime boss's son."

"And what do you expect from a crime boss's son?" asked Fleet, sailing to my rescue.

As it turned out, he had changed into a tux: a very nice one. He wore it well. Better than I wore mine. Mere mortals wore garments; Fleet exhibited them.

"What's a crime boss's son supposed to have that Johnny doesn't?"

"Oh, I don't know," answered the older man. He chewed his tofu. "More fervor. Harsher language. Different hair."

"Well, I can't attest to the hair," said my sponsor, "but you can't have missed the killer instinct in his expression. Look at it." Christopher Cotton looked at it. "He has the brooding intensity of a criminal, does he not?"

Cotton gave another sniff. "I guess. The accent seems about right. When we all joined the board, someone mentioned that the Herrings hailed from England."

"There you have it," said Fleet, and sallied us away.

We went into Malcolm Rosso's studio. It had been converted into an industrial-chic ballroom. The bleached pine floorboards never looked so good.

"Just keep it up, Johnny," offered Fleet, by way of encouragement. What exactly I was supposed to keep up, I couldn't guess. "I have to see a man about something. Excuse me."

The man he needed to see was standing over by the resident exhibits, admiring Christine Cotton's Minotaur painting. Admiring might be the wrong word. He wasn't exactly reeling back in abject horror, but he clearly wasn't enjoying himself either. He moved down the line to Chris Cotton's photos. These seemed to soothe him. I was struck how easygoing he appeared. In fact, he seemed to be the most relaxed-looking man I had ever seen in my life. I envied him. He was a few inches shorter than Fleet, clean-shaven, tanned, and about sixty-five I would have guessed, going by the graying temples. He also wore his tuxedo well. He looked like James Bond—a well-aged, very relaxed James Bond.

Fleet and he fell into conversation.

The door to the collection rooms was now open, as the occasional *oo* and *ah* drifting down the hall would indicate. Guests did not have to crawl through any crevices to see the masterpieces. I had spotted Vroom in the foyer earlier, strutting about like a square-headed rock star. I assumed that Hutton's key delivery had gone off without any hitches. I hadn't actually seen Hutton in the last hour.

What I did see was Jill, my future sis-in-law. I cursed freely, causing one of the jaded old men in my vicinity to spill his drink on his date. I darted over to talk to Jill.

There was a nervous-looking young man whispering to her. Thickset jaw, curly blond hair, vaguely English looking—but in my circle, who wasn't? I didn't recognize him. As I approached, he faded behind an ice sculpture and began consuming jumbo shrimp with a wary frown. A couple of times he peered out toward the room, but only for a split-second—as long as it takes to poke one's head out, bite a shrimp and recede behind an ice sculpture again.

"Jill!"

Jill jumped. "Johnny. Don't sneak up on me like that! What's the matter with you?"

"What's the matter with me? What's the matter with you? What are you doing here? You're supposed to be at a clambake." I froze. That ice had nothing on me. "Wait, is everybody here?"

"If by everybody you mean Mum, Dad, Ate and Lesley, then yes. Everybody is here."

I blustered. "I specifically wanted—they were strictly told—I, we—dammit!"

Jill looked concerned. "I don't exactly get what you're saying there, sibling-to-be. What's on your mind?"

"What's on my mind? We, I—you have to get out of here. It's not safe."

"You do keep saying places aren't safe, don't you, Johnny? And I'm sorry, but we can't go right now. Dad wouldn't like it."

"Dad?"

"He's the one who canceled the clambake. He wanted to see what you were doing instead. I don't think he trusts you."

This wasn't news. "Listen very carefully, Jill. Something is afoot here."

"You mean like a caper?"

"I need you to go collect everyone and—" I paused. Our nervous shrimp-eater had moved out from his hidey-hole and into our inner sanctum. He stood between us now, staring back and forth with large, bulging eyes. It was hard to tell where the crustacean in his hand left off and the studio guest began.

"Can I help you?" I asked.

He looked to Jill for assistance.

"Oh, don't mind him," she replied. "He's with me."

"With you?" I met his stare. "Who is he?"

Jill made the introductions. "Johnny Hathaway, Johnny Herring. Johnny Herring, Johnny Hathaway."

## 28 — Canon of Work

This was precisely what I needed. Couldn't be better. Johnny Herring. The killer Fishes. The gangster prince. Perfect. No one could find the man for months, and in two days Jill had not only found him but scooped him up and brought him to a party already fraught with obstacles; obstacles such as me posing as the man. Why should she quit there? Assuming she could lay her mitts on a shrimp fork of adequate sharpness, why not hand this off to Johnny H for him to jab into my jugular.

I gave him the once-over. He didn't look like he would be jamming anything in anyone's jugular. In fact, not to go all Christopher Cotton on anybody, but he didn't look like much of a crime boss's son. He was choking on some cocktail sauce. Jill patted his back.

"What's going on here?" I asked them.

"John and I met this weekend. He's been hiding out. I'm the only one he trusts."

"She rescued me with her womanly charm," said John Frederick Herring. "I would have gone insane had it not been for her."

I wouldn't have been crooning over that sound mind right away, if I had been him.

The girl with the womanly charm giggled. "Nobody else knows about him."

I don't know what it was—maybe it was the sea air—but I felt unusually attuned just then. Everything came together for me. Scenes from the weekend flashed across my mind: Jill standing in the Herring foyer with TWO martinis in her hand…Jill standing in the Herring upstairs, again with TWO martinis…Lesley screaming over red paint on the floor…Paint such as a certain holed-up gangster/painter might use to while away the hours…

"You've been hiding in your own house all this time, haven't you?"

Herring nodded. "There are these secret passages, you see—"

I stared. "*Your* house has secret passageways? *This* house has secret passageways."

"I know. It was designed by the same architect. My grandmamma."

"Your grandmamma designed this house?"

He nodded again. "It was quite a triumph for female equality. Oddly enough, her nickname was also Johnnie, spelled with an ie. Her full name—"

I held up my hand. The *Johnnie* was enough. "Why are you here?"

Jill reasserted herself. She was never one to be shunted aside in a conversation. Grandmamma Herring would have liked her. "He's got to get to Cornelis Vroom and warn him."

"Warn him?"

"About the art. The Locke Collection is in jeopardy. Someone's going to pilfer it."

"I know."

"What could you possibly know?"

"A lot more about that than you might think," I retorted. And with the first feeling of satisfaction I had experienced in days, I related the saga of Daniel Locke, Ariadne Locke, the board, the bribes, the blackmail and the impending heist of the heist. I even threw in the birch tree for good measure.

Jill was impressed. "Wow, you really do know the time of day."

"Thank you."

"Mum and Dad are quite wrong about you, you know."

"Thanks."

Johnny Herring was having trouble keeping up. "If you know all this, then why are you allowing this charade to continue?"

"Gotta be that way, I'm afraid. Enescu Fleet knows what he's doing."

"The private detective? He's here?" He looked relieved. "I've been trying to get in touch with him. I figured he was the only man who could help."

I had another brainwave: "That's why you arranged for Hutton to borrow your house?"

"Yes. That was rather serendipitous. I happened to hear someone was looking for a large house to rent for John Hathaway and friends, and I told my agent to get in touch and make the arrangements. I thought I could remain hidden while still soliciting Fleet's advice. Consult him without sticking my neck out. Unfortunately, it never seemed like a good time to approach him."

Well, he was a busy man. "But why are you, of all people, hiding? I mean, you're a don in training, aren't you?"

"His father was the gangster," said Jill. "That's what he wanted his son to be. John just wants to paint. And he's brilliant at it too."

Ain't that always the way, I thought—Vroom Sr. wishing his son would simply embrace his artistic side; Herring the Younger becoming an artist when all his father ever asked for was a son who was as much a ruthless killer as he had been. Fathers and sons. No one is ever satisfied.

"So are you hiding from Vroom, or your family's expectations?" I asked.

"A bit of both," answered Herring. "You see, I was on this board at this university—"

"The board that handed over the Locke Collection to Cornelis Vroom. Yes, I know."

"That's right." He, too, seemed amazed that I was so well informed. "That was the basic conspiracy, yes."

"A basic conspiracy you went along with."

"Yes. That is, I went along with it because Cornelis made such a persuasive argument for moving the art. He's not all bad, you know. Besides, it didn't seem to be any concern of mine. I didn't like to get involved."

"John's a bit of a recluse," said Jill.

The recluse continued, "Then this blackmailer came on the scene and Stothard Hope was murdered and I thought the best thing to do was to go to earth."

Seemed like a funny place for a fish to go, but he knew best. "You heard about Stothard?"

"My bodyguard Tony Rudd told me."

"Rudd was your bodyguard?"

"A legacy of my father's. He's a good man, Rudd. A bit harsh in his methods, I suppose. I can never be sure what he's involved in. Crimes, I guess. Nothing that's any of my concern. He has always been very good to my family."

I *you-betcha-ed* on the harsh methods. "He's dead too, you know."

Herring said bugger.

"He didn't happen to identify Stothard Hope's killer to you first?" I asked.

Herring said he hadn't. Then he said bugger again. "He was looking into matters on my behalf, but he hadn't found anything definite."

I saw Hutton approaching from the buffet table. He took me aside and confirmed that everything had gone smoothly with the key handoff to Vroom. The scene had gotten a bit tense when he failed to deliver either Herring or Hope, but the key was what Vroom really wanted.

"Vroom is the least of our problems," I replied. I turned to Jill's guest. "Hutton, Herring. Herring, Hutton.

The two men shook hands. Neither had a clue what was going on.

"You know Lesley's family's all here?" Hutton asked, shouldering his bewilderment better than most.

I said I knew. In fact, I needed to go deal with that now. "Everyone hang tight," I told them.

I had last spotted Fleet heading down the hall toward the collection rooms. I dashed off in that direction, ramming into Lesley and Ate. They were dressed to the hilt and looked fantastic, even with the air knocked out of them.

Airless or not, Lesley shot forward and threw her slender arms around my neck. "I've been looking everywhere for you." I detected a quaver in her voice. She probably didn't know the extent of the soup I was in, but judging from past experience it had to be pretty gloppy.

"Seen your father around?" I asked Ate. She pointed over her shoulder. "Thanks." I gave Lesley another hug and a kiss. As we broke from our embrace, I noticed Vroom's compact enforcer Basil watching from afar. He was standing in the back of the studio, dressed in a purple sharkskin suit. Very chic. He was staring in my direction, rubbing hand cream into his knuckles.

I peered across to the other corner. Lesley's mom and dad were talking with someone who looked like a county treasurer. Like Basil, Larry D was also staring in my direction. It was difficult to say which stare I liked less.

"Gotta go," I remarked.

I managed to snag Fleet in the corridor, just outside the main collection room. He was looking at some of Niles' found art.

Enescu Fleet never gets frazzled, but the news that his daughter had arrived certainly didn't delight him. Add the Darlingtons into the mix, along with the actual Johnny H, and you could take that delight, fold it up into quarters and stick it in your back pocket for the evening. We wouldn't be needing it. I might have taken this opportunity to ask him how he was enjoying that *moment* now, but I never got the chance. Probably just as well. Nobody likes a smirker.

We were joined by Niles Brisbane. "I see you have found my found art," he said. "Tell me, what do you think?"

I turned to fob off the question on my partner in crime, but found myself fobbing to air. My cohort had melted into the crowd.

I rotated back around to face Niles' art (which, curiously enough, was also rotating). There were a lot of mobiles. Tiny motors were spinning and humming, displaying everything from auto parts to wine bottles to various bits of bric-a-brac in copper and iron, all twirling about on piano wire. Our piece of driftwood was there. It was hanging by a thread opposite a rusted paint can with the words "Sold out" printed across it. This symbolized artistic complacency, Niles explained.

On the whole, it wasn't bad. I'd seen worse. There weren't any old urinals or toilet seats.

"And here are some pieces I'm really proud of," said the artist, ushering me down the corridor to see his toilet seat exhibit.

I was spared any further duress. The art movers had arrived, clanging ladders and sweating on guests. The head mover, a burly man with a mustache and a gut, asked that everybody vacate the collection rooms. His men needed the place clear to load the crates.

We complied with the man's wishes and filed down the corridor and back into the studio. I located Fleet and Hutton. They were standing at the foot of Malcolm Rosso's covered statue, discussing the sort of things men named Fleet discuss when I'm not around. Cornelis Vroom was up on a raised platform making a speech. I hadn't missed Jelena's unveiling.

I had to hand it to him, Square-head was a pretty good speaker. Nothing too flowery, but definitely not dull. (I wish I could remember the one he told about Seurat. It was hilarious.)

"And now, ladies and gentlemen," he said, winding it up, "as we wish the Locke Collection a cheerful *bon voyage*, counting the moments until we can meet again at the new and improved Vroom Gallery—corner of 4th and Main; parking free on Sundays—let us turn our attention to a little something new among the old."

He indicated Malcolm's hidden masterpiece. "The artist would have liked to have unveiled this himself, but he is of a shy and retiring temperament—"

Retiring was right, I thought. Retiring into some rat hole somewhere.

"—so it is my honor to take his place," said Cornelis Vroom. He took a deep breath. "Without further ado, I give you *Jelena's Caress*."

A wave of the hand, a startled jump from a pair of peons who weren't paying attention, and the sheet was whisked away from the statue.

We all stared up at it. I had to hand it to him, Stinky was a pretty good sculptor. Okay, he was a damn good sculptor.

I don't know how to describe the piece, really. You might as well ask a man to describe love, or the feeling he gets sipping his second single malt after a long day. It was definitely modern; a bit abstract; but the spirit of its inspiration was clear in every polished inch of stone. It was most certainly *Jelena*. Proud. Stirring. Bold. It was every bit a *Caress* as well. Warm. Tender. Necessary. It seemed to exemplify pure female charm in all its splendor. Beauty without expectations. Sexuality without lust.

Speaking for myself—the male perspective—it was like the first time you noticed girls. I mean, really noticed them.

And yet, the ladies seemed to be getting something out of it too. I don't know what this was—I didn't ask them—but there was a look of connection in their eyes. Sisterhood. I mean, it could have been sisterhood.

Jelena—the woman—was there, standing off to the side. Contrary to her popular habit, she was dressed. Her clothes hardly mattered. The entire room was gazing between her and her likeness, her likeness and her. There was no female jealousy, no male awkwardness. It was as if we had all agreed to set aside our preconceived notions about sex and male-female relationships, and were just, well, enjoying the moment.

It was cool.

I don't know how long we stood there, fifty people in tuxes and gowns, all locked in on the nude. Probably some considerable time, because I hadn't seen the movers arrive. And yet, there they were.

Vroom saw them. They were congregated in the entranceway behind him, gawking in at the splendor of female charm.

He snapped out of his portion of the trance. He growled at them, "Get back to work! This is not for you."

A balding man with no gut and a clean-shaven upper lip stepped forward.

It seemed to me their moving uniform had changed. Before, it was kind of a yellow, now sort of a beige.

"What work do you mean, pal?"

His "pal" Vroom turned purple. He moved closer to better contain his murderous rage. "I mean moving the masterpieces, you imbecile. The art in the collection rooms."

The mover responded with a universal gesture of agreement: he hitched up his jumpsuit. "That's what we were told we'd be moving—art—but so far all my men and me have been doing is milling about the kitchen, eating leftover snacks on toothpicks."

"You've been eating our hors d'oeuvres!"

"And milling about the kitchen," agreed the mover. "That's where the note we received told us to go."

"You got a note instructing you to go stand in the kitchen? You should have been in the collection rooms an hour ago!"

The mover rubbed his upper lip. "The musty rooms around the corner?"

"Yes!"

The man nodded. "The thing of the thing is, we made a walk-through of those rooms a couple minutes ago. There's nothing in there, pal."

## 29 — Cannon of Work

It was the first time I had ever seen a gangster barrel. He barreled off the podium, barreled through the peons holding the sheet (pausing to get entangled in said sheet), and eventually barreled out, past the movers and through the exit. When last observed, he was seen barreling down the hall, the sheet flapping behind him like a cape.

Fleet, Hutton and I followed. We didn't barrel. We walked. Quickly.

Vroom wasn't in the collection rooms more than a moment. Just long enough to see the bare walls, give voice to a searing oath and bound out again ranting something about a dock. The rest of the gala maintained a cautious distance behind, sipping cocktails at one another and raising the occasional eyebrow in well-bred inquiry.

"Why dock?" I asked, as we followed Vroom outside.

Fleet explained that the art was too heavy for a truck to bear across the soft sandbar. The Locke Collection was to be moved by boat.

I might have figured that out. "Then Ho! for the dock," I declared. Fleet and Hutton looked at me. "Not Ho! for the dock?" I wondered.

We arrived at the dock. There was no boat anchored here, only a single square-headed crime boss gazing out at the setting sun. His hoard was motoring off into the distance.

"They stole it," he said. "They switched movers on us, and stole the lot of it."

I nodded sympathetically. I patted his shoulder. "I know, I saw them." I suddenly found my hand dashed aside and Vroom's paw attached to my pleated tuxedo shirt.

"Who were they?" he growled.

"Um."

"What did they look like!"

"Uh." I paused to consider. "Movers?"

He released his grip and swung around to address his men, panting and gasping as they came over the ridge.

"Get the car!" he shouted.

His subordinates were not built for sprints. They hunched over, leaning on their knees.

Basil spoke for the lot. He was not panting or gasping. "Car won't do us any good at this point, guv." (I had never heard a person in real life use the word *guv* before. I liked it.) "Tide's in."

Vroom railed against the tide. According to his information, it wasn't due for another hour. "Then call for a boat! Do *something*."

"Phones are out. Somefing's jamming the signals."

"Jammer," mused Hutton, and Vroom shot him a homicidal glare. He probably would have grabbed his shirt too—which seemed to have smaller pleats than mine—but that would have required stepping through Enescu Fleet. He confined himself to verbal abuse: "This is what I pay you for, Fleet. [He meant Hutton.] Every minute we waste, my precious cargo is slipping farther and farther from my grasp. [He meant the Locke Foundation's cargo was slipping farther and farther.] *Do* something."

It was news to Hutton that he was actually on the Vroom payroll. "Not to put too fine a point on it, but I haven't technically received any funds—"

"Do something or I'll have Basil tear out your throat."

"Consider your account settled. Now then, as for a general plan of action, it occurs to me that a couple of your men could swim to shore and call the authorities there, outside the range of the jammer." He looked around. "Who, as they say at the fertility clinic, are your best swimmers?"

Vroom didn't hesitate. "You and you," he said, pointing to a pair of goons on his left. They didn't look like good swimmers. They sighed and took off their rented shoes. One of them said aw.

"Now that we have Plan B in hand," continued Hutton, pleased with the results of his suggestion, "I will spearhead Plan A."

"And what is that?"

"Locating the jammer. Care to assist, Gigi?" [He meant Ate, standing at the edge of the gathering crowd.] Ate sniffed, glanced at Lesley and said why not. She downed her drink and off they went. As they made their way through the bystanders, I heard her say, "Who the hell is Gigi?"

I took Lesley by the hand and off we went in the opposite direction.

"Where are we going?" she asked.

"In search of a very different Fleet," I said. I couldn't help noticing the aged one had disappeared again.

We tracked him upstairs. All we had to do was follow Pixie's barks. We found him standing in one of the larger McKnight depictions: an expansive room with many small sculptures scattered around. Sadly none of these were of Jelena.

"Someone was up here during the party," he informed us, watching as his dog did laps around the room. "I confined Pixie to these rooms so she could rove without disturbing the party. Someone must have come in here and confined her further." He pointed to an armoire. "She was closed up in there."

I followed his finger. Didn't seem like such a bad idea, really. Every house she visits should be equipped with an armoire such as this.

"Now what are you doing?" I asked.

His reply should have been: *standing in the middle of the room with my eyes closed*. He responded instead: "Something in here is off." He opened his eyes. "That desk has moved."

The desk was black, ornate and vaguely B-shaped. How he could know it had moved was beyond me. I looked at Lesley. Much to my surprise, she didn't share my derisive scowl. Instead, her head was tilted to one side. "It's not the desk," she stated. "It's the rug."

Fleet's face cleared. "You're right. I was going by the placement of the furniture, but you're absolutely correct. It's not the desk, but the rug under it. Well done."

Lesley smiled graciously. She had been looking at floors a lot lately, she explained. "You only have to step in one pool of blood—"

I was beginning to feel outclassed here. "First of all," I interrupted, remembering the scene, "it wasn't blood, it was paint. And second of all—what is everyone talking about?"

Lesley gave me the skinny. "Look at the saturation, Johnny. The carpet's all discolored from the sunlight. But it should be discolored on that side,"—she pointed—"where the light comes in from the window. Someone's rolled it up and then put it back down again the opposite way around."

I didn't see why they shouldn't. You rotate tires, why not carpets? I mentioned this.

"In a home with a regular cleaning staff," said Fleet, "perhaps. But I'm guessing this room hasn't seen a decent cleaning in decades. And yet the carpet has been turned around, and turned recently. I'd call that significant."

I supposed it was sort of significant.

"Help me roll it up," he remarked. I knew it would somehow come down to my crawling about amongst the dust bunnies. We got the rug rolled up, and Fleet knelt beside it, examining the floor. One of the floorboards was loose. Now *that* I found significant.

Running his hand down inside the crevice—you couldn't have paid me to do that—he followed the space along the floor to the wall. Nothing.

"I need to see the collection rooms again," he said.

This would prove to be a little difficult. When we arrived back downstairs we discovered that Vroom had ordered the door sealed up and locked. I couldn't figure the mentality there. It's not like there was anything left inside to heist. I chalked it up to wounded pride.

"Let's use one of the backdoors," suggested Fleet.

With the passage through the studio a tad too conspicuous, we decided to use the one in the McKnight gallery. This time, I was the one explaining the lay of the land to Lesley.

Several minutes and a pound of dust later and we were in the main collection room again.

It looked bizarre without all the art. As I had observed from the hall, the walls were bare. There was nothing but dusty square smudges now: the shadow of where untouched masterpieces had once rested for decades. Someone had certainly touched them now: a heavily mustached mover who could stand to lay off the calories. The question was, who had hired the 'stache and where had he and his men taken the art? Who was pulling the strings here?

Occasional muffled voices passed by the door: guests murmuring intrigues about the heist of the century; guests murmuring about getting stuck here; Cornelis Vroom yelling to Basil about having someone's throat torn out. Just like any museum you visit, really.

I wandered around to the other four collection rooms and found more of the same. More nude, cavernous walls, all the more vast without their artistic charges; lots of decrepit furniture; several half-drunk martinis and other remnants of the gala. In a word, nada.

I was curious how Enescu Fleet was getting along in his investigations, now that he'd had a moment alone with the scene of the crime.

Lesley and I rejoined him in the main room. He was gazing up at a giant mirror propped up on the mantelpiece: one of the few items still remaining on the walls (aside from the tapestry and garish paper). He swiveled around to greet us, and to my amazement wore a contented smile. This couldn't all be pleasure for how he looked in his tuxedo.

He beamed toward my fiancée. "I've been meaning to tell you, my dear, you have a butterfly on you."

I scowled. There had been some talk recently of Lesley getting a tattoo of a butterfly on her left *gluteus maximus*—or if not the *maximus* directly, somewhere in the *gluteus* area—and if this meant she had gone ahead with the program despite my protests—I was against the project—I wasn't gonna be any too pleased. I was even less pleased that Fleet had somehow spotted it from where he was standing.

It wasn't a butterfly tattoo. It was an actual butterfly, camped out on the back of her dress—a gentle flicker of red and gold against the slate fabric.

"How did that get there?" she asked, turning to get a look at it.

"Christine Cotton," I answered. "She keeps butterflies in the conservatory—and according to Hutton, also communes with whales.

One must have hitched a ride as we passed through. The butterfly, not a whale."

Fleet stepped over and relieved her of her tiny passenger, admiring the creature on his finger a moment before making a request. "How would you feel about fetching us a jar with some holes poked in the lid, Johnny?"

I replied that I would feel stupendous about it. When there are billion-dollar heists afoot, I like nothing better than to go about the place fetching jars. I pushed back into the makeshift passageway, slamming the tapestry shut on my way out.

I don't know whether it was ire over my errand—too foolish to be called a fool's—or just a rotten sense of direction, but I never did find my way back to the conservatory.

Somewhere between the dead rat and the McKnight gallery I got hopelessly turned around and had to come up for air. I found myself in one of the less flashy depiction rooms: a simple space of cooling colors, such as you might find in a typical suburban living room. (I later learned that the McKnight painting it was imitating was called *Suburban Living Room*.)

Ate was there. She was standing by the window with an uneasy smile frozen on her lips. She said hi.

I said hi back. "This isn't the conservatory, is it?"

She shook her head from side to side.

"Hutton around?"

She shook her head from side to side.

"I just left your father. He wants me to get him a butterfly jar, of all things. Can you beat that?"

She shook her head from side to side.

As riveting as this conversation was, I figured I should be off again. "Let us know when you dig up that jammer, right?"

She shook her head from side to side.

I had just about reached the door when she called back in a thin voice: " '*O what a noble mind is here overthrown!*' "

I paused. I knew that line. Shakespeare. *Hamlet*, spoken by Ophelia, Act Something, Line Something Else. "Say that again?"

She shook her head from side to side.

Ophelia—why was she talking Ophelia at me? And why did it seem so significant? Something about Shakespeare...the women of Shakespeare...Ophelia...Juliet...Desdemona!

"Are we talking a Maneuver?" I asked.

She didn't have a chance to shake her head. No sooner had I uttered these haunting words than a pair of bodies burst out from the curtains. Ate was shoved to the sofa, I was knocked clear of the scuffle, and the bodies smashed into a sewing table behind us. The combatants were Hutton and Malcolm Rosso (still dressed in his PJs). Evidently the AWOL sculptor had returned, getting the jump on them a few minutes before I arrived. As Hutton would later explain, the lunatic had taken him in a chokehold behind the curtain, threatening to break his neck should the *bella ragazza* fail to get rid of me.

The bella had failed to get rid of me alright—and a man of his promise, Malcolm was doing his darnedest to break Hutton's neck. Charging forward, he drove my pal into a supporting beam and began shaking the life out of him by the throat. Hutton slipped the stranglehold, but the artist's brawny arms impeded his escape. He eventually tied the sculptor up on the ropes, and they toppled backwards together and took out the sewing table for good. (Apparently that dilettante extraordinaire, Christine Cotton, liked to use the room for her fabric and crafts projects—which explained all the spools of thread, not to mention the antique Singer by the window.)

I felt it was about time I got in on the act. Ate was on her feet, making a run at Malcolm with a china vase. He smacked it aside and flung her back over the sofa. Now it was my turn. I sprang forward and drove a fist into his ribs. It was like punching one of his statues, except without the give. (The man was one well-knit little chiseler.)

He spun around and swung a heavy left, which I somehow managed to swat out of the way. Despite his innate physicality, honed from years hunched over blocks of marble, he wasn't much of a fighter. More puncher than boxer. No art. He went to the right next, then back to the left, trying to chip off bits of me without the hammer and chisel. Some I blocked or dodged, others I didn't.

One of the *didn't's* came out of nowhere, clipping me on the jaw and sending me careering back into the Singer. I never saw the punch.

I hit the floor and Malcolm, refusing to go to a neutral corner, pounced. Another punch, which I did see, and the lights went out. This wasn't all bad.

I needed the rest.

I awoke sometime later (which I suppose goes without saying). My arms were chained, my feet were wet and my head was throbbing.

I surveyed my surroundings. I appeared to be in some kind of underground cavern. Over a little to my left there was a bizarre contraption that looked like a set piece from a B sci-fi film.

The phone jammer? Probably was.

A little to my right was a dead man, slumped over in a heap. Tony Rudd? Yes, most definitely Tony Rudd.

I sensed a presence behind me. I peered over my shoulder pad and saw another shoulder pad lined up with mine.

"Is that you, Hath?"

"Is what me?" I asked.

"You? Hath?"

I said yes. It was I, Hath.

"Hutton here," said Hutton.

"What's going on?"

He explained that we were chained up in an underground cave with only a phone jammer and Tony Rudd's corpse to keep us company. I replied that I had gathered that much already.

"Did you see the ocean?" he asked.

I looked down. "There's ocean in here," I said. It was about up to my thigh.

"The rising tide," said Hutton.

I didn't care for the rising tide. "What happens when it finishes rising?"

"We drown."

Nope, definitely didn't like it.

I was about to suggest we formulate a plan when Malcolm Rosso came in. He was muttering incoherently to himself. He had a deranged look on his face, more deranged than usual. Add to that the tattered PJs and sleeveless tee, and it wasn't a pleasant picture. On the plus side, wading through all that salt water had given him a fresh, earthy smell.

"I can't let you take me down," he grunted.

"Say again?"

He directed his muttering my way: "I know who you are, Herring. You're going to try and pin this on me, I know you are. But I won't let you."

"Honestly, you don't have to worry about me," I said. "I'm not pinning anything on anyone."

"I know why you've been hiding out. You've been collecting evidence, twisting facts so I look more guilty than I am. You think you have me right where you want me. You plan on finishing me, but I'm the one finishing things."

"I'm not trying to finish you," I protested. "I'm not even Johnny Herring!"

"You think you're so smart."

"I don't!"

"This will finish it," said Malcolm, splashing around to check on Hutton. He twisted Hutton's head, and Hutton replied, "How's it going, mate."

I tried to reason with the loon (the artist loon): "Would you listen. I'm not Johnny Herring. I'm not trying to pin anything on anyone. Would you listen!"

He wouldn't listen.

"Everyone will think you drowned trying to swim to shore," said Malcolm.

I perked up for this. "But actually we'll be okay?"

"No, you'll definitely drown. It just won't be swimming to shore."

I perked up less.

"You can't do this," objected Hutton. "You can't drown us like a couple of sewer rats. This is a borrowed tux."

Malcolm agreed with him. "That's why I need to get my mallet, to bash you in the heads. People will think you hit your heads on the rocks and drowned. It's kinder than you actually drowning."

I appreciated his consideration, but had to raise another small objection: "Did you say we *both* hit our heads and drown?"

"Sure, why not?"

I snorted. For such a gifted sculptor, the man had no artistry for murder. It was like his fighting technique all over again. "It's no good," I said.

"Contrived," replied Hutton, supporting my view. "We can't both hit our heads."

"And what of Ate," I added. "She saw you. She'll know we didn't hit our heads."

"The young bella won't know anything," said Malcolm. "I couldn't carry all three of you at once, you see."

I saw. Frankly, carrying me and Hutton together was quite a feat. He was definitely a strong little monkey.

"I locked her in the wardrobe and will attend to her in a moment."

I said of course. "You didn't lock the dog Pixie in an armoire earlier, did you?"

"No, I did not."

That was too bad. It would have cleared up one of our minor mysteries. "Now where are you going?" I asked him.

Malcolm was halfway to the cavern entrance. "I'm getting the mallet now. Yell all you want, nobody will hear you. *Ciao*." He went.

Hutton and I were left to discuss the situation. I was of the opinion that we were screwed blue, but Hutton took a more tranquil approach.

"We just have to take it easy and ponder a bit." I couldn't see his face from my angle, but I suspected he was leaning back with his eyes closed, just like Enescu Fleet. I could feel the back of his head on mine.

"Get your scalp off me," I said. I had enough to worry about without getting his pomade in my hair.

"You have to chill, Hath. No ideas will come if you don't relax."

"You're not going to tell me to enjoy the moment, are you?"

"It couldn't hurt."

I was too weary to argue. I gazed around the cavern. It was a nice cavern. The water was cool and refreshing. The walls underground-chic. I felt surprisingly calm.

My life flashed before my eyes. Well, maybe not flashed. Strolled past, let's say.

"You know, you're right, you and Fleet both. I don't enjoy the moment, never have. When we were at school, I was only thinking how nice it would be to be done and graduated. When we had graduated, all I could think was how great it would be to meet a nice hot girl and settle down. And now that I'm engaged to a nice hot girl, all I can focus on is getting past the wedding, avoiding any future contact with her folks. I can never just relax."

"Well, perhaps this weekend will be a valuable lesson to you, then."

Perhaps it would. A lesson I would take to my grave, which should be in another five minutes.

"You're a good pal, Hutton."

Hutton said I wasn't too bad myself, but there was no reason to get maudlin. "This is no time for wallowing about in the moment. We have our futures to think about. I have an idea."

"Yeah?"

"Help me shift over a bit. If I can reach Tony Rudd's pocket with my foot, I might be able to kick the revolver to one of us."

"Do you think it's in his pocket?"

"Where else would it be?"

He had a point. Where else?

I shifted and he shifted and eventually, after nearly sawing ourselves in two with the chains, he reached Tony's pockets. "It's there. I can feel it."

"Excellent."

Business with kicking and pockets. He sighed.

"What's wrong?"

"I just kicked your phone out of his pocket."

This was good too. "Go for the gun now."

He wasn't up for it. "Kicking it out of his pocket might have been grossly optimistic on my part."

"You can't get to it?"

"I can get to it, but I can't *get* it. Not without growing talons on my feet." He settled back against our chains. "It's no use." The tide was about to our necks now.

"What is no use?" asked Malcolm Rosso.

I couldn't help noticing he didn't have the young bella with him. He explained that he had gotten turned around in the caverns. The secret passageways that led under the museum were confusing. "What is of no use?" he repeated.

Receiving no answer, he went to the corpse's submerged pocket. He pulled out the gun. "Ah, now I see what you seek." He smiled.

This would work too. "Goodbye, Johnny Herring." He raised the gun.

I shut my eyes. "I wouldn't do that," I blurted out.

When I opened them again, I saw Malcolm scowling at the revolver. "Why should I not?"

"You've gotten the firing pin wet. Gun won't discharge with a wet pin."

"This should make no difference. As long as the cartridges are airtight."

"Yes, but if some moisture seeped through," said Hutton, "that could have an effect. Also, if the bore isn't completely drained you risk a misfire. You wouldn't like a misfire, Malcolm. Guy I knew got moisture down in the bore of an antique revolver and he was never the same again—"

"Enough!" shouted Malcolm. He raised the gun once more. "Goodbye, Johnny Herring." He paused. "What was that noise?"

I had heard it too. Sounded like a woman's voice. A ghostly woman's voice echoing in from the caves. *"Art lives"*—that's what it had said. Or something along those lines anyway. It was pro art, whatever it was.

"Ariadne Locke," whispered Hutton.

Malcolm scoffed. He looked around and raised the gun a third time.

He frowned. The thought of that ghostly voice was clearly nagging at him. "Dammit! Stay here," he told us. "I must find out what that is." He left.

Hutton and I barely had enough time to shimmy against our chains before we had another visitor to our cave. Enescu Fleet stood in the cavern entranceway.

"Can I be of assistance?" he asked. Not waiting for our pithy reply, he hastened to our side. If ever the man had a key up his sleeve, it would be great if this was one of those times.

Sadly, he had no key to the chains. "I'm going to have to shoot off the locks," he said. He withdrew a Glock from his belt.

"Is that mine?" I glubbed, spitting out the rising tide.

Fleet said it was.

Hutton was also having a bit of trouble talking over the ocean. "But you, *glub,* told us that model Glock wouldn't fire underwater."

The Glock expert shrugged. "I say a lot of things."

"Then you think it will work?" I asked.

He replied that it was certainly a fifty-fifty chance.

He felt around under the water and down went the Glock. "Good luck, Johnny Hathaway."

A brief stage wait and then came a muted *blub* from the vicinity of the chains.

We were free.

We didn't hang around. Pausing to snatch my phone from the cavern floor—evidence— I led the way. I addressed our rescuer on dry ground. "How'd you find us?"

"Oh, that was easy. I followed the thread." He reached down and shined a flashlight on a thick red thread on the cavern floor.

"Oh, you saw that?" asked Hutton. "I managed to snag that off one of Christine's industrial spools before Malcolm knocked us out. I'm glad it was long enough to reach. And didn't snap."

I was too. God bless Christine Cotton. And God bless that thread. I was glad one of us hadn't snapped.

The withdrawal from the caverns didn't take as long as I would have thought. Down the tunnel, couple of rights, one left, and *bing* we had emerged in the basement. Up the stairs and *bing*, there was Malcolm Rosso waiting for us, wild-eyed in the kitchen.

"So it is an escape you want. I will give you your escape."

He sprang forward with menace, waving his sculptor's mallet. I sprang back to avoid the onslaught, Hutton sprang back to avoid the Hathaway, and the pair of us nearly took a header back down the stairs. Picking myself back up, I crawled up to the top step, peering out at the kitchen brawl. Fleet was right in the midst of it.

When last seen, he had snatched the artist's weighty left around the wrist. Up went the man's right, and Fleet snagged that as well. They were locked in an ancient and manly tradition now: just like my handshake with Lesley's father, only slightly more violent.

Fleet pushed forward, Malcolm staggered back. Malcolm shoved left, Fleet shifted right. Back and forth they went until Fleet, who had the power of the tux on his side, knocked the mallet from Malcolm's grip. Unfortunately it was the artist who seemed to benefit from the shift in momentum. He began moving Fleet our way, toward the precipice. I braced myself for another falling body, when a most remarkable thing happened. Just before he could muscle his opponent the last few inches, Malcolm lost his footing. His legs made a mighty split on the kitchen tile. He staggered back. He did a little slippy dance. Eventually he shot up in a lovely arc, feet first, hitting his head on the floor as he landed.

He was out.

Hutton went to assist Fleet with the body, while I lingered back, looking at the tile. There was a pool of liquid at my feet, right about where Malcolm had slid.

The dog Pixie crouching in the shadows told the story. Never underestimate the power of the piddle.

"If anyone asks," said Fleet, slinging Malcolm over his shoulder, "I knocked him out with a right cross."

## 30 — Pièce De Résistance

"So what was up with the ghostly voice?" I asked, as we arrived back in the museum's main foyer.

Fleet shifted the artist to the other shoulder and blinked at me. "Ghostly voice, Johnny?"

"It said, 'Art lives' or 'Go art' or something like that. You must have heard it."

"Sorry, no."

"Well, it was there. It bought us just enough time for you to splash to the rescue. Hutton said it was the ghost of Ariadne Locke."

"Perhaps it was." We had reached the studio, now cleared out. Fleet tossed Malcolm's sorry hide down on Jelena's platform.

Various interested parties began to wander in. Cornelis Vroom. Basil. The Darlingtons and Ate (guess someone had let her out of the wardrobe). I noticed Fleet's buddy in the nice tux was there. We still hadn't been properly introduced, he and I. A few more gala goers rounded out the lot. Jelena arrived. Also Johnny Herring. Then the rest of the board convened. The Cottons. Niles Brisbane. Pixie scurried in last, curling up next to Malcolm.

Lesley rushed to my side. "Johnny, you're all wet."

I agreed I was

"If everyone would find a seat," Fleet announced, "we can get started."

I doubted anyone in the studio had a clue what it was we were starting—I know I didn't—but we found our seats anyway. Some preferred to stand.

Cornelis Vroom moped. I had a feeling that his chances of recovering his boodle of art had gone by the wayside. This was confirmed a moment later when two very soaked henchmen squeaked across the threshold. His best swimmers.

"Where the hell have you been?" roared their employer.

The henchmen reluctantly explained. They had made it to land alright, but once they had gotten out of range of the jammer they discovered that their cells had been fried in the swim. They went looking for a landline, but then a mob of protestors—opponents of the move—swarmed them, hitting them with their signs and calling them philistines. The long and the short of it was, they had to beat it down the beach and swim back to the island.

Vroom appeared unimpressed. "You had guns, didn't you?"

"They got wet," answered the henchman on the right, sneezing.

Vroom sighed and sandwiched in next to Lesley and myself. We were on a lounge.

Enescu Fleet was at his best now: on stage. His tuxedo didn't look half bad considering he had waded through a swamp under the museum and wrestled a deranged sculptor in the kitchen. Mine looked like hell, but that was just me.

"As I was saying," he began, addressing the room, "I have gathered you all here because—well, where else do you have to go?"

Lesley and I smiled. The rest of the audience remained straight-faced. Someone coughed.

Cornelis Vroom grunted. "What can an *actor* possibly have of interest to say to us?" He spat as he said it. I could see he was going to be one of the tougher audience members to please.

Fleet smiled. "It is true, we all play many roles in this life—I more than most—but I am no actor, sir. I am Enescu Fleet."

Vroom twisted around and glared at Hutton, then at his men drying out in the corner. Apparently they had been the ones on the detail following the "false" Fleet. The crime boss shook his head and returned his attention to Fleet and nothing but the Fleet. "If you're really Enescu Fleet, then you can help find the people who have my art."

"I can."

Vroom bounded to his feet. "Then do it!"

Fleet said, "Sit." The other man blustered, but Fleet held strong. "Sit," he commanded.

Vroom sat.

"We must do this right," continued the orator, "or else a ruthless killer and blackmailer will go free."

I hated to burst his bubble but the ruthless killer and blackmailer was currently drooling on his Maltese.

Fleet had not forgotten about him. "Malcolm was an integral part of the plan here," he commented, reading my mind, "but only as a pawn. The real mastermind of the heist, and the deaths surrounding it, is someone else entirely."

"Next you're going to say that they're in this very room," smirked Lesley's sister Jill.

"I am, and they are," replied Fleet.

That held the crowd for the moment. The Darlingtons, her parents, looked shocked. This wasn't how they did it in England.

"Who is it?" demanded Vroom.

"In due time. First you have to understand the killer's motivation."

"And you say you're not an actor!"

"The blackmailer was not motivated by greed or lust for power," said Fleet, "but by a sense of duty to the Locke Collection—a misguided sense of duty, perhaps, but a sense of duty nonetheless."

"What are you talking about?" piped up Vroom again—it's amazing how often I wind up with seats next to the most priceless asses. "What sense of duty?" he asked. "Nobody has done more for the Collection than I."

"You have done quite a lot, it's true," answered Fleet. "And a lot for yourself as well. You stand to make millions from your control of the Locke Collection. Not to mention the cultural prestige, which is sometimes better than money. The Foundation will make some, but who's to say that it will get all that is owed it once the collection is under your purview?"

"I say it."

"And where does the line get drawn when guests tour the rest of your gallery, eat in your restaurants—you own five in the vicinity, do you not?—purchase your souvenirs, download the Vroom Gallery iPhone app."

"It is a very fine app."

"I have no doubt. And don't misunderstand, I do admire your technique. Racketeers of old made a living with brickbats and brass knuckles. The modern gangster uses trusts. It is a kinder, gentler crime boss you have become, Mr. Vroom."

Vroom settled back on the lounge and frowned. He seemed to be thinking that there was no reason to get personal about it.

"But it is not my intention to lecture you. Your means were devious, even a little underhanded, but you never technically broke any laws—that we know of."

"Thank you."

"That would come later, and from a very different source."

He paused now to tell the tale of the corrupted board, the advent of the secret blackmailer and how the residents unconsciously aided in the heist this evening.

Vroom grew hotter and hotter as the facts of their deceit were laid out. "I knew there was something going on with them!" He spun around and shouted, "I hand you everything you ever wanted, and this is how you repay me!" He was bright red now. "I should have you all arrested. There's such a thing as right and wrong, you know."

Fleet calmed him. "I said unconsciously, Cornelis. They were only pawns."

"They can't all be pawns!"

"No, you're right. One is a knight in pawn's clothing."

"The knight's the one that makes a move like an L?"

Fleet suggested they lay off the chess metaphors for now. Vroom nodded and retook his seat. "Do they have my art?" he asked wistfully.

Fleet went on without answering:

"It was initially thought that the brains of the blackmail, the mastermind behind the heist, was some outside party. That was what the victims here were meant to believe, but in fact the villain was amongst them all along. Tony Rudd figured this out, but he died before he could relay any kind of meaningful message relating to the blackmailer's identity. Stothard Hope also discovered the truth. He managed to get a message out, in the form of a cryptic postcard, but it was a code that no one could decipher. Until now, that is."

At this point, he picked out his friend from the audience: the relaxed-looking man with the nicely combed gray hair and the well-cut tuxedo. "You're on," he said.

Mr. Cool took his place beside Fleet. "Yes?"

The master detective thanked him for coming. And for getting all dolled up for the event.

The man thought nothing of it. He had dressed for the opera this afternoon down in New Haven—what was another few hours in the monkey suit?

Fleet said splendid. "Oh, Johnny."

Once I realized I was the Johnny he wanted, I stood and joined the men.

"Who is this guy?" I whispered, glancing toward my fellow inhabitant on stage.

Fleet whispered back, "My McKnight expert."

I said ah. "He any good?"

Fleet replied that he wasn't too bad, not too bad at all. He made the proper niceties. "Johnny, Tom. Tom, Johnny."

We shook hands. "Tom?"

"As in McKnight," said Fleet.

I gaped. "Tom McKnight? The artist Thomas McKnight?"

Fleet said indeed. None other.

I was amazed. "Your McKnight expert is Thomas McKnight himself?"

Fleet said of course, who better? It was official. Enescu Fleet truly did know everybody.

I continued amazed. "When did you meet? Not this weekend?"

"Oh no. We've known each other for years and years. We originally met at a White House Christmas party decades ago. And then there was that little business I helped clear up with those forged prints."

"The forged prints," laughed Thomas McKnight. He turned my way and chuckled. He immediately brought me into the loop. I felt like I had known him for years and years myself. "There was this counterfeiting ring, you see, pumping out prints of my work overseas. I finally got fed up and asked Ef to look into it."

"I didn't mind popping over for a look," said Fleet.

"So he goes over to the law firm I had hired to represent the matter, and what does he see as he steps inside the lobby of the firm—but one of the counterfeit prints hanging over the reception desk!" He chuckled again. I chuckled. The audience, all except Vroom, chuckled.

"It made locating the ringleader a lot easier," Fleet agreed. "Anyway, we shan't keep you much longer, Tom."

"No bother."

"As I mentioned to you the other day, we need your help interpreting one of your White House Christmas pieces."

"Green, red or blue?"

"The Red Room. Is there anything in that piece, any bit of symbolism or esoteric history that could have been used to convey a secret message?"

McKnight considered the question. He couldn't think of any real symbolism in the piece. It was only meant to convey an emotion, a sense of well-being. "It's not like the cat represents social unrest or something."

And that was when it hit me. I only get these kind of inspirations once, maybe twice in an investigation. I thought the can of kippers had been it this time. That proved to be a bust—Johnny H didn't have anything to do with Rudd's death—but this was no kippered herring. The moment McKnight had said *cat* it was as if some brawny sculptor had snuck up behind me and hit me over the head with his sculpting mallet. He hadn't, but that's what it was like.

"Cat!"

Fleet and McKnight paused. The latter had been telling an amusing anecdote about how the cat, Socks, had been shoehorned into the original painting by executive fiat. Upon my pronouncement they both turned and stared.

"Cat," I repeated, trying to make it clear that I wasn't having some kind of fit. "That's what was missing from the picture. Or rather what wasn't missing, but what was there when it wasn't there before."

Fleet and McKnight continued to stare. The audience joined them. Perhaps I was having a fit, after all. "I'm not making myself clear," I admitted.

I tried again. "The card that came from Stothard Hope didn't have a cat in it."

"He's right," said Hutton. I appreciated his support. "I only saw it for a moment, but there was no cat."

McKnight appeared intrigued. "Can we take a look at it? I always enjoy seeing what printers do with my work—the legitimate printers, that is."

I frowned and looked at my feet. "Actually it's not here."

"Hath lost it," chimed in Hutton again. That kind of support I could do without.

The visionary behind the card was unconcerned. "That's alright. It was red you said?"

"Very red."

"And it was a Christmas scene?"

"Incredibly Christmas-y."

"Then it's obvious what is going on," he said.

He addressed Fleet. "It wasn't a reproduction of the White House Red Room card, Ef. It was a reproduction of an earlier piece of mine called *Christmas in Connecticut.*"

There was a semi-long silence here as we all absorbed this revelation. Then a triumphant "Aha!" rang through the studio. It was Hutton again, on his feet and grinning from lens to lens. "I got it."

"Got what?" Fleet demanded.

"The solution to the puzzle. The Stothard Code decoded. The identity of a killer and blackmailer." He spun and twirled, then twirled back because he had overshot his mark. "There he is. The killer of Stothard Hope and Tony Rudd, the blackmailer of these fine people and the man behind the heist. He is and always has been Niles Brisbane."

"I wonder if you realize," said Hutton, strolling around his prey, "just how brilliant your parents were choosing that name for you." Like mine, his tuxedo looked like crap. He didn't seem to notice. "It really is very funny."

Niles' face remained as expressionless as the giant hen's egg it could have been modeled from. He was standing in the middle of the studio. "Funny?"

"With your name, yes," said Hutton. He let the room in on the humor: "We New Englanders take it for granted, but the name Connecticut actually comes from the Mohegan word *Quinne-something*, which loosely translated means 'beside the *long tidal river*.' "

"Quinnehtukqut," corrected McKnight.

"Exactly. The state of Connecticut, you see, is on a long tidal river, also called the Connecticut—which I suppose loosely translated means 'The Long River Beside the Place Beside The Long River.' But that is neither here nor there. The long river," he said again. "Now where have we heard something about a long river lately?"

"Niles!" cried out my fiancée from the audience.

Hutton said precisely. "The Nile. The longest river of them all."

"I thought the Amazon was the longest," I queried.

"Shut up, Hath."

"You got it."

"The Amazon is the largest, the Nile the longest."

"Gotcha."

"And the Brisbane is one of the longest rivers in Australia," spoke up Jill.

Hutton gave her a nod in turn. He didn't seem to mind *their* input.

"So what do we have? Connecticut. Nile. Brisbane. *Niles Brisbane.*" He laughed. "Stothard Hope had one chance to communicate your identity, Niles—the identity of the secret blackmailer—and he chose the perfect postcard for the task. What do you have to say to that, Mr. A-River-Runs-Through-It?"

The river Niles denied it. "This is preposterous."

"You deny killing Stothard Hope, the assassin Tony Rudd, and blackmailing half this room—not to mention stinking up the place with that insipid pipe of yours?"

"Of course I do."

"Well, I think you could have conceded the point on the pipe," said Hutton. "And now I guess you're going to deny pocketing several billion dollars' worth of art?"

Niles refused to dignify that question with an answer.

Hutton tossed up his hands. He couldn't work this way.

The accused snorted. "No one here has the collection, you nitwit. It's long gone now. Any simpleton would know that."

"I'm not so certain any simpleton would," said Enescu Fleet. He shuffled Hutton out of the way and addressed himself once again to the audience. "Leaving aside Hutton's theories for the moment—I agree, an absent postcard is hardly concrete evidence—let us focus our minds on what has become of that art."

"Finally!" uttered Cornelis Vroom. "Enough of this blather about rivers and amazons."

Fleet couldn't agree more. "Speaking of the Amazon," he said, and Vroom huffed, "there's an old expression about a butterfly beating its wings in the Amazon. It's a rather elaborate question of cause and effect. It proposes that a simple butterfly flapping its wings in the Amazon can have an effect on events across the globe."

"Now we have wandered into metaphysics?" asked Vroom.

"We're not in the Amazon," continued the PI philosopher, "but we do have the requisite butterfly. It's resting down the hall. I was wondering if everyone would care to take a look." Much to our surprise he led the entire audience down the hall to the collection rooms.

At the door, he paused again, mostly because Vroom was raising a fuss (again).

"But I never locked that door!"

"Actually, it's not locked," said Fleet, removing a metal wire wrapped around the handle. "Someone simply wanted it to appear that way."

We all filed in. One of Vroom's henchmen flung Malcolm onto a rug by the fire. We found our seats.

"Now for our next guest of honor," said Fleet.

In a slightly less dramatic reveal than *Jelena's Caress*, he went to the mantel and lifted a handkerchief off a jar. In this jar was a butterfly—probably the same butterfly from Lesley's dress, but on this I had no definite knowledge.

Fleet smiled at Christine Cotton. "I assure you no harm will come to your tiny charge, Christine. I require him for an experiment. You permit this?"

Christine nodded. "His name is Reginald."

Fleet said he would bear that in mind. He showed the audience the jar. "I'll now let this little bugger out so we can all follow the path of his flight. See what that gets us."

He began to turn the lid.

There was a commotion. From out of the blue a figure crashed through the assembly and snatched the jar from Fleet's hand. The figure was Niles Brisbane.

Huffing a bit from his outburst, he said, "I won't let you manhandle that creature. There's no reason for it."

Fleet smiled. "I'm happy to see I didn't misjudge you. I was hoping you wouldn't wait for Reggie to leave the jar. That might have gotten messy. You may be a murderer, but you would never squash beauty."

"Murderer?" Niles attempted a chuckle of his own. "We're not back on that?"

"We never left it. Hutton was correct. You're a killer, Niles, and thanks to my little experiment we have proven you are also a thief."

"I—"

"I knew one person here would kibosh the butterfly maneuver," Fleet explained. "Someone who couldn't afford it flapping around the room; someone who couldn't afford everyone peering up to follow its path. I just wanted to see if that person would be you."

"You're babbling. Why would I care where people peer?"

Fleet shook his head. "It's no good, Niles. The jig is up. Literally. Once the suggestion is out there, you can't bank on people's natural impulses. People will look up."

There was a gasp from the audience. Then another. Fleet was right. People were looking up. And gasping.

I figured I might as well follow them. I looked up. I gasped.

Dangling from the ceiling high above our heads were hundreds of masterpieces—THE masterpieces—connected to hundreds of metal threads.

Cornelis Vroom ran to the next collection room. "There's more in here! They're everywhere."

"Of course they are," said Fleet. "That's how you rigged it, isn't it, Niles?"

Niles didn't answer.

"You originally went through the floorboards upstairs. That's where you threaded the needle. Then, after you had instructed Malcolm to tunnel into this room, you wired up each and every painting over the last few weeks, connecting these invisible wires to a motor of some sort. I'm not entirely certain where you hid that, but I wouldn't be surprised if it isn't masquerading as one of your found art pieces. Once you had provided the proper distraction at the gala—the statue's unveiling—you slipped away and threw the switch. We are standing in the ultimate mobile, made with the world's finest found art.

"I suspect Pixie must have irked you when you came upstairs to check the threads—she does irk—so you locked her away in the armoire. Up went the art, and nobody was the wiser.

"The movers you hired, meanwhile, were never meant to move anything—which, judging from some of the men in that profession I have known, should have been right up their alley. They provided the sleight of hand for your heist. They would steal the real movers' boat, ditch it somewhere and disappear. More misdirection. All you had to do then was sit back and hope nobody looked up. It was a pretty good bet. Everyone was convinced the art was gone, and people don't usually crane their necks unless compelled to do so. The ceilings in here are unnaturally high: forty feet or more. I believe architectural digests have frequently commented on this."

Niles Brisbane did not speak. He took a seat on a settee and removed his pipe from his tuxedo pocket. He filled it.

"I assume," continued his nemesis, "that you would not have left the art dangling here indefinitely. Perhaps you planned on moving it while the authorities were busy chasing phantom boats? However you taped it out, you no doubt banked on hiding it somewhere else until the Locke Collection could live again in its only true habitat. Perhaps this was to be your private oasis, as it once was for old man Locke?"

Niles continued to give Fleet the silent treatment. His pipe filled, he raised this to his lips and chomped defiantly.

Vroom was busy congratulating Fleet, promising him a Monet or two on the house. Anything he wanted. "And as for you, Brisbane," said the crime boss, but what was for Brisbane we shall never know.

Those cold staring eyes, that giant unmoving head. Niles Brisbane was dead.

Hutton stepped over and whisked the pipe from his lips. He sniffed. "Poison." He shook his head. "The old poisoned pipe maneuver. They call that one—" He paused. "Actually, I don't think they have a name for it."

# 31 — The Artist Formerly Known as Gerome Lance

I won't bore you with the technical details of the wrap-up: the recovery of Tony Rudd's body from the caverns; the hauling off of Malcolm Rosso by the police; the police sergeant slipping on Pixie pee in the foyer; not even the prolonged goodbye the dog received from Christopher Cotton upon our departure from the Ariadne Locke Museum. It took hours, was very tedious (especially the Cotton part), and without Enescu Fleet probably would have taken days or even weeks. That man really knew how to smooth out the rough patches with the authorities.

We were back at the Herring mansion now—the Fleet, Hathaway and Darlington gangs all together again. The real Johnny H was playing host; which is to say he had adjourned to one of his hidey-holes and hadn't been seen for hours.

Fleet, Thomas McKnight and I were in the library, reviewing the last few points of the investigation. Drinks were at our elbows, our ties dangling stylishly open at the throat. I felt like one of the Rat Pack.

Fleet was explaining how Niles had strung it all together: "Once the authorities were convinced that the art had been whisked away, suspicion would naturally fall on the board. Niles was prepared for that. He had already framed himself for Christopher Cotton's embezzlement—he had to appear to be one of the victims in order for his plan to work—and he would have gladly submitted himself to that investigation, if it meant distracting attention from the real location of the collection. From the beginning, the board was setup to be fall guys (and gals). The crimes they had been framed for would eventually be dismissed, but everyone would go on believing that they had engineered the heist."

I had a question: "So, other than Niles, and technically Chris Cotton, everyone else was innocent?"

"All except Malcolm Rosso. The crime Niles held over Malcolm was drug smuggling, but he hadn't been framed for it. Malcolm really had been a smuggler in his youth."

"Which explains why he was so hep to do in his blackmailer?"

"Correct. Ironically, Niles himself wasn't the most violent one in the group. Not compared to Malcolm, or, for that matter, Tony Rudd."

"Yes, but Niles did kill Stothard Hope. Don't forget that."

Fleet refilled our drinks. "I'm not certain Niles did kill Stothard in cold blood. From the condition of his body, his death may well have been an accident, sustained during an argument or escape attempt. He may have simply hit his head and drowned."

I shook my own head. I had heard enough about hitting heads and drowning for one day. "So maybe Niles Brisbane shouldn't have offed himself, after all," I remarked. "Sounds like there may have been extenuating circumstances to the murders. And when you think about it, he didn't really swipe the collection. Not technically."

Fleet conceded the point. Still, he didn't feel all that sorry for Niles. "He never should have locked my dog in an armoire," he grumbled.

On the cue "dog" McKnight stood and said he should be getting home now. He had dogs of his own who would be glad to see him. (He had come in on the subject of cats, and was leaving on dogs.)

Fleet shook his hand. "Something wrong, Tom? You've been very quiet."

I had noticed this as well. The artist seemed pensive.

"Oh nothing, nothing at all. Before we left, I took a peek at that conservatory, the one with all my paintings in it."

Fleet nodded. "You're lucky it was Ariadne and not her father who took a fancy to you. Under the terms of the Locke Foundation, your paintings are there to stay."

"Yes." It was not the most enthusiastic yes. "Any chance they can be moved as well?"

"I'm sure it can be arranged. Why?"

McKnight did not hesitate: "I don't think I like the idea of my pieces getting singled out from the move. It doesn't seem right. Besides, have you seen the new Vroom facility, Ef? It's a beautiful gallery. The man has taste, you have to hand him that." And on that note, he bid us farewell. The two men shook hands again, and Fleet asked Tom to give Renate his regards. Ef still owed the artist and his wife a dinner.

No sooner had McKnight left than Jill and Ate came in. Hutton followed.

Jill went straight to the point. "You're both here. Good. We need help."

Fleet bowed. "Always glad to assist my daughter, my namesake and any new friends."

"Oh, it's nothing to do with them," said Jill, waving them off. "They're just fine. I'm the one with the problem. I'm pretty sure the folks don't approve of Johnny."

I already knew this. I saw no reason for her to rub it in.

"Not you, Johnny. My Johnny. John Herring. I don't think my parents like me falling for a mobster's son."

"Have you fallen for him?" I asked. Seemed a little quick.

"We're nuts for each other. We both love animals, art, England. And he's got the name of a fish—what could be better for a vet than to fall for a fish?"

I didn't get it. "Vets don't deal with fish."

Jill asked why not? Why couldn't they? "Anyway, we're thinking of running off together. Your thoughts?"

I replied that I wouldn't run off if I were them. It can cause riffs, running off. Just ask Mr. and Mrs. Darlington.

Evidently it wasn't my thoughts Jill wanted. She was staring up at Fleet, waiting for the great one to answer.

"I wouldn't run off together," he said.

"You're probably right," she agreed. "It's no way to begin a romance."

"I was thinking more of John. A boy with his reclusive tendencies wouldn't do well on the lam."

Jill supposed he wouldn't. "So now what?"

"Just be patient. I have a feeling your father will come around."

Jill sighed and said she wouldn't bet on it. Then with another sigh, she went to fetch her fish a snack.

Fleet watched her leave. "I have a little secret to share," he said. Ate, Hutton and I drew in closer. "I don't think Lawrence will continue to be quite the hard-ass he once was. Did anyone happen to notice me talking with Basil at the museum?"

I had. I wondered what he was doing speaking with that poisonous little pipsqueak.

"He told me something most interesting. He said he recognized Lesley's father. He said he was Gerome Lance."

"We've heard that one before," I scoffed. "He bears an uncanny resemblance to the one-time con artist Gerome Lance—so?"

"He bears a resemblance, Johnny, because he really is Gerome Lance."

"Say what?"

"It's not so hard to believe. After the gang broke up, Lance started a new life. This new life involved becoming Lawrence Darlington, respected barrister."

I couldn't believe it.

"Did you ever wonder, Johnny, why your prospective in-laws chose this moment to pay you a visit?"

I said no. Actually I had, but I felt like saying no.

"Stothard had gotten in touch with him. He was killed before the Darlingtons arrived so they never got a chance to speak. One wonders what he would have told his old crony."

I walked up one end of the room and returned rubbing my hands together mischievously. "I'm going to enjoy this," I said.

Fleet was shocked. "You're not seriously considering outing him, are you?"

"Why not?"

"He's made a respectable life for himself. He's going to be your family."

"He hates me!"

"Yes, but he'll come around. Hathaways are an acquired taste."

I hadn't bought that when he said it to Jill, and I didn't buy it now. I looked at Ate and Hutton. "What do you two think?"

"I'd let it go," she said.

"Be the better man," Hutton concurred.

"But don't you think Lesley should know?"

"Not your place to rat the man out," Hutton remarked.

"Just let it go," said Ate.

I said fine. "But I'm keeping this in my back pocket, just in case."

Hutton was frowning, not about my pocket but on the Gerome revelation as a whole. "So I was right all along?"

Fleet didn't care to admit it, but yes. He was right.

While we were on the subject of clearing things up: "I have three more questions—" I announced.

Ate rolled her eyes. Hutton shook his head.

"One," I said, "if Johnny Herring wasn't the murderer or blackmailer, why in the hell did Tony Rudd grab a can of kippers to identify him?"

"You only assumed he grabbed kippers," Hutton pointed out.

That was true. "I guess you're not the only one who can make a hash of things."

"It was no hash," said Fleet. "I'm quite sure the kippers were Rudd's clue."

"Then why—"

"It wasn't the herring aspect of the kippers he was trying to indicate. The label didn't even say herring. I checked. It was another word: 'Smoked.' Kippers are *smoked* fish."

"Smoked?" I couldn't help laughing. "Niles' pipe." I was beginning to hate Tony Rudd.

"What was question two?" asked Fleet.

"Two," I said, and turned to Ate, "why did you quote a line from *Hamlet*, when you were trying to tell me that Malcolm was pulling a Desdemona Maneuver? Why not quote *Othello*?"

"I don't know any lines from *Othello*."

"Three," I said, and offered this one up to the room. "What would Niles have done if Malcolm's sculpture had been below par? Everything depended on the gala going all gooey over the statue, as a distraction, but what if his sculpture had sucked?"

"In that instance," explained Fleet, "Jelena had been instructed to disrobe."

"That works," I agreed.

"She should have tried it anyway," Hutton spoke up. We all looked at him. "I'm just saying, better safe than sorry. And it's not like she was shy or something. She kept doing it all weekend."

Ate squinted. "Just how much disrobing are we talking about here?"

Hutton considered his reply carefully. "Not much. Just the occasional treat. Nothing too bawdy." He paused, that great mind working in overdrive. "Besides, it was Hathaway who saw the most of her."

Ate left.

"Seriously, Hath was ogling her naked body way more than I was. I'm amazed he got anything else done."

They faded off into the distance.

I must have been frowning again because Fleet laid a hand on my shoulder and told me not to worry, he wouldn't tell Lesley.

"It's not that," I said. "It's all the coincidences."

"Coincidences?"

"I mean, what are the odds that my father-in-law would turn out to be one of the very con men we're trying to find—a con man you once knew?"

"Of him, Johnny. I knew *of* him. We never met while he was Lance. And I still don't understand why you should call it a coincidence."

"Isn't it?"

"Not at all. I already told you, Stothard contacted Gerome—and you, and me, and possibly even Hutton with that postcard of his. He was the mastermind behind our reunion. As for your father-in-law turning out to be an old associate of mine, there is nothing coincidental about that. You have to realize, in my prime I was involved in thousands of investigations. In fact, it would have been far more inexplicable if your father-in-law had turned out *not* to be an ex-con artist I once knew of."

I nodded slowly.

"It makes perfect sense, really," said Fleet. "And so, when I tell you one final secret—that our friend Jelena was actually Celeste Hope, Stothard's long-lost granddaughter, you will see it as you should: not as a coincidence, but as the logical cause and effect of a complicated adventure. Remember the butterfly in the Amazon."

I must have been staring, because Fleet poked me in the stomach.

"Jelena is Celeste Hope?"

"Absolutely. Jelena, or I should say Celeste, was not Malcolm's original model. When her grandfather went missing she made arrangements to take the first girl's place. She began investigating his disappearance on her own. She started with the Vroom gallery—she was feeding him information, which is how I was able to learn so much about your exploits before I arrived. She then worked her way to the Ariadne. Along the way, she met up with Herring, became his model, but they never met face to face. Well, not Johnny's face. He painted her once but from behind a screen. He's a shy boy. That's her there." He pointed to the topless mermaid painting in the corner.

I should have known it was her. I would have recognized those—that face anywhere.

"So she's not really Romanian or whatever?"

"So few of us are," said Fleet sadly.

"Then why pretend?"

"She was playing on Tony Rudd, posing as a girl from his village. It worked too. Rudd was putty in her hands."

I expected he had been. "Then she wasn't really a blackmail victim?"

"Not initially. She tricked Niles into blackmailing her with false evidence so she could get closer to the board."

"So she was one of the good guys?"

"For you especially. She was helping you all along. From what I understand, she let you out of the basement at one point."

I didn't want to talk about the basement. Or locks. "So *that's* not a coincidence? Jelena turning out to be Celeste Hope?"

"Of course not. She didn't *turn out* to be Celeste, Johnny. She was Celeste all along." He smiled broadly.

I thanked him and went outside. I needed some fresh air.

I'm happy to say that I spent the last evening of our visit at the Herring mansion with Lesley, out on that wondrous private pier I had heard so much about. Turns out it was really quite nice.

We were sitting there peering out at the night sky, when Lesley complained that something was poking her. (I had since changed out of my filthy tuxedo and back into a pair of jeans and my old sport jacket. It was from the right pocket that Lesley had felt the poke.)

I reached inside and pulled out four spa certificates, a pack of gum and Stothard Hope's *Christmas in Connecticut* postcard (Thomas McKnight, artist.)

"Is that—?"

It was. It had been there all along. I had stuck it in my pocket that first morning.

Lesley and I looked at the clue together in the moonlight. There was definitely no cat.

"You know, I still can't say who Stothard Hope meant this for—I mean, really meant it. It could have been for Fleet or Hutton. Hell, when he said 'old man' he could have meant Gerome Lance."

"Who's Gerome Lance?"

"Not important," I said.

She sighed contentedly and leaned her head on my shoulder. "I wouldn't fret about it, Johnny. These things are always open to interpretation."

"I suppose you're right. It's like that ghostly voice I told you about in the caverns. Fleet won't admit it was him monkeying about, and I don't care. Maybe it was the ghost of Ariadne Locke. Who knows, who cares?"

"That's the spirit."

"Although, maybe it was Jelena," I mused, straightening up. "Or Ate. She was nearby. Come to think of it, where were you—"

"Just enjoy the moment, Johnny."

I nodded and she put her head back. We looked out at the water.

"Speaking of Jelena," said Lesley, "what was this about you ogling her naked body throughout the weekend?"

I continued to peer out at the horizon. "Not ogling," I answered. "Just a fleeting glance."

## FURTHER READING

If you enjoyed *Fleeting Glance,* you may want to take a peek at *Fleeting Memory*, the first Enescu Fleet mystery. Also, don't overlook John and Lesley's adventure with the Azure Star in *Five Star Detour*.

www.ingramcontent.com/pod-product-compliance
Lightning Source LLC
Chambersburg PA
CBHW021621030826
48979CB00035B/1395/J
* 9 7 8 0 9 9 1 2 3 2 4 4 4 *